T0049789

the TIFFANY GIRLS

A NOVEL

SHELLEY NOBLE

WILLIAM MORROW
An Imprint of HarperCollins*Publishers*

This book is a work of fiction. References to real people, events, establishments, organizations, or locales are intended only to provide a sense of authenticity, and are used fictitiously. All other characters, and all incidents and dialogue, are drawn from the author's imagination and are not to be construed as real.

THE TIFFANY GIRLS. Copyright © 2023 by Shelley Noble. All rights reserved. Printed in the United States of America. No part of this book may be used or reproduced in any manner whatsoever without written permission except in the case of brief quotations embodied in critical articles and reviews. For information, address HarperCollins Publishers, 195 Broadway, New York, NY 10007.

HarperCollins books may be purchased for educational, business, or sales promotional use. For information, please email the Special Markets Department at SPsales@harpercollins.com.

FIRST EDITION

Designed by Diahann Sturge

Library of Congress Cataloging-in-Publication Data has been applied for.

ISBN 978-0-06-325244-8

23 24 25 26 27 LBC 7 6 5 4 3

To all the little-known Tiffany girls who helped
break the glass ceiling for those to come

Praise for *The Tiffany Girls*

"Under Noble's deft hand, Grace, Clara, and Emilie come vividly to life in turn-of-the-century New York City in her new novel, *The Tiffany Girls*. I couldn't help but root for the trio of heroines as they strived to become artists in their own right through their work for Louis Comfort Tiffany, renowned master of stained glass. Readers will revel in the fascinating and lavish details, and never look at a Tiffany lamp the same way again. An immersive, wonderful read!"

—Heather Webb, *USA Today* bestselling author of *Strangers in the Night*

"*The Tiffany Girls* sparkles with as much light, hope, and wonder as Mr. Tiffany's stained-glass creations."

—Kaia Alderson, author of *Sisters in Arms*

"Noble brings the late nineteenth century alive in her story of these young women from various walks of life who work and live together as they forge their own artistic paths while supporting each other through the ups and downs. An inspiring friendship tale of talented female artists and their search for independence in a world that wasn't too keen on female autonomy."

—Eliza Knight, *USA Today* bestselling author of *Starring Adele Astaire*

"A historical fiction of bold new beginnings and the creative courage of three women artists who forged their careers at Tiffany's glassworks."

—Tessa Arlen, *USA Today* bestselling author of *In Royal Service to the Queen*

"*The Tiffany Girls* is an engaging story filled with unforgettable characters as incandescent as the iconic Tiffany stained-glass designs they helped create. Brimming with passion and reverence for the artistic mastery of the Tiffany style, Shelley Noble's excellent storytelling presents a portrait of turn-of-the-century New York City and Paris that illustrates the dedication and determination of women to gain recognition for their contributions within the art world and take control of their lives. A must-read!"

—Monica Kilgore, author of *Long Gone, Come Home*

"*The Tiffany Girls* is a fascinating look into the art world, and the working conditions of women, at the dawn of the twentieth century. A sweeping cast of characters, comprised of both historical figures and fictional ones alike, brings the high-stakes world of the Tiffany glassworks to life in vivid detail. Richly researched and utterly captivating, a must-read for fans of turn-of-the-century historical fiction."

—Aimie K. Runyan, bestselling author of *The School for German Brides* and *A Bakery in Paris*

Chapter 1

July 1899
Montmartre
Paris

Emilie Pascal wipes her hands on the cleanest cloth she can find and carefully places the sheet of stationery on the desktop. It is her last one. She had managed to secrete two sheets from the d'Evereux writing desk this past fall when her father was finishing the chevalier's portrait.

She'd already had to use one.

This one will be for her.

She aligns the sheet just so, pulls the inkwell closer. Takes a breath and slowly touches her cheek. The bruise will be gone before she arrives in New York with her letter.

But she must hurry.

She must also be very precise, something that she has learned over the years. One mistake could cost her everything.

Emilie pictures the letter she will write in her head, like a scene on a canvas before she begins to paint. A florid, but masculine script. Just enough explanation, not too much praise. She touches the pen's tip to the page.

My Dear Mr. Tiffany . . .

The pounding on the door comes just as she is about to sign her near perfect forgery. She lifts the pen instinctually from the paper and, *Dieu merci*, it does not blotch the paper.

Carefully now . . .

Mes sincères salutations,

Le Chevalier d'Evereux

The door begins to shake under the increasing pounding. She has no blotter. Emilie blows on the signature, then folds the paper. She will not seal it with a wafer. Too much or too little is the one slip that will always give you away.

She stands and hurries to her bed and the black portfolio that awaits its last work of art.

Now the shouting begins. "Dominique Andre Pascal! Open the door in the name of the Sûreté de Paris!"

Emilie slips the letter into the portfolio.

The door will give soon. They won't find him here. He is gone. She doesn't know where, but good riddance. She throws a cloak over her shoulders and grabs her portfolio from the bed. One quick look about to make certain she has left nothing, and she races to the window.

She has planned for this moment. It seems her whole life she has planned for this moment. The window is open, and she slides her most precious possession onto the little balcony. Hoists her skirts, dark in color but light in weight, for her escape. One leg over the sill, then the other. She pulls the window closed just as the door gives.

She scoops up the black case, throws it onto the next balcony, and throws herself after it.

Jean and Marie are waiting to help her inside. They have heard the gendarmes in the hallway. Without a word, Marie helps Emilie into her cloak; they lead her over to the ladder to the roof, and she climbs up, gripping the handle of her portfolio as if it will sustain her in everything. And it will.

Jean wants to see her safely away, but Emilie shakes her head. "*Non, tu dois m'oublier.*"

"*Mais je t'aime.*"

"*Non.*"

Marie hands up the valise they have been keeping for this moment. "We'll send your trunk when you're settled."

Emilie nods. She cannot speak.

Marie begins to cry. Jean snaps a warning look. Marie wipes her tears in case the gendarmes come to question them about their neighbors.

Emilie looks out only long enough to make sure she is alone, then she climbs onto the rooftop.

Jean looks longingly up through the square opening. This is the way she will remember him. Framed in light.

Then the darkness closes over him, and Emilie is off over the rooftops of Paris.

She has only one last stop to make on her way to the docks and the ship that will take her far away from here. From her memories, good and bad, her friends and her enemies, and most of all from her father.

She climbs down to the rue Suger. The lights shine on silent cobblestones; no one is about. She hears no sound of searching police.

Clutching her belongings, she starts north toward the river. It is a hot night even for July and Emilie is slick with perspiration from her exertions and her fear. And she still has a distance before her.

Already the shadows of men and women appear in doorways, workers on their way to the factory, the river boats, the sewing shops, the flower market, where they will sell their wares to the few souls who will venture out in this weather.

Emilie walks faster, though her whole body fights her. She wants to sit down, to hide her face in her hands, but that will come soon enough.

And then she sees her, the little flower seller at the foot of the Pont des Arts.

The woman sees Emilie approach and grins her crooked smile. They are old acquaintances. She looks over her bucket of chrysanthemums, lilacs, and daisies and pulls out a long-stemmed rose from their midst. Emilie can see in the first rays of light that today it is red, a perfect symbol for parting.

Emilie drops a coin in the woman's palm and takes the rose. She doesn't even know the flower seller's name.

She moves on measured steps to the crest of the bridge. Slows while two men, late from carousing the night away, pass her in their hurry home. Then she turns to look down at the deep waters of the Seine. She will not cry.

"I leave France tonight, Maman. I may not visit you for a long while. '*Ne m'oublie pas.*'" And she drops the rose into the darkness.

July 1899
Tiffany Glass and Decorating Company
Manhattan

Clara Driscoll sat at her desk, squinting at the week's expenses and thinking about dragonflies. *Dragonflies.* Hovering in the air, their iridescent wings reflecting the sunlight for a second before darting away, then reappearing somewhere unexpected.

She'd seen them while cycling in Central Park on Sunday, and they wouldn't leave her alone.

She leaned back, pinched the bridge of her nose. Her eyes were already tired, though it was still morning, and she could feel one of her migraine headaches coming on.

As manager of the women's division of Tiffany Glass and Decorating Company, it was her job to make sure her figures tallied each week. Normally she could separate her work as manager and that as designer without too much trouble. But not this morning. The business manager, Mr. Pringle Mitchell, had just instituted a list of new requirements that added to Clara's aggravation; additional work taking up more of her time without actually being useful.

She and Mr. Mitchell were always at loggerheads over expenses. Mr. Tiffany insisted on quality unique art pieces. Mr. Mitchell was mostly interested in keeping costs down. Clara usually managed to navigate the waters between them well enough.

But this. The most egregious new rule was charging the women's division rent for the space they used working for the company. Fifty dollars a month! It was outrageous. Especially since she knew Mr. Mitchell had done it just to annoy her.

Mr. Tiffany told her to pay it once and not worry about it again; he would sort it out. Which was all very well for him to say, but he'd left for his family's trip to Europe. There he would consult with Mr. Bing about the Grafton Gallery exhibit the coming October. And, if Clara knew Mr. Tiffany, he would be in the thick of the *on dit* about the upcoming Paris Exposition Universelle to take place in April.

Clara considered herself a rational, understanding modern woman, and she was happy to both steer the ship, so to speak, and mentor the women learning their craft under her aegis—and do both while working on her own designs. But it was difficult to concentrate with dragonflies demanding attention. Especially on a headache day. And between the accounts, the loss of two workers to marriage in the past month, and the increasing summer heat stifling the fifth-floor workshop, this was decidedly one of those days.

Clara let her head roll back, closed her eyes. She would just rest them for a moment. Her eyesight had never been the best, and it was always exacerbated by her headaches.

And there were the dragonflies again. Flitting above her head, alighting on the stack of watercolors and sketches she had yet to file. Swooping onto the wooden mold for the lampshade she had just completed. Diving at the work tray of glass cuttings and tools that she'd pushed out of the way to make room for the accounts books.

Accounts. She opened her eyes and sat up. The sun was streaming through the window, making a perfect spotlight on the waiting columns.

Clara adjusted her muslin work sleeves, picked up her pen, and began where she'd left off.

Two large sheets of green opalescent glass #2435B. These she'd had to order directly from the Tiffany furnaces in Corona, Queens, since the triptych had already used a good portion of stock downstairs in the glass storage room. She'd gone to the furnaces herself to pick it up.

Round-trip trolley, ferry, and train fare. Though it hardly seemed fair that her department should pay for the trip just because the men couldn't keep up with their supply of glass.

Clara sighed. Between their normal number of commissions

and the extra work due to the additional pieces destined for the Paris Exposition, they were only halfway through July and already they were close to exceeding the monthly budget.

But there would be no scrimping on materials or construction. Mr. Tiffany had a bee in his proverbial bonnet about the Exposition. He had chosen not to exhibit in the last Paris world's fair ten years before, and John La Farge, his most encroaching competitor, had taken all the medals Mr. Tiffany was convinced would have gone to him.

This time, he was preparing to astound the world like they'd never been astounded before, and he would at last be recognized as the undisputed king of art glass.

Clara didn't disagree with the notion. Mr. Tiffany was a genius with a vision. The fact that making his vision of stained-glass windows, vases, lamps, pottery, mosaics, and all the other commissions Tiffany's studios took on required teamwork among several departments and a myriad of individual craftsmen and artists to complete didn't matter in the least.

He was their guiding force. And they all knew it.

Clara had never met anyone like him. She didn't believe there was anyone else who could even come close to Louis Comfort Tiffany.

And Clara Wolcott Driscoll and her Tiffany girls were an indispensable part of his process.

She had just finished tallying the first row of figures when there was a quiet knock at the door. Clara dabbed at the perspiration on her upper lip and slipped her hankie into her sleeve. "Enter."

Annie Phillips stood timidly in the doorway.

"Well, come in, Miss Phillips. Is there a problem?"

"No, ma'am. Not a problem . . . exactly. It's just. Well . . ." She thrust out her hand, revealing a cheap gold-looking ring with a tiny glass stone faceted to its surface.

Clara's heart dropped; her head throbbed in response. Annie was one of her better glass cutters. This was the third engagement her department had suffered this month. And when a girl became engaged, married, or, heaven forbid, got herself in trouble without the legality of marriage, she was let go immediately.

Mr. Tiffany might be an excellent employer, paying his "girls" on a par with his men, even going so far as to say they made better cutters and selectors than their male counterparts. But he sided with the other business owners and the law on one point. No married women were allowed to work in the studio.

Which seemed utterly shortsighted on his and the law's part. Most married women had even more reason to stay employed than not.

"And who is this young man?"

"Jack Mills, ma'am. He's respectable and comes from a good hardworking family."

Which most likely meant they were as poor as church mice.

"And he's ever so handsome, Mrs. Driscoll."

"Ah." How many times had Clara heard variations of this speech? How many girls had left to pursue their dreams of marriage and home and family and had never been heard from since? She used to try to talk them out of it. She had learned from her own experience that the promise of love and security could become a harsh reality.

"And what does Mr. Mills do for a living?"

"He's a carter, Mrs. Driscoll. Over in the garment district. He plans to work his way up to manager."

They all did, Clara thought, despondently. And he most certainly earned less than the girl standing hopeful before her. Clara was above all else a practical woman, and if she did usually side with the philosophy of the New Woman, she also understood the allure of handing over your responsibilities to a wider pair of shoulders. After all, she had done the same thing herself.

"Well, if you're certain this is the right decision for you . . ."

"Oh, I am, Mrs. Driscoll. I am."

"In that case, we'll all be sorry to see you go, but wish you the greatest happiness." Clara stood, ending the interview and Annie Phillips's employment.

Annie's lip quivered.

"Now, now," Clara said, coming around her desk. "Chin up. You're embarking on a wonderful new adventure." Why had she said that? It was stupid to think that this girl would have anything but an ordinary life of drudgery, having baby after baby and working her hands to the bone, while her husband made his way in the world . . . or didn't.

It must be her headache and the heat that were making her so pessimistic. She didn't as a rule allow herself to be negative. It wasn't useful or helpful to others.

"Have all the girls seen your ring?" It was a superfluous question. Of course they had. Sometimes Clara felt the studio was no better than a train station, a temporary place where young women waited for their next journey to begin.

She smiled reassuringly and walked the girl to the door. Watched her hurry back to the other girls, then Clara closed the door.

She'd barely sat down at her desk before another knock sounded on her door. She groaned. *Please heaven, not another one.*

July 1899
Mrs. Bertolucci's Boardinghouse
Manhattan

GRACE GRIFFITH BARELY made it back for eleven o'clock curfew. Mrs. Bertolucci was standing at the door, key in hand, when Grace slipped inside.

"Whew," Grace said. "I was afraid I was going to have to climb in the kitchen window."

Mrs. B, as the boarders all called her, gave her an arch look. "You better not be out carousing with some young man."

"You know I'm not," Grace said truthfully.

"What was it tonight?"

"Who. A woman named Emma Goldman. She was giving a talk on birth control, free love, and women's emancipation. She was magnetic."

Mrs. B crossed herself. "That woman. She's a notorious anarchist, causing trouble wherever she goes. Don't get yourself mixed up in that nonsense. They're violent people, those anarchists. I saw it myself in the old country. Oh *dio mio*."

"I would never," Grace insisted. "I'm all for women's right to vote, to get equal wages, for owning our own properties and not being bullied by husbands—but Miss Goldman . . ." Grace shrugged. "She makes for excellent caricature."

Mrs. B cut her off with a wave of both hands. "Maybe, just make sure you don't get swept up in things you can't control."

Her vehemence took Grace by surprise. "I promise. No violence for me. I make church windows all day."

"And you'll be getting fired if you fall asleep over your glass."

"Not if I find a husband first," Grace quipped.

"You're a pretty girl, Grace. Smart, maybe too smart. Maybe a little tall for some men, but you just find one tall enough and rich enough."

Grace opened her mouth—

"I know. Not if you have to give up your work, both your works, but I worry about you."

"And I appreciate it, but you're a modern woman, too, Mrs. B. A model for us all . . . even if you won't admit it."

Mrs. B could have remarried after her husband died. She'd been a reputable widow with a comfortable inheritance of a boarding-house in a nice, safe neighborhood. But she hadn't, though she'd had plenty of opportunity.

"Bah. Your dinner is in the warming tray but don't blame me if it's as hard as shoe leather."

"I won't. You're a dream, Mrs. B." Grace bent over and planted a kiss on her portly landlady's cheek.

"Now get on with you and turn out the lights in the kitchen when you're done."

"I will, thank you." Grace hurried down the hall, relieved and thankful. She was starving, and the idea of trying to sleep on an empty stomach in this heat was daunting.

She carefully removed the covered plate from the warming oven and placed it on the table. Lifted off the cover and breathed in the heavenly aroma. Pork chops, roasted potatoes, and cabbage. She slipped her sketchbook out of her knapsack, and alternating between fork and pencil, the pork chop and potatoes disappeared, and the firebrand anarchist, Emma Goldman, became a recognizable caricature.

And a good one at that. The gold-rimmed spectacles, the prominent, somewhat bulbous nose, and the hair that sat like a mushroom over her forehead, all exaggerated under Grace's pen.

It was not flattering, but it captured her spirit and features fairly well, if Grace did say so herself.

Grace sat back, satisfied. Now to come up with a pithy caption and get some newspaper to buy it.

Until then she would go each morning to her other "cartoon" work. It was ironic really that the large-scale drawings she made of the small watercolor window designs at Tiffany Glass and Decorating were also called cartoons. She supposed because they were line drawings. But they couldn't be further from most of Grace's other cartoons.

With the window designs she helped to bring art and beauty to scores of people, but with her political cartoons, Grace Griffith intended to change the world.

Chapter 2

Emilie sat upright on the bed in her second-class cabin, valise still packed and sitting at her feet, her portfolio on the narrow bed beside her. As if she thought there would be any escape if she was found. Were the authorities even looking for her? She had done nothing wrong. Not willingly. But they might want to question her, have her attest to her father's guilt. She hadn't been able to go that far, though she'd known from the beginning that one day she would have to make him stop.

But surely she was safe now. No one had prevented her from boarding the train to Le Havre or the *Gascognia* just before it sailed. But even so, she had made up her mind. Her future lay in New York in the studio of Louis C. Tiffany. She would turn light into art, her way, her vision, all hers.

She heard the ship's engines change from their rhythmic chug to the steady hum of power that told her they were well underway, out of the harbor and into the sea. Into safety.

Emilie let out her breath, not expending it all at once but slowly, as if the slightest ruffle of air might set things she couldn't control into motion.

The last time she'd sailed, she and her father had a first-class suite, a cadre of ship's personnel to see to their every need. A beautiful dining room and library; deck chaises where one could sit sipping lemonade or champagne before dressing for dinner or a ball or a salon. Of course, then her father had been an established portrait painter, much in demand.

Before the world discovered how he really could afford such a lavish style of life: copying the lesser known old masters—and some of the new ones—and selling them as originals to gullible, mostly foreign, collectors.

He was an adequate painter in his own right, but it was the appearance of affluence that made people think he had to be excellent to be so much in demand. Which brought more clients who wanted their own portraits painted by an artist who was au courant—and were willing to pay for it.

And there, Emilie might be considered guilty. For when her father got too busy with his illicit art endeavors, he left the finishing of details on the portraits to Emilie.

She hated it. She hated portraiture. And most of all she hated her father.

Those people didn't see the other times, when they fled in the night because they couldn't pay the rent, or when he came home enraged and took it out on his wife and daughter. And then on Emilie alone, when her mother could take no more.

Emilie shuddered. She couldn't remember when she'd last had an untroubled sleep. She was tired to the bone, but she knew sleep would elude her. Once she was safe in America, she could sleep.

So she sat in her cabin, so small she could almost touch the opposite wall. Sat as the ship shuddered and rolled beneath her. Sat until they were well out from shore and she could hear movement outside her door, which meant it must be noon or later.

A steward knocked on her door to ask if she wished to have luncheon in her cabin. She said yes, knowing it would cost her extra, unlike the people above her in first class. She pushed away the thought. She needed to watch her money, but she also needed to eat, and she wasn't ready to face the world just yet.

When the tray came, she opened the door, face averted while the steward put the tray on the desk and departed.

She drank the water, dipped a bit of bread in the wine, but her stomach rebelled. Nerves or the sea, she couldn't eat.

Emilie pushed the tray aside, hoisted her valise onto the bed, and pulled the key out from where it hung around her neck. Slowly she unlocked it, irrationally listening for the final sounds of the chase. They didn't come.

She had packed two serviceable skirts and shirtwaists and two work aprons that she hoped would make her fit in with the others. She shook out the skirts and hung them in the narrow closet. Next came a visiting dress that should suffice until she was settled and could send to Marie for her trunk. She stowed her undergarments and nightdress in the little set of drawers on the wall.

And there at the very bottom of her belongings was what she wanted. Her sketchbook and several gallery catalogs and art magazines. From these she would continue learning the fine art of stained glass. She'd been reading and practicing ever since discovering Tiffany's work in Monsieur Bing's Maison de L'Art Nouveau months before.

She'd never dared go into the gallery before. She couldn't afford to buy anything, and his displays of the new art were ridiculed by the members of the Académie des Beaux-Arts, where she studied, and abhorred by her father, whom she feared. But she was walking by one day when a flash of color from the window caught her eye. And in an act of defiance and curiosity, she strode bravely inside to see what had caused it.

And stopped dead as she came face-to-face with a mounted window made of glass unlike any she'd seen before. "Favrile" glass, they called it. In the most amazing patterns and colors imaginable, from inside the glass itself, not painted and enameled on the surface. Not at all like the dreary windows of the cathedral or myriad old churches that dotted Paris neighborhoods.

Set on pedestals, vases of impossible fragility seemed to embrace the air around them, vibrant and moving, and alive. And as Emilie stood awed, the sun shifted outside and needles of magical light refracted in all directions, flooding the floor and walls with moving color.

Louis C. Tiffany.

After that, she returned again and again. She searched Paris for more examples of his work, learned that he kept a large studio in New York where scores of artists and artisans designed, created, and constructed these wonders. And that one particular atelier was composed entirely of women.

Emilie scoured magazines and catalogs for examples of this glass, read about how it was made. Jean managed to "confiscate" several from the Académie library where he worked to support himself and Marie while they both pursued life as painters.

Dear Jean, loyal and honest and talented; his love for Emilie had made him a thief. Her need had tainted his life, too.

Among the cache was a copy of *The Art Journal*, an American magazine that explained how it was all done. And Emilie was determined she would learn.

Then her world exploded.

No matter, she would just have to teach herself on the voyage over. Learn enough to get a toehold in the Tiffany workshop. It could be done if she set her mind to it. It would *have* to be done. Just enough to get her an audience with Mr. Tiffany, and then she would convince him to hire her. Oh, how hard she would work.

Emilie closed the valise but didn't remove it from the bed. Its hard surface would make an acceptable desk for the work she needed to do while at sea.

But work receded from her brain almost immediately. She yawned, then yawned again and curled against her valise and portfolio, her arm draped protectively over them, she fell asleep.

When Emilie awoke again, all was quiet except for the rhythmic churning of the engines. She wove almost drunkenly to the door, bracing herself on the wall when a particularly large swell threatened to throw her off her feet. She poked her head into the hallway and seeing no one about, crept out to the second-class deck to breathe in the cool fresh air.

Night had fallen. It was dark. A kind of dark you never saw in Paris. In Paris, someone was always awake, reveling and lighting up the sky. But here, not a hint of the harbor lights of Le Havre shone through that inky black. No coastline of France was silhouetted against the night sky. That was good.

She turned away from the past, knowing the darkness would follow her west, like a shadow that refused to let her go. But for now she would work and work until she was so tired, she would have to sleep. And when she awoke again, it wouldn't matter if it was day or night.

The deck swelled beneath her feet; her stomach swelled with it. She would have to go to the dining room tomorrow or she would be too weak to do anything when they arrived in New York.

How had she come to this place of exile? One drunken accusation thrown out in anger on the street, repeated at Madame Hubert's salon several nights later. "A rumor, you understand. Nothing more." But the damage was done, and the news spread, quietly at first, some not believing, some brushing it aside as idle gossip or jealousy.

It was jealousy, but it was also true.

Dominique Pascal was an art forger.

And then the speculation turned toward Emilie. She noticed it first at the Académie where she was training as an artist and would sometimes sit for established painters. A statement whispered under the breath. Surreptitious glances in her direction, quickly darting away when she returned their look.

They were wondering if she knew. If she had helped him, if she was as guilty as he. And it all supported what they had known all along. Women had no place in the Académie des Beaux-Arts.

At first Emilie tried to ignore them. Her stubborn streak forced her to lift her chin and continue to study even as they shunned her, snickered as she passed by, grumbled when she entered a room. And still she went every day though it shredded her heart.

And then Dominique Pascal had disappeared, leaving his only daughter (at least the only one he claimed) to face Parisian society and the police on her own. If she had had a family or even powerful friends, she might have been able to weather the storm, but she didn't. So like the father, the daughter had fled.

And now she was free.

For the next four days, Emilie remained in her cabin, shunning the sunlight and curious eyes. Sometimes she would go to the dining room and force herself to converse with the other passengers just to practice her English. Sometimes she would take her sketchbook to the deck, but it didn't lend itself to the careful work she needed to do. Mostly she stayed in her cabin and drew, copying the photos from the gallery catalog and the other magazines.

She began with the art nouveau posters. With their dark accentuated shadows, they were well suited to understanding how to turn a painting into a puzzle of glass pieces. At first Emilie copied straight from magazine to sketchbook, then she would grid out a smaller section and draw it to a larger scale. And then a smaller section and an even larger scale.

It was painstaking work and sometimes she just wanted to explode with lines and color until they ran off the page and curled in the air like the vases she'd seen. But she kept her discipline. Precision and attention to every detail would eventually far surpass whatever need to create she possessed now.

But someday. She could already see her work in her mind's eye. *Someday.*

She bent her head and realized that she was moving her pencil in tune with the rolling ship. Very rarely did she lose control of the line, except when a sudden lurch sent the tip slashing across the page.

One night there was a storm; the ship rolled so violently that Emilie had to leave off drawing or even reading. There were very few people in the dining room that evening. Emilie found it difficult to even contemplate eating, but she forced down a few morsels of meat and pudding. Only to lose it back in her cabin in waves and waves of nausea.

She didn't attempt to ingest anything but liquids for the next two days, and then miraculously the seas calmed. And a day later the engines shut down and they were towed into New York Harbor.

SHAKY AND WEAK from not eating, from nerves, from excitement, Emilie dressed in her best work skirt and shirtwaist. Paid special attention to her hair, which she braided and twisted into a coil at the nape of her neck. Not the usual sweep of red-brown curls she favored, but flattering enough, and the style would show her serious intent.

She went to the dining room, determined to have a good breakfast before she left the ship. But when the food appeared, she could manage only a small roll and some black coffee.

Well, no matter. As soon as she was employed, she would treat herself to a steak dinner in a nice restaurant where you didn't have to chase your silverware each time you wanted to take a bite.

Then suddenly the ship slowed, the engines stopped altogether, and the passengers made their way on deck. The first thing she noticed was the heat. Much hotter than Paris. She was wearing the same cloak she'd worn the night of her escape. There was no room for it in her valise, and it was too heavy to carry along with her valise and portfolio. She was already perspiring by the time she reached the front of the line and presented her carte de visite to the customs man.

"Traveling alone, are you?"

Not that it was any of his business. "Yes."

He took a second look at her carte.

All the fear Emilie thought she'd left behind flooded over her. She swayed slightly on her feet. But he handed the carte back to her and passed her on.

"Can you tell me the way to Fourth Avenue?"

"Take Fourteenth Street across town. That's Fourteenth right out there." He jabbed his finger in the direction of the street. Gave her a quick scrutinizing look, and Emilie froze.

"It's about seven blocks, so if no one is waiting for you, you'd best take the trolley or a cab. Don't think about walking it. We're in the midst of a heat wave, worst in years if you ask me. And if you're carrying all that luggage and wearing that coat . . ."

She thanked him and hurried away, his muttered "foreigners" echoing in her ears.

Seven blocks to Fourth then from Fourteenth to Twenty-Fifth where the Tiffany studio was located. A long walk and it *was* unbearably hot. She didn't want her first impression to be one of a frazzled, disheveled waif. But a cab . . . it was too dear. If it became too hot on the way, she would merely stop at a fountain to cool her face.

Emilie had never been to New York before. But her mother had been English and made certain that her daughter was raised with English manners as well as French. But that was only until Emilie was eleven, when the river took her from them.

But Emilie even at eleven knew that it wasn't the river's fault. Her mother in desperation had been the one who chose the river.

Now, suddenly Emilie was afraid her English wouldn't be good enough. That her accent would put people off. That she should have brought better clothes. They might think she was some poor, uneducated immigrant like those souls aboard the *Gascognia* who had watched from the lower deck as the first- and second-class passengers disembarked. Knowing that they would be turned around and sent to immigration where they would be poked and prodded and have their names changed, some to be admitted to quarantine and some to be sent back without ever setting foot in America proper.

She'd felt their energy, she, one of the lucky ones, as they watched, their hope and fear piercing a hole in her back. She'd heard the stories passed around the neighborhood, complained of loudly in the bars where her father spent many evenings and where Emilie was sometimes an unwilling companion. That's why she'd spent so much of her meager savings for a second-class ticket. She was here, feet solidly planted. And here she would stay.

Tears welled up in her eyes, tears of relief and hope and fear that she wouldn't know how to survive on her own.

But she wasn't on her own. She had her portfolio and her talent and her ambition.

And with that, she shifted her valise and portfolio and started off down Fourteenth Street. She was sorry not to be able to make an "entrance," but she'd sold most of her hats and gowns to have enough money for the trip.

Never mind, that was all behind her. She was a working girl now. Emilie looked both ways then stepped out onto the street. Maneuvering between handcarts and delivery wagons and horse-drawn carriages, she made her way to the opposite side.

Then she lifted her chin and started resolutely toward her future.

It only took half a block in the heat, being jostled by people in a hurry, the smell of horse manure and human sweat cloying her nose, to realize the blocks in this city were longer than she had anticipated. And the heat was overpowering.

Emilie paused under a grocer's awning, but there was little respite. If she took off her cloak, she would have to put down her two cases and someone might snatch them away. And even if they didn't, she would have to carry the cloak in addition to her already heavy belongings.

And if all the blocks were as long as this one appeared to be, she would never make it. Already she was perspiring and feeling a little unsteady on her feet, her skirt hanging loose at her waist. And it was getting late.

A trolley passed by her, going toward the docks. And she knew that if she didn't want to present herself to Mr. Tiffany with her coat hem lined in dust, her shirtwaist sticking to her back, and her hair wet against her face, she would have to take the trolley. She didn't dare splurge on a cab.

Thinking of her dwindling purse, she switched her cases to opposite hands to relieve her shoulders and crossed the street. After a few minutes' wait, she climbed onto the next trolley going east.

When the conductor came to collect her fare, Emilie drew herself a little taller and asked in her best English if this was the correct trolley to "333 Fourth Avenue, Tiffany Glass and Decorating Company."

"Change at Union Square to the northbound," he said, and handed her a ticket. "Show this to the conductor."

"Mer— Thank you."

Emilie sat back and took several long breaths. Soon, soon she would be there. And looking around her, she began to accustom herself to America.

It wasn't much of an introduction. Fourteenth was a wide, dirty street, with nothing much to recommend its architecture. Rows of squat buildings of a dark brown stone were interrupted by an occasional warehouse or factory. One would think that a visitor's first view of the famous city would be more impressive. In Paris the main thoroughfares were lined with trees and stately buildings . . . *But you're no longer in Paris*, she reminded herself. And might never be again.

After several minutes, the conductor called out Union Square and a string of names Emilie didn't recognize.

They were at a park, a pretty-looking respite from the crowds and the heat. Normally she would have enjoyed a stroll beneath its trees. But she followed the other passengers who appeared to also be taking the northbound trolley.

The next trolley to stop was already crowded, and if a smallish gentleman hadn't offered Emilie his seat, she would have had to balance her cases while attempting to keep her feet as the trolley clattered up the avenue.

She craned her neck at each stop looking for a street sign. Eighteenth, Nineteenth . . . not long now. . . . More passengers got on and Emilie could barely see past their heads . . . Twenty-First . . . Twenty-Second. Twenty-Third. She was barely taking in her surroundings so afraid that she might miss her stop, even though the trolley seemed to stop at every corner.

At Twenty-Fourth she stood. Threaded her way through the other passengers, her valise and portfolio creating additional obstacles. But by the time the conductor yelled "Twenty-Fifth!" she was ready to descend.

She waited for the trolley to pass, then looked around.

She was on another wide avenue, but unlike Fourteenth Street, this one was flanked by large business and apartment buildings. Fewer people strode up and down the sidewalks.

Emilie scanned the businesses across the street, then turned and searched those on her side of the avenue. Just as she was beginning to panic, she saw it, one building away, cast in bronze over a double door. Tiffany Glass and Decorating Company.

Her nerves raced. *Calmly now. Be professional.* She risked putting down her valise and portfolio while she patted her hair, rebuttoned her cloak, which she'd unbuttoned on the trolley ride, and dabbed the perspiration from her face with her sleeve.

This would have to do. She picked up her belongings and marched up to the door.

"You'll be wanting the Twenty-Fifth Street entrance," the uniformed doorman said and directed her back up the avenue.

Emilie went around the corner and came to a less impressive door, though it was impressive enough. Once again, she collected herself and stepped inside.

The porter here was dressed in workpants, collarless shirt, and suspenders. He looked up from his stool when she stopped in front of him.

"Good day, miss," he said, a slight question to his voice.

Emilie sighed, wishing she wasn't so hot, so weak, so unkempt, but she hadn't dared stay overnight at a hotel or the YWCA as someone on board ship had suggested. Surely a great artist wouldn't hold it against her that she was weary and mussed from her voyage, even if his porter did. It would convince Mr. Tiffany she was serious about working, anxious to begin. He couldn't turn her away. She had the letter. The letter, if nothing else, would convince him. No matter that it was no more real than the paintings her father passed as originals.

"Yes, miss?" the porter repeated.

"I—" Emilie steeled herself and started again. "I have an appointment with Mr. Tiffany." Which wasn't exactly true, but what was another little lie after so many? This would be the last. At least as soon as she got the job, it would be her last.

"That is not possible, miss."

"Of course it is. I have an appointment."

"Well, there's been some sort of mix-up then," the man said. His eyes were kindly, but wary, as if he thought she might be a bit mad. "I'm sorry to say, Mr. Tiffany sailed for Europe . . . must have been a week or so ago."

Emilie swayed back on her heels.

The porter jumped to his feet. He was tall and angular. "Are you quite all right, miss?"

His words sounded very far away. *Sailed for Europe.*

"But I . . . I . . ."

He glanced at her portfolio. "You're an artist, miss?"

She nodded as the world righted itself again, and she pushed down the panic that threatened to drown her. Where would she stay until he returned? How would she survive on the little money she had left? Of all the things that she'd imagined could go wrong, she'd never imagined this.

"Did you come to apply for a job?"

"Yes . . . Mr. Tiffany . . ."

"Perhaps then you should speak with Mrs. Driscoll. She's head of the ladies' division. She's on the fifth floor. The elevator is just back there." He frowned, his mouth curving into a contortion that was almost comical.

"Here now, let me get Alfred to watch the door and I'll see you up, myself."

"Thank you."

Emilie put down her cases, stretched her back. *She would have to talk to Mrs. Driscoll.*

It seemed an eternity before the porter returned with a boy wearing a worn suit that he hadn't quite grown into. He nodded and took his place on the stool.

"This way, miss." The porter escorted her into a large elevator and closed the grille.

"The ladies are up on the fifth floor. I know for a fact they're looking for new cutters. So you've come at a good time."

Emilie just nodded; she was busy thinking of what she would say to the woman who wasn't Mr. Tiffany.

The elevator came to a stop, the porter opened the grille, and they stepped out.

"You just stand right here." He raised his hand and called in a hushed voice, "Miss Griffith. . . ."

A young woman who was standing on a stool in front of one of the large-scale drawings—*cartoons*, Emilie reminded herself—looked over and stepped down. She leaned her maulstick against the easel, put her pencil away, and came to meet him.

"This here is a young lady seeking employment."

Miss Griffith gave Emilie a quick appraising look. She was about the same age as Emilie, maybe a little older, and a little taller, with thick brown hair and a well-formed face. "I'll just let Mrs. Driscoll know." Miss Griffith smiled, hurried down the length of the room, and knocked on a narrow door at the far end.

"You just wait right here. Mrs. Driscoll won't be but a minute." The porter nodded and took himself back to the elevator.

Light-headed and attacked by alternating relief and anxiety, Emilie stood at the entrance to a new life. Afraid to put down her valise or portfolio and risk the whole scene disappearing like a magician's act.

Two rows of long worktables were placed down a center aisle to the door through which Miss Griffith had disappeared. At each table, two or three women were sitting on stools or standing, all dressed in aprons over their shirtwaists and skirts, and bent over trays that held hundreds of pieces of colored glass.

Two others, like Miss Griffith, were standing at large easels re-creating drawings that would become scenes of stained glass.

The room had windows on three sides, lighting the room to its far corners. Huge rectangles of glass were placed before several of them—windows in progress. Only partially finished, a kaleidoscope of greens, reds, yellows, and colors Emilie had imagined but never seen, they radiated the sunshine in a dazzling display, dappling the walls, floor, and workers in color.

It was almost too much.

The door at the end of the workroom seemed much farther away than it had before. But a woman was walking toward her, tall, large-boned, and very serious looking. The name, *Mrs. Driscoll*, floated in Emilie's head. She was followed by Miss Griffith and another woman, shorter and softer, and Emilie concentrated on her until Mrs. Driscoll stood before her.

"Yes?"

"*Je*— I'm— I have a let—" Emilie couldn't seem to form the word. *A letter. She has a letter.* She grasped the portfolio tighter. Mrs. Driscoll tilted her head and frowned.

Emilie fumbled at the portfolio's closures.

"I have a . . ." *She can't reach the letter. She thrusts the portfolio forward. It falls from her hand, spilling her sketches onto the floor, and taking Emilie with them.*

Chapter 3

Good heavens, she's fainted," exclaimed Miss Gouvy from beside Grace. Mrs. Driscoll had already knelt down by the recumbent figure and began to dispatch orders. "Smelling salts, Miss Evans. Top shelf, medicine cabinet in my office. Miss Hodgins, a glass of water. Alice, let's get her out of this coat."

It was the first time Grace had ever heard Mrs. Driscoll break what they called the "Miss" rule, a form of address they used in the workshop to keep everything professional.

Miss Gouvy didn't blink an eye but immediately knelt on the other side of the girl and efficiently began to attack the buttons.

For a moment, Grace just stood where she was, mesmerized by the young woman on the floor. She itched to capture her on paper, not as an exaggerated social figure but as Ophelia, painted by John Everett Millais, the sketches spreading around her like the flowers in poor Ophelia's watery grave. Otherworldly, her skin so pale as to be almost transparent with a serene beauty that barely managed to hide the turmoil inside.

She would make a great window.

Throughout the workroom, attentions were drawn to the spectacle and soon everyone had slipped from their places and edged closer to get a better look.

Grace was so captivated by the scene, she only saw their encroaching feet when Miss Kruger's overly large boot came into view. Grace barely managed to snatch a handful of the sketches away before they were trampled on by everyone trying to help. She tossed the renderings to the top of the nearest worktable and went back to save the rest.

Everyone had gathered around the fallen girl. She sighed, stirred, groaned, and tried to rise.

Mrs. Driscoll held her back and said in her no-nonsense way, "Don't get up, you fainted, but you'll be fine directly. Miss Hodgins!"

"Coming, Mrs. Driscoll." Dora Hodgins hurried back, holding a glass in front of her and sloshing water as she ran.

Mrs. Driscoll lifted the girl's head and held the glass for her to drink, before handing it back to Dora, and Grace took the time to straighten the sketches and take a closer look. What she saw made her catch her breath.

Precisely rendered details of what must be larger sketches: pen and inks, watercolors of perfectly formed flowers, fields of lupine and figures from gallery posters, all copied and transformed by dark lines representing pieces of stained glass. They were miniature cartoons. And good ones. Work of this caliber would certainly be a welcome addition to the women's Glass Cutting Department.

She began to return them to the portfolio when from inside a splash of vivid color caught her eye. Not everything had fallen out. She carefully reached inside and extracted two larger cardboard-backed paintings.

Well, thought Grace, *I wonder if she meant to show these?* Mr. Tiffany abhorred modern painting. And these were definitely modern. One was a portrait of a woman, not in the pastels of the sketches, but rendered in garish colors and harsh, thick applications of color.

The other painting was a street scene of two women sitting at a small table at a sidewalk café. Here, too, instead of the soft peach tones of the impressionists, they were depicted in cobalt blue, red, and yellow. One chair was deep purple, the other orange. And the brushstrokes were laid down in an almost random, frenetic fashion.

These were a far cry from the other more classical sketches in the portfolio. Strong and bold and, it seemed to Grace, a little irreverent. The word *raucous* came to mind.

So she hadn't been wrong, Ophelia had a rebellious streak.

They were like nothing Grace had seen before. Of course, she wasn't that knowledgeable about art movements. When she studied art for its own sake, she studied journalistic cartoonists.

Mrs. Driscoll and Miss Gouvy finally helped the girl to her feet. But she pulled her arm away and reached toward Grace. "*Mes croquis.*" Her voice was low, weak, but not timid.

Their eyes held. The girl seemed to realize at the same time Grace did—and probably the others as well—that she had spoken in French. "My sketches," she repeated.

Grace hastily slid the newest paintings under the others. "They're here on the table. No harm done."

"Nothing will happen to your work," Mrs. Driscoll said. "Now, come sit over here until you're recovered a bit. It's this monstrous heat wave."

Between the two of them, Mrs. Driscoll and Miss Gouvy maneuvered the girl across the room and helped her to sit on a bench by the wall, Miss Gouvy managing to quietly slip the coat completely off in the process.

Dora handed her the glass of water.

Emilie took a sip and revived a little. "I came to work for Mr. Tiffany. I have a letter of introduction." She tried to stand, but Mrs. Driscoll pushed her gently down.

"Soon enough for that, once you've recovered."

"It's in my portfolio." The girl looked quickly around.

"Over here," Grace called. She scooped the now empty portfolio off the floor and held it up. Then she placed it on top of the sketches before hurrying to join the group.

"Forgive me. It is the heat, I just came from the ship and had to take the trolleys."

This garnered gasps from the others.

"I wished not to be late, so I didn't have a proper breakfast, but I am fine now and ready to work."

Her accent was strong, definitely French. So that's why she showed up with a valise and full portfolio. Had she sailed from Europe to work for Mr. Tiffany? Excellent. They could use another experienced artist. And if she could cut glass, all the better.

"You just sit here," Mrs. Driscoll said. "And someone please find her something to eat."

"I have an apple," Maggie Wilson volunteered.

"Thank you, Miss Wilson, that will be an excellent beginning."

One by one the girls came up with a piece of cheese, a bit of bread, and Miss Evans, finding no need for the smelling salts she'd fetched, hurried off to make tea.

"You're French," Mrs. Driscoll said matter-of-factly.

"Yes, but my mother was English. And I am schooled in oils, watercolors, pastels, and pen and ink."

I'll say, thought Grace.

"And your name?"

"Emilie . . . Pascal."

Her name rolled out like a song and at least one of the girls sighed. No doubt they would all be pronouncing their own names with that French lilt by the time they left for the day.

"And you say Mr. Tiffany was expecting you?"

"I have a letter. And examples of my work in my portfolio."

Mrs. Driscoll turned to Miss Gouvy. The two of them not only worked together but were childhood friends, and Grace sometimes thought they could communicate without speaking.

Like now, when they simultaneously moved a little away from the group, who took the opportunity of crowding closer around the girl.

Grace approached them. "Mrs. Driscoll?"

"Yes, Miss Griffith."

"Before you decide what to do with her, I think you should look at these." Grace motioned them over to the portfolio. Moved it aside to reveal the sketches.

Both women looked from her to the artwork.

"These are all hers?" asked Mrs. Driscoll.

"Yes. They were on the floor. I picked them up so they wouldn't be damaged."

"Quick thinking on your part, Miss Griffith," said Mrs. Driscoll, leaning over to peer at the scale drawing of a single peony. She pushed the papers around until she found the original sketch. An eight-by-eleven watercolor of a peony bush growing against a brick wall. She pulled a magnifying glass from her pocket and studied the two, going back and forth from original to scale detail.

"Impressive," she said, glancing toward their visitor, who was being subjected to excited questions about what it was like to live in France. "There's no doubt that she's a talented copyist. Her scale is near perfect." Mrs. Driscoll looked through the top few pages. Then she came to the painting of the women at the café.

"Good heavens."

"A modernist," Miss Gouvy said, not able to keep the slight disdain from her voice.

"Certainly interesting," said Mrs. Driscoll.

"We really shouldn't be looking at these without her permission," Miss Gouvy pointed out.

"True," Mrs. Driscoll said, not making any move to put them away. She glanced at Grace, and Grace understood that she was about to be dismissed.

"Miss Griffith, could you keep Miss Pascal company while Miss Gouvy and I confer?"

"Gladly . . . I'm sure she will be an asset to the workroom."

Mrs. Driscoll flashed a smile. "Are you volunteering to show her the ropes, as they say?"

"I'd be happy to," Grace said, wanting to kick herself for taking on extra work when she already had more than she could handle. But if it would get them another designer, copyist, or even a cutter, it would be worth it.

Grace peered past them to where the newcomer sat, very straight, regaining confidence by the moment. She'd pushed the escaped tendrils of hair behind her ears, but already they were beginning to curl around her face, as if breaking free from confinement. Her skirt and waist were a little worse for wear, and not of the first or even second quality; but definitely in keeping with the rest of them. There was even a smear of paint on the cuff of one sleeve. But the coat, ridiculously out of place in the summer heat, was of a fine quality, if in need of cleaning.

Interesting. Working girl clothes, a debutante's spring coat.

The detailed copying and the sectioning of the art nouveau figures showed admirable adherence to discipline. But those wild-colored paintings? Those came from someplace deep and a little frightening.

Which one was Emilie Pascal?

There must be a story to tell. And Grace was already imagining it.

"In that case, come with me."

Grace nearly jumped at Mrs. Driscoll's voice, she'd been so immersed in her speculation about Miss Pascal. She fell in step with the manageress as she strode over to the group still gathered by the newcomer.

"Ladies." Mrs. Driscoll had to clap her hands to gain their attention. "Back to work, please, before the day gets any hotter. I've asked Mr. Mitchell to send up additional fans. Be sure not to aim them directly at your glass. The glass dust wreaks havoc on the eyes and throat."

With a collective sigh they all returned to work, except Maggie Wilson, who continued to stare worshipfully at Emilie Pascal.

At twenty-three, Maggie had the understanding of a young child. She'd been taken on to sweep and run simple errands when her sister, Lotte, was hired. And though she was adequate at sweeping, she was easily distracted, especially by the "jewels" of glass surrounding her.

She had the same look of wonder now, looking at Miss Pascal, that she did when wandering among the glass samples.

"Maggie, back to work," Grace whispered. Maggie jumped.

"Nice to meet you," she said to Emilie, dipped an awkward curtsy, and hurried away.

Grace was shocked to see the French girl smile and blink tears from her eyes.

"Miss Pascal," said Mrs. Driscoll. "This is Miss Griffith, who has offered to sit with you while I look over your portfolio, if that is acceptable to you."

Emilie started to rise, but Mrs. Driscoll waved her back down. "No need to get up, your work will be quite safe with me, and you seem to have gathered quite a feast. Please enjoy it while you wait. And drink some more water. You must be parched."

The girl looked at the bench to either side of her. It seemed everyone had had some little morsel to donate to her lunch. She nodded at Mrs. Driscoll.

"Excellent. We'll be in my office at the end of the workroom. It's less dusty there." She walked away, leaving Emilie staring a little apprehensively after her.

The girl was as high-strung as a racehorse. Grace hoped to heaven she wouldn't always be getting the vapors or dropping glass in an attack of the fidgets if they did hire her.

Grace sat down beside her. "I'm so glad you agreed to sit here. It will keep me from having to climb back onto that stool for a little while longer. The sweat was dripping off my nose so fast, I thought I might float away."

This earned her a smile from Emilie.

"You came in the middle of the worst heat wave in years," Grace continued.

"Then it is not always like this?"

"Well, it is summer, but not usually as hot as this."

"I couldn't fit my cloak in my valise."

"I figured that, and it was too cumbersome to carry all the way from the docks," Grace said sympathetically.

"Yes, and I had to take the trolleys to come here." Emilie smiled ruefully. "I'm not sure exactly where I am. It is my first trip to America."

"Do you have family here, Miss Pascal?"

Emilie shook her head.

"Friends?"

Again Emilie shook her head.

"Then where are you staying?"

"I was hoping that after I saw Mr. Tiffany, there would be a place for me in the women's dormitory."

Grace frowned at that. "We don't house our workers. Do they in France?"

"Sometimes, but women have no such opportunities as this." She gestured toward the workroom. "But where do you all live?"

"Most live at home with their families; mother, father, and siblings. You're not allowed to work here if you're married. You're not married, are you?"

"No. Never."

"Good. I mean . . . it's good that you aren't married now."

A soft sound escaped from Emilie's lips, and Grace decided it was a laugh.

"Some of us live in nearby boardinghouses or rent rooms at the YWCA or the women's hotel. If Mrs. Driscoll hires you, we'll help you find lodgings."

"Thank you." Emilie picked up a bunch of grapes and offered it to Grace.

"Thanks, but I don't want to have sticky fingers when I get back to my cartoon. That's mine over there in the corner. It's for a triptych that needs to get done by yesterday."

She caught Emilie's look of confusion and said, "That just means I need to finish it really, really fast. We're starting next on a series of four panels that we'll be exhibiting at the Exposition Universelle in Paris in the spring. The 'Four Seasons.' Mr. Tiffany designed it. Miss Northrop's sketches made it possible to be rendered in glass."

Then remembering Mr. Tiffany's warning not to discuss the new projects with anyone except one another, Grace added, "She's really wonderful but can be a little intimidating. She lives all the way out in Queens and has to take the ferry to work."

Grace saw Emilie's perplexed look and elucidated. "It's just across the East River." She leaned a little closer. "She's in her forties and she lives in a boys' school."

Emilie's eyes widened.

"Her father is headmaster there."

"Oh." Emilie looked past her to the triptych cartoon. "Could I see it up close?"

"Sure, if you're up to it."

"I am very strong. It was just a . . . an aberrant occurrence."

Artistic and stubborn, too, thought Grace. "In that case, finish your lunch and I'll show you."

"These are exceptional," Clara said, spreading Emilie Pascal's drawings across her desktop.

"True," Alice agreed.

"So what is troubling you?"

Alice glanced at the closed door. "Nothing specific. But there is something a little secretive about Miss Pascal. Didn't you notice it?"

Clara, who had braced on her hands to peruse the details of a particularly complicated drawing, stood up. "It was an unusual entrance, I agree."

"And coming unannounced like that, when most of the girls are recommended by either the Metropolitan's art school or the Y's art program for women."

"True," Clara agreed.

"And Mr. Tiffany didn't mention having offered anyone a position on his last trip abroad, did he?"

"No, but he was preoccupied with his latest voyage, especially since he decided to take his entire family." She moved a rendering of a lavender stalk out of the way and took a closer look at the cartoons of a theater poster. When Alice didn't respond, she looked up.

"What are you saying?" Clara felt a twinge in her temple; soon her head would begin to throb. *Not now*, she thought. She didn't have time for one of her headaches now.

"I'm just remembering Mr. Tiffany's order right before he left."

"Which one? There were so many."

"That we have to be exceptionally vigilant about guarding what we are working on. That his competitors would love to get their hands on the latest designs."

"Oh, Alice. You think Mr. La Farge has sent that young girl to spy on us?"

"It sounds ridiculous when you say it out loud," Alice agreed reluctantly.

Clara pulled her hankie out to wipe her forehead. Standing beside her, Alice looked as cool as a cucumber. Her hair was still perfectly coiffed, no damp wisps hanging about her neck. Even her shirtwaist was still crisp and dazzling white.

Clara always felt large, owlish, and somewhat dowdy in Alice's presence. Mr. Tiffany had once mentioned that Clara had an exotic look about her, and she clung to that idea in her darkest hours. But Emilie Pascal was truly arresting. Those dark eyes, the unblemished complexion. It was perfectly reasonable that his love of the exotic would be moved by her person, even more so by her attention to detail, which would inspire him to offer her a position. Clara just wished he'd told her about it.

"It does sound like something he would do," Alice said, breaking into her thoughts. "Though it hardly speaks to her favor that she came in and fainted at our feet."

Clara laughed. "It did get our attention." She pushed a detail of the peony toward Alice. "These scale drawings are impeccable."

"They are, but what do you think these two are?" Alice nodded at the two expressionist paintings that Clara had moved out of the way.

"They make me shudder," Alice said and pushed them ever farther out of the way.

"That's because you are the mistress of pastel nature study, and all these loud colors and stark brushstrokes disturb your higher sensibilities."

Alice pursed her lips. "Don't be ridiculous. But don't you find it strange that she shows up just after Mr. Tiffany leaves? And with perfect examples of stained-glass drawing. *And* those." She lifted her chin at the paintings.

"Alice, I can't afford to lose any more girls. We're behind as it is, and I'll be swaneed if I have to let the men take over any of our work. They would just love to see us shut down altogether."

"You will never let that happen."

"Absolutely not."

"Said like a true general," Alice said, and she saluted, her eyes twinkling. "I suppose you could give her a temporary try, like you usually do."

"Yes. We'll call her in and interview her. If we both like what we hear, she can have a week's trial at three-fifty a week."

"Equitable," Alice agreed. "And just pray no one else decides to get married."

"Perish the thought," Clara said. She had to do something about speeding up the work schedule immediately. Please God, that Emilie Pascal would be the answer to her prayers.

Emilie was too excited and nervous to eat much, but she forced down some fruit and bread and cheese. It wouldn't do to keep fainting, something she never did. But she was anxious to get started.

Miss Griffith helped her fold up the leftovers, then led her over to her workstation.

"So I'm what they call a cartoonist," she told Emily. "Which just means I take small watercolor renderings and turn them into a full-size drawing that can be used as a pattern to cut the templates for the glass pieces that make up the final windows."

She paused, giving Emilie a chance to understand. Emilie did understand. She'd read all about how a cartoon was made, but seeing it up close made her realize how little she actually knew, and a wave of apprehension rolled over her. What if it was too hard?

Then she steeled herself and thought, *Just get the job and then worry about keeping up.*

"We're lucky to have these big windows on three sides of the workroom. We can put glass easels in front of them and work on several stained-glass windows at a time while still having enough light for the decorative arts people to work on their projects."

Miss Griffith swept her arm to the far side of the workroom to other rows of tables where women were creating all manner of decorative items, which caught the light like a hundred jewel boxes. All around Emilie, girls were working, their heads bent over their work, and a thrill coursed through her.

"Vast, isn't it?" Miss Griffith said. "And this is just the fifth floor. There are departments on the other floors, though they're all staffed by men."

"And the vases?"

"They're all blown at the furnaces in Corona, out in Queens." Grace moved on. "At this next window is Miss Hodgins, who brought you the glass of water."

Emilie nodded. "I remember."

At the mention of her name, Dora Hodgins turned, pencil in one hand, maulstick in the other. She was quite pretty, Emilie thought. Her nearly black hair was swept back with a flair of wings before being confined in a tight chignon. Her eyes were a bright blue, a surprising contrast to her dark hair.

She gave Emilie a quick smile and went back to work.

"Miss Hodgins is tracing a finished cartoon. We always make two copies, one that will go behind the large plate glass, and one to be cut into individual templates for cutting the glass. Each gets numbered so you know how to put it back together again."

"And you cut the templates with double-edged scissors that allow room for the solder," Emilie added. "That's why she's painting the lines so thick."

"Exactly," Miss Griffith said.

Emilie breathed a little easier. It looked simple enough.

They stopped next at a table where one lone young woman was nipping the edges of a small piece of glass. There was a wooden tray before her filled with bits and pieces of what Emilie assumed were the trimmings.

"And this is Miss Wilson."

Lotte Wilson, quite thin and already slump-shouldered—probably from constantly bending over her work—looked up and smiled, but kept working. The stool and work tray next to hers were empty.

"We just lost Miss Phillips to marriage," Miss Griffith explained. "So perhaps if they hire you, you'll start here."

Emilie nodded, suddenly mystified. She'd assumed she would be hired as a copyist or even a designer. It hadn't really occurred to her that she might have to actually cut the glass. A moment of panic seized her. She breathed it away.

It would be like cutting paper, only with glass and that thick-handled blade Miss Wilson was using.

"And that's pretty much what we do, day in and day out," Miss Griffith said cheerfully.

"There are other girls who select the glass. We have thousands of pieces in the basement. It's all quite beautiful. Mr. Tiffany can do things with glass you can't imagine. No one knows how they do it. It's a secret. He has his own furnaces. They say he keeps all the formulas locked in a safe and only he and Mr. Nash, the foreman and head chemist, have ever seen them."

"He sounds like a smart man."

"I suppose. But a suspicious one to be sure. And that's about it." Miss Griffith glanced toward the closed door of Mrs. Driscoll's office. She was probably anxious to get back to work.

Why were they taking so long to decide?

As Emilie thought it, the door opened and Mrs. Driscoll stepped out. She looked around and, seeing Emilie, raised her hand. "Miss Pascal, would you come in, please?"

Chapter 4

She had the job! Even with Mr. Tiffany in Europe *and* without having to show the chevalier's letter of introduction.

Mrs. Driscoll had taken Emilie on her sketches and detail work alone. She hadn't even asked about the letter of introduction, and when Emilie started to mention it, survival instinct held her tongue. She took that as an omen. No more lying, no more cheating, no more fear twisting her guts every time she heard footsteps on the stairs.

She'd been so relieved she'd even agreed to let Mrs. Driscoll keep several of her sketches to show to the "higher-ups." But she needed to get her portfolio back to make certain the letter was still inside. And make sure they never saw it. She wouldn't destroy it, not yet. But, please heaven, she would not ever have to use it.

She'd managed to get through all their questions almost truthfully.

She'd only had to stretch the truth a bit about her appointment with Mr. Tiffany, but she was hired! Emilie wanted to jump for joy, but she maintained a calm decorum born of years of hiding her true life and her father's behind an impenetrable façade of sangfroid. Only this time *this* would be her true life. Just hers, on her own merits, on her own talent and discipline.

A week's trial. But she wasn't worried. She knew how to

work, and she would make herself indispensable in this atelier of women.

"Right now I need a cutter," Mrs. Driscoll was saying. Emilie dragged her attention back to her new employer. She was a tall woman, rather plain, wearing a pair of spectacles that looked like they pinched her nose. "In this workshop we all pitch in where we are needed. Cutting is a very important job. It depends on precise, detailed work. I'm sure you can handle it. When I hire another cutter or two and if you prove a good fit, then we'll see about moving you to the cartoons."

Emilie nodded. She would cut glass. She would do anything they asked her, if they just gave her a home.

". . . half pay for a week . . ." She would need a place to stay. Miss Griffith said she would help. Emilie had a little money left and she'd soon be making a steady salary. To think of it. She'd be paid for making art.

"If you'll excuse me for a moment, Miss Gouvy will explain your duties, the hours, and other points of business." Mrs. Driscoll stood from behind her desk, looking formidable and a little tired.

Emilie swallowed and watched her walk out the door.

GRACE RESTED HER hand against the maulstick she used to support her drawing hand and wiped the sweat from her chin. The air that was pumped throughout the building had turned oppressive in the afternoon heat. The two electric fans they'd been allotted whirred by the door but did little to cool the air in the room.

And it was bound to be even hotter out on the street for the walk home. No wonder Emilie Pascal had fainted at their feet. Grace considered taking a quick break to sip some of the tepid tea left in her thermos; but she was behind, and it was nearing the end of the workday, so she kept going.

She moved the maulstick over and started on the next section of her panel. She'd had to render the top fourth of the cartoon while standing on a step stool to keep her eye straight to the design. Any foreshortening or angle could throw off the scale, which at best would mean redrawing a second corrected sheet and gluing it on top of the offending spot. Or at worst, starting the whole blinking cartoon over again.

"Miss Griffith."

Grace looked over her shoulder to see Mrs. Driscoll standing behind her. Mrs. Driscoll stared up at the six-foot cartoon, then over to the twenty-four-by-eight-inch watercolor design. "It's coming along well."

"Thank you." Grace had carefully calibrated each petal, leaf, and stem. Had placed them in near perfect juxtaposition. Even Miss Northrop, who demanded perfection, had been pleased so far.

"Miss Northrop is anxious to get started on her part of the 'Four Seasons' window. She's requested that you be the one to draw the cartoon."

"That's a great honor." Grace was flattered, but it added another layer of stress to her work. Miss Northrop was an excellent designer, also a demanding one. Well, Grace wouldn't let her down. She would just have to work faster.

"I've placed Miss Pascal on a week trial. She's in the office finalizing her duties with Miss Gouvy."

Grace waited patiently for Mrs. Driscoll to get to the point.

"Considering her portfolio, I think she would be of more use on the cartoons. But I need more cutters, so I will put her on the 'River' window with Miss Wilson."

Where was this going? Mrs. Driscoll didn't usually consult with her "girls" over artistic decisions. Extra hours maybe, or plans for a company picnic, but the assignment of individual workers? Never.

"If it wouldn't be too much additional responsibility, do you think you might just keep an eye on her? I'm sure Miss Wilson will be helpful getting her started, but could you just make yourself available in case she . . . runs into trouble."

"Is there something in particular that concerns you?"

"No, but it must be bewildering to find herself in a new country where she has no family or friends as far as we know. She is undoubtedly an accomplished painter, but quite frankly, I need to know how adept and efficient she is in glass."

Grace thought that beggars couldn't be choosers, especially after having seen the girl's sketches, but she merely nodded. "Of course."

Mrs. Driscoll started to move away, but turned back. "From what she's said, it appears to me that Miss Pascal has made no arrangements for a place to live."

"She mentioned that," Grace said. "Annie Phillips just moved out of Mrs. Bertolucci's. If she hasn't let the room yet, I'm sure she would be glad to have another Tiffany boarder. We are notoriously on time with our rent money. Most of us, anyway."

"Very good. I'm not sure the girl has any money at all. She was very closemouthed about her situation. Pride, most likely. But tell Mrs. Bertolucci that if Miss Pascal is acceptable after a week here, she will get a full salary."

"I will," Grace said.

"And make sure to get her to work tomorrow morning."

"We'll see that she makes it. She seems eager to please."

"So she does. Very eager."

Mrs. Driscoll turned away and clapped her hands to get everyone's attention. "I think considering this heat and it being close to quitting time, let us make this a short day and be all the more prepared tomorrow. Dismissed."

Grace reluctantly balanced her maulstick against the cartoon, the tip of the long wooden implement resting gently against the drawing, and placed her pencil on her work desk. She'd hoped to finish today, but the disruptions had eaten up the time and thrown off her rhythm. Now it would take her well through tomorrow morning or longer to complete the panel.

But Mrs. Driscoll was right. The day was so hot she'd heard some of the girls complaining that they were afraid the wax they used for attaching the glass pieces to the easel would melt and cause the work to become unstable.

Miss Northrop had hoped to start on the "Four Seasons" soon. She wouldn't be pleased by the delay of even a few minutes.

Grace had seen the watercolor sketches for the four-paneled "Seasons" window. Even from the small watercolor, she could imagine the power of the finished work.

That's why, when she was most perturbed by Mr. Tiffany—his lofty search for beauty and his unflagging self-importance that he alone could dictate that beauty—Grace remembered how he wanted to bring his art to people of all walks of life. And whether his motives were altruistic or egocentric, she had to say, hip hip hooray.

All over the workroom, brushes and pencils and glass cutters were cleaned and put neatly away. Work trays were covered with sheets of muslin. They'd taken to protecting their glasswork overnight. In spite of the meticulously closed windows, coal dust and other miasma managed to drift up five floors where it would settle on the glass pieces in a sticky, dirty goo.

When all was put away, there was a mad rush—barely more

than quick walking with your arms held to your sides, lest you upset the glass in your haste—to the cloakroom.

Grace picked up Miss Pascal from the office and took her to the cloakroom; she was clutching her valise and portfolio as if she expected they might fly away.

"You can have Annie's cubby," Grace told Emilie. "You can leave your apron and anything else you don't want to carry back and forth." Grace loosened the ties of her own apron and slipped the straps over her head.

Grace's cubby held a small cloth bag containing her "after hours" sketchbook, and a supply of freshly sharpened pencils that she carried everywhere. She put her thermos inside and hung her apron on a hook.

"Ready?"

Emilie had taken out two work aprons from her valise but was holding them to her chest as if she was afraid to let go.

"It will be fine. All the rooms are locked each night. Mr. Tiffany insists on it. Glassmaking is a competitive business and he is certain that there are spies everywhere trying to steal his ideas. So you can see, we are all perfectly safe here."

Emilie Pascal slowly put her aprons in the cubby and they joined the exiting throng.

As soon as the workshop had emptied out and the last of the girls had descended to the street, Clara closed the accounts books and prepared to make the trip she had been avoiding all day.

Before she even finished cleaning up her desk, the door opened, and Alice ducked her head inside. "Are you leaving? Shall I wait for you? I'll walk you halfway home; then I'll take the trolley crosstown."

"You go ahead," Clara said. "I have to requisition more fans for the workroom. If this heat keeps up, the wax on the easels will melt and the glass pieces will slide right to the floor."

"Heaven forbid." Alice's lips pursed in consternation. "But even if Mr. Mitchell okays them, where will we place them?"

"We'll figure that out once we have them." Clara pushed herself out of her chair and stretched. "First I need to talk to Agnes, get her opinion of the situation, and ask her to come take a look at Miss Pascal."

"She's probably left for the day," Alice reminded her. "It's a long way to Queens. I don't envy her in this heat."

"The ferry will be cooler than the street," Clara said. "Though I'd better hurry. See you tomorrow."

She walked Alice through the workshop and left her waiting for the elevator.

To tell the truth, Clara rather hoped Miss Northrop had already left for the day. That would give her time to find two new cutters somewhere and move Miss Pascal to the cartoons.

Miss Northrop's office was at the end of a veritable maze of dimly lit hallways. Clara suspected she'd chosen it to be as far away from the others as possible and thus avoiding the constant interruptions Clara dealt with all day long.

Agnes Northrop was the only one of the designers who had her own studio, even though it was barely larger than a postage stamp. She had been the manager when Clara returned from her brief marriage to Francis Driscoll and had been more than willing to hand over the day-to-day running of the workshop to Clara.

Agnes was a designer first and foremost, and yet she willingly helped out whenever they needed an extra pair of hands. And Mr. Tiffany had asked her to be especially helpful during his current absence.

Still, Clara hated to ask. Agnes was always polite, but she wasn't warm. Or particularly friendly. Maybe it was because, at forty-two, she still lived with her parents.

Clara made a last turn and arrived at Agnes's door. She knocked, not really expecting an answer, and was surprised when a soft, throaty voice called out, "Come in."

Clara turned the knob and stepped just inside. "Sorry to bother you."

Miss Northrop turned from where she stood at a wooden easel that held a watercolor painting of magnolias. Clara stopped where she was to admire the subtleties of the light pink, green, and ivory of the petals, how the blossoms seemed to drift down toward the bottom of the page.

And she allowed herself a moment of envy. Clara was a good designer but her drawing skills left something to be desired. Fortunately she had Alice to render her ideas into the form Clara imagined.

"They're exquisite," she managed.

Miss Northrop turned, her light brown hair catching the sunlight and framing her face in a lovely wisp of soft curls.

"Alas, they are still not quite right. You know how you can see it in your mind, but on paper it manages to keep just out of sight?"

"I do," Clara agreed. Oh, how she knew. She'd been working on two separate lamp designs for weeks, one of which still eluded her, the other hovering just beyond her grasp. "I do indeed."

Agnes huffed out a sigh. "Well, that's where I am with these petals. But you didn't come to talk about my magnolias."

"No. I came to discuss a new young woman who came in today."

"Please tell me she can cut glass. How many cutters have we lost this past month?"

"Three," Clara said. "It's an outbreak."

"And I hear tell all the projects are falling behind."

It was no secret, but where had she heard it? Agnes had Mr. Tiffany's ear. They were sometimes thick as thieves. Had he been discussing the state of the workroom with her before he left?

Clara pushed down the niggle of jealousy that he might confide more in Agnes than he did in her. A fruitless and immature thing to feel. "I've called the Met school and the Y program and they're looking for experienced or even merely potential cutters to send me. This girl is a true talent, a rare talent, but I'd like your opinion before I move her into a more permanent position. That is, if she works out."

"And why wouldn't she?"

"For one, she walked in out of the blue and fainted at our feet."

"Oh dear, is she sickly?"

"I don't think so. She's French. It seems she had just arrived from Paris and came straight to the studio from the docks. I think she was merely overcome by the heat. I'm going to start her as a cutter, because we're desperate. But she brought sketches, amazing ones."

"Ah," said Agnes. "I see. Why don't I stop in tomorrow morning to take a look." She glanced at a shelf clock. "Oh my goodness, is it that late? I'll be late for dinner if I don't hurry."

"So will I. Until tomorrow then." Clara left Agnes busily putting away her brushes and pencils.

She hurried back down the hallway, wondering at the absurdity of someone Agnes Northrop's age, a comely woman with a good disposition, still not married and rushing home every night after a long day at work to dine with her mother and father.

A shiver of what she suspected was dread ran up Clara's spine at the thought of the same thing happening to her. Not going home to parents, but going home . . . alone.

Home. . . . Mrs. Owen's boardinghouse was her home. She liked living there, but she would also like to remarry. Not just for a couple of years to a much older man as she had done before. And not to Edwin, who had asked her to marry him, then disappeared before they ever tied the knot. Bless Mr. Tiffany, for taking her back for a second time.

And yet, she might one day find someone to love her until death did them part. She really loved her work and was devoted to Mr. Tiffany, and she wouldn't want to give up either of them again. Life wasn't the same without Mr. Tiffany, without his vision, his ambition. His passion.

Clara just wished she could have both.

Chapter 5

After their aprons were hung up and bags and lunch pails retrieved, the Tiffany girls made a mass exodus to the elevator. Grace and Emilie were in the last group, and when they reached the sidewalk, they found Dora Hodgins and Lotte and Maggie Wilson waiting impatiently for them.

"What took you so long?" Dora drawled. "It's like a furnace out here. I think the soles of my shoes are cooked."

"Then stop your grousing and let's go," Grace said.

Dora stuck her tongue out.

"We always walk home together," Lotte explained to Emilie. "Those of us who live at Mrs. Bertolucci's. It makes the walk go faster when you have others to walk with."

"Is it very far?"

"A few blocks. It hardly makes sense to take the trolley and then transfer, unless you're too tired?"

Emilie shook her head.

"I can carry your case," Maggie volunteered and lifted the valise from Emilie's hand.

"But it's heavy," Emilie said, looking wary.

"I'm strong, and I'm good at carrying things," Maggie said. "Aren't I, Lotte?"

"Yes, you are, and you're very careful."

Maggie smiled proudly and started off down the avenue.

"Hold up, Maggie," Lotte called and ran after her. "Miss Pascal will think New Yorkers gallop like horses down the street, instead of walking like regular people."

Maggie skidded to a stop and looked around. "I'm hungry. I bet Miss Pascal is, too." She grinned at Emilie.

"Oh heck," Dora drawled. "We're off work now. I'm Dora. Do you mind if we all call you Em-ee-lee?"

Emilie shook her head. Grace thought she looked like she was about to keel over. Grace gently removed the coat she was carrying and guided her down the sidewalk. Emilie came docilely enough. She was so busy looking around, they probably could have left her on the sidewalk and she wouldn't have realized it.

They reached the corner of Twenty-Third, waited for a trolley to pass, then hurried across, Lotte pulling Maggie away from a tempting ice cream cart.

"I can't believe Annie Phillips is getting married," Dora said as they started off again. "And she's not even that pretty."

"It's wonderful, isn't it?" Lotte said.

"If you think working extra hours to make up for her leaving is wonderful," Grace said. "Then yeah. Wonderful."

"Oh, Grace, I don't think you have a romantic bone in your body." Dora's southern accent had a way of intensifying at the most annoying times.

"Well, you'd be right. Show me a married woman who can keep her profession, have charge of her own money and freedom to move about as she pleases, and isn't enslaved to some demanding man, and I'll reconsider."

"What would you do instead, Grace?" Lotte asked.

"Me?" Grace said. "Right now I'd just like for this newsboys strike to be over so I can keep abreast of the scandalous press."

"Grace reads to us out loud sometimes after supper," Maggie volunteered. "Look, Grace, there's a newsboy right on the next corner!"

"Yes, but he's only selling the *Times* and other respectable and newsworthy papers. We like the more exciting tales in the *World* and the *Journal*, don't we, Mags?"

"Oh yes," Maggie said, nodding vigorously.

"Complete sensational trash," Grace said in an aside to Emilie. "But entertaining."

"Why are the newsboys on strike?"

"Because they're treated like dirt. Hearst and Pulitzer make a fortune off their scandal sheets, but they're tightfisted employers, so the newsies have gone out on strike for better wages and to be able to return unsold papers. Until now they've had to pay for whatever they didn't sell.

"And the thing is, they're still publishing but you can only buy copies at the big hotels or directly from the papers. Which of course I wouldn't do. Any boy caught selling their papers during the strike gets beaten up and their papers stolen."

Grace huffed out a sigh. "And I get no news until it's over."

As for Emilie, she was glad the newspaper boys were on strike. She wished they'd all go on strike. No news from Paris was good news for her.

She shuddered as a wave of fear swept over her. Would she never be free of that sudden sickening moment of overwhelming panic brought on by a word, a sight, a passing stranger?

By Twenty-First Street, they'd all grown quiet while they concentrated on putting one weary foot in front of the other. They turned east off the avenue and passed a small park.

"How lovely." Emilie had begun to think that the park she'd seen from the trolley was the only park in the city.

"That's Gramercy Park, but you have to have a key to get in," Dora drawled.

"How do you get a key?"

"You have to live in one of these posh town houses."

"Oh."

"Only another block and a half," said Lotte, sounding as exhausted as Emilie felt. And she was beginning to worry. What if Mrs. Bertolucci didn't have room for her? What if she didn't like foreigners? She'd heard that many Americans didn't. Where would she sleep if she was turned away?

Finally, they stopped in front of a plain brownstone building whose only adornment was a white granite pediment over a dark wooden door. Grace went ahead, and the others trudged up the three steps behind her. Emilie followed more slowly and stepped into a wainscoted foyer filled with coatracks, side tables, and stacks of mail and magazines.

Grace was talking to a short, round woman with black and silver hair pulled back in a braided bun at the nape of her neck. She nodded and frowned as Grace explained the situation to her, all the time wiping her hands on a much-splattered apron.

Emilie settled her portfolio at her feet and had just straightened up when the landlady turned toward her. "Is this the young lady?" She had a thick Italian accent, and Emilie began to feel more at home in this strange city. Mrs. Bertolucci, like her name suggested, was a foreigner, too.

"Oh, *caro è troppo male*. And you just arriving on the boat . . . all that way. Oh dear, oh dear. But there is nothing I can do. *Niente.* I have nothing for you. *Mi povera bambina.* I rented out

Annie Phillips's room just this morning to a friend of Miss Vanderheusen."

For a moment there was utter silence, while Emilie's hope died and despair settled over her. She looked wildly around for her valise, which Maggie was still holding. "I must—"

All faces were turned toward her—like a court of accusers, it seemed to Emilie.

"She can stay with me and Lotte," Maggie said.

"No, Maggie, she can't," Lotte said. "I'm sorry, Emilie, but there's barely room for the two of us."

Mrs. Bertolucci tsked and shook her head. "It is true. Very, very small."

"*Je comprends*." Without a thought, Emilie groped for her portfolio and lifted it from the floor. She stepped resolutely toward Maggie, pried her valise from her hand, and turned blindly toward the door.

"Wait," Grace said.

Emilie stopped, almost afraid to turn around.

"We'll think of something. There must be somewhere," Grace said.

The others nodded and looked from Emilie to Grace to Mrs. Bertolucci.

Then the landlady motioned to Grace and the two of them stepped through an archway to what must be the parlor.

"They'll find you somewhere to stay," Lotte assured her. "Grace is very clever."

"I think we should find her a place *here*," Dora said. "Then she can tell us all about living in Paris, and all the fashionable gowns and the balls."

"So do I," said Maggie. "I want to hear about ball gowns, too."

Emilie barely heard them as she tried to discern what Grace

and Mrs. Bertolucci were saying, standing close, their heads bent toward each other.

After a few minutes, they returned. The other girls moved to stand at Emilie's back as if they could prevent her from leaving.

Mrs. Bertolucci bustled over to the group and threw up her hands. "*Successo!* Grace has agreed to share her room until another becomes free. It isn't a large room, but it has a nice window. If that is to your liking."

Emilie darted a tentative glance at Grace.

"*È fatto.* It is done. And, uh, *reciprocamente vantaggioso*!"

"She means you get to split the rent," Dora said. "Say yes. It will be ever so much fun."

There were murmurs of encouragement from the three girls, but Emilie was intent on Grace. She looked uncomfortable, and Emilie didn't want to make any enemies on her first day.

"Are you certain this is what you want, Grace?"

Grace gave her a quick nod. "Mrs. B will up the rent from five to six dollars a week, so that we each pay three dollars, room and board. It's okay as long as we honor each other's privacy, and we can save some money." She swallowed, Emilie could see her throat tighten with the action. "And it will only be until a room opens up or you find someplace you like more, or . . ." Grace shrugged, and Emilie filled in *or if you're not kept on at work*.

"Then, thank you. That will be . . . acceptable."

"*Va bene*," Mrs. Bertolucci said. "I will have Nessa and Jane get the spare bed out of the closet and set it up so you can move in when you've finished eating." She clapped her hands. "Now, *sbrigati*!"

"That means hurry," Maggie said, and they all propelled Emilie up the stairs to the second floor, Grace and Mrs. Bertolucci following on their heels.

But when they would have crowded into Grace's room, Mrs. B shooed them away. "Go wash up for supper. Pot roast."

The other girls dispersed to their own rooms, and Emilie followed Mrs. B and Grace inside.

It was a small room, but it did have a large window that faced the street. A narrow brass bed, painted white, was pushed against the wall beneath the window. It was covered in a chenille spread and two needlepoint pillows. A washstand and a small chest of drawers with a mirror above stood against the side wall at the foot of the bed. A desk and narrow bookshelf took up the back wall. Emilie couldn't imagine putting another bed in this space.

"You'll see," Mrs. B said. "Before Grace came, three girls who worked over at the Altman's department store lived in this room. Such a noise they made. I was glad when they moved out, I can tell you. So you see, little one, do not worry. There is plenty of room for you. If Nessa and Jane move the desk away from the wall, there is just enough room for another bed.

"Do you have a trunk? More cases?" she asked, frowning at Emilie's lone valise and portfolio.

Emilie shook her head. "Not at the moment."

"That is good. There is this wardrobe. You can share until you need more space."

Emilie nodded. She had no need of more space, she had no need of tea dresses or ball gowns. She probably didn't even need the trunk that awaited her back in Paris.

"Now, there are a few rules that all the girls must obey." The landlady held up a forefinger. "No men except in the parlor."

Emilie nodded. She didn't know any men here.

The second finger joined the first. "No cooking or eating in the rooms."

Emilie shook her head.

Third finger. "No washing of clothes in the sink. A girl comes in to do the wash each Saturday. Every piece must be marked and taken to the basement the night before.

"Do not look worried. Young working ladies ought not have to do their own laundry, and the cost is quite reasonable."

"And keeps us from flooding her bathroom with underwear caught in the drains," Grace said, so seriously mischievous that Mrs. Bertolucci snapped her apron at her.

"Keep your room neat, and no loud noises when others are sleeping." Her eyes were dark and bright, like obsidian catching the light, as her attention darted from Emilie to Grace and to her own finger.

"I lock the door every night at eleven o'clock. You must be back before that or have good friends to take you in until the morning. That includes Saturday and Sunday."

Emilie just nodded. She didn't have anywhere to go, though one day she would venture out to a museum or to find a park that didn't require a key to enter. If there was such a thing.

"I expect my girls to be well behaved, and not get themselves into trouble. Treat Mrs. B's just like it was your own home, with respect and love, and it will love you back. And I might like you a little." Only the appearance of a dimple in her rounded cheek gave her smile away.

"*Oui* . . . yes, I understand." Emilie reached for her purse.

"You can pay after dinner. Which will be soon. So wash up and come downstairs. We'll see about getting you settled in after dessert. Rice pudding, tonight." Mrs. B snapped her apron again and hurried out of the room.

Emilie turned to Grace. "Thank you. I won't be a . . . a . . ." She couldn't think of the word. "I will try not to take up too much space."

Grace laughed. "Now go get washed. We don't want to be late for dinner. They'll start without us. Take that spare towel over there."

Emilie nodded, pushed her valise and portfolio hard against the wall, and went down the hall to wait her turn in the bathroom.

She longed for a bath, but there were five girls that she knew of on the second floor and only one bathroom. She'd gone without baths before—when her father had drunk or gambled away the rent money. But there had been other times. . . . She sighed. It all seemed so long ago.

As soon as Emilie returned with the borrowed towel and a clean face, neck, and hands, they hurried down the stairs to the dining room where a long mahogany table was set for eight. In addition to the Tiffany girls, two other women, well into middle age, were introduced as Miss Vanderheusen and Miss Burns, both professional seamstresses.

"Sit here, Emilie," Dora called. "It was Annie's place."

Emilie dutifully took her place next to Dora. When they were all seated, Mrs. Bertolucci came to stand at the table. Everyone bowed their heads, and Emilie had a vision of one of Mr. Tiffany's church windows as it might portray Michelangelo's *Last Supper*, only with the eight women as the apostles.

Mrs. B blessed the food, beseeched "*nostro Signore*" to watch over them and have mercy on them. Then the food was passed.

The pot roast was tender and served with small boiled onions, potatoes, carrots, and peas. Slices of thick bread were piled high in a wicker breadbasket.

Emilie ate and listened to the women around her. She was too tired to contribute much to the conversation. A full day of English had numbed her ears and her brain. She was grateful when the plates were cleared and a sweet pudding was served in heavy cut glass compote bowls. Emilie thought the cut glass was a nice show of respect to these women who had to fend for themselves, even though it only made more work for the kitchen staff, which she guessed must consist of Mrs. B and the as-yet-unseen Nessa and Jane.

As soon as dinner was over, the girls dispersed, some up to their rooms, others to the parlor. Dora stopped Emilie at the foot of the stairs. "Oh, do come play Parcheesi with us."

"Thank you, but I am very tired and I still must arrange things with Mrs. Bertolucci. Perhaps tomorrow." She started up the stairs and met Grace coming back down.

She was carrying a cloth bag and stopped long enough to say, "I'm going out. I'll try not to wake you if you're sleeping when I get back."

"Going to visit your great-aunt?" Dora said.

"Yes. She's expecting me, and I don't want to be late." Grace hurried past.

Dora pursed her lips and watched until the door closed behind her. "Her great-aunt. Ha. My aunt Fanny."

"She's your great-aunt, also?" Emilie asked.

Dora rolled her eyes. "No. Of course not. I just meant— Oh, never mind."

Someone called from the parlor. Dora hurried away. Emilie continued upstairs to pay Mrs. Bertolucci and hopefully get to bed.

Grace set off briskly toward Second Avenue, but as soon as she was out of view, she began to run. She would have to take the trolley downtown to New Irving Hall where the newsboys were holding their rally. She had wanted to get there early, but between being so behind at the studio, then getting Emilie Pascal settled . . . *and pot roast.* Mrs. B's pot roast was the best and not served often. Grace had given in to temptation. And now she was late.

There was bound to be a mob. She just hoped they didn't turn her away. Because she'd decided yesterday that if the newsboys couldn't sell her their papers, then she would go to the newsboys.

They were a colorful bunch with their distinctive caps and hobnail shoes. Their funny English and their enthusiastic hawking. But they were also a very mistreated bunch, comrades in the fight for fair wages and decent working conditions. They were perfect for her pencil.

Grace had just reached the corner as a trolley pulled away. Undaunted and not taking the chance of having to wait for another, she grabbed her skirts and ran after it. She managed to jump onto the back step just as it picked up speed. She threw her arms around the rail pole and hung on until she could get her balance. Then she found a seat in the back and had her change ready when the ticket taker came round to collect her fare.

"We don't recommend that kind of foolishness, miss."

"Sorry, but I was running late and . . ."

"And it was pretty impressive," said a young man from across the aisle. He winked at her.

Grace pretended not to see. She had no time for flirtation tonight . . . or any night. Time enough for that when she was working as a full-time newspaper cartoonist.

By the time the trolley let her off at Broome Street, Grace was sweating profusely. She would have liked to stop for an iced lemonade, but immediately saw the impossibility of doing so. Ahead of her, the street and the sidewalks around the hall were teeming with newsboys, many wearing or carrying signs written with slogans like "I ain't a scab," "Don't buy the World," "Hearst ain't fair," "50 cent for 100." The latter alluding to the price the boys had paid for their papers before their cost had been raised to sixty cents, cutting into their profit and setting off the current strike.

Grace plunged into the crowd, squeezing between them until she managed to make her way to the entrance, where a man was explaining at the top of his lungs that they had already "got you boys hanging from the chandeliers in there. Ain't no more room."

Undaunted, Grace fought her way to the front. "Press," she barked at the man who barred her way.

"Yes, ma'am." He tipped his hat and moved aside; Grace hurried inside before he asked her to prove it.

The hall was even more crowded than the street outside. Not only was the main floor packed like sardines, boys were crammed into every niche and windowsill. Even the stairs were impassable with seated newsboys. The guard outside hadn't been exaggerating by much when he said they were hanging from the chandeliers.

From her previous attendance at rallies, lectures, and the occasional free-for-all, Grace figured there would be an area set aside for the press, if she could get to it. Luckily, two men with notebooks cut through the crowd of boys right in front of her. Grace slipped in behind them and followed in their wake to a group of chairs near the speakers' platform, roped off and already packed with newsmen, and two newswomen, yelling out questions to the newsboys around them.

Grace spied a seat in the back row, which was exactly where she wanted to be. She didn't care about getting the latest scoop, reporting every last word. She wanted to capture the energy, the characters, and create a world—the essence of that world—in one picture. Like Mr. Tiffany did with his windows.

She climbed past two reporters, one who pulled his knees to the side for her to get by, and the other, completely unaware or purposely ignoring her need until she landed one foot on the top of his instep.

He let out a "What the hell? Oh, pardon me . . . miss."

Grace didn't look at him, just nodded and kept going to the end of the row. She sat down and pulled out her notebook, careful to turn it to an angle so none of the others could see that she was sketching and not reporting. The attending "press" might not take kindly to her occupying the space of a "legit" reporter, meaning male, uncouth, and reeking of cheap gin.

It was hard enough for women to get a decent reporting assignment. But female cartoonists were virtually unheard of. The few that did exist were mostly relegated to illustrating women's magazines and children's books.

Not that those occupations were bad as far as they went, but . . . Grace opened her book and began sketching.

A line of men, some merely older boys, took their places on the platform, and bedlam broke out across the hall. It took much banging of the gavel and shouting by the chairman and his two dozen assistant chairmen to finally bring a semblance of order.

During the introductions and speeches of the invited guests, while her fellow reporters were busy scribbling down names and positions held, Grace concentrated on quick sketches of the boys closest to her. She could have spent hours capturing their quirks and personalities, but when the chairman announced Mr. Symonds, president of the union, Grace turned her attention to the stage. The president was no more than a typical-looking newsboy, and Grace made a quick sketch of his mobile face as seen through a row of newsmen's heads. She chuckled at the juxtaposition.

It was then that she felt someone watching her. She glanced

down the row, in time to see the reporter whose foot she had trod on quickly turn away. Grace shifted farther to the side and held her notebook out of his view.

Mr. Symonds finished a list of demands, and the chairman took a moment to ask the press not to quote the speakers using words like *dese*, *dose*, and *youse*. He then introduced "Kid Blink, our master workman." The newsboys gave Kid a rousing show of support.

Kid Blink was an undersized boy with a black patch over one eye. Grace's pencil flew over the page, as he began to talk. "I don't agree with you boys about going up and taking papers away from people. What we want to do is stick together and not sell the *Journal* and *World*. I'll tell you the truth. I was one of dem boys who knocked over the carts in Madison Street last night. But it ain't right. Just stick together and we'll win. Am I right, boys?"

The crowd was his. A tussle of exuberance broke out near Grace, and when she drew her attention back to the stage, someone sat down in the free seat beside her. Grace moved her notebook to a sharper angle, as the chairman called a Park Row news seller, Annie Kelly, to speak. "One of our own, boys!"

Annie was pulled to the stage by a group of boys to the chant of "We've got Annie." The news seller looked like she'd rather be anywhere but on that platform, but she stepped up to the microphone and the crowd immediately quieted.

"Annie ain't got no *World*s or *Journal*s under her skirts!" yelled Kid Blink, which set off more wild applause that had to be quelled by numerous bangings of the gavel before Annie could speak.

Grace leaned forward. She'd seen a few women selling newspapers on the street, but she hadn't thought about them being part of the strike. Now that took courage. Grace's pencil moved quickly, capturing the shy expression, the adoration of the boys.

Annie looked up. "All I can say, boys, is stick together and we'll win. That's all I've got to say to you." And she left the stage.

"So what rag do you write for?" The question came right in Grace's ear.

Grace snapped her sketchbook closed. It was the guy with the big feet. Younger than she'd expected. About thirty. Thirty and smug.

From the corner of her eye, Grace saw Annie Kelly disappear into the crowd.

"'Cause I don't recall seeing you in the press box before."

Grace turned away, determined to ignore him, which was a little hard to do, since he had bright copper hair and blue eyes, brimming with mockery.

"Let me guess, *Ladies' Home Journal*."

Grace shot him her most withering look. "Do you mind? I'm trying to listen."

He managed to move a little closer. "Why? Nobody's talking. What are you doing in that notebook? Not taking any notes."

Grace moved her notebook to her far side. "I'm doing my job, and if you were doing yours, you wouldn't notice what I was doing."

The reporter grinned.

Grace thought, *He'd be handsome if he wasn't so obnoxious*. And if someone hadn't broken his nose, though she could understand how someone might be provoked into putting that little crook in an otherwise perfectly straight feature.

There was a burst of applause and Grace's attention was pulled back to the stage where a large floral horseshoe was being presented to Kid Blink—he of the eye patch—for giving the best speech.

Grace's fingers itched to get the image down, but Mr. Bigfoot was still looking at her and grinning.

"Don't you need to take notes?" she countered. "Or do you depend on that big head of yours to remember everything?"

The grin broadened.

Grace rolled her eyes and concentrated on remembering every detail of the floral horseshoe dwarfing the diminutive Kid.

The rally began to break up; Grace jammed her notebook and pencil into her bag and stood up.

"Might as well relax," her unwelcome companion said. "It will take a while to clear out. I'm Charlie Murray by the way. From the *Sun*."

The *Sun*, Grace thought. A large paper, if smaller than the *Times* or *Herald Tribune*. At least he was a serious journalist.

"And you are?"

"In a hurry. So if you'll excuse me . . ."

He just stretched his legs out and settled back to wait her out. "So what's your real line?"

"I don't know what you mean."

"Sure you do. You're no dummy. Nobody who can concentrate like you have for the last hour could be very dense."

"I'm so relieved that you have such a flattering opinion of me."

He laughed out loud. "I do. I think most people are dummies."

If Grace had been less mature, she would have been tempted to say, *It takes one to know one*. But being a mature nineteen-year-old career woman, she merely nodded brusquely and trampled over his feet on her way out.

But when she got to the end of the row, she did the most infuriating thing. The one thing she had ordered herself not to do. She looked back.

Mr. Murray was watching her. He wasn't grinning now but frowning quizzically. He tipped a finger to his forehead. "See you at the next one. I hear the messenger boys are the next to strike."

Grace lifted her chin, kicking herself for succumbing to vain curiosity, and pushed through the last stragglers and onto the street.

She was still steaming when she hurried up Twenty-First Street to the boardinghouse. It had to be eleven. She crossed her fingers and prayed that Mrs. B hadn't closed up for the night.

When the knob turned, she could have clicked her heels, except that she was too hot, too tired, and too full of ideas.

All was quiet downstairs. Grace locked the door, turned off the table lamp, climbed the stairs to her room—and walked smack-dab into her desk. It had been shoved into the center of the room and left there. Rubbing her thigh, she squinted into the darkness and saw a narrow iron bed where her desk had been. Emilie Pascal lay curled tightly in her sleep under one of Mrs. B's chenille spreads. The room was stifling hot. Grace was amazed that Emilie hadn't roasted to death.

Though perhaps she had. She didn't move at all. Grace tiptoed over to take a closer look. She'd almost reached the bedside when Emilie bolted upright. Grace and Emilie both let out shrieks, followed by Grace's "Shhh. You'll wake everyone up."

Emilie sat as rigid as Mary Shelley's monster, her breath huffing in and out in short, sharp gasps. Finally, she calmed enough to say, "I'm sorry. I thought I was . . . someplace else."

That much was obvious, thought Grace. And wherever Emilie thought she was must have been pretty damn bad.

It was going to be a trial to have a roommate, especially one so skittish and prone to nightmares, not to mention the fainting. What had she gotten herself into? She'd have to be even more careful about her "secret" cartoons than she had before. She'd surely lose her job at Tiffany's, not to mention her reputation, if word of her clandestine activities got out.

So tonight, instead of leaving her sketchbook in her desk drawer, Grace slipped it beneath her pillow where it would be safe. Then she crawled into bed, cursing the heat, and trying hard not to think of Charlie Murray's mocking grin.

Chapter 6

Emilie dressed in her clean shirtwaist and skirt. She only had two of each, but she didn't want to go into work her first full day with the dust and dirt of the sidewalks, trolley, and the workshop floor still clinging to her. She'd just have to alternate them until Saturday and hope she had enough coins left to afford the washer girl. And maybe after a few paydays, she could afford to buy another blouse.

Grace looked tired this morning; her eyes were swollen . . . from lack of sleep? Was she uncomfortable with Emilie sharing her room? Did she not trust her?

Emilie had been asleep long before Grace returned from her aunt's and she wondered if she'd dreamed Grace standing over her bed, or later sitting at her desk in the center of the room, a small light casting shadows on the wall and shining on her hair as she bent over whatever she was writing.

She did remember her other dream . . . Even now, it was trying to pull her back in. *She is running. Chased. Stoned by the mob. The mob is dressed like the trustees of the Académie.* Only last night the stones had turned to shards of colored glass.

Emilie slipped two handkerchiefs into one skirt pocket and a few coins into the other, snatched up her art satchel, and hurried to catch up to the others who were already heading noisily downstairs, where they stopped to pick up thermoses and sandwiches wrapped in waxed paper from the hall table.

She started to walk past, but Mrs. B thrust one of the sandwiches and a thermos at her. "When you have a full salary, I will add it to your bill. It is a pittance."

"Come on, Emilie," Dora drawled and pulled Emilie toward the door so quickly that she could only cast a grateful look at Mrs. B over her shoulder.

"It's so hot," Maggie complained, the minute they stepped onto the sidewalk.

"Another scorcher," Lotte said brightly and slipped her arm in Maggie's to keep her moving along.

Grace had run ahead of the others and Emilie hoped she wasn't avoiding her on purpose. *Not that it matters*, she reminded herself. *You are here to work, not to make friends. Friends. Could these become her new friends?*

"Em-ee-leeee, stop daydreaming," Dora prodded.

Emilie shoved her thermos and lunch into her satchel and hurried after the others.

They caught up to Grace just as she slipped a brown envelope into the slot of a lamppost mailbox.

"See? I told you she has a sweetheart," Dora confided in Emilie, drawing her closer. "All that 'visiting her aunt' and writing letters all the time. She can't fool me."

Emilie was inclined to say that it was none of their business, but she just shrugged and smiled and walked faster.

When they arrived at work, two more electric fans were crowding the doorway to the workshop. Emilie didn't hold out much hope of them making a difference, hence the two handkerchiefs in her pocket.

She imagined her first week's half salary dwindling away in

rent, sandwiches, extra hankies, and, if anything was left over, another set of lingerie.

Eventually she would have to send for her trunk, but she was almost afraid to allow even the briefest contact with her old life. Perhaps it was superstitious, but she didn't want anything from the past to taint her new life—even clothes.

Emilie stored her things in her cubby and followed the others into the work studio. This would truly be her work, no matter that she had to share it with the whole group of Tiffany girls.

But when she stepped into the workroom and everyone dispersed to their places, she felt a sudden shyness.

"Come, Emilie," Lotte said. "Though you'll be Miss Pascal until we're back on the street again. I'll help you get set up."

Emilie followed her to the worktable where she had seen Lotte working the day before. Lotte pulled off the muslin cover and neatly folded it before putting it away beneath the table. Then she reached over and pulled the cover off a second tray already filled with pieces of glass in various stages of cutting and polishing.

"This belonged to Annie—Miss Phillips. Look under the table; there should be a pair of work sleeves and a basket of tools. Then pull your stool closer and I'll show you what to do."

Emilie smiled gratefully, found the tools—"her" tools—and slipped the muslin sleeves over her own sleeves. Then she pulled the stool closer to Lotte—Miss Wilson—and sat down.

"That' s our window right over there. We call it the 'River of Life' window. We do a lot of water windows."

At this distance Emilie could see the stream running downhill through trees and bushes, all delineated in a myriad of black lines indicating the individual pieces of glass. "It must take so many pieces," she exclaimed.

"It does, but don't worry. Many hands and all that. You'll get the hang of it soon. Have you worked as a cutter before? We didn't get a chance to talk much last night."

Emilie shook her head and stared down at her tray of glass. She glanced over to the other women who were steadily working their way through stacks of similar glass pieces. "But I've read a lot about how it is done."

"Well, that puts you ahead of most of the girls when they first come. It's easy, really, once you get the knack of it, but it's important to be very precise. The hardest part is making sure you choose the right section of the glass before you start cutting."

"How do you do that?" Emilie hated having to ask. She'd thought she could just learn by doing, but it was more complicated than that.

"Don't worry. The glass has already been selected by someone else. You just have to make sure you get the template positioned correctly on the glass before you cut. Here, I'll show you. And you can ask me questions anytime."

Emilie peered at the puzzle of glass pieces clinging to the glass easel. "It looks just like water."

"It's called ripple glass. There's a piece in your tray. Annie was working on that part, so I'm thinking Mrs. Driscoll will want you to continue."

Emilie picked up a piece of the blue ripple glass. It wasn't flat as she'd expected but rippled against her hand. In Paris, she'd never been allowed close enough to any of the exhibits to know for certain, but this glass actually mimicked flowing water.

How had they made it? And how could she possibly cut with precision when the glass was literally undulating in her hand?

"Speaking of Mrs. Driscoll, here she comes."

At Lotte's announcement, Emilie popped off the stool, still holding the glass, and stood at attention waiting for Mrs. Driscoll to reach them.

"I see Miss Wilson has already gotten you started," Mrs. Driscoll said. "Miss Wilson is one of our most proficient cutters and I'm sure she'll be able to answer all your questions."

Emilie and Lotte both nodded and smiled.

"Then I'll leave you to it."

As soon as she left, the two girls exchanged looks.

"She must think you're good. Usually she oversees your first day more closely. But things have gotten so hectic around here with the Exposition in the spring and everything falling behind with all the girls getting married—" Lotte frowned slightly as if she'd forgotten what she was saying. "But don't be surprised if she keeps coming out to check on your progress."

Emilie shook her head and concentrated on breathing.

"So . . ." Lotte reached across her to pick up a square piece of paper. "This is the section of water you're working on now. It's all numbered and coordinated with the glass color. See?"

She held up the paper, which was a square jigsaw of shapes and numbers.

"This section," Lotte continued, "corresponds to that section on the easel."

Emilie searched the glass, then hopped off her stool and took the paper over to the window to get a closer look. There were hundreds, maybe thousands, of individual parts all delineated with thick black lines. And even with Lotte's direction, it took some time to find her small section. Once she found it, it seemed so obvious.

And she realized it wasn't just a question of cutting precisely but adjusting the glass in just a way to perfectly reflect the actual picture. She hurried back to her place, holding that detail in her mind's eye.

"Don't forget to number each piece," Lotte reminded her. "Or you won't know where it goes on the window and will have to start again."

"I won't," Emilie said, only half attending, so immersed was her mind in the process of creating water from glass.

She picked up a cerulean blue sheet of ripple glass.

She looked across the worktable to where their window stood, thanking her lucky stars—if she had any—that she hadn't just started cutting before she had studied the original cartoon. If she hadn't seen—and understood—the whole, she might have cut the pieces so that the water flowed upstream or straight across the window. It would have ruined everything.

Always see the whole, she reminded herself. Just like in a painting, so that the details become that whole.

With Lotte standing over her, Emilie placed the ripple glass on the table, selected one of the templates, and placed it on the glass. Comparing it to the window, she adjusted it until she knew she'd found the perfect place to begin cutting.

"Now hold it down with one hand," Lotte said calmly. "Take the blade of the cutter . . ."

Emilie picked up the heavy glass cutter, breathed in, slowly exhaled.

"Try to keep the cut steady without too many stops and starts. Easy now."

Emilie placed the blade at just the right angle to score the surface. And when she made the first cut, it was as if she could feel the glass flowing in her veins, just as she'd once felt with a brush in her hand.

She belonged here. She'd expected it all along, and now she knew for certain.

But cutting glass turned out to be more difficult than the *Art Journal* article or Lotte would have her believe. Keeping the blade moving in an arc when it would rather go in a straight line was difficult enough, but not letting the pattern slip while fighting with the instrument was even harder. Emilie came close to slicing her own fingers more than once.

By the end of the first half hour her arms, fingers, and back were aching.

But she wasn't daunted. She was surrounded by art-in-the-making. On every worktable in the room, in every window, art was alive. If the sun went behind a cloud even for a moment, everything changed. The colors darkened, softened, only to flare back to life when the cloud had passed. It was hard not to just sit back and watch the changing sky through all the pieces of colored glass.

When she finally had her first piece cut and trimmed and the edges covered in a thin layer of copper foil, Emilie expelled a long, satisfied breath.

"You know, you'll have to work faster than that once you get the hang of it," Lotte said.

Emilie nodded. She numbered her first piece, took the template for her second, and started again.

Mrs. Driscoll made several appearances during the next couple of hours where she merely stopped and nodded or muttered, "Very good, ladies," and continued through the room.

Each time when she left, Lotte and Emilie pulled out their handkerchiefs and wiped their faces, then dried their hands on their skirts to keep a good grasp on the glass, and started up again.

Once Emilie became accustomed to the cutting blade and the

nippers, which cleaned up the ragged edges that were sometimes left by even the most meticulous break, she settled into an even rhythm. It was mesmerizing, though no doubt it would eventually become tedious after days, weeks, and months of repetition.

But for now, she reminded herself that her little pieces of cut glass would one day become part of a glorious stained-glass window. Not as a static work of art but ever changing with the sky outside. She silently thanked Mr. Tiffany and Mrs. Driscoll and even the girl who got married for making it possible for her to be a part of it.

It didn't matter that no one would ever know which pieces of glass were hers, or Lotte's, or any of the others. Emilie Pascal was not here to make a name for herself, but to lose herself and her art in the safe haven of Mr. Louis C. Tiffany.

Clara felt a little bad about passing off Miss Pascal to Miss Wilson without doing her usual introductory exam. But she would know soon enough if the talented painter was ham-fisted when it came to glass.

In that case there would be nothing she could do but let her go. But if she didn't hear the breaking of glass, she might at least get a few more minutes to work on her own designs.

She sat back and looked over the series of sketches that littered her desktop. She'd come in this morning before the others arrived, to beat the heat and have a few minutes to herself to work on the design for her new lampshade.

She distractedly dabbed at the sweat accumulating on her brow. Already the day was sweltering. Mr. Mitchell had made good on two new fans, though they hardly seemed to make a difference.

Clara had been working on this same design for months and still hadn't managed to get it exactly the way she imagined it. In her mind, she saw her dragonflies stretched in flight creating a border around the bottom of the glass shade. Above them, almost as if the breeze created by their wings was lifting them up, long blades of tender grass tapered to the top of the glass cone.

At the moment, the dragonflies looked more like static paper dolls lined up wing tip to wing tip, while above them, the tender stalks of grass stuck upward like a green picket fence.

She tossed her pencil onto the desk in disgust. She wasn't the best artist, she didn't pretend to be. She depended on Alice to turn her ideas into beautiful watercolors.

Clara was a good designer. Maybe a little better than good. She was a patient designer . . . except these days there was no time for patience. No time to experiment and change her mind and try again until what was in her head was transformed like a miracle into glass. She needed results now, which was made doubly impossible by the continual specter of Mr. Pringle Mitchell looming over her shoulder.

Mr. Tiffany would have told her to ignore him, take her time, let the creative genius strike when it was ready. Clara was trying, but lamps and decorative arts weren't like the majority of the windows they made. With those one decided on a religious figure then surrounded him, or occasionally her, with some lilies and cherubs and sent the girls to pick the glass.

Her lamps were different. They were meant to bring nature into people's homes, so they would always be surrounded by beauty, day and night, not just on Sundays or at funerals or on an occasional walk in the park.

She didn't like to think she was in competition with Agnes Northrop. She wasn't. Agnes designed windows and Clara designed lamps and decorative arts. They both loved nature and they both respected Mr. Tiffany. They loved his passion for nature and for art and for bringing the two together.

Windows suited Agnes. Seen from a distance, rarefied, to be contemplated in one's holiest moments. Clara's mirrors, inkstands, and toilette sets were handled and used and kept always just within reach. To be used, to be part of a person's everyday life.

Clara shoved her latest attempt out of the way—she was collecting quite a pile. Between her sporadic attempts to capture the essence of the flight of dragonflies into a lamp, she'd made two additional designs. One that she was particularly pleased with. She'd used a dandelion motif with a white-flecked globe of favrile glass supported by a copper base, repousséd with all the parts of the dandelion plants from the leaves and stems to the puffballs that seemed to burst open and float in the light. Yes, she was very pleased with that one.

She pinched another clean sheet from the paper tray. Measured out the area that would be one of three repeated sections to make the shade. And began again.

Mr. Tiffany was right. You couldn't force inspiration, it had to grow organically from the spirit. But she didn't have much time if she was going to have a model of the actual shade in time for Mr. Tiffany's return.

And there was the rub, to paraphrase Hamlet. She wanted to complete it in time for it to be chosen to appear at the Paris Exposition.

There, she'd admitted it. Her little lapse into pride. She wanted the honor of being chosen by Mr. Tiffany to represent his art at the most important exhibit in the world.

But it wouldn't come like this, and she had other duties that needed her attention, other projects to keep on schedule, girls to oversee. With a sigh of resignation, Clara returned her latest attempt to the folder and went to check on Miss Pascal's progress and await Agnes's visit.

Agnes was coming through the outer door just as Clara was coming out of hers. She hurried to meet her, merely glancing in Miss Pascal's direction as she passed, though she did notice that the girl was already busily working. A good sign.

Agnes was wearing a smart new shirtwaist with a soft, high-standing collar and a bib of precise little French tucks down the front. Agnes liked nice clothes and she dressed in a quality above most of the others, not because she wanted to show off, but because she appreciated fine things.

But Agnes lived with her parents and probably had her entire salary at her disposal. Which was a good thing for Agnes, who was also an avid photographer and owned an expensive camera. Clara also enjoyed photography but the cost of developing the photographs alone was prohibitive.

Clara admitted to being a bit of a tightwad; she had her clothes made over . . . and over, though part of that was her middle-class midwestern upbringing. She earned a nice salary but never seemed to have enough for frills. Though she had to admit her bicycle had set her back for quite a few months. But she wouldn't trade it for all the soft collars and French tucks in Manhattan.

Though perhaps this weekend she would walk over to Stern Brothers or maybe even splurge and look in at Lord & Taylor to see what the new fall fashion would be. Clara dabbed at her forehead. Ridiculous to be thinking of fall when they were sweltering in summer. Where had her brains gone roving?

Agnes had stopped to talk to Miss Griffith, who was responsible for the border of Agnes's religious triptych. The figure itself had been designed by a male artist and sent to the women's division for the floral surround.

Clara went to join them. "Very nice," Agnes was saying. "Do you think you'll be able to start on the 'Summer' panel for the 'Four Seasons' window soon?"

Miss Griffith raised both eyebrows. "I'm not certain; once I get this cartoon transferred to the glass easel for patterning, I believe that Miss Egbert and Miss Byrne have been assigned the selecting and cutting— But here is Mrs. Driscoll, who will be able to tell you more."

"Ah, good morning," Agnes said.

Clara smiled as they made room for her to observe the cartoon. She liked Grace Griffith. She was smart and polite and very efficient, but Clara always sensed a little reserve, not in her manner but in something she couldn't quite place. Which made absolutely no difference to Clara as long as she kept doing what she was doing and didn't suddenly decide to get married.

"Yes," Clara said, pulling her mind from that horrific possibility, "we're a bit backed up at the moment, but hopefully . . ." Catching sight of Emilie Pascal at work several tables away, she reminded herself that a faucet with a steady drip could soon fill a glass to the brim and added, "But that will soon be remedied."

She nodded to Miss Griffith and she and Agnes moved away.

"The borders on that triptych are beautiful," Clara said to Agnes.

"I'm quite pleased with them."

"Do you ever want to do the main figure? There's no reason you shouldn't."

"Except that those designers are mainly men. And quite frankly, I for one am very happy drawing flowers. There is not a happier place than a garden."

Or an open field of wildflowers, thought Clara, remembering spring in Ohio.

They walked toward Clara's office.

"I take it that's the new girl next to Lotte Wilson?" Agnes said.

Clara nodded. "But before I introduce you, I want you to see her finished work. I thought we could move her to the Exposition pieces if she does well on the 'River' window. I'm afraid her talents are wasted on cutting, but that's what I need at the moment."

They made their way to Clara's office, nodding greetings as they went. As soon as they were behind the closed door, Clara motioned to a chair. "Please have a seat. Wait until you see these."

Agnes smoothed her skirt and sat down.

Clara reached for the samples of Miss Pascal's work and spread them on the desk before Agnes.

Agnes took a moment to study them, holding each one up to the light of the window. She didn't speak, but after a few seconds she looked at Clara, eyebrows raised.

"She also had some examples of very different oils. Rather expressionistic."

"Good?"

"Well, if you like the expressionists."

Agnes laughed. "Not particularly. But you're wondering why a talented artist came all the way to New York from Paris to work in the anonymity of the workshop cutting glass."

"It did cross my mind."

"It's a great opportunity for an artist. Especially one new to the country and without family or friends?"

Clara nodded. "And she said she had a letter of introduction."

"Oh? From whom?"

"I have no idea. In my relief, I hired her on a half-pay trial without looking at it. I suppose I shall have to ask to see it, if I keep her on."

"Well, my vote, if I have one, is to keep her regardless. Perhaps she can work with Miss Griffith on 'Summer' where she can be overseen. But these sketches . . . the nuance, the touch, the eye . . . probably the most talent we've had in many, many years."

"I agree," said Clara. "I know you're busy with your own work but with Mr. Tiffany still out of the country, I wanted your opinion and to make sure we all stay apprised of our progress."

"Thank you, but now I'd better get back to my studio. The Grafton show is just over the horizon. And my bet is Mr. Tiffany will return to oversee things before it's time to ship the artwork that isn't already at the gallery."

Clara sighed. "I've been thinking that myself. I'll be glad if he does, but I just wish we were a little more ahead of schedule and not so ahead of our monthly budget."

"We always are, and yet we—you—manage." Agnes smiled sympathetically. "You have a thankless job, Clara, I know. But you're the only person who could manage both business and designing and make it all work."

Clara laughed and resisted rubbing her forehead, which was already beginning to throb.

"Well, I say keep the new girl, and if you can find two more just like her, hire them, too." And Agnes left her alone to her task.

Chapter 7

It wasn't until after the lunch break that Grace finally finished her cartoon and oversaw its transfer to a glass easel next to Emilie and Lotte's landscape.

While she was waiting for Miss Byrne to arrive, Grace stopped for a moment to see how Emilie was faring.

"It seems like such a long process for one window."

"It is," Grace agreed. "But getting everything precise is of the utmost importance. And precision takes time. One slip of the pen or the cutter can ruin everything. Think of it this way, if a template is minutely off, then the glass cut from that template will be a little off, and the next, until the whole window is thrown off."

"But when the pieces are soldered . . ." Emilie began.

"Soldering can fix some inaccuracies, but the templates have already been cut with double-edged scissors to create the space for solder into account."

Emilie shook her head, and Grace knew in an instant what she was thinking. "I know. Not much leeway for bursts of creativity."

"No," Emilie agreed.

Grace smiled, remembering her own first days at the workshop. It was tedious beyond words, copying flowers and leaves and trailing vines for hours on end. Making them just the right size, applying a color wash in shades only similar to the original design and that were not always to Grace's taste.

Gradually she'd developed an appreciation of the process. It was satisfying in its way, but would never afford the rush of excitement of sketching real events as they happened. The thrill of knowing that you'd captured a special moment among all the rest. Nothing in the glass studio had come close to that. And that would never change.

She found herself wondering about Charlie Murray. If he felt moments of pure inspiration or whether he just wrote what happened, taking it for granted that his articles would always be accepted. Whether his article would appear in this evening's edition of the *Sun*, and if there would be an accompanying illustration.

Grace had sent hers off that morning on the way to work, but she didn't fool herself into expecting it to be accepted, nor remunerated. She should have gotten it in last night but she didn't have the means to rush back to the newspaper office to make the deadline. Even if they would take her seriously, which they wouldn't.

Miss Byrne arrived with her stylus while Grace was ruminating over the state of journalism. She turned the project over and went back to her worktable to prepare for the next.

As soon as the day ended, Grace hurried her housemates to their cubbies, then into the elevator and onto the sidewalk.

"What's the rush?" Dora complained. "I have a blister on my heel."

"You shouldn't have worn your new shoes to work," Lotte told her.

"Where am I supposed to wear them? All we do is work."

Lotte sighed. "Maybe we'll all go to the beach on our next day off."

"I want to go to the beach," Maggie said and led the way home.

They plodded along in the heat, Dora limping and complaining. The only time they slowed was for Grace to buy a newspaper from the boy on the corner.

"I thought the newspapers were on strike," Emilie said.

"Only the *World* and the *Journal*. This is the *Sun*."

"You must be desperate," Lotte said.

"The *Sun* is boring," said Maggie.

"True, Mags," Grace said. "But I gotta read something."

"Why?"

"I don't know, I just do. I like to know what's going on in the world." And she was dying to see what kind of writer Charlie Murray actually was.

She found out soon enough.

Everyone went straight upstairs to get ready for dinner. Grace practically shoved Emilie inside their room, before she shut the door and tossed the newspaper on her bed. She sat down, untying her shoes and pushing them off her feet, then climbed on her bed to open the paper.

She found the newsboys' strike on the second page. *Three whole columns.* She started to read. And six inches down the first column she knew. "Damnation."

"*Que'est-ce que passe?*" asked Emilie, alarmed.

"Huh? Oh, sorry. Everything is fine. Just this article."

"Is it terrible?"

"No, it's good. Very good." Though Grace did notice that Mr. Murray hadn't bothered to follow the chairman's request not to quote every "dem, dese, and dose."

Reports of the most encouraging description were received from various localities. An envoy from the Brooklyn union

brought this good word: "District Master Workboy Spot Conlon says here's lookin' at youse noble strikers, an' he can't bring his forces over to-day like he said he would, 'cause he's got an engagement to break scab heads over dere. De hull push is out, an' de kid wot tries to sell Woilds an' Joinals gets his slats kicked in. Dat goes. By order of de union." Up rose then Cross-Eyed Peters, representing the uptown boys.

Grace had to admit, it made colorful copy. When Mr. Murray wasn't indulging in recounting the boys' dialects, he delivered quite a bit of actual information, *and* while making the reader feel like she was right there. But it would have been even more successful if it had an illustration.

And she'd sent in a good one: Mr. Pulitzer and Mr. Hearst, standing on the backs of sprawling newsboys struggling to catch at the dollar bills that were falling from the publishers' fists as they "duked" it out. And at the very bottom of the pile, Kid Blink still holding a battered floral horseshoe. It didn't even need a caption. It spoke the message loud and clear.

It would have been perfect. She would just have to figure out how to get her cartoons in early enough to make the midnight deadline while not—yet—revealing her sex, the idea of which just made her angry. If you could do the work, why couldn't you just get the job? Look at Mr. Tiffany. He hired women and they made some of his most praised designs.

Grace flopped back on the bed. Sometimes it was plain out hard not to get discouraged. "Tell it to Nellie Bly," she mumbled.

"Pardon?"

"Nothing. Just talking to myself. My weaker self. I try not to pay attention to her. But sometimes . . ."

"I'm sorry, I don't quite understand you."

"It's nothing. I was just rambling. I wonder what's for dinner."

They went downstairs a few minutes later, where dinner passed with little conversation. It seemed even hotter than it had been on the walk home, and as soon as dinner was over, Lotte declared that she and Maggie were going to walk down to the park. Dora called dibs on the tub and Emilie said she would go to bed. Grace didn't blame her for being tired. Her first day on the job had been long, especially after the night she'd passed. Grace hoped she wouldn't be having nightmares every night.

Grace stayed downstairs in the parlor and pulled out the copy of the *Sun* to read Charlie Murray's article again—and again . . . and even again.

EMILIE HAD JUST hung her shirtwaist and skirt in the wardrobe and was standing in her shift by the window hoping to get a breath of air, when a quiet knock sounded on the door. Before she could answer it, much less throw something over her shift, the door opened and Maggie slipped into the room.

"Oh, hello, I thought you were going on a walk."

"Too hot. Whatcha doing?"

"Looking out the window."

"Is this where you sleep?" Maggie walked over to Emilie's bed.

"Yes."

"Me and Lotte only have one bed."

"Oh."

"And it's hot at the back of the house."

"I think it's just hot everywhere, Maggie."

"Is it hot in Paris?"

"Yes, it is." In so many ways that she knew Maggie and most

people would never understand and, hopefully, would never learn.

Another knock, the door opened and Lotte stuck her head in. "Is Maggie—?"

She saw her sister. "Maggie, don't bother Emilie. She's getting ready for bed."

"I'm not bothering her. We're just chatting."

Lotte mouthed *Sorry* to Emilie.

And though she wished them both elsewhere, Emilie smiled and said, "We were just chatting."

"About Paris," added Maggie.

Lotte took that as an invitation and stepped in, closing the door behind her.

"Won't you have a seat?" Emilie gestured to the only place to sit, her little bed, and prayed that Grace would soon return and shoo them away.

"Tell us about Paris," Maggie urged.

"Well," Emilie began, accepting her fate. Before she'd even begun, the door opened. Dora bustled in wearing a light blue gauze robe and her hair turbaned in a towel.

"I thought you were all in here. What did I miss?"

By the time Grace came upstairs, Emilie had woven a description of Paris that sounded like a fairy tale to her ears, but it was just what the others wanted to hear.

They had also discussed the spinsters in the workshop. Of which there were only a few, since most girls found husbands as soon as possible and moved on.

"Not to mention Miss Gouvy and Miss Northrop *and* Mrs. Driscoll."

"But she's a Mrs.," Emilie pointed out.

"Married some old man who died after three years," Dora said. "And Miss Gouvy . . . well, I don't think she's even stepped out with a gentleman. She's very proper."

"She's very nice," retorted Lotte, who had grown somewhat quiet during this conversation.

"I want to get married," said Maggie.

"No, you don't," Lotte said. "You stay away from men. You like working for Mr. Tiffany, don't you?"

"Yes, but . . ." Maggie frowned at Emilie.

"You liked Annie," Lotte reminded her. "And Annie got married so she couldn't work at the workshop anymore."

"Yes, but . . . Do you want to get married, Emilie?"

A sharp, anxious look from Lotte, and Emilie understood. Lotte wouldn't be finding a husband anytime soon, if ever, not with the responsibilities of taking care of Maggie. And Maggie . . . it was best not to even travel down that path.

"Not I, Maggie. I want to work for Mr. Tiffany. Besides, I'd rather have a sister. You're lucky."

It was an odd sensation, thinking about someone rather than herself for a change. Lately, Emilie hadn't thought much of the plight of others, so busy was she, trying to relieve herself of her own.

"And now tell me about Mr. Tiffany. I've never seen him."

"He's gone to Europe," Maggie said.

"He's rather short," Lotte volunteered, obviously happy to change the subject from marriage.

"No, he isn't," Dora said. "He's tall."

"He's tall to you because you're short."

"Humph. I'm petite."

"Fat, thin? Young, old?" pressed Emilie.

"Not exactly fat, but stocky," said Dora. "And old."

"He's thin and not that old," Lotte corrected.

Dora made a face. "He has blue eyes."

"No, he doesn't, they're brown."

"Blue," retorted Dora.

"He walks with a stick," Lotte said.

"But he doesn't need it," Dora countered. "Just uses it to beat people with if he doesn't like your work."

"He does not!" Lotte retorted adamantly. "Dora is just teasing you."

Dora pouted her lips. "Well, he does sometimes knock the glass onto the floor if he thinks it's wrong. He does have a temper," Dora said and shivered.

"He's temperamental," Lotte said. "Most creative men are."

Emilie could attest to that. At least the creative men she had known—and some she'd loathed.

"He has a beard," said Maggie.

The other two agreed to this and before they could argue about the beard's attributes, Grace returned and herded everyone out of the room. Maggie stopped at the door. "I'm glad Annie got married and had to move out. I like you better, Emilie."

"I like you, too," Emilie said and gently closed the door behind her.

"Why didn't you send them away? You look completely knackered." Grace tossed her newspaper on the desk and began to undress.

"I didn't want to be rude."

"So what have you been talking about this whole time?"

"I asked about Mr. Tiffany."

Grace pulled her shirtwaist over her head. "And?"

"I learned that he is a tall, short, old, not so old, blue-eyed, brown-eyed, stocky, thin man who has a beard, the one thing all three agreed on. Oh, and he walks with a stick, which neither Lotte nor Dora thought he really needed for support."

Grace shimmied into her nightdress and reached for her toothbrush. "Huh. That sounds about right." With that, she grabbed a towel off the dresser and padded off down the hall.

Chapter 8

By the end of her trial period, Emilie was beginning to dream in glass and double-edged scissors. Her back hurt, her eyes hurt, her fingers were crisscrossed with tiny little cuts from handling the glass.

On Saturday half day, she waited in line to receive her half pay and tried not to be anxious. No one had mentioned anything about her staying or going. Though Mrs. Driscoll had complimented her several times on the tidiness of her work.

Tidiness was not exactly the kind of praise an artist lived for, but it would do. Emilie had already begun to feel at home here. Everyone was nice enough. And though Mrs. Driscoll wasn't one to show much personality, she didn't seem cold.

Emilie reached the front of the line and Mrs. Driscoll handed her half pay. "We're very pleased with your work, Miss Pascal. And would like to offer you full salary of five dollars a week."

Emilie grasped her few dollars in her hand and sent a grateful prayer to the saints whose names she'd never learned. "Thank you, that would be acceptable."

"Excellent. And once your landscape window is completed, you will be assigned to a new project. Do not let us down, Miss Pascal."

"No, Mrs. Driscoll. I won't."

Lotte, Dora, and Maggie were waiting for Emilie in the cloakroom. They were all going to celebrate the end of the week with ice cream in Madison Square Park just a block away. Emilie's first response was to refuse. She was still a little apprehensive about going out into the world, though that fear, she knew, was mostly in her mind. She'd been in Manhattan for over a week, going from work to boardinghouse to work to boardinghouse. She longed to see the rest of the city. To visit the museums and art galleries. It was said in Paris that the Metropolitan "for a new museum" had a respectable collection.

She would save her money for the museum fare . . . but a park . . . one not locked against the public. She couldn't resist.

"Aren't we going to wait for Grace?" she asked as the four of them crammed into the last space on the elevator.

"No, she has to visit her great-aunt today." Dora scrunched up one side of her face in an exaggerated wink.

As soon as they were on the street, Maggie struck out ahead of the others. She obviously knew the way. But Emilie took her time trying to absorb everything she saw as they walked west down Twenty-Fifth Street. There were apartment buildings and row houses, and even a small art gallery squeezed in the ground floor between two sets of steps. This was more like what she'd been hoping for. And suddenly she was anxious to see more.

Grace waited until the others were well away before she took the elevator downstairs. She really would have liked to go to the park, but her weekends (half day Saturday and full day Sunday) were when she had the most uninterrupted time to work at her other profession. Not that it was much of a profession.

It had been days since she'd sent in her newsboys cartoon to the *Sun*. She'd bought every evening edition since then and it hadn't appeared. Considering how much she made on her last cartoon for *Suffrage Weekly*, she couldn't keep shelling out two cents a day much longer before she was paying out more than she took in.

She'd buy this afternoon's edition and if it wasn't there, she would know that once again, she'd been ignored. There had to be a way to get a foothold in the newspaper publishing door.

She made her way down to Union Square where the Police Department was presenting its annual parade. Not something that she was particularly interested in, but you couldn't pick your news, and a smart journalist, especially a smart political cartoonist, understood that even the most mundane event could turn into a big story.

Besides, Grace had heard several reporters at a political rally the week before saying that Thomas Edison would be filming with his moving picture camera. Now there was an angle that might present some material. Of course, if she had been one of their group she would know just where Mr. Edison would set up his camera. But she wasn't one of them. She would just have to find it herself.

Grace walked the seven blocks to the square wrestling with the one question that seemed to consume her every thought these days: how to earn a place in the male-controlled publishing world.

She bought a bottle of root beer and drank it while she strolled through the park, keeping her eye out for a camera or a group of journalists. Crowds were lining the street and she could hear a band playing behind her. She squeezed past the spectators and reached the south sidewalk as the bicycle squad rode by, followed by the horse brigade. She stretched up on her toes and spied Mr. Edison and his camera, surrounded by several reporters, just across the street.

She moved to the edge of the crowd just as the policeman band turned the corner, their white gloves and shiny helmets gleaming in the sun. She was about to attempt to cross the street ahead of them when she caught a glimpse of a bright copper head directly across from her.

Charlie Murray. Other journalists were watching the parade, but not Mr. Murray. He was standing right next to the camera and seemed to be interviewing the photographer. That would have been *her* angle, Grace thought with disgust.

She didn't cross the street. She didn't want him to see her, though she didn't take the time to analyze why. She pulled out her sketchbook and hastily drew in the camera, the man behind it, Mr. Edison himself, and several newsmen, none of whom would be Charlie Murray.

The brass band marched past, blocking her view momentarily. She hastily sketched what she remembered. Then she flipped the page and sketched the line of marching trombonists.

When the band cleared, Charlie Murray was gone. She quickly looked around to make sure he wasn't heading her way, but he had totally disappeared, probably already running back to the newspaper building to write his copy.

Well, so much for that. Maybe if she had told him what her profession was the first time they'd met, he might have introduced her to his editor. But she knew better. From the moment their paths crossed, she had no doubts as to what his opinion would be about newspaperwomen. Mr. Murray was a newspaperman, which pretty much said it all.

She was glad now she hadn't told him. She was a woman and should be hired on her own merits. She didn't need a man. Especially one of Charlie Murray's ilk. A tall, cheeky lout.

Who, she had to admit, was also a darned good journalist. *She* was good, too. She was even tall, and she'd been known at times to be pretty cheeky herself. The only thing she lacked was a pair of trousers.

MONDAY CAME AROUND all too quickly, but Emilie was just glad to have clean linen and a long bath to face the new week. And though her half pay had quickly dwindled with rent, laundry, ice cream, and other sundries, starting today she was a full-fledged, fully paid member of Mrs. Driscoll's Tiffany girls.

And it struck her that she had never been a member of anything before. Certainly not of a family, her mother's family having disowned her and any progeny she might have when she ran off with the—in those days—dashing Dominique Pascal. And certainly not with her father's family, if he even had any. Not at the Académie where they barely tolerated her and the handful of other women who studied there.

There was Jean and Marie, of course. And it surprised her and saddened her when she realized she hadn't thought about either of them in days.

This morning everyone seemed slower than usual as they put away their things and donned their aprons. Only Grace and Emilie hurried into the workroom, Emilie to her landscape memorial window, and Grace to her new project, which everyone seemed very excited about—a window called the "Four Seasons."

Conceived by Mr. Tiffany, it had been rendered into a watercolor design by Miss Northrop, and Grace had been chosen to draft the design to the actual window cartoon. Grace seemed to be the only one not caught up in the anticipation. Perhaps because she was now carrying the biggest responsibility.

As soon as Miss Northrop arrived with her small sketch, all the girls at nearby tables craned their necks to see.

Emilie marveled at how supportive they were, how they applauded one another's successes. The Académie was all backstabbing intrigue, sarcasm, and snobbishness—jealous of everyone's talent but one's own.

Lotte came to stand next to her. They were soon joined by Dora, who sighed heavily. "It's all great for our work to be going to Paris, I just wish it was us."

Lotte sighed, too. "I don't expect to ever see Paris. Or anyplace else."

"Are you homesick, Emilie?" Dora asked. "I sure would be."

"Not at all," Emilie said. The only thing she longed for in Paris was to be near her mother.

"Not even a little bit?"

"No. I'd rather be just where I am."

Dora shook her head in disbelief and wandered back to her work.

Lotte and Emilie returned to their window, which would be headed, not to Paris, Lotte had told her, but to a church on the Upper West Side of Manhattan. A place she had yet to see.

Really, next weekend she would have to do some sightseeing, maybe even hazard the museum.

A FEW DAYS later, Emilie positioned the last glass piece on the window, and both she and Lotte stood back to admire their work.

"It's turned out well, don't you think?" Lotte asked.

"I do," said Emilie.

"Especially your water. It almost looks real."

While they were standing there appreciating their handiwork, four burly men entered the workroom and walked straight toward Emilie and Lotte's worktable.

"This the church window?" one asked.

Lotte and Emilie nodded.

The man motioned to his companions and they surrounded the easel.

"What are they doing?" Emilie asked as she watched them lift the easel and tilt it until it was almost parallel to the floor.

"They have to take it downstairs to solder the pieces together," Lotte explained.

"And they just carry it like that?"

Lotte nodded. "Down the stairs to the fourth floor. They do it with all the windows."

"What if the pieces drop off? What if they drop the whole window?"

"You just pray they don't," Lotte said, beginning to frown as the men carried the window down the aisle toward the door. "Actually it's the most nerve-racking part of the job. Best not to watch and hope for the best." Lotte sighed as she watched as they maneuvered the window out of sight. "I suppose this must be what a mother feels when she watches her little ones leave home."

"Do you think so?" Emilie didn't think she would ever experience that feeling. She'd learned firsthand that artists as parents only caused heartache and worse.

"Maybe," Lotte said and began brushing the glass shavings from their worktable.

Emilie had barely returned her tools to the tool basket when Mrs. Driscoll came from her door accompanied by Miss Northrop.

They were headed in her direction and for a moment Emilie panicked. Had they changed their minds about hiring her? Had they somehow reconsidered her work and decided it was inferior? Impossible. She was as critical of her own work as the next person and she knew her cutting had been very competent.

And she'd taken great care to place the pieces just so that it flowed across the landscape like a cool, refreshing brook. It was good. Emilie knew it was good.

"Ladies," Mrs. Driscoll said. "Very nice work. Miss Wilson, you will join Miss Egbert on a new commission. And you, Miss Pascal . . ." She turned to give Emilie a serious look.

Emilie swallowed. She would refuse to go. She would beg them if she had to. It wouldn't be the first time she'd had to beg.

"Seeing the progress you have made in the time you've been here, Miss Northrop and I have decided to move you to the 'Four Seasons' window."

Emilie heard Lotte gasp behind her.

"It is a major project. Usually we would appoint our most experienced cutter and selector to something of this importance, but we've been impressed with your work thus far. It's a big responsibility."

Mrs. Driscoll seemed to want some kind of assurance so Emilie nodded. "I am ready."

"Excellent. Now, let us take a look at what you'll be doing." Mrs. Driscoll turned away and she and Miss Northrop moved down the aisle toward Grace's cartoon.

Emilie cut a quick glance at Lotte.

"Go," she whispered, and Emilie hurried after them.

They stopped at Grace's easel where she was transferring a small watercolor to scale on a large piece of manila paper. Grace acknowledged them with a nod and continued working.

"This is Mr. Tiffany's 'Summer' panel," Mrs. Driscoll explained. "One of four, each depicting a different season. And which will eventually be combined into one large window with internal and surrounding borders. Miss Northrop is responsible for the excellent sketches of his ideas and Miss Griffith has started work on the cartoon of 'Summer.' Appropriate of the weather, I think we can all agree."

Emilie murmured something; she hardly knew how to react. She was to work on the "Four Seasons" panel.

"So this twelve-by-eleven-inch sketch," Mrs. Driscoll continued, gesturing to the watercolor that was propped up on a small table at Grace's elbow, "will become . . ."

Her voice grew distant as Emilie leaned in to get a better look at the sketch. Bright red poppies growing against a cobalt-blue sky, lush green leaves, dark trees in the distance, and the whole placed within an ornate oval of opalescent pearls and ribbon with "Summer" scrolled above—as if anyone would have to guess. So much was evident in that one small watercolor that Emilie was prompted to take another good look at its creator.

Pretty, but not dynamic, Miss Northrop didn't talk loudly or call attention to herself but seemed perfectly content to draw flora and decorative motifs. And yet these were the boldest colors Emilie had seen in watercolor.

"It will be the centerpiece of Mr. Tiffany's Paris exhibit," Miss Northrop added. "But it will take a precise and sensitive eye to color." Her own eyes had taken on a brightness that hadn't been there just moments before..

"Miss Griffith should be able to finish the cartoon and get it traced by tomorrow. We are disgracefully behind schedule and we can't pull any of our more experienced selectors off their current projects. You have a special talent and a keen eye for the properties of the glass, Miss Pascal. Miss Northrop and I have been observing your work on the river panel. With the way you've cut the ripple glass, and placed the colors and contours to create a seamless flow of the water, we are assured that you are up to the job."

Emilie heard Mrs. Driscoll but couldn't form a response. She was to cut *and* select the glass?

Even Grace stopped at that and looked from one woman to the other.

"We, of course, will assist you with the selection," Mrs. Driscoll said. "I realize it's a daunting task even for an experienced cutter. But small steps will get the job done. If you think you are up to the task."

Emilie nodded.

"And Miss Griffith will be here to guide you through."

A look passed between Mrs. Driscoll and Grace, but Emilie was still too shocked to discern what it meant.

"As soon as we have an available cutter she will be assigned to help you. Until then, you'll have to be both selector and cutter. . . .

"And now if you'll follow me and Miss Northrop, we will introduce you to the basement."

The storage room was indeed in the basement. Shelves and shelves of glass sheets, lined up like books in the *bibliotheque*, rose on all sides as high as Emilie could reach and beyond.

Rows and rows of every shade from the palest yellow to the deepest violet. And in their center, several "girls" sat at tables, choosing between one shade and another so subtle that Emilie could hardly make out the difference.

How would she ever be able to choose the correct one? Her river glass had already been chosen before her. She'd like to think that she would have chosen as well, but suddenly she didn't know. With oil, pastels, and even watercolors she knew how to combine light, shadow, and color into representations of life.

She understood how the impressionists created scenes without ever drawing a line. Just brushstrokes of a variety of colors so that when viewed close, they appeared to be random splotches of hues. But when you stepped back, the strokes took shape, became people, objects, entire scenes. Even the expressionists and their bold slashes of thick color seemed arbitrary when compared to stained glass.

With glass you had to be precise. One bad cut and you most often had to begin again. Edges were sacrosanct, and though she'd been introduced to "plating," the technique of layering pieces of glass to enhance the depth of tone, the color still didn't stray beyond the solder line. No blending. No meshing. It was all in the glass.

And suddenly far from home, from her normal tools of the trade, Emilie felt a wave of uncertainty. It was a vast undertaking. Had she been too cavalier with her belief in herself, belief that she could outrun her past, that she could really succeed on her own?

The other two women had stopped at a section of the greens. Now they motioned her over. Miss Northrop held up a sketch of a branch of leaves. Emilie recognized it as a detail of the top arch of the "Summer" sketch. Miss Northrop pulled out several sheets of glass and asked the male attendant to carry them to an unoccupied table.

"What do you say to these?" Mrs. Driscoll asked.

Emilie moved closer, studied the leaves in this detail, but in her mind she was remembering the full sketch, how the arch of leaves canopied the cobalt sky. Miss Northrop had chosen one with too much brown, one with red, and one fairly pure. None of them were right.

This part of the panel called for the green of Seurat or Pissarro, the yellow green of spring already deep and maturing into the ripe green of summer. Light, but bold. The answer to a promise.

Did she dare speak her mind or did they expect her to agree with their choices?

"I—" Emilie studied the selections, closed her eyes. "None of these." She held her breath.

"Show us what you would suggest." Mrs. Driscoll walked over to the wall of glass and motioned to Emilie to choose one.

It took several attempts, and Emilie was certain the attendant was losing his patience when he finally pulled out a sheet that she knew was perfect, a play of light spring green becoming viridian then olive, all within the glass itself, as if the glass were the canvas.

"This one," she said.

The attendant carried it to the table where Miss Northrop was waiting.

"And this one," Emilie added, pulling out a darker, more heavily veined piece. The attendant added that to the first, then he tilted one selection to stand on edge so that they could see the light shine through.

Emilie was vaguely aware of the two women exchanging looks as she mentally cut the glass into leaves. If only they saw it the way she did.

Miss Northrop pulled a sheet from behind the leaf detail. "And this?" It was the background of darker trees behind a row of poppies. "What would you do for the trees?"

"I would borrow minute traces of the foreground leaves, leading to deep, deep green, almost black, interrupted by bits of light blue-green, as if glimpsing the faraway sky." They didn't agree or disagree, so she kept explaining. "The light green invites the viewer to enter the garden, but the dark trees draw them farther and farther inside."

Mrs. Driscoll merely lifted her hand to gesture Emilie toward the shelves. She went, no longer unsure. She knew just what she was looking for, but had the glassmakers envisioned it, too?

She walked slowly down the last rows of green. This time took quite as long as the first choices had. She deliberated on some and didn't hesitate on others. Halfway down, she found her touch of blue, sparsely veined with threads of deeper green, just enough. "This one," she said and kept walking while the attendant pulled the chosen sample.

She found the last one in the very last section of greens. Oh yes, this was what she envisioned. Emilie nodded to the attendant and followed him back to where the other two women waited.

He placed this sample next to the others and moved way.

Neither woman spoke and for a heart-stopping moment Emilic was afraid she had misjudged her own eye. But she had no choice. Like a gambler who, with his last sou, bets everything to save himself from having nothing.

"From these to these," she said, tracing the pieces with her finger. "And if I remember correctly, reintroduce the first at the bottom with the red of the poppy flowers."

Then Miss Northrop smiled. "Just as I saw it in my watercolor sketch and as Mr. Tiffany saw it in his mind."

Mrs. Driscoll nodded to the attendant. "Please hold these aside for me." She turned to Miss Northrop. "Shall we move on to the poppies?"

As the days passed and the design started to take shape, Emilie could hardly remember that last vestige of panic she'd felt as she'd faced those greens in the basement. Gradually the glass became an extension of herself. She stopped thinking and let the color guide her.

Several yards away, Grace had begun "Autumn." Outside the

weather began to change. And Emilie wondered if it was the seasons outside or the ones they were working on that ruled their lives.

As the garden of poppies began to take shape, Emilie began to think ahead about the decorative surround. Completed on all sides by a scroll pattern and colorful opalescent beads against a deep antique marigold.

And there were three more panels to come. It seemed like a herculean task.

Miss Northrop made daily visits to the workshop to check on their progress. Mrs. Driscoll made her usual rounds, but she seemed a little preoccupied.

And there was talk of Mr. Tiffany's return.

Clara stared out the window at the clouds scudding by; the sky was turning grayer by the second. Every cloudy day slowed the work down. Colors that looked perfect in the sunlight transformed into something you didn't expect, became murkier or changed color value completely. It took concentration to keep the memory of the actual color foremost in the mind. Electric lighting had been installed years before, but it didn't give the same light as sunshine.

The Met school had promised to send over a new candidate that week, but the girl had changed her mind and enrolled in secretarial school instead. Clara had to settle on a complete novice and she was still two cutters short. Thank heaven for the new French girl. She was a wonder and she worked well with Miss Griffith, though to be fair almost anyone did. Miss Pascal, after her memorable first day, had settled in nicely. She was a bit opinionated. After all, wasn't that the mark of a good artist? Clara was a bit opinionated herself.

She turned from the window as the sky lit up briefly, then the rain began to fall. She almost didn't hear the knock at her door, an occurrence that was beginning to cast her into dread.

"Come in."

Miss Hodgins burst into the room. "He's here. He just walked in without notice."

"Who? Who walked in?" Clara asked, feeling slightly alarmed.

"Mr. Tiffany. He's back from Europe. Early. And he's standing outside."

Clara sprang up. He wasn't supposed to be back for another two weeks.

"Is he on his way to my office?"

"No. He stopped to look at the 'Summer' window. I slipped away to tell you. He's just standing there, staring at it."

"Well, this is a happy surprise," Clara said, pulling herself together. She would be glad to see him, glad of his return, but she'd hoped for a little warning. Hoped they'd be a little further along in the schedule, have more to show him of the "Seasons" windows. That she would have her dragonfly lamp finished instead of still in its nascent design. But she hadn't had a moment to give to her own work. Nonetheless, he was home and she felt her spirits lift.

"Thank you, Miss Hodgins. I'll be out directly."

Dora hurried away.

Clara took a couple of deep breathes, patted her hair, and straightened the front of her shirtwaist; she hesitated for a moment, then pinched her cheeks before striding across her office and out the door. She made it halfway down the room before she slowed. Then stopped altogether.

He was standing several feet away from where Miss Pascal was applying glass leaves around the red poppies. Clara had kept a close eye on her progress and so far the girl hadn't let them down. In fact, she'd brought amazing contrast to the garden scene. Already, even with big unfilled holes in the display, Clara could tell it was going to be a cut above.

Even so, she wished she'd had the opportunity to tell him about Miss Pascal, before he introduced himself. He was always mercurial and generous but quick to leap to decisions. She could feel his energy from where she stood, hands clasped behind his back, one hand holding his ever-present walking stick, his compact body alert. Clara knew he was analyzing the girl's every move.

In a word, he was mesmerized.

Clara had rarely been under such scrutiny herself, and in the present case she wasn't sure what it meant.

The rain ran down the windows behind Miss Pascal and her garden. If this had been opera, which Clara attended whenever she could, the strings would vibrate with a low tremolo, the basso would step into the garden and sing in his lowest voice, sending a thrill over the audience.

But Mr. Tiffany stood motionless. Around the workroom, the girls had noticed him and stopped to watch. But he paid them no mind. She doubted that he was even aware of the stir he'd caused. He didn't even acknowledge Miss Griffith, who was standing a mere six feet away with the almost completed "Autumn" cartoon.

All his energy was held by the unaware girl who carefully placed another leaf precisely into place. Clara was loath to interrupt the magnetism between them.

Don't be a ninny, she chided herself. *Introduce them.*

She started forward only to hesitate again when she saw his hands unclasp, the cane move, and she thought, *Not now.*

And then his voice, so persuasive, so passionate, broke the fragile atmosphere.

"You, who are you?"

At first Miss Pascal didn't turn. She seemed unaware that he was speaking to her. Or even that he was speaking at all.

"You must be new. I don't believe we've met."

Miss Pascal turned, and in Clara's mind the sky grew even darker.

She watched as the girl's expression changed from surprised to curious, then to recognition.

"I am Emilie Pascal." Her words were low and barely carried across the workroom.

"I see that you are working on my window."

"Yes."

"I don't like that color of green you're using." The cane came up.

Clara broke out of the stasis that had held her in place. She knew what would follow.

"It is the green I chose for the leaves," Miss Pascal said, lifting her chin.

"You should have chosen something brighter; those are anemic leaves."

"They are bright in the sunlight, but they change with—"

She never got a chance to finish her explanation, that they changed with the overcast sky, which Mr. Tiffany knew well enough, if he had stopped to think.

The tip of the cane swept across the table and the glass pieces it held. A green teardrop flew off and hit the floor with that horrible crack they all dreaded.

Clara started toward him.

But she had waited too long.

Emilie Pascal stooped down and picked up the pieces. Stood and held them up to his face. She was almost as tall as he, and their eyes met, hers sharp with anger, his full of fire.

"How dare you. I cut this glass with my own hands. It took time and precision and you fling it away as if it is nothing? It is the perfect green for your leaves."

From the corner of her eye, Clara saw Miss Griffith move toward the girl, and she gave a sharp shake of her head to stop her.

Clara rushed forward. "Mr. Tiffany, how wonderful that you've arrived ahead of schedule." Her forced enthusiasm did absolutely no good. But she needed Emilie Pascal and so did he, which he would realize in an hour or so after he'd sent her packing. Clara couldn't let that happen.

She stepped in between them, blocking his view, and smiled like someone demented. "We're all so glad that you had a safe journey, Mr. Tiffany. I wanted to introduce you myself, but I didn't get the chance. Miss Pascal is new to us. She came all the way from Paris to study the craft and learn."

Clara was distracted by his breathing, puffing in and out like a pair of bellows.

"Mr. Tiffany," she urged quietly. "She still has to learn our ways, but she is a great talent."

Now he turned to give her his full attention. "A great talent? A great talent?" He looked back at Miss Pascal. "*I* can see that she is a great talent.

"What she must learn is that she is *my* great talent." And with that he spun away and strode to the door, his cane *tap, tap, tapping* into the silent room.

Chapter 9

"It was the green we decided on, you and Miss Northrop and I," Emilie said, lifting her chin despite the urge to climb inside her cubby and hide until everyone had gone home. Her knees were quaking so much that she was afraid she would disgrace herself as she had on her arrival. She locked them against the possibility. She'd made it all the way into Mrs. Driscoll's office with everyone watching and she hadn't faltered. She would not falter now.

She would plead, beg if necessary, because she must. Clasp her hands and go down on her knees if need be, though she'd discovered years ago that acting pitiful rarely succeeded, especially when you needed it to most desperately.

"I know, my dear." Mrs. Driscoll sat down. "It was the overcast clouds, and he wasn't paying attention; you caught him by surprise.

"Please sit down. I can see you are a bit shaken." She gestured to the chair across from her.

Emilie hesitated, but Mrs. Driscoll merely began straightening sketches that littered her desk. It was only the second time she'd been in Mrs. Driscoll's office, and the first time she hadn't noticed how crowded it was. Open shelves held a jumble of molds and models, small decorative pieces: inkwells, mosaic boxes, clocks, candle screens, pottery. Papers, tools, and glass pieces cluttered the desk. The only relatively clear space was right in front of the manageress, where several sketches depicted large double-winged insects lined up wing tip to wing tip like a row of paper dolls.

Emilie sat. "Is he going to fire me?"

"No, dear, not if I can help it. But you must learn not to confront him head-on. He has to fight his business manager and the company's board and even his own father, all of whom think they know better than he. They don't but they still harass him, and sometimes . . . Well, sometimes he doesn't think before he speaks."

"He is a man."

Mrs. Driscoll merely raised one eyebrow. "A trait that isn't the whole proprietorship of the male sex."

"Yes," Emilie said, lowering her gaze, but biting her tongue not to answer. She knew she was being reprimanded, gently, which was new to Emilie but stung nonetheless.

"What will happen to me?"

"If you can keep your thoughts to yourself until asked for them, I believe you will become a great asset to the workshop. Can you do that?"

She must do that. "Yes."

"Mr. Tiffany is a great genius, and he knows best."

"Then I shall go pick out different greens and show him." Emilie glanced out the window. "But when the sun is out."

"I will take care of the green situation."

"No, please. I will show him that I . . . defer to his . . . greater wisdom. And . . . and . . . apologize."

Emilie sat still, forcing herself to keep quiet while Mrs. Driscoll's eyes raked her. Too much deference and the balance could tip against her. Just like in a good forgery, know when to quit. But she was not a forger. No longer. She bit her lip, keeping the words she longed to say from spilling out. *Please keep me.*

Here, I am the true me. Here, I am safe. Here, I will do great art. And added *For Mr. Tiffany* to the end of her silent prayer.

"Very well, tomorrow if it is sunny, we will both go to the basement and choose a selection of greens and present them—and you—to him."

Emilie wanted to argue that she must do this herself, but she merely said, "Thank you, Mrs. Driscoll."

Mrs. Driscoll stood. Emilie stood.

"*Libellules*," Emilie said, pointing to the insect drawing on the desk.

"I beg your pardon?"

"Those insects. We call them *libellules* in France."

"Oh, dragonflies," said Mrs. Driscoll, pulling one sketch out from the rest. "I've been fighting with the little devils for weeks now. I see them flying in my head, but on paper they just come out static." She puffed out a small laugh. "Sometimes the best ideas are elusive."

Emilie understood that she was talking to herself and not to Emilie, but she answered. "Perhaps if you try overlapping the wing tips." For another heart-stopping moment she was afraid she had overstepped . . . again. But it seemed so obvious.

"I believe you're right," Mrs. Driscoll said. "Amazing how an outside eye can suddenly see things that you haven't seen for all your looking."

Emilie didn't respond, as she tried to understand if Mrs. Driscoll was talking about herself and Emilie, or Emilie and Mr. Tiffany. It was too complicated in English. She would let it go and concentrate on her glass.

"Now if you will get back to your window, I shall take a minute to redraw these . . . *libellules*?"

Emilie nodded. "Dragonflies."

"Yes. Now back to work, and Miss Pascal?"

Emilie turned from the door. "Yes?"

"Perhaps you might like to start with the poppies for now?"

DAMN, IF THE girl wasn't right, Clara thought as the door closed and she pulled her latest rejected sketch to the center of her desk. *And tarnation*, she added as she reached for a clean sheet.

Half an hour later she had the beginnings of a new lampshade design. A border of dragonflies, wings spread and slightly overlapping at the tips. It hadn't taken much to turn a static rendition into a three-dimensional display.

She couldn't help make the comparison between Emilie Pascal's reaction to herself and to Mr. Tiffany. No doubt things would be livelier around here with her presence.

She went back to her drawing and in spite of the overcast light, she could see it clearly, all of it, the shape, the border, the blades of glass. Bodies of light blue tapering toward the sky. The overlapping wings shaded from dark to light. The light tips of the front wings popping out from the darker color of the wings behind—and overlaid with . . . filigree . . . bronze filigree.

Yes. Brilliant. And all of it shimmering around the base of the shade, while the grass rose like flames of green to the bronze top ring.

And the base. She hastily grabbed another sheet of paper. It wouldn't be just a bronze tube or an oval large enough to camouflage an oil container, but a bulb-shaped mosaic, echoing the hues and tones of the shade, just color, no figures . . . just . . .

A smile parted her lips. Brass dragonflies, *libellules*, set at a diagonal against mosaic tiles.

Her business self immediately interrupted her artistic zeal. She would have to check with the metal department to see if it was feasible. Well, it would have to be. Even if it cost ten times what Mr. Mitchell would want to pay. Fine and elegant and long-lived.

Mr. Tiffany was right. You couldn't push inspiration. Sometimes it just took you by surprise. Lifted you and carried you to new heights all because of one suggestion. She could hardly wait to get started.

She was still bent over the design as the light grew darker and she leaned closer to the paper to see better. The world outside dropped away and Clara didn't even think to wonder if she was needed in the workshop or in one of the offices. No one had knocked on her door, not that she'd heard anyway.

So she was startled upright when the door opened and Alice stuck her head in. "I was beginning to worry, when I saw your light and realized you were still here," she said. "May I come in?"

"Of course," Clara said, jumping to her feet. "I've got it. At last I've got it. Come look. It was thanks to the new French girl. She and Mr. Tiffany had quite the dustup."

"I heard. I also heard you smoothed it over."

"Well, I didn't have a choice. We need her. I mollified him for the moment and brought her in here to explain how one acts while in the studio. Strange girl, but as she passed by on her way out, she casually suggested overlapping the wings. And the whole design fell into place, blossoming like one of Agnes's peonies."

Alice moved toward the desk. "Well, let's take a look then."

"I WAS AFRAID she was going to fire you on the spot," Dora drawled as they headed for home. Lotte and Maggie had gone ahead, and Emilie really wanted to catch up. She didn't want to relive that moment when she turned around and realized who was standing before her.

He'd knocked her glass piece off and she'd reacted without

thinking. But for the wrong reasons. Not because he didn't like her choice of glass but because of all the times she had been tossed aside just like that piece of glass. If he had been another man, she might have thrown herself at him and scratched his eyes out. But he was Mr. Tiffany. He held her future in his hands.

And he'd been wrong. She knew it. And soon he, too, would realize it. Then where would they be? Madame Duchamps had once told her, "Never prove men wrong; they will destroy you for it. Just manipulate them until they think your idea was their idea." Emilie had taken that advice to heart. And had used it before. But she wouldn't have to do that with Mr. Tiffany. Tomorrow in the sunlight he would choose the glass to use. She had no doubt it would be her glass.

Ahead of her, Grace didn't even slow down when they passed the corner where the newsboy sold his papers. The strike had been over for several weeks after they'd come to a compromise. Grace had stopped buying the papers every day. But she seemed distracted and a little distant. Emilie tried to be an unobtrusive roommate. Not that Grace really noticed her. She'd moved her desk from the middle of the room over to the window, shoving the bed at an angle to make room for it.

She said it was to take advantage of the sunlight, but Emilie wasn't fooled. She just didn't want Emilie to see what she was writing every night after she went to bed.

Emilie didn't understand her roommate. She'd gone out at least once a week since Emilie had moved into Mrs. B's. She hardly ever came with them to the park or shopping on half days. Even one Sunday when they took the ferry out to the beach on Staten Island, Grace begged off, ostensibly to visit her ailing great-aunt.

These days, she certainly looked tired enough to have been

nursing an invalid relative, but Emilie didn't believe her. It takes a liar to know one, and Emilie had done her share of lying.

Though she couldn't fathom any nefarious reason except what Dora had suggested. A man. Surely Grace wouldn't be so stupid as to get herself in trouble that would lead to her immediate dismissal. She didn't even seem interested in love, though as Shakespeare rightly pointed out, maybe she "doth protest too much." But Emilie didn't really believe that, either. Grace seemed too smart to fall under the spell of any man. Not even Mr. Tiffany.

Emilie was even more curious about the notebook Grace wrote in every night and slept with beneath her pillow. But Emilie wasn't about to interfere. Sometimes it was better not to know. Besides, she had her own life to worry about.

When they reached the boardinghouse, Emilie was astonished to see Mrs. B slip an envelope to Grace, which she quickly stuck into her skirt pocket. By the time the rest of them had asked about mail and magazines, Grace had already bounded up the stairs.

Emilie didn't wait to see if she had any mail. Of course she wouldn't. She had written to Marie and Jean but had only said she was staying with some of the girls and would write when she had a permanent place to live. It wasn't exactly a lie. If no one moved out of the other rooms and Grace got tired of having her encroach on her living space, she might have to move.

Though why would anyone want to move from Mrs. B's? It was modest, which was fine by Emilie, and more steady and comfortable than the roller coaster that had been her life in Paris, going from riches to abject poverty and back again in the blink of an eye. She would stay with Mrs. B for as long as possible; hopefully, one day, she would get her own room where she could set up a small workspace and paint again.

She shuddered. It was too soon to think about her own work.

She had more than plenty to do working on Mr. Tiffany's, which reminded her that tomorrow she would have to face him. Offer to use whatever colors he desired and hope that she'd been right and that her choice would also be his.

She went upstairs and entered her room.

"Emilie!" Grace squeaked and shoved a letter in her pocket.

"Who else?" Emilie tried not to look at Grace's pocket; she didn't want to appear a snoop. But she could tell by Grace's effort to control her facial expression that it must be . . . "Good news?" she asked.

"Yes, at last, I mean . . ."

Emilie waited for her to continue, hoping she wasn't going to announce an engagement or something equally disrupting. But Grace merely turned and began moving things around on her desk, so Emilie went to the closet and looked at her second shirtwaist.

She wanted to look smart tomorrow, but her shirtwaist was dull and wrinkled. The one she was wearing was worse.

So as soon as dinner was over Emilie carried her skirt and shirtwaist downstairs to spot clean and push the unwieldy iron over the fabric, careful not to leave it in one spot too long and chance burning a hole in the fabric. Then she moved to the skirt, brushing out dust and particles of glass until it looked, if not good as new, at least better.

By the time she carried them both back upstairs, the bathroom was free so she gave herself a sponge bath, pulled her hair out from its coil, and brushed it until it shone. Then she changed into her nightdress, rebraided her hair, and went back down the hall to her room.

She found Grace lying on her bed, smiling at the ceiling. A wave of unease settled over her. "Grace, you're not going to leave Tiffany's, are you?"

Grace turned her head to look at her. "Of course not. Why would I do something so stupid? This job pays better than most I could get."

"Oh, good. I just thought . . ."

"Well, don't think. Everything is going to be fine. Just fine."

GRACE WAS STILL staring at the ceiling when Emilie climbed into her bed. The beds were much closer now that Grace had moved her desk to the window. But she had to work and she didn't want to take the chance of Emilie walking in or waking up and seeing what she was doing.

She felt a little guilty, as if she owed Emilie an explanation, but she didn't. And if it seemed a bit rude to exclude her, well, she'd just have to appear rude. She couldn't very well confide in Emilie. A slip of the tongue and Grace would be sunk.

But the *Sun* had bought her cartoon of the policemen's parade. They'd sent a check for one dollar and twenty-five cents, nearly an entire day's pay for a half hour's work . . . if she didn't count the time it took for the parade and for transportation, and the root beer she'd drunk on the way. Or the several working sketches it took to achieve just the right interpretation. But they *had* paid her. A real respected newspaper.

She held still until she was certain that Emilie was sleeping, then got out of bed and slid onto her desk chair. She pulled the check from the top drawer and looked at it in the moonlight. Then she reread the letter.

Dear Mr. Griffith,

We received your latest cartoon depicting the Police Parade and are pleased to inform you that we will be printing it with a com-

panion article in the evening edition of the Sun. *Enclosed please find a check for the amount of $1.25. We also received your previous work about the newsboys strike, but unfortunately not in time for publication. We would be happy to speak with you about further association, if you could make an appointment to visit our offices at your earliest convenience.*

Direct your call or letter to Mrs. Petry at the editorial desk to arrange.

Most sincerely,
The Editors

Grace wanted to shout her good fortune from the top of rooftops, but she couldn't even celebrate because it had to be kept a secret. Grace couldn't take the chance of appearing as herself, and she didn't really believe all those stories of girls dressing up as men and actually getting away with it. Not close-up and observed closely by fellow journalists.

She'd have to come up with an alternative plan.

She returned the letter to the drawer and flopped back on her bed. They liked her. And to think she would have never sent in something to the *Sun* if it hadn't been for Charlie Murray and his oversized feet and his annoying attention.

Well, it would serve him right when he found out they were both working for the same newspaper. *Ladies' Home Journal*, indeed.

Emilie woke the next morning to glorious sun, an auspicious start to meeting Mr. Tiffany. Grace was still sleeping so she slipped out of bed and tiptoed to the dresser to retrieve her toothbrush and towel, then headed down the hall to wait her turn in the bathroom.

When she returned, Grace was just stirring.

"It's past seven," Emilie said out loud.

Grace mumbled something and turned over, pulling the sheet over her head.

Emilie loosened her braid and pulled her brush through it to untangle the ends. Then she stood in front of the mirror and carefully rebraided it, before wrapping it at the base of her neck.

She didn't feel like being severe today; she wanted to leave it loose and wavy and tied up with a ribbon with tendrils flying about her face. But she was to meet Mr. Tiffany formally this morning and she would be her neatest. He would find no fault with her this morning. She knew how to be . . . demure.

She dressed in her freshly ironed and brushed work uniform and went downstairs to breakfast, leaning forward over her plate so as not to spill a drop.

The day was humid and promised to be hot again but at least the sky was blue and the sun was shining and Emilie took it as a good omen. She struck off at a crisp pace, anxious to get to work.

"What's the hurry?" asked Lotte. "We'll have to start going in early soon enough."

"What do you mean?" Emilie asked, not breaking stride.

"When fall comes and the days start getting shorter, Mrs. Driscoll will ask us to come in an hour early to take advantage of the extra light."

"All this extra work makes me plumb tired," Dora complained as she tried to pin a stray lock of hair and still keep up.

"Well, get used to it," Lotte said. "And be thankful it keeps a roof over your head. And ribbons in your hair."

Emilie glanced over at Dora. She was partial to hair ribbons with big bows and flounces; today's was yellow with black dots.

"Why are you in such a hurry to get to work?"

"Because," Emilie said, beginning to huff a little, "I have to choose more green glass for Mr. Tiffany's window."

"That green you chose is fine."

"Mr. Tiffany didn't think so."

"Oh, he's always spouting off about something or other."

"Dora," Lotte scolded. "He's our employer and a great artist."

"I know. But he didn't have to frighten Emilie. She's new and isn't used to him yet. You don't have to be afraid, Emilie."

"Oh, I'm not afraid. I'm apologizing." And she really wanted to know what color he would choose today in the sunlight.

As soon as they arrived at the Tiffany building, they put their things away, and Emilie went directly to Mrs. Driscoll's office.

"I'd like to go to the glass room now before I get started if that's all right."

"Mmmm." Mrs. Driscoll sat frowning over several sketches that Emilie couldn't quite see from where she stood.

Emilie waited.

Mrs. Driscoll looked up. "Oh, Miss Pascal. You must see what Miss Gouvy painted for me last night. You were absolutely right."

"Pardon?"

"Overlap the wings. I took your advice—"

"Oh, but it wasn't—"

"And everything fell into place. Have a look."

She motioned for Emilie to come closer. Miss Gouvy had made several sketches, but the one in the middle was a completed lamp with a glass shade trimmed with dragonflies. It was beautiful, and the base . . .

"Are those mosaic tiles?" Emilie asked.

"Yes, in complementary colors."

"And these?"

"Well, I know that the powers that be will balk when I introduce these. Filigree dragonflies."

"It's so delicate. They can do that?"

"I'm going to consult with the metal department. But I'm sure they can figure out a way."

"It will be very dear, I think."

"Yes, it will. But I hope to convince them it will be worth the price. Now, what did you want to see me about?"

"The glass for Mr. Tiffany's window. I want to get some samples to show him. Remember?"

"Ah yes. Of course. Well, go down and tell them that you need several selections, which you will return, then come to me, and I will take you down to Mr. Tiffany's office."

"Thank you."

"Mm-hmm." Mrs. Driscoll's attention had already returned to her lamp.

Emilie quietly retreated to the door. As she stepped outside, Mrs. Driscoll called after her. "Come to me first."

Emilie chose three small pieces of similar greens from the green section, signed for them, and carried them upstairs, stopping only long enough at her worktable to add another sample before she carried all to Mrs. Driscoll's office.

Mrs. Driscoll stood and straightened her skirts before accompanying Emilie to the second floor to Mr. Tiffany's office.

"Are you going to tell him about your lamp?" Emilie asked.

"Not yet. I want to have a finished model first so that he can see it as it will be. So not a word. It will be a surprise."

Emilie nodded.

They came to a heavy dark door. Mrs. Driscoll knocked firmly, then opened the door and gestured Emilie and her armful of glass samples inside.

He was sitting at a large desk but stood as they entered. Emilie was only half aware of the man because of the exotic furnishings that surrounded him.

"Mr. Tiffany," Mrs. Driscoll was saying. "This is Miss Pascal, whom you didn't quite meet yesterday."

Emilie drew her attention back to the man.

"Yes, well. Miss Pascal."

"Sir," Emilie said. She was still holding the stack of glass samples so she couldn't very well shake hands. "I'm very glad to meet you and happy to be working on your windows," she added demurely.

"She's brought some samples for you to choose for the summer window," Mrs. Driscoll explained. "Please put them on the table by the window, Miss Pascal."

Emilie carried the glass over to an already crowded table and deposited her stack with the others.

Before she had time to straighten and surreptitiously wipe her hands on her skirt, Mr. Tiffany was standing next to her, peering at the different hues.

Emilie held her breath.

"These would be for the foreground leaves," Mrs. Driscoll said, moving to Emilie's other side.

Emilie suddenly knew what a cheese wheel must feel like as the moisture is pressed out of it. She was just that weak. But she knew she must be right about what he would choose.

He lifted each slice of glass to the window and examined it closely, then chose another piece and did the same, repeating this with each sample.

"It's very important, Miss Pascal, to see how the light will affect your choice. Sunlight will give you the purest color, but it must stand up to the cloudiest day."

Emilie barely breathed.

"I am hearing good things about your work. So you're from Paris."

"Yes, sir."

"Ever heard of Siegfried Bing?" His focus switched from the glass to her face, his eyebrows raised. He was standing not two feet away, close enough for her to see the white among the dark whiskers of his beard.

"Oh yes, that's where I found you." She snapped her mouth shut. And cast a quick look toward Mrs. Driscoll. His interest and her enthusiasm had caught her off guard. Never volunteer information about yourself. And never overstep, at least when your future is at stake.

"Found me, eh? Well, that's good to hear. I think this one." He picked up one of the greens, handed it to her. "This is a bold, mature, vibrant summer green. It will be perfect for the foreground leaves."

"Thank you," Emilie said. *Thank you, thank you, thank you.* She hadn't been wrong about him.

"Now get back to work; time is precious. Leave the rest of this lot. I'll have them returned downstairs. Now *vite, vite*!"

There was a quick exchange between Emilie's two superiors, then the two women were walking down the hall together.

As they waited for the elevator, Mrs. Driscoll said, "Am I correct in thinking that the green he chose today was the same green he hated yesterday?"

Emilie nodded. She tried to look contrite, but she felt triumphant. "But today he saw it in sunlight."

"That was a low trick."

"Was it? I knew he would change his mind."

"How do you know what he would have chosen? Just because you and, I confess, Miss Northrop and I thought it was right for the window doesn't make it right."

"Because I know his work, his mind. I studied for months before I left Paris. He doesn't always choose as I would, but I would not choose against him."

"Well, I must say, you were right on this occasion. Please accept your victory, but don't gloat; his patience is not infinite and I would hate to lose you."

"Oh, but it isn't a victory. And I would never gloat. Yesterday he was just being temperamental. Because he was surprised. He is a man, after all, and their intensity often leads them to make snap decisions, not always the good decision." Emilie had to fight the automatic urge to touch her cheek.

"He does know what's best," Mrs. Driscoll cautioned.

"Oh, I know. I knew that the first moment I saw his work in Paris. And now I am happy because we both chose the same. And I know that we are . . . are . . . *de meme sensibilité*."

"Oh lord, do not get any ideas above your station."

"I don't understand."

"You are his employee and he is . . ."

"He is Mr. Tiffany," said Emilie.

Chapter 10

Clara sometimes wished she could go without sleep and could do it without causing her head to pound, and her stomach to crash like waves on a stormy sea.

She'd left for the workshop before light this morning. It was quiet now; the girls wouldn't be coming in for another hour, and she'd done so much work on the dragonfly design that she almost wished someone would come in so she could crow.

She was actually expecting Alice to appear any moment. Clara had managed to divide the lampshade pattern into thirds fairly evenly, but it would take Alice's talent as a watercolorist to transform her flat sketch into a paper for a curved surface.

Clara was especially excited to get started on the lamp base. In general, the table lamp designs were being geared more and more toward the medium-price buyer. They had switched to thinner brass designs, thanks to Mr. Edison's incandescent bulbs and the insistence on economy by the powers that be.

There would be nothing economic about her bulbous mosaic base. Or her glass dragonflies with their filigree wings and cabochon eyes. That's why she wanted to have a finished presentation before she showed it to Mr. Tiffany.

She didn't mind creating items for efficiency and economy,

pretty pieces to be enjoyed by the owner. Those were important. But so were the finer art pieces.

And her dragonflies were certainly one of those. This design was special. She was pleased. If she could just convince the others.

Her door creaked open.

"Ah, there you are, Alice."

Alice Gouvy slipped inside. "Sorry, am I late?"

"No, not at all. I've just reached a place in the rendering when I need your expertise."

Alice put down her bag and peered over Clara's shoulder. "I almost overslept. If it hadn't been for the milk truck, I might still be in bed."

"Thank goodness for the milkman," Clara said. "I need your opinion. I'm having a heck of a time getting this pattern edge to overlap with the next one. It seems the only logical place is along the side of the body."

Alice scooted an extra chair next to Clara's and peered more closely at the drawing of the parts. Then she picked up the line drawing Clara had made of the section. And looked around the desk.

"Is that the mold you're using?" she asked, pointing to a plaster cast balanced precariously on a stack of invoices.

"Yes, and you don't need to tell me I'm running out of room. This office seems to grow smaller every day."

"It's because you're taking on more and more work every day."

"It's true, and I live in dread of someone else getting married."

"Do you ever think of leaving it all and doing something else?"

Clara frowned at her friend. "Do you?"

"Actually, I have been. Oh, don't worry, not for a while. But I think I would like to go back home one day. Mother is getting older, and it would be nice to be around my family again. The city can be a lonely place."

Clara nodded. She lived with a group of people, men and women, whose company she enjoyed. And yet Clara understood. She often felt a deep longing for the simpler life. Where trees and flowers and streams had attributes other than represented in glass. The park was nice, and her bicycle rides with the Palmié sisters, Lillian and Marion, were godsends. "I'd like to start a craft workshop back home someday." She laughed a little. "Put the whole family to work making things that we could sell to support ourselves. But . . ."

"But you would never leave Mr. Tiffany," Alice finished for her.

"I did," Clara said. "Twice."

"But it didn't last."

"Not for lack of trying."

"No," Alice agreed. "Well, I hear the girls coming in. Why don't I take this pattern and the mold and see what I can do with them?"

"Wonderful. What else are you working on today?"

"Hollyhocks. For some reason, Mr. Tiffany wants a study of them. He sent a whole vase."

"He's restive since he's been back."

"Like a racehorse in the last stretch?"

Clara laughed. "What do you know of racehorses?"

Alice laughed, too. "Next to nothing. I read it in a story this past weekend. But it's apt, don't you think? This is his year. You can feel it every time he comes into the workshop. He's not content to be well respected. He must stand head and shoulders above the rest."

"Oh, that he were a little taller and we had less stress in our lives."

"Clara!"

"I know. But sometimes I find it necessary to make him less

godlike in my mind. Especially right before I'm about to convince him to let me do something that will be very expensive to produce."

"And this looks like it will be that."

"Yes, that's why I'd like to have it look as much as possible like the finished product, so he and the 'powers that be' won't have to wonder if it will work."

"Then I'd better get started." Alice gathered up the sketch and the mold, and Clara hurried ahead to open the door.

Clara stared at the door long after Alice had gone. And allowed herself a moment of sheer possessiveness of her rambunctious dragonflies. They were in good hands. Alice would create what Clara saw in her mind.

In the meantime, she would have to go out and find a cutter and selector somewhere within her already overworked staff to start on Agnes's "Magnolia" window. Mr. Tiffany had decided to push it to the front of the queue, because he was convinced it would show spectacularly at the Paris Expo.

Clara said a little prayer not to heaven, or Mr. Pringle Mitchell, not even to Mr. Tiffany, but to the creative powers that be that her lamp would be there, too.

EMILIE AND GRACE hurried ahead of the others up Fourth Avenue. Emilie was anxious to get started on her work. Each piece she cut on the "Summer" window led her further into a place where she knew she belonged. Last night she'd almost brought out her sketchbook, though she hardly knew what she would have drawn. Her pastels were down to nubs. Maybe she would buy some watercolors . . . after she bought a new shirtwaist, maybe two.

Dora, Lotte, and Maggie were lagging behind, busy making

plans for a final day trip of the summer to Midland Beach, which they promised was only a half-hour ride on the ferry.

Grace pulled the street door open and stepped inside, and Emilie noticed that the others were quite a ways behind. She let the door close behind her and walked right into Grace, who had stopped suddenly.

Grace let out a muffled sound; Emilie regained her balance and peered around her shoulder. Mr. Tiffany was waiting for the elevator and talking to another man, who looked vaguely familiar. Both men turned toward them, and after a startled second Emilie recognized him.

Leland Bishop, art dealer with galleries in London, Paris, and New York. She had never met him, but she'd seen him from afar at various events before the Pascals' last nightmare had begun.

Mr. Bishop was hard to forget. The darling of the art-minded men and women of Paris. Young. They said he was not yet thirty and already had made his name in the world of art dealers. And handsome. A head taller than Mr. Tiffany, with thick sable brown hair and blue eyes that took in the newcomers, so quickly that Emilie barely managed to duck behind Grace.

Grace didn't seem inclined to continue toward the elevator, and Emilie deliberated between backing out the door onto the sidewalk or staying half hidden behind her friend until the men went upstairs.

The door opened, and the other three girls jostled inside.

"Oh, good," Dora said. "Hold the eleva— Oh." She stepped to the side of Emilie and sighed. "Who is that?" she whispered.

Emilie ignored her.

"Why are you stopping?" Maggie demanded. "I don't want to be late. Mrs. Driscoll will scold."

Unfortunately she said it loud enough to catch Mr. Tiffany's ear. "Ah, the ladies of the glass department. Good morning."

"Good morning," they all said as if they'd been rehearsed and Emilie couldn't help but think of all the downstairs maids she'd encountered. They had no reason to act so subserviently or to act like well-trained schoolgirls; they were artists.

"So these are the famous Tiffany girls," Bishop said, and he turned a charming smile on them all. Beside Emilie, Dora simpered. In front of her, Grace's shoulders straightened.

"Yes, Leland, I employ, I believe, thirty-five women in the glass department."

"And when are you going to show me this renowned department?"

"Perhaps next May, once the Paris Exposition is up and running."

Leland Bishop laughed, a clear amused sound that Emilie thought was free of jealousy and suspicion, unlike Mr. Tiffany.

Though she didn't blame him. She knew firsthand what people would do for money, power, or fame. He was right to be distrustful. And though she'd never heard anything spurious about Leland Bishop, she didn't think Mr. Tiffany should be showing him anything that he wasn't ready to show the world.

"Ah, you trust no one with your creations," Bishop continued.

"Excuse us, Mr. Tiffany," Grace said. "But we don't want to be late."

"Of course, do go ahead." He made a slight bow in their direction.

Grace nodded and started for the elevator, Emilie on her heels.

"Oh, Miss Pascal. How is my window coming along?"

Emilie froze. Her name, "Pascal," was echoing so loudly that she wanted to cover her ears. Could she pretend not to hear? She had almost made it to the elevator.

"It is progressing . . . sir . . . very well, I think," Emilie answered, keeping her chin tucked in a way that he might think was shyness instead of an unwillingness to look up. Which she had little hope of since he already knew she wasn't afraid to stick up for herself.

"Perhaps I'll stop in at the studio today, to have a look."

She did look up then and in that instant her eyes caught Leland Bishop's. She quickly looked away. "We'll be happy to see you." She turned to go. Had that been a flash of recognition in Leland Bishop's eyes? They had never met. Had he noticed something that would give her away? Pascal was a common name.

Emilie was pierced by a stab of fear that she hadn't felt in days, maybe longer. Was she overreacting? He had no reason to know her . . . but that look. She couldn't tell. Judgment was useless when it was clouded with fear.

She hurried Grace into the elevator. The others pushed in behind them.

As soon as the elevator man closed the grille and they started their ascent, Dora sighed theatrically. "Who was that Mr. Dreamy?"

"A friend of Mr. Tiffany's," Grace said.

"How do you know?"

"He called him by his first name."

"I think he was gorgeous."

"Me too," said Maggie.

"Well, you can forget him," Lotte said. "Though Emilie might have a chance."

"What do you mean by that?" Dora countered.

"If you hadn't had your head in the clouds, you would have seen the way he watched her as she passed."

The relief that was just beginning to settle over Emilie shattered.

"He was definitely interested."

"Stop it, both of you," Grace said sharply, glancing at Emilie. "Dora, keep your mind on your work or we'll all be staying late. There's little chance of any of us seeing him ever again."

Which was fine by Emilie. She took a deep breath. There was nothing in what Lotte was saying. He hadn't recognized her. Surely he would have looked more shocked. *She was safe. She was safe. She had to be safe.*

THE DAYS BEGAN passing more and more quickly. Everyone focused intently on their own respective projects. Emilie completely immersed herself in finishing the "Summer" window panel. All in all, she was pleased with it. And because of the nature of glass, you couldn't overwork an idea until your colors grew murky and the shapes lost their identity.

There was something immediate about working in glass. Not in the actual construction but in that split second when you decided where to place the pattern and how to begin the cut. And then you held a little piece of potential magic in your hand. Waiting to join the other pieces until it became the essence of itself.

All around her, artisans were doing exactly what she was doing. In one far corner, they were working on various lampshades, all florals, which she had learned were the particular domain of the women's division. The men were responsible for lamps of geometric design, which seemed arbitrary to Emilie. But it didn't bother her: you had a lot more freedom in the depiction of real life than you did in squares and triangles, no matter what the modernists said.

Emilie had looked among the lampshades in progress hoping to see Mrs. Driscoll's dragonflies, but so far it hadn't appeared. As for Mrs. Driscoll herself, she was looking a bit fatigued, arriving early and staying until the others were gone, and was making more trips down to the basement than before.

Miss Gouvy was in and out of the office more than usual; Miss Northrop came several times a day to check on the progress of the "Four Seasons." And Mrs. Driscoll hired a new cutter, a Miss Zevesky, whom she assigned to assist on the "Summer" panel.

Mr. Tiffany also appeared more often, not only on his habitual Mondays when he surveyed the work before going out to the Corona furnaces. Some days he would stop to address the group, deliver a short piece of advice or philosophy about art. Which was all very fine and inspirational, but Emilie wondered if it went in one ear and out the other since the "girls" stopped long enough to be polite, but their minds never left the pieces that waited on their work trays.

By the time they collected their wages on Saturday half day, they were all footsore and ready for a day to themselves.

Lotte knew of a small store that catered to working girls, and Emilie bought a white-and-blue-striped percale waist originally forty-nine cents but that was on sale for forty-two and considered it a bargain. She would have liked to have a nice summer frock to wear for their excursion the following day, but she wouldn't spend her last cent on one day at a beach.

She would need winter clothes soon enough. She should send for her trunk, but a last little thread held her back. Perhaps it was superstition that her old life would follow with the trunk.

Late Saturday night, Lotte knocked on Emilie and Grace's door. She held out a simple muslin dress dotted with little flowers.

"I know you haven't sent for your clothes and might want

something cooler to wear at the beach. If you wouldn't take it amiss, I thought you might wear this. It isn't fancy or anything like that, but it would be comfortable and cooler than your work clothes." She held it tentatively toward Emilie.

Emilie smiled, feeling inordinately touched by Lotte's gesture. It was something she had not felt for a long time "That's so thoughtful . . . but I . . ."

"Wear it," said Grace from where she was sitting at her desk. "Or you'll be depositing beach sand on the studio floor until next washday."

She sounded gruff, but she turned on her last word and grinned at them. "Besides, I've wondered what you would look like in a 'summer fra-a-aah-ck,'" she said, imitating Dora's accent to perfection.

Dora had spent most of dinner musing about which one of her summer frocks she was going to wear until Miss Vanderheusen told her that they'd had enough of fashion talk for one meal.

Dora pulled a face but that didn't stop her the next morning from knocking on Emilie and Grace's door while Emilie was still doing up the buttons of Lotte's dress.

"Hurry up. We don't want to miss the nine o'clock ferry."

"It runs every hour," Grace said from her desk. "So if you miss the nine o'clock, you can take the ten."

"But . . . oh, just hurry up. And don't forget your hat or you'll get windblown and sunburned."

Emilie reached for her head as if she thought a hat might magically appear there. She only brought to Manhattan the black felt beret that belonged to Jean, who had stopped her on a snowy walk by the Seine one afternoon to pull it from his head and put it on hers, securing it over her ears in a moment of tenderness that she would cherish always.

"You better take mine." Grace produced a straw boater from the bottom of the closet and tossed it to Emilie.

So dressed in Lotte's flowered dress and Grace's boater, Emilie hurried downstairs, where the three others were waiting impatiently for her.

Lotte and Maggie were dressed in simple dresses and straw hats with narrow brims. Dora posed like one of the popular Gibson girls who were featured in so many advertisements. Her hair was curled and poufed under a wide-brimmed straw hat trimmed with ribbon and flowers. When she saw Emilie, she twirled around showing off her ensemble, a white lawn dress pleated down the front and cinched at the waist with a light blue grosgrain belt.

All she was missing was a matching parasol.

As for herself, Emilie couldn't remember ever wearing white, even as a young girl. Her father abhorred the color. Of course, she couldn't remember ever wearing little flowers, either, and yet here she was.

Mrs. B came bustling out from the kitchen carrying a covered wicker basket. "Lunch. You don't want to spend your hard-earned money at those stalls along the boardwalk. And you certainly don't want to go into the hotel restaurant. You won't have fare for the ferry once you're done. Get a lemonade from one of the carts and find a nice place to share the sandwiches and fruit." She handed the basket to Lotte.

"And don't stay too long in the sun."

"Come on, come on," Dora cajoled. "We don't want to miss the ferry."

The ferry, Emilie was surprised to find, left from the East River instead of the docks on the Hudson where she had landed. She didn't have a clear idea of where Staten Island was but she was content to feel the breeze in her hair and the sun on her face. Each time she closed her eyes, she was somewhere else. Cannes when things were going her father's way. Biarritz when he was painting the portrait of a local dignitary.

They seemed like someone else's life, and she was glad that she was on a ferry to a place called Midland Beach.

A half hour later, the ferry bumped against the ties of the St. George Terminal and they all disembarked, following the other passengers who crowded onto the gangway and onto land. From there they took a tram to the beach.

They traveled along the shore through marshlands and a wooded area filled with what Lotte explained were campers who liked to live rough. A few minutes later the tram stopped at a long wooden pier.

"We're here!" exclaimed Dora and hustled them out.

Emilie took a quick look around. The boardwalk stretched a long way, culminating in a Ferris wheel at the end. Benches lined the seaside and were filled with women in sun hats and summer frocks, some with black umbrellas shielding them from the sun.

On the shore side, game stalls and eateries led up to a large hotel and restaurant.

There were already people on the beach. Blankets were stretched across the sand where women were sitting, their skirts spread around them, watching children who ran and wove among the crowds. Only a few women had forgone their shoes and stockings and held their skirts above the surf to bathe their ankles. The men, more adventurous in their one-piece swim clothes, swam and lounged and dripped down on their female companions.

Dora held one hand to her eyes, blocking out the sun, and stretched from one foot to the other as if in search of something . . . or someone, Emilie realized when a group of young men lounging around a bench at the entrance to the pier all stood up and waved.

"Of course," Lotte groused. "That's why she was in such an all-fired hurry to catch the nine o'clock ferry. She'd made plans."

"Who are they?" Emilie asked, looking over the odd assortment of half a dozen men, tall and short, bony and chubby, dressed in a version of trousers and shirtsleeves, and an assortment of headwear.

"Guys from the pottery department downstairs. She must have made a date with them during lunch one day."

Dora hurried toward the men. And after admonishing Maggie not to wander off, Lotte and the picnic basket followed her.

They caught up to Dora, who was already holding court among her attentive audience, some blushing, others cocky and sure of themselves. Young workingmen on a lark.

"There you are, you slowpokes. Look who I ran into." Dora gestured to a guy with overly large teeth and a shock of blond hair. "This is Jack. And Paul," a freckle-faced man, who looked still in his teens, "and Sandor . . . you all introduce yourselves later."

The men and Dora started off toward the beach without waiting. Maggie hurried after them, and, resigned, Emilie and Lotte brought up the rear.

The "boys"—Emilie couldn't help but think of them that way, she supposed in complement to the Tiffany "girls"—had staked out a place in the sand, covered by blankets and faded quilts. They waited until the girls had seated themselves then filled in around them, mainly closing in on Dora and Maggie, who had plopped herself down on Dora's right side.

Emilie had thought about bringing her sketch pad but had changed her mind at the last minute. She wasn't ready to go back to painting quite yet. She might not want to ever go back. And where would that leave her? But every time she'd almost picked up a brush, she stopped herself, as memory overtook her desire to paint. Finishing the last details of some stranger's portrait, every detail she'd added, filled with her own disgust.

She shivered, just thinking about it.

"You can't be cold," said the boy on her right. Peter, she remembered.

"No," she said. And not being able to think of anything else to say, Emilie closed her eyes and lifted her chin to the sun.

Dora soon announced that it was time for lunch and sent Frank and Sandor off to buy lemonades. She wrested the sandwiches from Lotte and added them to a store of other provisions contributed by the men. It was quite a feast. And they ate until every morsel was finished.

Lotte hardly spoke, from shyness or something deeper, Emilie couldn't tell. And for the first time since arriving, Emilie felt alone. She missed the worldly vivacity of the artists and the intellectuals, and even the hangers-on. She felt ancient, not at all amused by the bumbling efforts of Jack and Peter and Sandor to vie for Dora's attention.

Jack soon gave up and directed his attentions to Maggie, who blushed and giggled and moved closer to him, while Lotte scowled.

Emilie understood. It wasn't jealousy that Lotte, worn out though still young, felt toward her sister, pretty enough and rounded and soft. It was fear that her lack of reasoning powers would lead her down a perilous road.

But it was just a day at the beach.

After lunch, Lotte settled down to a book, and the boys cajoled Dora into taking off her shoes to wade in the water.

"I'll come, too," Maggie said.

Lotte closed her book and started to get up.

"Oh, she'll be fine," Dora drawled. "I'll watch after her."

"I'll watch them both," Jack said and squeezed both women around the waist.

Lotte looked relieved. "If you're sure."

"Of course. You read your old book. Come on, Maggie, let's race the boys." And they took off, Dora squealing as the boys laughed and pretended to trip and stumble and Maggie held up her skirts to run faster.

Lotte groaned and glanced over to Emilie. "I guess I should go after them."

Emilie watched them cavort in the sand. What harm could a few hours at the beach do? Soon they would go their separate ways, summer would end, and they'd all be safely back where they belonged.

"You can see her from where you are," Emilie said. "Read your book." *You deserve some time for yourself, too.*

When Dora and Maggie returned, Dora was looking prettily disheveled and Maggie's skirts were drenched up to the knees. They took their leave of the boys, and after stopping by the bathhouse to freshen up for the ferry ride home, the four women jumped on the tram back to St. George.

Chapter 11

Grace came downstairs just before five o'clock, her sketch bag slung over one shoulder. She was on her way downtown to the rumored seamstresses strike. This would be her first "serious" outing. Serious in that it was well known that sweatshop strikers were often set upon by hired thugs. And if those strikers were mostly women—who better to report on their plight than another woman? She could say in one picture what would take several columns from a man's perspective.

As luck would have it Mrs. B was just coming out of the parlor when Grace reached the foyer.

"And where would you be off to, miss?"

"I'm going to the mailbox on the corner." Grace did have a packet of cartoons to drop off in the post on her way.

"Ah, Grace, what am I going to do with you? Why you not go with the other girls to the beach? You should be out having fun with your friends on your day off. Not working away in your room for—" She broke off, her eye catching the sketch bag slung crosswise across Grace's chest.

"And what's that over your shoulder? You need your sketching bag to walk to the corner?"

Grace glanced down at the bag. "You never know."

"I know," Mrs. B said. "I know you. Do not try to get around me. What terrible thing are you about to report on now?"

"I thought I might look in on the women's garment strike on the Lower East Side."

"Oh, Blessed Mother and all the saints. What am I going to do with you?"

Grace shrugged. "Just give me a place to come home to. Feed me. And try not to worry. I know, Mrs. B. I just can't help myself. I'm on a . . . I guess you'd call it a mission."

In answer, Mrs. B crossed herself and muttered another invocation, bypassing the saints and going straight to the top.

"Think of it, Mrs. B. We're lucky, but these poor women spend fifteen to sixteen hours a day crammed into unspeakable excuses for workshops. Paid by the piece, which is docked for the slightest mistake. Surrounded not by windows of sunlight but dark, airless holes that often make them sick. They are underpaid, cheated, and subjected to the worst possible kinds of assault on their persons and their souls. Some of them are just children. What kind of life is that?"

"Oh, Grace, where do you learn such things?"

"From the papers, from talking to people. But things can change. I read that they are trying to form a Ladies' Garment Workers' Union. Too late for most of these poor women, but things *will* change. I just know they will. But I also think it's going to need us women to push that change. And I want to be a part of that."

Mrs. B patted Grace's cheek. Her palm was rough with work; Grace put her hand over her landlady's and held it there, feeling suddenly homesick for a home and childhood that she'd left behind.

Because even then, she had wanted to change the world. She just hadn't known how hard it would be.

"Don't worry, Mrs. B. I know how to take care of myself." She slipped out of reach and headed for the door. "I'll try not to be too late."

Mrs. B sighed and twisted her hands in her apron. "I'll keep your dinner warm and the kitchen window unlocked."

Grace thought her voice might have caught on the last word, but she didn't stop or dare look around. She knew Mrs. B had her best interest, all their best interests, at heart. But you couldn't play it safe in this world; if you did, it might swallow you up. Push you to the back of the line, shut its ears against you.

Well, that wouldn't happen to her. She would make her own way, or die trying.

That thought made Grace trip over a fissure in the sidewalk. Best not to think of dying or any other kind of violence. She'd keep well away from it, if it did happen.

She posted her cartoons and took the trolley downtown.

By the time she arrived on Delancey Street where a group of about forty women, men, and children had gathered, a tiny woman had been hoisted onto a barrel and was yelling out a list of their grievances. Only a few people were listening, and no one who would do one thing about it. All the sweatshop owners in the area, having learned of the plan to strike, had merely gone about their usual Sunday: breakfast with the family, church, and an afternoon of leisure.

They took it for granted that the workers would docilely return to work the next day, after having their pay docked for the work they had missed on the day of rest, leaving the foreman and paid guards to prevent the crowd from getting out of hand.

Grace fell in with the group, some of whom were carrying

signs, but most of whom seemed to be more concerned with keeping their children out of mischief.

Grace had to hand it to them. It was hard enough to fight for your rights without having to mind your children while you were at it.

They marched down Delancey to Orchard Street where a row of known sweatshops occupied floors and basements and whatever space they could cram people into.

They were followed—at a safe distance—by a small group of reporters, which Grace intentionally avoided, though she had as much right to be there as they did. They weren't very attentive to the march, some occasionally stopping to write something down, most just chatting and waiting for "something to happen."

And something did happen. They rounded the corner to find a gang of men, thugs most likely, barring the way. The thugs' presence did not deter but instead inflamed the marchers, who began yelling "Fair wages! Fair hours!" and pumping their signs.

For a moment the thugs seemed to step back. After all, there were mostly women and children. Even thugs might think twice about attacking them.

Grace moved off to the side to be able to see the confrontation if it happened.

The reporters who had been nonchalant moments before had caught the scent of incipient news and closed in on the group of strikers.

The sound of a window shattering was heard from the far side of the street.

"They've thrown a brick!" a high-pitched voice yelled. The strikers surged ahead. The thugs raised clubs and hammers and rushed the crowd. Several policemen appeared at the end of the street, but Grace couldn't tell which side they were on. They didn't seem to know, either, and blew their whistles and waved their truncheons in the air to no avail.

Women screamed and tried to pull their children out of the melee; the few men left were quickly knocked down. Stones and bricks appeared from nowhere.

Knowing that the strikers only had a short time before they were dispersed, Grace pressed herself into a niche between two doorways and drew as fast as she could, capturing the look of horror on one side, and the animosity and aggression on the other.

A woman fled past, holding a younger girl before her, trying to shield her from the onslaught of every imaginable thing being flung through the air. She was overtaken by the crowd, staggered, and fell to her knees. The girl tried to pull her up, but the thugs were advancing, and Grace knew she couldn't stand by and watch them trample her. She shoved her sketchbook into her skirt pocket and rushed into the street, stretching her arms out to the woman.

She pulled the woman to her feet and grabbed the girl's hand, before they were swept along by the mob. Something hit Grace hard across the cheek, and she staggered, letting go of the child's hand. Grace was pushed and pummeled until she tripped and fell down a stairwell and crashed, lying motionless in a basement doorway.

She huddled there listening as the crowd ran by, the screams and shouts. When the worst of the attacks had passed, Grace crept out. She recognized several newsmen running after the crowd; others were already walking away, not even waiting to see how the evening ended.

Grace clutched her side, her only thought to get away. She hadn't known how it would be. Even Charlie Murray would have a hard time imparting just how awful the mob had been. To attack women and children much too young to be out at night. *But not too young to spend their every waking hour sewing piecework in bad light until their fingers were swollen from needle pricks and their eyes were strained to painfulness.*

Grace became aware of the throbbing in her left shoulder and her head. She was shaking from anticipation, and fear, and the fact that she hadn't eaten since breakfast.

She'd been so sure of herself after selling her parade cartoon to the *Sun*. She had planned to dazzle them with her depiction of the strike. Now she wasn't even sure she could hold a pencil, much less a maulstick.

She limped out of the shadows. The street was mainly clear except for broken signs, injured people, and a couple of policemen who stood talking and laughing beneath a streetlamp. There was no sign of the woman and girl she'd tried to help.

Grace kept close to the buildings as she groped her way along the street, sticking to the shadows, praying that she would encounter no one until she reached home.

Mrs. B had been right. She had rushed in without an idea of what might happen.

By the time she doubled back to East Broadway where she hoped to find a trolley, her knee and her shoulder were throbbing. The sleeve of her shirtwaist was torn, her skirt was filthy, and her hair was falling in her face. God knows what the ticket taker would think, if he'd even let her aboard.

But a trolley didn't come, and she started walking north toward home.

It must have been an hour later when, sore and aching and asleep on her feet, Grace turned up the steps of the boardinghouse. She didn't have much hope that Mrs. B had left the door open this late. It was well after midnight. The door was locked.

Grace trudged back down the steps to the sliver of alley that led to the back of the house and the kitchen window.

But when Grace reached up to push open the window, her shoulder jerked and a searing pain spread through her arm and down her side. Somehow she managed to pull the trash box over and climb on top so that she could reach the sash with both hands.

It was always hard to open, but tonight it seemed almost impossible, and for the longest time she could only kneel on the top of the box, her cheek resting against the cool windowpane.

Maybe she slept, maybe she passed out, maybe she was dreaming, because the window began to move against her flushed skin. She swayed away and there was a face in the window. Emilie Pascal was on the other side of the glass, a horrible expression on her face. The window opened and Grace came to her senses. Emilie was letting her in the window.

Grace used every ounce of strength she had left to push herself through the opening; she would have fallen to the floor if Emilie hadn't caught her and held her on her feet, until she reached a chair at the table.

A strike of a match and light shone into the room. Emilie had found the oil lamp.

"Oh, *mon Dieux*, are you all right? What happened?" Emilie's voice was low, but urgent.

Grace touched her face and the hair streaming across her eyes. She pushed it away. "The trolley didn't come. . . . A long walk."

Emilie went to the sink, found a glass, and poured Grace some water, which she gulped greedily.

When she put the glass down on the table, she looked up to find Emilie staring down at her and looking angry.

"I don't know who you are meeting and it's none of my business perhaps. But I'll give you advice anyway. You obviously need it. Stay away from him. He will never change. Promise me." She grabbed Grace's shoulder.

Grace flinched. "It's not what you think."

"My god, it never is."

"No, no really. I was just . . . I fell, and I couldn't get a trolley."

Emilie stepped back. "You're a terrible liar. You may have fallen, but you had help and they took advantage while you were down."

"Is there any food? I didn't have time to eat."

Emilie looked around.

"Sometimes Mrs. B leaves dinner in the warming tray."

Emilie searched for a cloth, then lifted a plate out of the oven. She placed the plate on the table in front of Grace.

Grace sighed; it hurt her ribs. "Heaven."

"Does Mrs. B know about this?"

Grace nodded. "She does. She doesn't approve, but she's understanding. She leaves the window unlocked if I can't get back in time."

Emilie made a little noise that might have been disappointment. "I wouldn't have guessed." She handed Grace a fork. "Has he ever hit you before?"

"What? Oh, Emilie. It isn't that."

"No? Surely your aunt doesn't beat you. Dora thinks you have a secret lover."

Grace would have laughed, but it hurt too much. "I don't. It was an accident, truly." She stopped long enough to cut a piece of stuffed cabbage and shove it into her mouth.

Emilie waited for her to finish chewing and asked, "Do you even have a great-aunt?"

"I do."

"That you visit several times a week?"

Grace looked up. "Not exactly. She lives on a farm in Connecticut."

"And you swear you're not meeting some man?"

"I swear. Though I hardly think it's anybody's business but my own."

"It is if you're sneaking in at all hours and jeopardizing Mrs. B's reputation."

"I'm not. I wouldn't."

Emilie didn't answer, and Grace shoveled in another forkful of cabbage.

What did she do now? She hadn't thought about Mrs. B suffering because of her clandestine career.

"It won't happen again."

Emilie sighed in a world-weary way that made Grace stop to give her a deeper perusal. Grace knew for a fact that Emilie was only seventeen. Why was it that she sometimes seemed so much older than the rest of them?

And how could Grace possibly explain. Make up another lie that Emilie may or may not believe? It was fine when the other girls thought she was out "seeing some young man." They couldn't really imagine anything else.

But not Emilie. Sometimes she looked at you like she was seeing your inner soul. And now that she had somehow stumbled into part of Grace's secret, did Grace dare trust her with the rest?

She was aware of Emilie standing very still, waiting for an answer that she could believe, and suddenly Grace wanted to tell her. Wanted to be able to share her real feelings about what she was doing. Somehow she thought that this strange girl might actually understand her drive to become a political cartoonist.

Because she sensed that Emilie wanted to become an artist of another sort in her own right.

"You'll have to promise not to tell."

Emilie frowned at her. "Okay, I swear."

Grace put down her fork, pushed her empty plate away. Now that her belly was full, she felt every pain, bruise, and scrape. She took a deep breath and was relieved that it didn't hurt. "I have a second profession."

"*Bon dieu au paradis*," Emilie cried.

"Shh. Not that kind of profession. I'm a cartoonist."

"That is no secret."

"I'm a different kind of cartoonist. One who tells the news in pictures. I draw cartoons for journals and newspapers. Here." Grace reached for the sketchbook that she'd shoved in her pocket. Tried the other pocket. Stood up so abruptly that Emilie had to catch the chair before it fell over.

Grace felt her pockets again, checked her waistband, the empty bag that still hung across her chest. It wasn't there. Heat raced up her body, flared in her cheeks; her stomach roiled. "It's gone!"

"What? What is gone?"

"My sketchbook. I must have dropped it when I fell. Oh my god. I have to go back." She stepped toward the window not knowing quite what she was doing. And nearly fell; both her ankle and her knee were throbbing.

Emilie pushed her back into the chair. "You're not going anywhere else tonight. You can barely walk. You must come upstairs and clean up, and try to get some sleep."

"I have to find it. All my sketches are in that notebook."

"Then we'll go tomorrow after work and look for it."

"It will be too late. If it isn't already too late. It's my whole life." Grace leaned on the table and dropped her head onto her arms. "My whole life."

"Well, if we can't find it, then you will start a new life. It's not as hard as you might think. Now come."

Emilie quickly put the plate in the sink and locked the window, then she helped Grace up the stairs and into bed.

"I'll go down to the bathroom and get some water for that bruise on your face."

Grace grabbed her sleeve as she moved away. "Thank you, but how was it that you were in the kitchen?"

"I was watching for you out the window by your desk. I saw you come in but knew the door was locked and then you moved away and I thought what I would do in that case. And you were there. Right where I thought to find you."

"You were watching for me? Why?"

"Because I was worried, of course."

"You didn't need to be."

"No? Well, I was. It is one of the problems of being a friend."

Before breakfast the next morning, Grace and Emilie concocted a story to explain Grace's black eye, though Emilie wasn't convinced anyone would believe it.

"I was putting my clean clothes away and dropped a pair of knickers. When I bent over to pick them up, I hit my eye on the opened drawer. It hurt like the dickens, I don't mind telling you," Grace said.

Emilie had to fight not to roll her eyes. Grace was obviously uncomfortable having to prevaricate. Emilie envied her in a way. She herself had found it necessary to lie since she could remember and had no trouble still letting a tale slip off her tongue.

Really, if it hadn't been for her, nobody would have believed that far-fetched story. Everyone but Mrs. B, who gave both girls a look that said they wouldn't get off without the real explanation.

All the girls were enthralled by Grace's black eye: Maggie at the pain, Lotte with sympathy, and Dora at the thought of Grace having to walk to work with a black eye. She offered her face powder to help camouflage the bruise, which Grace accepted, though Emilie doubted it would do much good.

The front bell rang just as they were all getting up from the table. Mrs. B went to answer it, and the others followed behind her. Emilie and Grace were the last two out, and Emilie just caught sight of a tall, ginger-haired gentleman as he held out a notebook to Mrs. B and said, "I'm inquiring about a Mr. G. L. Griffith. I believe he lost his sketchbook."

Emilie immediately recognized Grace's sketchbook. Emilie had seen it often in the lamplight of their room. She turned to Grace, but Grace had ducked back into the dining room.

Lotte and Dora had turned on their way up the stairs. "That's Grace's sketchbook!" Dora exclaimed.

The man looked up. He was quite handsome except for a slightly crooked nose. He reminded Emilie of the participants in an Irish boxing match, whose depiction in oil had been payment for a certain young French painter's bar bill at the local café on the rue Suger. He'd staggered into the street after that and was never seen or heard from again.

"I beg your pardon. One of my colleagues found this in the street. The name is written on the front." He opened the sketchbook to the first page. "And I recognized Mr. Griffith's work from our paper. I'm a reporter for the *Sun*."

Mrs. B nodded and said, "Won't you have a seat in the parlor, Mr. . . ."

"Murray," he said.

Mrs. B turned toward the stairs. "Ladies, you'll be late."

The Tiffany girls ran up the stairs, a reluctant Dora being tugged by Lotte.

Emilie and Grace exchanged looks, turned back to the door, and came face-to-face with Mrs. B.

"Grace, I believe there is a gentleman to see you."

Grace shook her head.

"Shall I go?" Emilie asked. "I'll tell him that Mr. Griffith has already left for work but I'd be happy to take—"

"It is time for Grace to face her future."

Grace touched her cheek, and Emilie relived her own pain from every time she'd had to face the world after her father had struck her . . . oh, so many times.

Grace straightened up and walked past them. Emilie started to follow, but Mrs. B held her back.

"I expect he is in for a big shock, that one. You get ready for work. I will wait close by. But he seems like a polite young man—and he's very tall." She gave Emilie a gentle push. "*Ora vai.*"

Emilie had no choice but to go upstairs to get her things for work.

Charlie Murray was standing with his back to the door when Grace stepped into the parlor. She took a breath, and he turned around.

For a moment they just stared at each other. Grace didn't try to explain.

After an excruciatingly long silence, Mr. Murray simply said, "You."

It didn't really seem to call for an answer.

"You?" He shook his head as if to clear it. "You're G. L. Griffith?"

The jig was up. Grace had to admit it. She had fooled them once, but now it would spread among all the newsmen. She'd be laughed out of their ranks, before they even knew she was one of them.

"That was your cartoon of Edison and the Police Parade?"

Grace nodded.

"Unbelievable."

The word escaped from him in a near roar. And Grace flinched.

"So now you know. I thank you for returning my sketchbook." She reached for it.

But he pulled it out of her reach and grabbed her chin between his fingers to turn her head. A half laugh escaped from his full lips. "You got a shiner, G. L."

"Yeah," Grace said. "This woman had fallen down trying to protect a young girl; they just ran over her."

"And let me guess, you tried to help her and they ran over you, too."

Grace shrugged.

"What a damn fool thing for you to do. Everybody knew there was going to be trouble, why do you think all the reporters there were well out of the way?"

How did she tell him that she was so eager to get her images that she hadn't noticed until they had all gone running from the back of the pack as the group was dispersed?

"Well, I didn't know," she countered, suddenly feeling like she deserved more. "If any of you newsmen had bothered to talk to me except to make ribald or dismissive jokes, I might have known that."

He made a sound that might have been a groan. "You'd better rethink your longevity in the business if you don't reevaluate your ability to survive the mean streets."

"I will, but I have to get to work now. Or I'll lose that job, too. Thank you for returning this."

He finally relinquished the book.

"Lose it, too? Have you lost the one at the *Sun*?"

"I will once you tell them I'm a girl—woman."

"I won't tell."

She stared at him. "Not even over a beer at the bar?"

"Not even there."

"Why?"

"Because you're good. You draw like a man."

Grace would have been insulted if she hadn't caught the twinkle in his eye. He was teasing her.

Dora's head appeared at the parlor door. Her eyes widened. "We have to go. We're going to be late."

"I'm coming."

"I'll make a bargain with you."

"One that I can live with?"

"I hope so."

"Grace?"

"I said I'm coming. What is it?"

"I won't tell anybody. I'll even try to expedite your work, if . . ."

Grace braced herself. If he made some oafish suggestion, she'd deck him and accept the consequences.

"If you agree to have dinner with me."

"Gra-a-a-ce," Dora called.

"I have to go."

Grace ran to the door where Emilie was waiting with her coat and lunch bag. Grace grabbed them and they both hurried outside.

Charlie followed close behind. Grace was running down the steps when he called out after her, "Tonight! Seven o'clock. I'll pick you up here."

"I have a black eye."

"We'll go someplace with bad lighting."

"I can't tonight," Grace called.

"Then Saturday night. You'll have run out of excuses by then. Seven o'clock."

Grace looked back long enough to see his grin before Dora and Lotte each took an arm and propelled her down the sidewalk.

Chapter 12

As soon as they reached the corner, Dora stopped and turned back to look down the street. "He's still there."

Grace pushed past her. "Keep walking."

"Yes, please," Emilie added and took Dora by the arm to keep her moving forward. Lotte, taking the cue, did the same with Maggie, who walked backward until her sister had to forcibly turn her around.

"You have a date!" Dora said. "Of all the unfair things. You don't even want to get married."

"It isn't a date." Grace walked faster, head down, and the others had to rush to keep up with her.

"But how did he get your notebook?" Dora demanded. "Where did you meet him? That was a lie about hitting your eye on the drawer, wasn't it?"

They turned the corner and Emilie knew she had to do something. "No, it wasn't," Emilie said. "I was there, and Grace probably left her notebook in the museum."

"Museum?" Dora asked incredulously. "You'd rather go to the museum than to the beach?"

"Uh," Grace said, her step stuttering. "Yes. I wanted to do some sketches of a statue I like."

"Well, I never. The museum, of all places. You know, Grace, sometimes I just can't figure you out."

"You know, Dora, some of us want to be artists and not just get married." With that, Grace surged ahead.

Emilie could see that her face was flushed but whether it was because of seeing Charlie Murray or being caught out at her lie, she couldn't be certain.

But no harm had been done, and it would protect Grace from the repercussions for a while longer. Though Emilie didn't think it could be for much longer. Then again, her father had been forging artworks for as long as she could remember. She wondered for a moment if he'd been caught. She didn't care and it was best not to know.

WHEN THEY ARRIVED at the workshop, Miss Zevesky was already at work. Emilie rushed forward. How dare she start on Emilie's window without her. Then she pulled up short and took a breath. *It is not "your" window. None of this is solely yours.*

Emilie understood that. She'd thought it was what she wanted, but the intensity of her anger at seeing the work progress without her had taken her aback. This would be her new life. Dreams of finally being able to sign her own work, of having her talent recognized, faded from possibility.

Oh, did you see the latest Emilie Pascal exhibit? She's the first woman to be given such an honor from the Académie.

She will be one of the great artists of the decade.

Her use of color is striking, heralding a new movement.

None of those accolades would be hers. Did it matter? Surely it was better to be here without a name than to fall prey to the egotism, the treachery, the self-doubt that came with fame. And yet . . .

Miss Zevesky glanced up. "Good morning, Miss Pascal. I arrived early and thought to finish these pearls. We are almost done."

We. We are almost done. Emilie had selected, cut, and constructed the main scene on her own. She'd even risked standing up to Mr. Tiffany to have her vision re-created in glass. *We.* She had to get used to that. We.

Emilie forced a smile and looked at Miss Zevesky's tray where a half-dozen opalescent glass rounds were set to one side. She had to admit the girl did neat work. Just like her person. Starched apron, blond hair braided and pinned in a coronet around her head.

"Excellent." Emilie should be grateful to have been relieved of the boring task of cutting tiny circles for hours on end. They would still be days behind if Emilie had had to do it all herself. But still . . . *her window.*

On Wednesday morning the last piece of "Summer" went into place. Mr. Tiffany came in to make a final appraisal before it was sent down to be soldered and wait for its companion pieces.

The entire workshop had hummed with quiet tension as they waited for Mr. Tiffany to arrive. It was always so. If one of them failed, it was as if they all failed. So when the first minute sounds of *tap, tap, tap* slipped into the room, all casual chatter died; it seemed that even the clinking and cracking of glass became subdued.

Mr. Tiffany was accompanied by Miss Northrop.

Mrs. Driscoll appeared from her office and met them at the "Summer" panel.

Emilie thanked her lucky stars that it was a sunny, crisp day, with just a hint of the fall that was to come. A perfect day for sending "Summer" away.

Mr. Tiffany stopped in front of the easel. Emilie eased slightly aside, not so much to be polite but to place herself strategically in front of her window in case his cane came too close to the fragile glasswork.

"Hmm," he said. And then, the dreaded cane lifted. Emilie braced herself to fend him off bodily if he tried to mar the glass.

But he merely used it to motion her out of the way.

For an eon they stood, eyes connecting. It seemed to Emilie everyone was holding their breath. Emilie certainly was.

Then from the corner of her eye, she saw Mrs. Driscoll tilt her head. Emilie moved away. Reluctantly. Still at the ready.

Mr. Tiffany moved closer to the window, leaned over as if he meant to smell her glorious red poppies.

Then he straightened up, turned to Emilie. "You were right to plate these so heavily. How many layers?"

Emilie swallowed and searched for the word. "Three. I thought they would look more . . ."

". . . like real poppies," he said.

Emilie let out her breath.

"They're lovely," Miss Northrop said.

Mrs. Driscoll kept mum, but she gave Emilie a quick, appreciative look. She approved of Emilie's window. Hers and Miss Zevesky's . . . and Grace's and Miss Northrop's. But above all Mr. Tiffany's.

"Beauty is nature, Miss Pascal. And beauty is in my glass. *Within* the glass. It is my deepest desire to bring that beauty together and make it one."

Emilie cut a quick look to his face. He was frowning at her. Was he saying that he was pleased, or that she had missed her opportunity to bring that beauty to life? Did he expect a response?

What did she say? *Of course it is. That's the whole point of making art.* Did he think she didn't understand that? But not just beauty, but also hope, and hopelessness, fear, and ecstasy.

"You understand."

She dipped her chin and held her tongue not to argue that art was always beautiful, if sometimes a terrible, gut-wrenching beauty.

He turned to Miss Northrop. "Will 'Autumn' be ready to cut tomorrow?"

Miss Northrop looked past him to where Grace was working on the "Autumn" cartoon. And who, after a brief look up at their entrance, had paid them no more attention. "Yes, I think so."

"Good, good. Miss Pascal will do for 'Autumn.'"

Mrs. Driscoll blinked in surprise.

"Bring the glass to my office after lunch." With that, he made a quick sweep around the room and tapped his way toward the door.

But when he reached it, he stopped and turned. "I was right about the green, Miss Pascal." Then he turned and they listened as the *tap*, *tap*, *tap* receded to silence.

And Emilie thought, *And so was I, Mr. Tiffany.*

WITH MR. TIFFANY's exit, the workroom soon returned to that hum of activity that said all was going well.

An hour later the men arrived to carry "Summer" downstairs. The process caused even more hand-wringing than the first window Emilie had relinquished to the solder department.

"Careful," Emilie said. "This pane is very heavy. There is much plating, some parts up to three or four sections."

The men, of course, ignored her. They did this with every window and lamp, and it was just another duty in a day of work. But she had heard stories of someone tripping and an entire window crashing to the floor.

Emilie followed them out as if she could single-handedly save the work.

Grace met her at the door. "Let it go. It's out of your hands. If they fall, there is nothing you can do. It's better not to watch."

"But—"

"Don't get possessive, it will only lead to frustration." Grace turned away, picked up her maulstick, and went back to her drawing as if nothing had happened. But Emilie remembered Lotte saying it was like watching your child leave home. If that was true, Emilie would stick to glass.

Two men appeared with a new glass easel, which they hung in the space left by "Summer" and which would soon hold her—Mr. Tiffany's—"Autumn" panel.

Miss Zevesky was cleaning up her tray and the surrounding area. Miss Northrop and Grace were leaning over the sketch of "Autumn." Mrs. Driscoll was on the far side of the room talking to a small group of workers. Perhaps they were discussing the base for the dragonfly lamp.

Everyone seemed busy, except Emilie, and she felt oddly bereft, between projects even for a few minutes, as if she might float away if not anchored by the glass and cutters in her hands.

But soon Mrs. Driscoll turned, still smiling, and saw her. "Ah, yes, the 'pumpkin' glass. I'll be with you shortly." She hurried off toward her office.

She soon returned, carrying her small ledger book for tallying each piece of glass borrowed, returned, and used. She swept Emilie along, stopping briefly before Miss Zevesky. "Please go aid Miss Hodgins until I return. She's the one with the dotted bow in her hair. Cut whatever she needs and I will be back to you when I return. Come, Miss Pascal."

Emilie followed her out to the elevator. Mrs. Driscoll didn't speak on the ride down. She seemed to be preoccupied, but when the elevator doors had closed and they were alone in the hall, she said, "Miss Northrop was hoping to have you and Miss Wilson for her 'Magnolia' window, but it seems Mr. Tiffany has usurped you for 'Autumn.' He doesn't usually interfere with personnel, but he is like a freight train in a tunnel as time passes and the Exposition nears. How is Miss Zevesky settling in?"

Emilie was caught off guard. Mrs. Driscoll was asking her opinion?

"She's a neat cutter, though I've had her doing the pearls, mainly."

Mrs. Driscoll smiled. "Hard to let go of your domain, is it?"

"I'm trying not to get attached."

"Oh dear, we all do. When we stop caring, it will be the time to hand in our cutters and our sketchbooks and . . ." She trailed off, leaving Emilie to wonder if there had been more she'd decided not to say. "If she can keep up, I'll keep her on 'Autumn' with you."

The glass selection went much faster this time. Emilie was more sure of herself. She and Mrs. Driscoll compared and discussed, agreed and compromised, and before long they had two large stacks of samples to show to Mr. Tiffany.

"Please send these up to Mr. Tiffany's office immediately. He is quite anxious to get started on this piece."

The attendant shook his head. "Wants to see all these himself, does he? Would be easier on the men if he would just take the elevator down here."

"You know he likes to choose in the sunlight."

"You all do. I'll have someone haul them upstairs, then haul the ones you reject down again." He shook his head, a solitary, sensible man in the world of air dreamers.

"Too much time in the basement," Mrs. Driscoll commented as she and Emilie waited for the elevator. "Sunlight is as necessary as air to the soul."

THEY ARRIVED AT the door to Mr. Tiffany's office all too soon, and Emilie concentrated on not being nervous. If the truth be known, she'd been quaking on her first visit and hardly remembered most of what she said, or any of her surroundings, just that it was a very cluttered room.

Mrs. Driscoll knocked and entered. Emilie swallowed and stepped in behind her.

There was another man with Mr. Tiffany, about the same age, though heavier, taller, with a neat mustache and a receding hairline that created a shiny dome above a kindly face. She didn't recognize him and breathed a sigh of relief.

"Mr. Nash," said Mrs. Driscoll, "how lovely to see you."

"Delighted as always," Mr. Nash returned. "You haven't visited the furnaces in quite a while."

"We've been quite busy here," Mrs. Driscoll said, shaking his hand. "What brings you into town?"

"Delivering several new pieces going to the Bishop Gallery next month." He stepped aside to reveal a display table filled with—

Emilie's breath caught. Vases. Glorious vases. Blown favrile glass like the ones that had arrested her walk past the Bing gallery that long-ago day in Paris. She moved closer without thinking.

Mrs. Driscoll cleared her throat.

"You like my vases, Miss Pascal?" said Mr. Tiffany.

"They changed my life," she said, bending down to bring her vision level with these new wonders. Even up close she couldn't tell how they managed not to float away. Or how they supported themselves. One curved upward like the neck of a swan that seemed to hover above its base by magic. "I saw them in Mr. Bing's gallery in Paris, ones like these. I couldn't believe they could stand on their own. They moved like air creating color."

Mr. Nash chuckled. "Now there's a young lady who has eyes to see with. Air creating color. Ha."

"Indeed," Mr. Tiffany said, looking quizzically at Emilie.

Mrs. Driscoll stepped into the momentary silence. "Let me introduce Miss Pascal to you. This is Arthur Nash, the manager, overseer, and inventor of all the glass that we use in the workshop. He holds the secret to it all."

Pleasantries were exchanged, though Emilie could barely keep her eyes from the vases.

"How do they do it?"

"Miss Pascal," Mrs. Driscoll said quietly.

"I'm sorry. It's just so . . . I beg your pardon."

"You are from Paris, then?" Mr. Nash asked delightedly. He spoke with a definite British accent.

"Yes. I came to New York this past summer."

"Well, have Louis here bring you out to the furnaces some week and I'll show you how it's done." He cast an amused look to Mr. Tiffany, who was looking disgruntled.

"No trade secrets, mind you, but have you ever seen glass blown?"

"Never. I've only read about it."

"Bring her out next Monday. These ladies should know more about where their materials come from and how they are made." Nash nodded sharply, as if that settled the subject.

"And I hope that you will join them, Mrs. Driscoll. It's been much too long."

"Perhaps," Mr. Tiffany said, "but for now we have colors to

choose. We've started on the 'Four Seasons' but there's much work to be done yet."

"I'll let you get to it, then."

Mr. Nash nodded to the ladies, and Mr. Tiffany walked him to the door. "Bishop is coming a little later today to decide which ones he wants; I'll send the rest to the showroom."

While they exchanged a few more words, Emilie took the opportunity to look past the vases and to the office, the space where Mr. Tiffany spent most of his time, developed his ideas, created new art.

Paintings—landscapes, oriental markets, desert oases, and rowboats on a lake—hung in every space and Emilie wondered if they were painted by Mr. Tiffany himself. A glazed urn stood in one corner holding a spray of peacock feathers, iridescent in blues and green and black, the domain of the male peacock.

Her musings were cut short with the arrival of the men with carts of glass. They rolled them to the far side of the office to a large table, unloaded them, and placed them in neat stacks in a row at one end of the table. Then they left without a word, the last man touching his finger to his forehead as he closed the door behind them.

"Now then," Mr. Tiffany said as eagerly as if it were Christmas morning. "Let's get to it."

And be finished and away before Mr. Bishop arrives, Emilie added silently.

Grace was just finishing her lunch when Lotte came to lean over her and whisper, "Have you seen Maggie? She disappeared halfway through lunch. I thought she had gone to the WC but she isn't there and she hasn't returned."

Dora, who was sitting at the table across from Grace, perked up. "Probably off flirting with Jack or Paul. She had plenty of practice last weekend."

"I should have watched her more carefully," Lotte said.

"Oh, Lotte. Let her have some fun," Dora said. "Those boys are harmless enough."

"Dora," Grace said. "No boy is harmless when they're around women. Something you'd do well to remember yourself."

"Oh, pooh. You're both such spoilsports. You'll never find husbands with that attitude." Dora tossed her head as if she had curls to display instead of a bun knotted tightly at her neck.

"Just be quiet," said Grace and stood up, wrapping the remains of her sandwich and shoving it into her skirt pocket for later. "We still have a few minutes. Let's take a look."

Dora didn't volunteer to help, which was just as well, because they found Maggie and some young man in a deserted corridor past the WCs. Maggie was backed against the wall and giggling as the boy braced himself on one hand.

Grace bounded forward not waiting to see what the other hand was doing.

"Maggie!" Lotte snapped.

The boy jerked away.

"Jack Ratner, how dare you!"

"Aw, Lotte, we were just talking."

"Well, do your talking in plain sight and preferably not with my sister."

"Don't be mean to Jack," Maggie said.

"Don't you tell me what to do," Lotte countered. "And don't you go hanging around with Jack Ratner or any of the others."

Jack took the opportunity to sidle away. "See ya around, Maggie."

"You'll be sorry if you do," Grace said as he sauntered away.

He just smirked in her direction and strolled off down the hallway.

Lotte grabbed Maggie by the elbow and pulled her down the corridor. Grace fell in step with the two women.

"Your sister's right, Mags. Jack is no good for you. He'll take advantage."

"He likes me," Maggie said, wresting her elbow from Lotte's grasp.

"Jack Ratner likes anything in skirts," Lotte said.

"You're just jealous because he likes me more than you."

"Maggie, you don't understand."

"Shut up, Lotte. I'm going back to work now." Maggie flounced away.

"What am I going to do?" Lotte asked, watching Maggie trundle down the hall. "She doesn't have the judgment to know what can happen."

"You've talked about it, though?"

"Yes, over and over again. Then she listens to the girls like Dora and thinks she can dream the same dreams, have the same future. But she never will. She'll only have me."

And Lotte would only have Maggie. Grace gave her a quick squeeze. "We'll all just have to be more vigilant."

"Thanks. You're a good friend. But I'm afraid that she's my responsibility. All mine."

They walked the rest of the way back to the studio in silence. There wasn't much for either of them to say.

The glass selection lasted for a while. They made it through the sky, which echoed the cobalt of the "Summer" panel sky; the lush, heavy grapes ranging from almost green to blue to the ripeness of deep purple. Decided on several reds more powerful than the full summer poppies. Then the heavy golds, yellows, and ochers of earth. All deeper and fuller than their summer cousins. The light playfulness of summer giving way to the bounteous maturity of fall.

The three of them pulled and discarded, examined and compared, until Emilie almost forgot that she wasn't an equal here, but an apprentice, one who, unlike Icarus, knew the dangers of flying too close to the sun.

She glanced at her two superiors, Mrs. Driscoll and Mr. Tiffany, both arguing like old friends, colleagues, equals. Dependent on each other to create the art that made Mr. Tiffany famous. And Emilie felt once more the twinge of anonymity. The more she became comfortable, fit in, knew she was doing the work she was born for, the less she was willing to accept that her name would never be known. Then she remembered why she had fled France. Her name was exactly what she didn't want known. How hard it was to remember that now, when things were going so well.

It wasn't until she and Mrs. Driscoll were back in the elevator on their way up to the fifth floor that Emilie realized all this. That today for a few short hours she had worked alongside the world's great genius of art glass.

Emilie spent the rest of the afternoon helping with the installation of the "Autumn" cartoon on its glass easel and overseeing the delivery of the glass they would start cutting first thing in the morning.

And as the workday drew to a close, she felt as if she were putting an end to one chapter of a somewhat tumultuous story and beginning a new, fresh one, one perhaps with a happy outcome.

Chapter 13

Summer tumbled into fall. With the oranges and browns and deep purples of the window waiting for them, the Tiffany girls bundled into their coats and scarves and set off to work.

Thanks to the diligent brushing by the laundry girl, or possibly Nessa or Jane, Emilie's cloak had miraculously appeared in the wardrobe looking almost as good as new. But she would soon need her winter coat and boots and warmer clothes.

It couldn't be put off any longer. She must send for her trunk. She would go to the telegraph office as soon as she was paid on Saturday. It would take at least a week before her trunk would arrive. She'd just have to make do until then.

She had deliberated long into the night about the best way to ask for another favor. She had finally chosen to send a telegram because a telegram would arrive much faster than a letter and by nature would have to be short and terse. She wouldn't have to explain or tell too much about her new life. How could she ever explain her new life to her old friends?

A telegram. Emilie took the coward's way out.

And there was the other thing. The really cowardly thing.

Marie and Jean had been good friends. Jean had been more than a good friend. He loved Emilie. And she'd loved him. But it had taken too short a time after leaving France to forget her heartache at leaving him behind. Jean had been the first man to show her real kindness. She would always love him for that. But not as much as he had wished. What she had mistaken for love and safety she knew now were just the first steps to suffocation. And as the water that separated them grew wider and deeper, her heart had turned from regret to relief.

She would never be able to explain that she was not the girl he had known. That girl was as dead as if she'd joined her mother in the Seine. The new Emilie had a future, a life. Marie and Jean had helped her find it, and for that she would always be grateful. But she would never return to what was before.

But on the Saturday half day when she returned to the cloakroom to tell the others she would not be walking home with them, none of Mrs. B's girls were there. It was not like them to leave Emilie behind, but perhaps it was just as well. Now she could slip out without explaining to anyone what she was doing.

She put on her coat and was just leaving when Lotte came in, dragging a mulish Maggie behind her, sucking on a lollypop.

"Get your coat and hat on and give me that." Lotte yanked the lollipop out of Maggie's hand and threw it into the waste bin.

"Hey!" Maggie rushed to retrieve it, but Lotte stepped bodily between her and the bin.

Emilie had never seen Lotte lose her temper with her sister, but she was angry now. And Emilie could guess why. Things hadn't been the same since the day at Midland Beach. Maggie's attention had turned from her work to men. And that would be dangerous, because Emilie didn't think Maggie had the wherewithal to say no if one of them stepped out of line.

She cast a sympathetic look toward Lotte, who looked haggard and tired and bereft of hope.

Emilie vowed to help in some way, but right now she needed to get to the telegraph office.

"If you can manage," Emilie began as soon as Maggie stomped off to her cubby, "I need to run a quick errand."

"Of course," Lotte said. "She was down the hall that leads to the stairs to the men's division. I don't even know how she found her way, it's like a rabbit warren back there."

Lollipops, Emilie thought.

"You go on," Lotte said. "Dora went out with some of the other girls. They're going over to Stern Brothers. Not that any of them can afford a piece of dust from that store. And Grace is staying late to finish up her cartoon, though if you ask me it's more to do with her avoiding dinner with Charlie Murray."

"I'd almost forgotten. Are you sure you'll be all right by yourself?" Emilie asked.

Lotte nodded, her eyes downcast. "Thanks, but this is mine and mine alone."

But it shouldn't be, thought Emilie. In a better world . . . but there were no better worlds and they would all have to figure out a way to make do in this one.

Emilie left Lotte buttoning up Maggie's coat and Maggie complaining loudly that it wasn't fair that she lost her "lolly."

Emilie walked directly to the telegraph office on Twenty-Third Street, transferred her handwritten message she'd been working on for days to a telegraph form, and thrust the message through the window without looking at it. She'd worried over it long enough. She slid the payment after the form and left the office without a backward glance. It was done.

She didn't know why she should feel so depressed, since soon all her earthly possessions would be with her again. That should make her happy. But her cowardice had made her cruel and she took her time going back to the boardinghouse as the words she had sent shadowed her every step.

Marie Please send trunk in care of Mrs. Bertolucci 200 East Twenty-First St., New York, New York. Un million de merci, Emilie

Emilie had meant to go straight home, but guilt kept her walking along the sidewalks, even though her fingers and nose grew cold and her feet, already tired from a week of standing, balked at every step. She walked past Twenty-First Street trying to shake off the sense that she had slighted her dearest friends. Past Twentieth. She owed them more than a terse request for another favor after all the trouble and loyalty they had shown her.

She would go back to her room. Write them a letter that would get there long after they had fulfilled her need. Words that would somehow make up for the way she had neglected them, had thrust them aside as she pursued her new life. A life without them. And still she walked.

It was growing dark when Emilie finally climbed the stairs to her room at Mrs. Bertolucci's.

And stepped into a commotion on the second floor.

Dora swept out of Emilie and Grace's room just as Emilie reached the landing.

Catching sight of Emilie, Dora threw up her hands. "I don't kno-oo-w why she just won't let me help her," she drawled. "She looks like the worst side of a spinster the way she dresses. No one wears work clothes out to dinner. Especially not to a nice place where someone else is paying."

She turned from Emilie, long enough to yell at the closed door.

"Don't blame me if he thinks you're a frump." And she stalked off down the hall to her own room.

Emilie proceeded to her room and opened the door to find Grace busily pulling pins out of a lopsided cloud of hair.

"Ugh," Grace growled, espying Emilie in the mirror. "I know she means well, but really she's so annoying. First she couldn't believe that I stayed so late to work, when I had a . . ." She lowered her voice and drawled out, "Da-a-a-ate with an absolutely dreamy man even if he doesn't dress very well. Ugh!"

Grace pulled out the final handful of pins, and her thick, wavy hair came tumbling down about her shoulders. "Charlie Murray is as far from dreamy as a man could get; he's an arrogant, self-assured . . ."

"Certainly," said Emilie, dropping her workbag on her bed and taking up the brush from the dresser.

Grace reached for it, but Emilie lifted it out of the way. "Between the two of you, you've made such a tangle that you'll never get back to normal before Monsieur Murray arrives to fetch you." She began to brush the long tresses, which were indeed a tangled mess.

"*Monsieur Murray.* Ha. He's nothing but a brawling Irish newspaperman—"

"And also a 'damn good journalist,' I believe you said." Emilie brushed vigorously at Grace's hair, then twisted it expertly into a knot at the top of her head. Long stretches of time without a maid had taught Emilie to learn those things for herself. She pinned it so that when she took her hands away the twist settled onto the crown of Grace's head among a tasteful mound of thick brown hair.

Grace had grown quiet.

"Well?" Emilie asked, peeking over Grace's shoulder to study her friend's reflection. Grace had beautiful hair and did absolutely nothing to accentuate it. "Not too Gibson girlish, but better than schoolgirl braids."

"It does look nice," Grace conceded. "Better than that silliness Dora tried for."

"Well, you can't blame her for wanting to help. Maybe she'll be able to capture Mr. Murray's attention if you don't want it."

"Never. He would never fall for someone so free of ideas." Grace unconsciously tugged at the wisp of hair that fell against her cheek.

"Well, if you won't be nice to him . . ." Emilie teased.

"I'm perfectly polite to the man. I'm letting him take me to dinner, aren't I?"

"True," said Emilie, hiding her smile. "Where you'll talk about covering current events and the importance of journalism."

"Of course," Grace said. "What else would we talk about?"

"Nothing," Emilie said. "And I totally understand," she added, going over to the wardrobe to look for a suitable dress for Grace to wear.

"I already have my work clothes laid out on the bed."

"I saw them. But they make you look like a working girl."

"I am a working girl."

"But you want to be a cartoonist. And to do that you need to dress for the occasion."

"This occasion is probably some chop joint with Charlie Murray."

Emilie pulled out a visiting dress, elegant looking but not too formal, a deep shade of green with brown velvet trim that would complement Grace's hair and complexion. "This will be perfect for pub or fine restaurant. Always be prepared. What if you run into someone he knows who could further your career? You don't want to look like a clerk in the haberdashery department."

Grace grimaced and tilted her head, considering Emilie's choice. "Are you sure it isn't too ostentatious?"

"Not at all, very professional and shows that you're making an effort."

"I don't want to show him any effort. He's just someone I work with."

"Someone you *might* work with if he takes you seriously. But you'd better decide because time and hungry men wait for no one, not even you."

"Oh, all right. But it's just a dinner, a business meeting."

"I know." Emilie plopped herself down on her bed and, with feigned indifference, picked up a magazine she'd borrowed from the parlor.

A few minutes later, Nessa knocked on the door to say that a gentleman was here to see Miss Grace, before bursting into giggles. "Oh, I am sorry, but he's ever so cute."

"Ugh," Grace groaned.

"You'll be fine," Emilie said, not looking up from her magazine. "Just pretend it's me sitting across from you and we're arguing about art and society."

Grace sighed. "At least you understand. Here goes." She slipped out the door.

As soon as Grace was gone, Emilie tossed her magazine onto her bed and hurried to the door. She counted to five, then peered out.

She wasn't the first with the same idea. Not only were Lotte, Maggie, and Dora lined up peering over the banister rail, they had been joined by the two seamstresses, who looked from behind the others with expressions somewhere between longing and amusement.

Emilie joined them, safely at the back so if Grace or Charlie happened to look up, Emilie wouldn't be seen as part of the interlopers.

So much to-do over a man and a dinner. Not at all like her life in Paris, where every night was dinner somewhere with someone. Going out with men was nothing out of the ordinary. At least not in her social set of artists and their circle.

She repressed a niggle of what might have been envy. Dinner in a nice restaurant with interesting conversation seemed an impossibility.

Charlie Murray looked perfectly presentable, clean-shaven and wearing what from the landing looked like a plaid suit. His hair was slicked back, though one curl had fallen over his forehead in spite of the pomade, which had probably gone a long way toward Nessa's "cute" description.

Thank heaven Emilie had convinced Grace to wear her best visiting dress.

Grace, on the other hand, standing ramrod straight, her expression tense, looked quite radiant in the lamplight of the foyer. In Emilie's experience, no woman was that nervous about her appearance unless a man was involved.

Oh, dieu pardonne! The last thing they needed was for Grace to fall in love and run off to get married.

Below them, Charlie Murray was grinning like Mr. Carroll's Cheshire cat. And suddenly Emilie wished he would, like the cat, just disappear. But he merely opened the door and ushered Grace out into the night.

The last thing Emilie heard before the door closed was Grace saying, "I don't know why we couldn't have just met at the restaurant." And Emilie breathed a sigh of relief.

Mrs. B, who had chaperoned the proceedings, glanced up at Emilie. "He is very tall." And with a satisfied smile, she returned to her kitchen.

They all reconvened downstairs for dinner a few minutes later. The middle-aged ladies seemed somewhat subdued, but there was much speculation between Dora and Maggie about Grace's "date." Lotte held her tongue.

It seemed to Emilie that something had changed between the sisters. Did Lotte begrudge a man's interest in her sister? Could Jack Ratner's interest even be real? Maggie didn't have much to recommend her as a wife, loving perhaps, but was she capable of getting dinner on the table or discussing the future of their family? *Family.* Maybe he wasn't thinking family at all, but having a good time with a girl who didn't have the judgment to say no.

Emilie smiled sympathetically across the table at Lotte, who didn't seem to be aware of anything that was going on. Was she envying Grace at a restaurant with a decent-looking, employed young man while she was here, sitting between two older women who were beyond the age of marriage and were still having to work to keep themselves in room and board and knowing that she would one day be one of them?

No one lingered after dessert.

It was strange having the room to herself. A little empty. But a good opportunity to do something she'd been thinking about for a while.

Emilie leaned over the edge of the bed and pulled out a piece of cardboard, several sheets of coarse paper, and a box of cheap pastels. She'd bought the paper and pastels on one of her weekend shopping excursions. The cardboard she'd rescued from the rubbish heap.

She propped her pillow against the bed frame with the cardboard balanced against her bent knees to serve as an easel. Primitive, but with the telegram on its way she would soon have oils, watercolors, and good paper stock in her trunk.

She stared at the blank paper. The length of pastel felt strange in her hand, light and ephemeral after weeks of handling heavy cutters and nippers and pieces of glass.

The page stayed empty. Emilie didn't want to sketch florals or streams, though those images immediately popped into her mind. She didn't want to draw cartoons, whether glass or political.

She wanted to draw colors. The bright, bold, aggressive colors of . . . Paris. No. The new colors of her new world. New York. Tiffany. She looked around her room. Letting her eyes blur from what was to the way they were. Form over function.

Across the room, Grace's desk lamp cast nearby objects in a kind of shadow, picking out certain shapes, muting others. Emilie squinted until the shadows and objects became a dance of dark and light. She touched the pastel to her paper, let her hand follow her eye. And when she had filled the page she realized the inkwell, the bottle of pencils and pens, all the objects on Grace's desk became more than they had been and something stirred inside her. Something she hadn't felt in a long time, even on her happiest days working in glass.

She wished she had oils with which to explore the depth of color, light streaming through the window, an easel of her own. She started another study, moving the lamp so that it highlighted the patterns of Grace's quilt, then let the color flow out of the delineations and into planes of color.

She was engrossed in this experiment when she heard the downstairs clock strike ten. And then the half hour.

Grace had been gone for over three hours. Emilie pushed her papers aside and got to her feet. She was stiff and cramped, but she went over to the window and looked out. The street was quiet. An old man, hunched against the night air, slowly made his way toward Fourth Avenue. Another man hurried by in the opposite direction.

And for some inexplicable reason, Emilie felt a wave of homesickness.

She cleaned up her work, dressed in her nightgown, and waited for Grace to return.

When the clock struck 10:45, Emilie went to the window again, wondering what Charlie would think if Grace had to climb in the window to get inside.

But just when she was about to give up and go downstairs, she saw them coming up the street with unhurried steps. They appeared deep in conversation.

So they had gotten along after all.

They turned up the steps and a few minutes later the bedroom door opened and Grace came inside. She was flushed from the autumn air and perhaps just a little from Charlie's company.

Emilie looked up from her magazine, which she'd grabbed as she made a dash for her bed. "You're back."

"Yes," Grace said as she bustled about the room, dropping gloves and hat and pulling pins out of her hair.

Emilie waited patiently. It was none of her business, but they were friends and friends took an interest. She also had learned by now not to push Grace.

Grace began undoing the buttons of her dress. "He's not so bad when he isn't being a jerk," she said, as if Emilie had asked.

She slipped out of the dress and dropped it over the back of her desk chair, then sat down at the desk to finish unpinning her hair. "I don't know how it is that I can wear my hair pulled tight enough to give me a headache just fine," she said, scrubbing her scalp with both hands. "But something this loose and comfortable makes me feel downright light-headed."

Emilie suspected it might have been the—formerly—annoying journalist or possibly a glass of wine that had contributed to her friend's light-headedness, but she didn't mention it.

"He's really smart, as it turns out," Grace continued.

"You thought he might be."

"I did. And I was right."

A few moments of silence passed. Then Grace flopped back on her own bed. "Actually, he was pretty nice."

Emilie rolled over to brace herself on one elbow. "So will you see him again? I mean, other than at rallies and strikes and such."

"Maybe. He has an interesting take on the place of journalism. And he has nothing against women working. And even complimented me on my perspicacity."

"Oh? I don't think I know that word."

"It just means that I have a ready insight into things that matter."

"Oh. That's a good word. And it suits you." Emilie recited it in her head several times. It was a word she should remember.

"Anyway. He said he'd help me past the women cartoonist dilemma . . . as soon as he figures out how. And, Emilie, we talked about so many things that matter to both of us."

"And he won't give you away?"

"He said he wouldn't."

"Good," Emilie said. And they could only pray he kept his word.

Chapter 14

On Monday, Mr. Tiffany made his usual weekly visit to the women's workshop. Emilie wasn't sure how it happened that with all the normal sounds of the workroom—the clicks of the cutters, the rattles of paper, the scrapes of the files, the swish of skirts, and the low murmured conversations—the *tap*, *tap*, *tap* of Mr. Tiffany's cane penetrated through, dulling the normal sounds like the staccato beat of a tin drum.

The moment that everyone became aware of his approach, silence descended on the studio, movements and work arrested, as if even the walls were holding their breath.

And like every Monday, Mrs. Driscoll came from her office and hurried to meet him, joining him just about the time he reached Grace's easel. With her appearance, the workshop settled back into a quiet routine, while she and Mr. Tiffany made their rounds, stopping in front of various projects, where those artisans held their positions as if being photographed until he made his judgment, gave his advice, or showed his pleasure—or his displeasure. Then he moved on to the next and those women were held in stasis in their turn.

Emilie kept at her work. She and Miss Zevesky had made good progress on the drying corn and shucks, which were absolutely lighting up the bottom section of the "Autumn" panel and casting a spotlight on the deep purples and reds of the ripened fruits above them.

Emilie was adding a second layer to a deep red gourd and was considering one last darker layer when she heard it coming closer. *Tap, tap, tap.* Miss Zevesky turned to await her verdict. Emilie kept her hands moving as she held up the darker pane to the ones already adhered with wax to the easel.

The tapping stopped. Emilie glanced up and smiled. She didn't mean to. Fortunately, he was so intent that he didn't see. Merely motioned her aside with a gesture of his hand. The one not holding his cane.

He moved closer and leaned over the panel of glass she'd been contemplating. "Is this red plating for the gourd?"

Emilie searched for her voice. "That was my intention."

He nodded. "Good. It is what I would do. Richer, but not so dark as to lose the color."

As if she would be guilty of losing color. "If it loses color, it will be the sun's fault."

"Humph. And this?" He pointed to a scrap of green-and-gold patterned glass.

"It will go among the darker fruit to draw the eye and accentuate their depth." She picked up a piece only roughly cut but held it between two fingers and raised it to the window. "*Comme ça.*"

"With this." He moved another scrap of glass with the tip of his finger.

"And also this." Emilie pushed a fourth section to join the others.

"Use this behind them." He studied her work tray and arranged two scraps of the gold and green glass around several blue and purple samples.

Emilie nodded. She hadn't been sure about the two-toned color. Now she was.

He turned to Mrs. Driscoll, who always stood aside, waiting for his opinion. "And now where is the 'Magnolia' window? Miss Northrop said it would be started by now."

"And so it has been," Mrs. Driscoll said. "The cartoon is awaiting an easel and most of the background glass has been chosen, but the rest is waiting for a selector to become free."

"Send Miss Pascal. She has an adequate eye."

Emilie gritted her teeth. He was standing near to her. And could have asked her himself. But that was not his way. She was used to him by now. It was only natural that he would see them all as projections of himself, like a hundred pairs of hands for his brain. It was his way of trusting them. On a more effusive man, it would be a compliment, but Mr. Tiffany reserved his enthusiasm for the work and the art. And his vision of what they should be.

And that was fine with Emilie. She would be one of those pairs of hands as long as he let her use her sensibilities as well as his.

"Miss Pascal is quite busy and I need her for something else."

He raised an eyebrow at the manageress.

"Hmm," he said. "Then hire more girls if you must. I'll take care of Mr. Mitchell." And he tapped away, Mrs. Driscoll seeing him to the door.

The moment it closed, the workshop exhaled and the clicking, scraping, swishing, and conversation began again. The morning review had gone well. They all felt the better for his being there—and a tremendous relief now that he was gone.

On Wednesday, Mrs. Driscoll and Emilie went out to the Corona furnaces and workshops. Emilie had barely donned her apron before she was told to take it off again.

"I have business with the metal department and Miss Northrop is awaiting a particular color for her 'Magnolia' window now that the work has started at last. We'll pick it up and you can help me carry it back."

Emilie was glad to go, but she was loath to leave her panel even for a morning. Anyone could carry glass.

"Mr. Nash was so impressed with your attitude toward his vases that he mentioned it again to Mr. Tiffany. I think he would enjoy the company, and that will give me time to deal with the other departments while he shows you around the furnaces.

"The man doesn't get enough credit for all the work he does. Consider this a duty for us and a treat for him."

Mrs. Driscoll gave Emilie one of those no-nonsense penetrating looks, somewhere between a command and a promise of delight, that she often used to urge the girls onward—or before she announced that they would all have to stay late the following day.

So off they went, Emilie in her spring coat and Mrs. Driscoll wrapped up in a heavy wool coat and scarf with a roll of linen paper tucked carefully under her arm.

They took the ferry across the East River to Corona. Mrs. Driscoll seemed preoccupied and kept shifting the roll of what must be designs from her lap to her arm, sometimes cradling them as if they were an infant.

Emilie didn't mind. She spent the time looking at the passing water and wondering if they had put someone new on her "Autumn" window to cut while she was away. The idea created a kind of panic inside her.

She and Mr. Tiffany knew what they wanted. They didn't need to exchange words for her to know his mind. What if the replacement miscut a piece? Destroyed a part that Emilie had planned to use? She imagined returning to a disaster of color and ruined perspective.

She took a deep breath. At which Mrs. Driscoll glanced at her and smiled. Perhaps Mrs. Driscoll thought Emilie was afraid of the ferry and was trying to reassure her.

Emilie did fear the water but not in the way Mrs. Driscoll might imagine. Not because she feared drowning, but because it reminded her of her mother, not the beautiful, dark-haired woman who smelled of lilacs, but the one who stood on the Pont des Arts for the last time, looking down at the dark depths of the Seine. Had she been afraid at that final moment when she knew she would never return? Had she changed her mind when it was too late and fought with her waning strength to come back to Emilie?

"You should have a warmer coat," Mrs. Driscoll said, breaking into her thoughts as the ferry slowed into the landing.

"I have sent for my trunk," Emilie said.

"Excellent. Not long now. Just a short train ride and we'll be there." Mrs. Driscoll maneuvered them across the street to the train station and a waiting locomotive that carried them the last leg of their journey.

Emilie was relieved when a few minutes later they finally stepped off the train and into a street in a desolate area with only a two-storied brick factory building that spread out before them. Smokestacks of various sizes poured out smoke in colors that ranged from white to deepest black.

"Before we go in," Mrs. Driscoll said, "it is important to understand what an honor it is for you to be invited. No visitors without particular business are allowed in. In the words of one of our fellow artists, it is a place 'where no profane eye is allowed to penetrate.'"

"Really?"

"Quite really. Mr. Tiffany is acutely concerned with theft. Actually they've had to let several people go who attempted to steal designs and such for their own profit. It's said that the formulas for all the Tiffany glass are locked in a safe that only Mr. Nash can open."

"Not even Mr. Tiffany?"

Mrs. Driscoll, who had become somewhat sepulchral in her delivery, shrugged. "It's just what they say. I don't know that anyone could understand them if they did manage to get their hands on them. Each formula has a special code, so that even if someone managed to copy it, it would have no meaning without access to the code."

"And do they keep that in the safe as well?"

"I have no idea." She shifted her roll of paper, which by now Emilie was certain must be the designs for the dragonfly lamp.

Mrs. Driscoll led her to a door partway down the side of the building where they were immediately stopped by a serious-looking guard who barred their way.

"Ah, and it be you, Mrs. Driscoll, and a young lady. Is Mr. Nash expecting you?"

"Indeed he is, Jenkins."

"Come in. Come in. We ain't seen you so much lately."

"We're all very busy this season."

"Don't I know it. Seems like ever since the men got back from their summer break they been working twice as long and twice as hard."

Emilie followed close on Mrs. Driscoll's heels as the heavy door shut quickly behind them.

"If they're working so hard and long," Mrs. Driscoll said in an aside to Emilie, "it's a wonder they're so far behind."

The building was quite warm, a welcome sensation after the ferry and train ride. But as they made their way into the bowels of the building, the air became heavy and overly hot. A door opened down the way from them, and Mr. Nash stepped out to greet them.

"Welcome, my dear Mrs. Driscoll."

Mrs. Driscoll nodded. "And you remember Miss Pascal."

"How could I forget." He performed a quick half bow. "I hope you have enough time for me to show the young lady our factory."

"Not too much; I need to choose some sheets for the 'Magnolia' window, as we seem to be running short at the studio. And I need to check on some orders with the plateglass department and have a quick consultation with Mr. Gray of the metal department.

"But if you wouldn't mind, I'll just go on about my business while you introduce Miss Pascal to the factory. You'll have a rapt attendant, I assure you."

Mr. Nash smiled broadly. "Go right ahead. I should think you know your way around."

He turned back to Emilie, and Mrs. Driscoll took the opportunity to slip away.

"Shall we get started?" He gestured Emilie down a short secondary hallway and ushered her through the door to what proved to be a large brick-enclosed furnace room.

They were immediately hit with a burst of hot air that constricted her breath. The space was lined with windows and several open doors, but the sunlight couldn't compete with the blaze of several yellow suns that shone from the furnaces, or the smaller orbs of light that sat at the ends of blowpipes as men in shirtsleeves and thick aprons carried them from furnace to bench.

"The glory holes." Mr. Nash had to raise his voice to be heard. "Where they heat up the glass so that it can be worked. That's what those men at the benches are doing. Turning your glass into . . . what did you call it, color from air?"

At workbenches men in various states of cover were bent over their pipes, turning and lifting and cooling and returning them for another moment in the glory holes to be reheated. It was amazing, the immediacy of it all. One unsteady move, one turn too slow, one slip, and the glass would collapse, all their work for naught. Emilie automatically took a step closer for a better look.

Mr. Nash put up a restraining arm. "It's hotter than Hades, the glass. People have died from the burns."

And yet the men all went about their work in their shirtsleeves—or less.

She saw him first in silhouette, stripped to the waist but for the bib of a heavy leather apron. He was sitting on a bench before a metal bar, rolling and shaping a glowing glob of molten glass, called a "gather."

The intensity of his concentration was palpable. The muscles of his arms and shoulders flexed and glistened with sweat as his thick hands worked the glass with assurance. And more quickly than Emilie thought possible, the gather changed from a pulsing yellow mass to a graceful curving form, blue strands of color wrapping around it as easily and delicately as the smoke from the furnaces.

Emilie stood mesmerized. How could this rough man, his hair as black as the River Styx, his back powerful, his scowl frighteningly intense, make such fragile glassware?

Like mighty Vulcan at his forge with an artist's delicate touch.

"I see your eye has caught one of our most talented young glass artists. His name is Amon Bronsky."

Amon Bronsky. Even his name seemed rough, untamed. And Emilie couldn't pry her eyes away. Twice he went back to the glory hole to reheat his glass, carrying it at the end of the unwieldy pipe as if it were a mere bubble. Only the bulge of his arms belied the ease with which he seemed to make the journey.

On his second trip back from the heat, he caught her eye. His eyes were black and piercing and Emilie couldn't keep back a shudder. Then he turned, releasing her, and was back at the bench where the vase continued to lengthen and curve beneath his fingers. And like those she had seen in Paris, the vase took on a life of its own, glimmering in the stifling heat. Emilie wondered if any of the vases that had changed her life had been made by Amon Bronsky.

And the tiniest part of her wondered what those rough, creative hands would feel like on her skin.

CLARA WAS HAPPY to miss the furnaces and the sheet glass workroom. Though this was where all the magic of Mr. Tiffany's glass was produced, she always found it a bit depressing. The whole atmosphere was dark and gritty and stifling and made her long for the out-of-doors. And yet this pedestrian, dirty factory managed to create Tiffany's most uplifting glass.

She was just glad that her work was across the river and five stories up where the air was relatively clean. She stopped at the room where the plateglass sheets were finished and knocked on the door. The foreman greeted her by sticking his arm straight over his head and flapping his hand for her to approach.

They took a minute for their usual pleasantries then Clara got down to business. "Mr. Tiffany is adamant about getting Miss Northrop's 'Magnolia' window in production. It's quite a rarity and calls for whites of green and ecru shadings. Something delicate yet—"

"Yes, yes. Did you bring the design?"

Clara nodded and carefully placed her roll down on the worktable, untied it, and gently removed the "Magnolia" design. Then she carefully retied the remaining paper.

The foreman looked over the design. "I suppose they want it immediately."

"Of course, and we're still waiting for the border glass for the 'Four Seasons.'"

"We're working on it. Where is Arthur?"

"He's showing one of my selectors the furnaces and glory holes."

"Humph. Don't even think about sending any women over to do glassblowing or sheeting. The union won't stand for it: there will be an all-out mutiny."

Clara laughed. "Rest easy, we are all quite content with our workshop on Fourth Avenue." Actually, the thought of having to work here made her shudder with disgust.

"Just so we all understand how things lie. Come on back and let's see what we have that might work."

He led her through rows of glass that made the Manhattan storage room look like a pantry. A half hour later, they had chosen quite a few possibilities.

"Better run this by Arthur; I'll charge your account."

Clara let it pass; that was another of Pringle Mitchell's new rules. "I will. I expected him to have joined us by now. I need to get back, but I have one more quick stop to make."

"You go on. I'll see if I can curtail Arthur's sightseeing tour. And make sure he's not giving away any trade secrets." They both laughed at his little joke. The only person more secretive about the glass formulas than Mr. Tiffany was Arthur Nash.

"Excellent." Clutching her remaining scroll of paper, Clara slipped away and hurried down the corridor to the metalworks and Mr. Gray, whom she would have to consult about the dragonfly lamp's feasibility, before even attempting to convince Mr. Mitchell to pay for it. It would be very expensive to create.

Fortunately Mr. Gray was there and saw Clara the minute she

entered the room. She steeled her ears to the hammering, polishing, and cutting of the various metal projects being carried on in the shop.

"So what do you have for me? More lamp bases?"

Clara chuckled. "Always, except not today."

"Oh? Inkstands, candle screen, jewelry box . . . clock?"

"None of those. I was wondering . . . if you could possibly . . ." Slowly she unrolled her dragonfly lamp design and spread it on the closest empty worktable.

EMILIE WATCHED, MESMERIZED, as the finished vase was carried away. She'd followed every step as if she was the one transformed in Amon Bronsky's capable hands, and it left her weak with wonder.

Mr. Nash pulled out his pocket watch. "Mrs. Driscoll has gone to the metalworking department. I know she'll be wanting to get back to the city."

They traversed a labyrinth of rooms and came to another door, where they discovered Mrs. Driscoll and another man leaning over a design spread out on the worktable. They both turned as Emilie and Mr. Nash approached, and Emilie caught a glimpse of a watercolor sketch of Mrs. Driscoll's dragonfly lamp. Emilie had been struck upon first seeing it how detailed it was. The wings alone might consist of hundreds of pieces of glass. How would it be possible?

Mrs. Driscoll had come to the metalworks department.

And Emilie understood. Not many but one piece of glass overlaid with . . . "Filigree!" she exclaimed, forgetting decorum in her enthusiasm. "You're going to overlay the wings with filigree. That's brilliant!"

She clapped her hand to her mouth. "I beg your pardon," she mumbled through her fingers.

"No need," Mrs. Driscoll said, shooting her companion a triumphant look. "Mr. Gray and I were just discussing the efficacy of such an idea. I believe I have an ally in you?"

"Oh yes," Emilie agreed. "I've never seen that done before."

"Probably 'cause it hasn't been done before," Mr. Gray said skeptically. "I can make it work, no doubt about that. Just needs a little finesse, a steady hand, and a heck of a lot of money. The labor alone will cost plenty."

Mrs. Driscoll beamed, not deterred in the least. "I'll take care of the expense," she said. "As long as your department can and will be able to execute this as soon as the design is approved."

Mr. Gray huffed out a sigh. "For you, Mrs. Driscoll, I will see to it personally."

"Thank you, Mr. Gray. I knew I could count on you. Now Miss Pascal and I must rush. We still have several hours of work ahead of us back in Manhattan."

Chapter 15

Grace hurried along the street toward Webster Hall. She'd taken a trolley straight downtown, but she didn't begrudge the price of a ticket. Over the past few weeks she'd sold several cartoons to her usual magazines, plus one to the *Times* and two to the *Sun*.

She had Charlie Murray to thank for the last two. They'd met for lunch or dinner several times since he'd discovered that she was G. L. Griffith, usually after seeing each other at events they were covering. And most lately because Charlie had given her inside information about where the news was happening and where he inevitably would run into her.

They made a good team. His words and her drawings.

And Grace had Emilie to thank for her success. Emilie was the one who concocted a letter of introduction explaining that Mr. Griffith was not available for in-person interviews with the editors of the *Sun* but was content to continue their relationship through the post. Mr. Griffith agreed not to offer the cartoons he submitted to the *Sun* to any other paper.

The editors had agreed, and Grace suspected Charlie had something to do with that, too.

Grace was not too proud to accept help where she could get it. She would depend on herself to keep the position once it was hers. Tonight was a meeting of the Lower East Side cloak workers. Rumblings had increased about forming a women's garment workers' union, which was sorely needed. A union to protect the rights of women workers at work and, when necessity called for a strike, to protect them from being attacked by paid thugs like the ones who had attacked the woman and her child. Grace still shuddered remembering that night.

At least at Mr. Tiffany's, women were paid on a par with the men, and he openly depended on their good judgment and artistic abilities, giving credit where credit was due. To their faces at least. In public it was still a man's world. Mr. Tiffany's world.

Was it fair? No. But when balanced against the rest of the women's work lives, the conditions, the pay, the treatment, it seemed a small price to pay . . . for now.

Mr. Tiffany was no fool and he had a vision. And perhaps that vision would someday include the future of the women's workforce.

The rest of the working world was slow to change. But change it must. Already women were beginning to take their place in government and industry and art. And if men chose to stumble blindly along thinking they were the only ones making the world go round. Well, let them.

Grace hadn't covered another women's meeting since that night. It wasn't that she was afraid, but that she knew the importance of covering all the news. She didn't want to be pigeonholed in women's working rights, or suffrage, any more than she wanted to be chained to women's fashions or household tips.

She had almost reached the redbrick building where the meeting was to be held, when she saw Charlie leaning against the stair railing, munching on an apple.

Her heart lifted just a little at the sight of his slightly rumpled appearance and his cocky grin. She had grown to love that grin. Though she would never let on to him. He was too self-assured by half.

When she was a few feet away, he reached in his coat pocket, pulled out another apple with the flourish of a magician, and presented it to Grace.

"Thanks, I'm starving."

"I thought you would be," he said. "We'll have dinner after the meeting. I know a great little establishment nearby."

"How did you know I'd be here? And why are you here? Are you writing it up for the paper?"

"Thought you would be. And I am, but mainly I came because I wanted to see you."

Grace took a bite out of the apple, because she was hungry and it gave her something to do so she wouldn't have to react to his words.

He didn't seem embarrassed by his admission; she was learning that not much unsettled Charlie Murray. He just watched her eat the apple and when it was down to the core, he watched her eat that, too.

Then they went inside and sat at the back with two other journalists who were obviously bored with the assignment.

But Grace knew that this movement would soon lead to bigger news. She'd heard of several smaller unions already talking about organizing into a larger union, starting with the garment workers. It would soon spread to other professions.

Grace intended to capture the beginnings of what was bound to be a widespread movement.

She sketched the young woman who stood before a rather small group and tried not to be disappointed. There couldn't be more than fifteen people in the room if you counted the journalists, and Grace began to rue having spent her nickel on the trolley.

"You can't expect to get beaten up and trampled over in every assignment," Charlie said as they walked down the street after the meeting to a "little place" he knew.

Charlie knew all the good cheap places to eat, restaurants no bigger than a parlor, some smaller, with tables so crowded together that you rubbed elbows with other diners as you ate. Sometimes they talked while they ate rigatoni made by an Italian grandmother or chilled borscht by a Lithuanian soldier. Sometimes, when they were on a big story, they would write and draw over plates of chop suey and dumplings so that Charlie could get both their assignments in by the midnight deadline.

Everyone they met in one of Charlie's little places had their own story that they sometimes shared with the two diners. Most were immigrants from all over the world, some had exotic pasts, some horrific. But one thing they had in common. They all loved Charlie.

And much to her chagrin, they all assumed he was stepping out with Grace.

At first Grace tried to explain they were colleagues, but her explanations fell on deaf ears. They had made up their minds, and after a while Grace gave up trying to set the record straight.

She had no better success with her fellow boarders, since Charlie insisted on seeing her to the door whenever they met. "Just so you don't forget that I can be a gentleman," he'd say. And she would scrutinize his face for a sign of humility or sarcasm and always just found Charlie.

Anyone who was still up when she returned home would give

her sly looks, or envious ones, and she no longer attempted to explain their relationship.

At times she even wondered . . . what if?

EMILIE SAT ON her bed, sketching the things she'd seen at the Corona factory. Vases and ovens and a dark, intense man whose eyes had haunted her on the ferry ride home, had stayed with her through the rest of the workday, only to be broken at dinner when things became so tense between Lotte and Maggie that Emilie had fled to the solitude of her room as soon as the plates were cleared.

She had sensed tension between the sisters ever since that day they'd gone to the beach. Maggie was suddenly "mad for men," as Lotte accused her, so she sought conversation elsewhere in the guise of Dora, who was always ready to talk about men anytime, until tonight when she seemed to have realized that she'd helped create a monster.

Not that Emilie thought Maggie was a monster. She was a sweet girl, normally. But she needed constant supervision and would never be able to take on the duties of a household, much less make her own way in the world. There didn't seem to be a likely scenario for her happily ever after.

She didn't seem capable of keeping house. She wasn't even very thorough at cleaning the floors in the studio. Emilie suspected it was the kindness of Mr. Tiffany's heart, or perhaps Mrs. Driscoll's, that kept her on. Her wages helped Lotte to support them both.

Lotte was looking more and more haggard as the month drew on. Not at all how a girl on the cusp of womanhood should look. And Maggie, who had passed that time years ago, was looking healthy, radiant almost.

Emilie feared there was a man involved. And that boded no good. It had to be one of the men they'd met at the beach that day: Maggie had no time or opportunity to meet anyone else.

Lotte lived in fear of someone taking liberties with her sister's lack of judgment. And tonight over the raisin cake, her fears and frustrations erupted.

"I can't, I just can't," Lotte cried. She pushed her chair away from the table and rushed out of the room. Everyone watched, forks frozen in their hands, glasses held inches from their mouths. Only Maggie continued to eat, oblivious to Lotte's breakdown or the others' reactions.

So Emilie did what she had always done when she was upset or unsettled. She took out her sketch pad and drew.

But instead of calming her as painting often did, these sketches just caused more turmoil. Not the vases, not the ovens, but the portraits of Amon Bronsky. She hated portraiture, had never liked it even in the beginning, when her father had entrusted her with the finishing of his own work. She had thought in those days that it would make him kinder toward her, that his appreciation of her talent would make him love her, but she'd been wrong.

He'd forced her to do it, then resented her for doing it well. She couldn't please him. She doubted if anything or anyone could. She didn't want to wonder where he was, what had happened to him, if he had escaped the net being drawn around him and was living the gay life in Italy or Greece where many undesirables fled to escape retribution—from the law or from society in general.

Perhaps he was in jail and that would be fine with Emilie. If she was honest, deep-down-inside honest, she wouldn't cry if he was dead. The world would be a better place with him gone from it.

She mulled this over, her pen moving automatically as her pages filled with images. She was surrounded by papers when Grace breezed in just as the clock struck eleven.

"You're sketching," Grace said as she dropped her coat on her bed and came over to Emilie's bed. "Mind if I take a look?" She didn't wait for an answer. She was obviously still riding high on whatever excitement she had witnessed at whatever meeting she'd attended, most likely with Charlie Murray.

"Good god!" Grace exclaimed, peering over Emilie's shoulder.

It was only then that Emilie realized what she had done. What had begun as a simple rendering from memory—images from her trip to the Corona furnaces—had escaped the confines of brick ovens, glassblowers, and a profile of Mr. Nash before her pen strayed to one particular artisan rolling the glass on a marver table. On page after page he became more alive, more formed, until he was no longer a muscular man bending over the glass bench in his leather apron. He had transformed beneath her pen. Become larger than life. Dark hair flying, black eyes flashing, the apron gone and his nude form bending over a bed of flames. Intense, powerful. The mighty Vulcan. Hephaestus. Creator of the thunderbolts of Zeus.

"So those *were* your paintings in your portfolio."

"What paintings?" Emilie asked, wrenching her eyes from the sketches.

"I saw them in your portfolio when everything fell out on the floor that first day."

Emilie hesitated. "Yes. The Académie didn't approve. Did Mrs. Driscoll see?"

"I'm sure she must have."

Emilie's eyes filled with fear. She couldn't stop it. She could feel it as if it were tears waiting to overflow.

"Hey, she hired you. And they're good paintings, if a little weird."

"They use color, real color, aggressive color, if you will."

"Like these," Grace said, pointing to Emilie's last Vulcan sketch. Emilie didn't remember switching from pen to her pastels. The flesh of his legs and arms turned pink from the heat, as the red and black of the flames licked up around him. The deepest red worn down to a mere nub from trying to get a deeper color for the flames.

"I mean, I'm not an art scholar," Grace continued. "I'm mainly interested in illustrations, but these are so bold. And in pastel, not an easy medium; I've tried it a bit with no luck. You know Mr. Tiffany sometimes works in pastels himself."

"I saw one on the wall in his office. That was his? It was too tame for him. Everyone must be an impressionist these days, with their soft colors and softer lines. But life is not soft," Emilie said. "Color should be bold. Subjects, more than their outward image. Painting should take you inside to your innermost fear and bring it out to the light. Like Mr. Tiffany does."

"I get what you're saying, I think. But . . . Mr. Tiffany? He's as traditional as you can get except for his oriental themes, but they are mild compared to your paintings. And this . . ." Grace gestured to the Vulcan and the flames leaping around him. "This is almost heretical."

"And so is Mr. Tiffany," Emilie said. "For all his saints and virgins, he is a groundbreaker. His glass transforms light. He isn't afraid of color. It is the glass, though, that takes the light and makes it something more."

Grace huffed out a sigh. "A bit too esoteric for me."

"Not at all. You do it yourself."

"No, I don't."

"You take a real living person and distort them to mean what you want. To say something that you want to say."

"Oh, I suppose."

"Mr. Tiffany does, too. Though I think he is sometimes lost."

"Who? Mr. Tiffany? Never. He knows exactly what he wants and endeavors to get it. Good heavens, Emilie, don't ever let anyone hear you say that. He doesn't like to be thwarted."

"I know. And he is a genius, I agree." Emilie hesitated, then she smiled. "But don't ever let him hear that I said that, either." She slid her drawings into her sketchbook. "Now, tell me about the meeting you attended tonight."

"First you must clean off the chalk from your nightgown. Or Mrs. B will be wondering what you'vc been up to."

Emilie looked down. Her white nightdress was covered in black and red smudges. "I look like I've been consumed by the fires of hell."

"At least stuck in a chimney flue. But take that off and change into a chemise. We'll have Nessa wash it out tomorrow. Mrs. B won't mind if she does it in the sink downstairs. You'll have to give her a few pennies extra."

Emilie nodded and shrugged out of the gown. Shivering, she jumped beneath the covers. "Now tell me about the meeting and where Charlie took you to eat."

Clara Driscoll could hardly sleep knowing that she was ready to present her full-blown dragonfly design to Mr. Tiffany. Mr. Gray had agreed to make the filigree overlay. The cost for it all, the hours of construction alone, would be formidable, but it would be worth it when they saw the finished piece.

Getting Mr. Mitchell and the other "powers" to agree would take both her and Mr. Tiffany's compelling argument. And their approval depended on whether Mr. Tiffany saw its potential as Clara did. She wished she could have made a model to show him. In lieu of that, she'd had Alice draw up some watercolor transparencies that would give a better idea of what the completed lamp would look like.

Clara needed her sleep or she would be hobbled by one of her migraines while trying to be at her most persuasive. But the more she tried to fall asleep, the more awake she became.

And when dawn finally came, she had only dozed fitfully through the night and already her head was pounding.

She went early to the studio; she didn't dare eat, but she drank a cup of coffee, which did help a little. She spent her time alone in the studio gathering her displays and her wits.

She wouldn't be able to see Mr. Tiffany until ten. And though only hours away, it felt like an eternity. She didn't usually feel nervous about her work; the smaller decorative pieces were based on the same theme and were easily adapted and reproduced, ensuring a higher profit.

But this. Clara had invested more in her dragonflies than she had in any of her other designs. She'd also created the dandelion lamp in a flurry of creativity. And was overseeing at least eight other lamps, some of them bound for the homes of society ladies, others to be displayed throughout the home architectural exhibits at the Paris world's fair. But selfishly, she wanted her dragonflies to be chosen for the Tiffany Pavilion proper.

Clara never had false ideas about her own importance, nor ulterior motives, no more than most people, anyway, and she didn't feel she had to prove herself to anyone. She was what she had always been, Clara Wolcott Driscoll.

But even though no one might ever know that she made this lamp, she'd given it her heart and soul. She wanted it out in the world. She had drawn up a prospectus on hours and materials. It was dear, but not as dear as the dragonflies were to their creator.

Alice came in early as expected. "So today's the big day," she said excitedly, then immediately frowned. "Oh dear, one of your headaches?"

"I was too anxious to sleep, but it will go away once I have this lamp started in earnest."

"Which will be soon, I have no doubt." Alice immediately reached into her large carry bag and pulled out a thermos. "I made strong tea. It always helps with your headaches."

Clara smiled, suppressing the queasiness in her stomach. "You always think of everything. And I do appreciate it." Clara took the cup and sipped. It was hot and thc steam did indeed help.

She was finally beginning to relax, when a crash resounded from the workroom. Her headache rushed back. It was a sound they both recognized.

Clara pushed to her feet. "I swanee, if it isn't marriage, it's broken glass." Her head was pounding.

Alice murmured sympathetically. "Some days it does seem that way. But at least we know it isn't Mr. Tiffany having a temperamental freak. He hasn't come in yet this morning; I checked with the doorman."

"Thank heaven for that, at least. I dread to see what we've lost."

"Why don't you let me deal with whatever it is?" Alice said, moving to intercept her.

"We'll both go. I'm not sure I can meet whatever disaster is in store with equanimity without your calming influence." Clara straightened her muslin work sleeves, smoothed her work apron, and opened the door. And letting Alice lead the way, they went out to face the crisis.

At one of the tables, a cluster of girls were bent over with brushes and dustpans. Maggie Wilson lay flat out on the floor, her broom sticking out from her skirts like a witch's companion.

As they approached, Maggie flailed and struggled to sit up, and Clara's mind was brought back to the day Emilie Pascal had fainted at their feet, and she couldn't help but make the terrible comparison between the two.

"I feel funny," Maggie complained, sitting up.

"Because you hit your head when you fell," Grace said.

"Because you were air dreaming and not paying attention to what you were doing," added Lotte, sounding exasperated, which was unusual for her. "Now look what you've done."

"I'm sorry, Lotte. I didn't mean to. I didn't see Dora get up."

Grace Griffith rose like a phoenix from the cluster. "No harm done," she said brightly and glanced down to where Maggie huddled, her face lifted toward Clara's and looking frightened.

"I didn't do it. I didn't mean to, Mrs. Driscoll." She clambered clumsily to her feet, setting off another series of glass crunches.

"As long as you're not hurt," Clara said.

"No one's fault," Grace continued. "It's mainly Dora's work tray. There are enough large pieces salvaged to recut the broken ones."

"Which I just cut and now have to recut. Well, it's coming out of your pay, Maggie, not mine."

"Dora," Grace snapped.

Dora Hodgins held out two pieces of broken glass. "Just look at this." She sighed, screwed up her face, looking at Maggie. "Oh, I guess I can work around the break. It wasn't totally Mag— Miss Wilson's fault. She just turned toward me as I stood to go to the easel, and somehow she lost her balance."

"You tripped me." Maggie made a face at her.

"I did not," Dora retorted.

"I'll take care of the breakage." Lotte stood more slowly, probably counting up how much of her salary would be retained to make up for breakage and the extra work.

These kinds of accidents happened. It was the nature of working in glass. Unfortunately, when they happened to Maggie, they tended to be cataclysmic. There was nothing graceful about poor Maggie Wilson. And when she erred, she took a great deal of materials with her.

If she could continue to work without too much loss, Clara was happy to keep both sisters employed. It was a hard burden placed on Lotte. She was only nineteen, pretty enough, with a mild personality, and under other circumstances would have found a husband by now and left. But because of the vagaries of life, none of which were her fault, Lotte's whole life would have to be dedicated to taking care of her older sister.

"Well, clean that up, then. Everyone take a minute to drink some water so as not to get overheated."

The other girls had turned back to their work, their curiosity not outlasting their concern.

"I'll stay late to make up for the breakage," Lotte said.

"First see to your sister."

Maggie still appeared unsteady on her feet, and Lotte and Dora helped her toward the bench by the door.

Clara watched them for a second to make certain they needed no help then gave a final look around the studio where everyone was back concentrating on their own work.

And now it was time to concentrate on hers.

"Time to go," Alice reminded her.

"Good." The two of them walked back into her office where

Clara gave herself a quick look in the mirror and gathered up her designs. "Wish me luck."

"With all my heart, dear friend. Though your design needs no luck; it is perfection itself."

"From your lips to Mr. Mitchell's checkbook," Clara said and left to give Mr. Tiffany her best sales pitch.

Chapter 16

Mr. Tiffany's door had never looked so foreboding, Clara thought as she stood, designs in hand, like a schoolgirl awaiting an important test. Which was ridiculous. She had spent many happy hours behind that door, discussing art, design, and business with Mr. Tiffany.

Of course, "the powers" were usually not there, but she had come armored with renderings, numbers, and a good argument, which she had practiced before several of her boardinghouse friends the night before. Actually she'd been rehearsing it in her head from the first time her pencil had touched the page.

There were lamps, and there were lamps, but this one would be special. She could feel it. And she wasn't one to fantasize too far from reality.

As she opened the door and saw who was awaiting her, her mood slipped and her headache, which had subsided somewhat, threatened to revive. Mr. Mitchell, he of the checkbook, was wearing his usual aspiration-squelching black suit and matching expression. He stood with his back to the window, which made his silhouette even more formidable.

Clara refused to be cowed. She knew when she was right, and as far as she was concerned, Mr. Mitchell would not be able to hold out against her arguments. At least Mr. Belknap, one of the managers, and one of Clara's staunch supporters, was there as well. He gave Clara a hearty good morning. She smiled at him and lifted her chin to Mr. Tiffany.

"Good morning, Mr. Tiffany, gentlemen." Clara strode straight to the desk where Mr. Tiffany was sitting and felt her optimism soar.

She unrolled Alice's watercolor sketch and weighted it down with inkstand and paperweight.

"Ah," said Mr. Tiffany.

"Another dragonfly lamp," Mr. Mitchell said, begrudgingly looking over the sketch.

"Unlike the other prototypes that had to be made under certain strictures, I propose this one, which will appeal to the most discerning of our clients."

She turned away and addressed Mr. Tiffany directly. "And I think it will also be appreciated by art connoisseurs."

"Appreciated?" exclaimed Mr. Belknap. "It's remarkable. Unique. And the shape of the shade with that band around the bottom. It could start a whole new line."

Bless Mr. Belknap and his artistic sensibilities. Clara could always count on him for a discerning and artistic eye.

"What is this base?" asked Mr. Mitchell, in his most skinflintish tone. Clara imagined him counting up the costs as they stood there. Well, she had beat him to it. The costs were written out in the second sheet of paper she had brought with her. And it was going to cost a lot.

"It's mosaic. A pond represented by small rectangular tesserae reflecting the diaphanous wings."

Mr. Tiffany nodded.

Mr. Mitchell asked, "Why can't you put a bronze base on it like the one that went to the Grafton Gallery?"

"Because," Clara said, "I always felt that base took away from the fragility of the shade. It felt bottom heavy." She handed him a separate sheet of paper. "Here is an estimate of hours, materials, and workmanship. I think it will be worth every penny."

"And so do I," said Mr. Belknap. "Mrs. Driscoll is absolutely right. It's the most interesting lamp design of the season. The lamp we sent to London sold for . . ."

"Over two hundred dollars," Clara interjected. "I daresay this will fetch much more."

All three of them turned to Mr. Tiffany. "Mosaic. I like it. The colors reflect the creatures. As it should. And their wings?"

Here was the part she was most insecure about.

She lifted her chin. "Filigree. I've talked with Mr. Gray at Corona and he's agreed that he can do it in time."

She heard something like a groan from Mr. Mitchell.

"Superb," exclaimed Mr. Tiffany. "A breakthrough. Entirely different. I like it. Mitchell, see that she gets what she needs."

"But Mr. Tiffany—" Mr. Mitchell said.

"Can you have it ready in time to ship to Paris?"

Paris. Clara couldn't get the words out fast enough.

"Most certainly."

"Excellent. Get started on it right away. I like the look of it. Captures their . . . their motion, their brilliance. Filigree. Perfect for a lamp. Let me know when it's done. Does Nash have the right glass? If you can't find it downstairs, you'd better go out to Corona and have it made."

"I already have. I was there on other business and thought two birds with one stone in case you liked it."

"I like it, now get to work."

Clara nodded to the others and headed for the door. She heard Pringle Mitchell's first complaint as the door shut behind her.

She'd done her part. The dragonflies, God willing, were going to Paris.

As the "Autumn" panel took shape, Miss Zevesky moved from her beads background to join Lotte in cutting the American eagle whose wide-open wings would fly above the panels. Others had been pulled from their current projects and set to work on the border panels of golds and bronze vines growing from five massive urns depicted on the bottom border panel.

Dora was assigned to cutting the titles, "Spring" and "Summer," that arched over the top two cameos and "Autumn" and "Winter" curving at the bottom of the lower frames. She'd just started on the legend, "Abundance, Peace, and Prosperity" that would appear between spring and summer. Mr. Tiffany had even managed to insert the word *favrile* beneath one of the eagle's wings, and *L.C.T.* beneath the other with the date in bold Latin numerals in the center.

"My eyes are fairly poppin' out of my head," Dora complained each day as they put their aprons away. "All the pieces are so minute and have to be cut with such precision, I've sliced my fingers as much as the glass, I'm sure."

"It will be well worth it, when we see the finished window," Emilie said. She just hoped the beauty of the medallions didn't get lost in all the added details.

"How will I ever find a husband with hands like these?" Dora moaned.

"When do you even have time to find a husband?" Grace quipped. And Dora burst into tears.

Lotte rolled her eyes. "Come along, Dora, we'll give your hands a good soak before dinner, then apply some hand salve before bed. Sleep with your hands in socks and they'll be picture-perfect in the morning." She took Dora's arm and started off. "You, too, Maggie. Don't dawdle." Lotte turned back. "Maggie? Where has that girl gotten to now?" She trudged out of the room in search of her sister.

One day rolled into the next as the Tiffany girls trudged each day to work and back again. Their whole world centered around the glass studio. And for Emilie, the "Four Seasons" window. She imagined the response it would receive when it debuted in Paris.

How Emilie longed to see the faces of the academicians when they saw her window. How she would love for them to know that she, Emilie Pascal, woman and daughter of an art forger, had been a part of such beauty.

But they would never know. No one would.

Of course, even if they were impressed, they would never admit it. They were trained not to show enthusiasm but to tear down. And she, regardless of their reaction, most certainly would never see Paris again. That part of her life was over. She hardly thought about it except sometimes at night when she pictured the dark waters of the Seine and the loneliness her mother must feel with even her daughter gone from her.

Then she would turn over and dream of the future, which she couldn't see past the next panel. Inevitably, her mind would slip into images of the Vulcan glassmaker, and she'd nestle down in the covers and pretend she wasn't alone.

Only at the workshop could she lose herself in work. Each day sped by so quickly that Emilie couldn't see how they would ever finish in time.

Mrs. Driscoll seemed to be everywhere at once, overseeing the fancy goods work at the back of the room. Hurrying along the finishing of lamps and fire screens along the far wall, all the decorative items that would be sold in the showroom as well as ones intended to fill out the rooms of other decorative arts exhibitions at the world's fair.

In between her rounds, she would disappear with Miss Gouvy into her office where Emilie was certain she must be working on her dragonfly lamp. And Emilie confessed to being curious as to how it would turn out.

Even Grace seemed tired and distracted. Of course, she was going out more nights now that she had Charlie to brief her on the news events in advance. Emilie didn't see how she could be on her feet all day and then again all evening, dragging in just before eleven several nights a week.

Twice Emilie had to let her in the kitchen window.

"You're going to make yourself sick," Emilie said one night as Grace sat at the kitchen table shivering and wolfing down hot soup that Mrs. B had left in the oven for her.

"Well, what do you suggest?"

Emilie shrugged. "I don't know. You can't quit Mr. Tiffany. For one thing you can't make enough money at the newspaper. Even if you'd rather be there."

"I could if I were a man."

"But you're not. You could do anything you set your mind to if you were a man. The point is until women change that, we won't be able to do it. Even working at the glass company is because of Mr. Tiffany."

"Another man," Grace said and slurped soup.

"But at least we're doing good work and get paid well."

"It isn't the same. I mean the work is okay, but it's just work. I started on Miss Northrop's 'Magnolia' window today. The design is beautiful. I'm sure the window will be beautiful, but it doesn't change anything."

"Sure it does. It brings joy to others."

"Some rich person will probably buy it, and then only their family will see it."

"True, I guess. But we're bringing nature and serenity and inspiration to lots of people."

"What about you, Emilie? Are you really content to cut glass for someone else's ideas, even someone as insightful as Mr. Tiffany or Miss Northrop?"

"I have to be," Emilie said.

Grace looked up from her soup. "Why?"

"Just because. Now finish up and let's get to bed. We have a long day ahead of us."

"I know. You shouldn't have waited up for me."

"I don't mind," Emilie said. *That's what friends do.*

THEY FINISHED THE "Autumn" panel the day before Thanksgiving. And since Mr. Tiffany had been so busy making arrangements for his daughter's upcoming wedding, which kept him and Mrs. Driscoll from finishing the glass selection for the "Winter" panel, Mrs. Driscoll let the girls go home an hour early. They would get the whole day off tomorrow.

But even the thought of a holiday couldn't spur them to walk faster. They were all dragging, too tired even to fight the wind that cut through winter coats, and in Emilie's case, her spring coat, wrapped with a thick woolen shawl that Mrs. B had loaned her to ward off the cold.

Emilie longed for her winter coat. She didn't know why it was taking so long for her trunk to arrive.

"We should have taken the trolley," Dora complained.

"It wouldn't be any warmer," Grace told her. "And you'd be out a nickel to boot."

"Maybe Mrs. B will have some hot cider waiting for us," Dora said.

"I want hot cider," Maggie echoed.

"We'll keep our fingers crossed," Lotte said and bustled them both ahead of her.

Mrs. B met them at the door. "Good news, Emilie. Your trunk has arrived. I had them put it up in your room."

Emilie had been expecting it, but she wasn't prepared for the tumult of relief and dread that she felt at the announcement.

She couldn't really remember what was in the trunk. She'd already purchased a new shirtwaist and a third skirt. She really didn't have need of visiting dresses, evening dresses, or any of the other things she suspected were in the trunk. Except for her winter coat, and perhaps some underthings. She would just peek in and take what was absolutely necessary. She wasn't ready to let whatever else might be lurking there invade her new life.

"Was there a charge? What do I owe you?"

"I gave the two men ten cents each. The rest had been taken care of."

Marie and Jean had refused to take money before Emilie had left. She would need all her money. It would be their gift to her, so she wouldn't forget them.

But she had . . . forgotten them—or at least pushed them to the back of her mind and heart. There was no place for them here, and she would never go back to them.

She reached in her purse and handed Mrs. B twenty cents.

"Are you going to unpack it now?" Dora asked. "Did you bring any ball gowns?"

"Ball gowns? What would I do with ball gowns?" Emilie would just have to make sure Dora never saw the one gown she had, in a moment of optimism, stuck at the very bottom. It was probably wrinkled beyond repair by now.

"I want to see a ball gown," Maggie said, clapping her hands.

"Girls, leave Emilie to unpack in peace. I made hot cider. Come into the parlor and I'll have Nessa and Jane bring it out. And tomorrow we will have a feast."

Emilie stood where she was. Torn. Should she rush up and take what she needed while everyone was downstairs? But the thought of hot cider was very tempting. Cider won. She shed her coat and shawl and followed the others into the parlor where the two seamstresses were already seated, reading their magazines.

The cider was steaming, spicy and sweet, and Emilie enjoyed it in spite of her suddenly pounding heart. While the others crowded around the punch bowl for a second cup, she quietly slipped away to face her past.

But when she reached her room and saw the trunk sitting there in the center of the room, she stumbled back as all the horror of those last few days in Paris came roaring back at her. As if her trunk were a Pandora's box brought to ruin her future. She couldn't even touch it. It seemed to be alive, with everything she feared, and loved, and hated, and wanted to remember and forget pulsing to get out.

She leaned over and shoved it against the wall. It took all her might. But denial gave her strength.

It was with trembling fingers that she extracted the key from her bag and dropped to her knees in front of the trunk. It took several attempts to find the keyhole and the clasp popped open. Slowly she lifted the lid. The top tray was filled with paper, oil paints, and brushes.

Emilie removed the tray from the trunk. Then she saw it, the rolled-up piece of art paper she'd snatched from the fire. She'd tied it with a ribbon and hid it—and treasured it for six long years.

Tonight she pulled it open, the paper unrolled just a bit, its charred corner brittle to the touch. Carefully, she stretched it out just as the door opened.

She let go and the paper rolled in on itself.

"Oh, I'm sorry," Grace said. "I didn't know you were unpacking. Let me just climb over to my desk and get out of your way."

Emilie grabbed the top and slammed it closed.

"Emilie, what is the matter?"

"Nothing. Nothing at all. It's just there's no room for any of my things and no room for the trunk. I'll ask Nessa and Jane to take it to the basement."

She had put the key down when she opened the trunk and now she couldn't find it. Her fingers groped along the floor and in the folds of her skirt.

Grace didn't move. "If it's space in the closet you're worried about, we'll make room. Why don't I help you unpack, and we'll see what can be folded and what needs to be hung."

"There's nothing important in there. Nothing I really need."

"Not even a winter coat?"

Emilie shrugged; she was suddenly so tired of trying to sever her past. Why wouldn't it just go away? Why couldn't she at least get her clothes out without unleashing the ghosts that haunted her? When would she be able to look forward to holidays and young men and hot apple cider without always fearing they would be snatched away before they became hers?

Because she would never be free as long as she let it control her.

"I know you value your privacy, and I don't want to pry," Grace said, coming to sit at the end of the bed near the trunk. "But if you ever want to talk about it."

Oh, how Emilie wanted to talk about it, bare her soul to someone, Grace maybe, and she wouldn't feel so alone. "You would despise me."

"I trusted you with my story, Emilie; won't you trust me with yours?"

Emilie felt the tears seep into her eyes and she knew the time had come. She could trust Grace, surely she could trust her. "My father is an art forger."

Grace's eyes opened a little wider and she blinked, but that was all the reaction she showed, and Emilie blessed her for it. She knew Grace's fairness might soon turn to distrust.

"He was a portrait painter, a decent one, but he spent more than he made and not on his family. After professing his love to my mother, he seemed to resent that she had accepted it." Emilie slumped against the trunk, its hard metal edges digging into her back.

"It was always feast or famine with him, and when he was broke—or drunk—he got mean. My mother protected me from him, but it wore her down, sucked the life out of her, and one day, she just gave up."

"She left you?"

"She . . . she drowned herself in the Seine."

Grace slapped her hand over her mouth, but it was too late. Emilie had seen her horror that a mother could leave her child.

"Don't judge her. She'd taken more than she could bear. He drove her to it. I hate him."

"Where is he?"

"I don't know."

"And the woman in the sketch that you so hastily hid away. Is that her?"

Emilie turned and opened the lid enough to pull out the sketch. Stretched it out so Grace could see. "I saved it from the fire." Seeing Grace's questioning expression, she said, "He was burning all her things."

Grace slipped off the bed and onto the floor next to Emilie and held up one corner of the sketch.

Emilie traced her finger down the ragged charred edge of paper. "This is all I have of her."

She took a shuddering breath. "That kind of passion kills everything around it. I was twelve, he was crazed. We sometimes lived in splendor and sometimes in squalor and I never knew from one day to the next what I would be coming home to. Home." Emilie spit out the word. "We had no real home—ever."

And now that she'd started, it all flooded out. The deceptions, the fraud, the beatings, the women and the late-night carousing when he dragged her along and she practiced the language of her mother, sitting in a corner or under the stairs among the fumes of alcohol and sex. How he cheated patrons of the arts. How she had to finish the portraits when he was too drunk or too busy with his forgeries to complete. It all came out. His disgrace, how she was shunned from Paris art circles and the Académie where she studied.

All of it poured into Grace's unsuspecting ears. "They came to arrest him. I knew they would be glad to arrest me in his stead."

"But you've done nothing wrong," said Grace.

"It doesn't matter. Once the Académie turns against you, your career is ended. No one will trust you, not even the police. My father was guilty, but he disappeared before his arrest. I had no choice but to disappear also. They would have ruined my life, and they may still, if I ever go back. They are vindictive at the best of times; people in power often are, even artists. And if you are a woman who desires to paint, they are particularly cruel."

"Well, no matter," Grace said. "Your secret is safe with me. Truly. Now, let's unpack your clothes and tomorrow we will enjoy Mrs. B's Thanksgiving feast. And on Friday we will go back to work as if nothing has changed, because for me, it hasn't."

BUT THINGS HAD changed for Emilie, and when she and Grace went downstairs the next day for Mrs. B's Thanksgiving feast, she felt the first stirring of freedom—and hope that the bonds of her past had loosened just a bit. And that she might have a future worth living before her.

It was her first Thanksgiving and she wasn't even sure of the reason they were feasting, but feast they did. Mrs. B had outdone herself. Tomato soup served alongside a relish of celery, pickles, and olives. This was followed by roast turkey with a stuffing of oysters. Jellied cranberries that were tart and sweet at the same time. Peas and carrots in cream sauce and Mrs. B's own handmade rolls. All this was followed by minced pie with cream.

The whole dinner took an hour and was marred only by Maggie stuffing herself on so much pie that she had to run from the room to be totally sick in the kitchen.

And Lotte, looking resigned, apologized and followed her out.

There was a moment of quiet commiseration, before their attention was drawn to tiny glasses of anise-flavored digestif, which they sipped to great satisfaction before retiring to the parlor to sigh and try not to think about the cold walk to work the next morning.

Chapter 17

When Emilie stepped out of the boardinghouse on the morning after Thanksgiving, wearing her heavy coat and hat, it seemed that overnight the world had turned from autumn into winter. Even the air felt different. The crispness of November was suddenly cold and damp. The gusts of wind no longer sent leaves scurrying.

Now the trees were bare. The people they passed, heads ducked against the weather, seemed more in a hurry than they had the week before.

It was the holiday season; the windows in the stores they passed had suddenly become cornucopias of wares, buoyed by sprigs of holly and red berries and mistletoe.

"Oh look," Dora exclaimed, "Perkins has ice skates in the window."

"A little premature if you ask me." Grace punctuated the statement with a yawn.

"Don't be such an old spoilsport. As soon as the pond in Central Park freezes over we'll all go."

The others huddled deeper in their coats and plodded ahead.

"Well, Maggie and I will go skating, won't we?"

"I want to go skating," Maggie said, enthusiastically.

Lotte pulled at Maggie's sleeve, urging her to walk faster. "Maggie, you don't know how to skate."

"She can learn," Dora said, undaunted. "I learned to ice-skate. And I'd never even seen snow before I moved up here. Did you ice-skate in Paris, Emilie?"

Emilie shook her head. She had ice-skated but it had been years before and felt like it belonged to someone else's life.

"I like your coat. It's *très chic*."

"It's very warm," Emilie said, trying not to encourage more talk of Paris. Paris, which she had truly loved, now felt like an albatross. Her life belonged here.

"Definitely winter," Grace groused as they were hit by a gust of frigid wind as they hurried the last block to Twenty-Fifth Street.

They met several other Tiffany girls all piling through the doors to the glassworks building. Everyone seemed to have benefited from the day off, and they laughed and compared their Thanksgiving feasts on the elevator ride upstairs.

They stepped off the elevator to warmth and they all breathed sighs of comfort.

"Mr. Tiffany always makes sure we are comfortable," Lotte explained to Emilie.

"Sure he does," agreed Dora. "Since cold fingers are clumsy and slow and apt to drop things."

"Oh, Dora, you have a saucy answer to everything," Lotte said with disgust. "We are lucky to have such good working conditions. Many don't."

"Well, if we had an ounce of sense, we'd find suitable husbands and we wouldn't have to work at all," Dora said and marched off to her worktable.

Emilie had to agree a bit with Lotte. Mr. Tiffany was a good businessman as well as an artist. At least he knew to hire people who could run his business and act so that his ideas were well executed. But she also chose to think that it was because beneath the bluster, and the preening and the short temper, he was kind. He could certainly be annoying and overbearing, but she truly believed his spirit was pure.

The studio had been transformed on their day off. The curtains had been pulled back to make fewer partitions, completely exposing the windows to make best of the winter light.

The "Autumn" panel was gone and in its place was a new easel with the cartoon of "Winter" waiting to be traced and filled with glass.

Already, a daunting amount of sheet glass was stacked at Emilie's worktable ready to be cut and positioned.

She had no time to worry about how the men were handling "Autumn"; they had removed it without her being there. And while she felt a pang of annoyance and hurt, she also felt a release that she was accepting her place in the vast world that was Mr. Tiffany's.

Two windows down from the "Winter" easel, Lotte and Miss Zevesky worked in tandem on the "Four Seasons" border panels, comparing measurements and colors as they went.

In the window next to Emilie's, Grace stood before Miss Northrop's "Magnolia." Miss Northrop stayed beside her, earnestly giving directions.

All around her, the girls had taken their places and picked up work they'd left two days before as if they'd never stopped.

A creative human engine.

Emilie turned back to her own work. She had the watercolor design displayed on a small easel. The selected glass was stacked according to shade and tint. But for a while, she just stood before her rectangular pane of glass, imagining.

She was looking forward to "Winter," as it was the furthest yet from realistic representation that she'd seen in the studio. In a way, more impressionistic, and yet more than impressions. Almost as if the artist expected the viewer to create the visual from the essence.

Oh, yes, she was very excited about this panel. And just a little nervous.

Grace listened to Miss Northrop explain her vision for the "Magnolia" window. It wasn't really necessary. Miss Northrop's meticulous watercolor rendering was perfectly clear. And since she had picked out the glass herself, Grace had no doubt that it would be well thought out before Grace ever placed a piece of glass.

Glass cutting was the least favorite of Grace's duties at the Tiffany studio and she wasn't called on to do it very often. Her talent as a cartoonist kept her in projects constantly. But it seemed as soon as Mrs. Driscoll hired more cutters and selectors, more left to get married. She could never catch up.

Grace didn't envy Mrs. Driscoll. She was constantly being pulled in all directions, while trying to run an efficient shop and create her own designs. Lately she and Miss Gouvy had been secreting themselves in Mrs. Driscoll's office, and word had it that she was hurriedly completing a new lamp for the Paris Exposition.

"And this cream glass highlighted by the pearl pink should be plated with . . ." Miss Northrop reached past Grace to choose a piece of green.

Grace smothered a yawn. She wasn't bored listening to Miss Northrop's directions. She was just tired. She really didn't know how long she could manage full-time employment in two professions. But she couldn't see a way out. Even though she was drawing cartoons almost exclusively for the *Sun*, she knew her tenure there was tenuous. Safe as long as they didn't find out who she really was.

Charlie said that she already had a following. "And not just with readers," he expanded. "Just the other day, the guys in the newsroom agreed. 'This G. L. Griffith has a sharp wit.' That's what they were saying. And that you make an article come alive. And they're about the hardest nuts to crack you can find."

His eyes had grown soft then. Alarmingly so. "My articles are better because of you—your cartoons," he finished gruffly. Then they'd started talking about something else.

But Grace still felt unsettled every time she thought of that one momentary look. Unsettled, and mortified at the shiver of pleasure that ran through her, one that had nothing to do with cartoons, but everything to do with Charlie Murray.

"So that the overall effect is one of . . ." Miss Northrop had turned to look at her. What had she been saying? The subtle shift of color at the bottom of the spill of magnolias. "Yes, Miss Northrop."

"I know you understand and you'll do an excellent job. Your cartoons are always impeccable. I'm sure your glasswork will be, too."

Grace smiled. Would Miss Northrop be so effusive over Grace's "real" cartoons? What would she think if she knew Grace longed to be not here, but out on the street following the latest story? She knew she was blessed to have a well-paying, safe job. But her heart belonged to another profession. And maybe just a tiny bit to Charlie Murray.

"I will give it my most rapt attention," Grace assured her, though she longed to say, *I am an artist, too. My cartoons may not stand forever in great mansions or churches or museums, but I reach thousands of people every day.*

I am G. L. Griffith. I am a political cartoonist. I am a woman.

But that would be professional suicide.

Sometimes, life was really unfair.

CLARA FINALLY ESCAPED into her office where Alice was sitting at her desk arranging mosaic tesserae on a wax mold.

"This is beautiful," Alice said.

"That was my intention," Clara said, frowning at the lamp base.

"Though quite labor-intensive," Alice continued. "I've been at this for two hours and at this rate will have several hours to go."

"I know that, too, but this will be my pièce de résistance. After that, they can codify the shades and add slender brass bases to accommodate electric light. Plus I drew up a few designs that assuaged the powers that be." She reached over to her notebook and took out several pages that she spread before Alice.

"Vanity sets, inkwells, hair combs . . . I love those. You were always a persuasive person, Clara, even when we were students."

"Just organized and . . . determined."

"Well, they can't complain about these. They'll sell faster than we can make them. And if you ask me, the original will fetch a very nice price. They might even make a profit on it."

"I'm hoping so, but more than that, I'm hoping that—"

"It will be finished in time to send to Paris," Alice finished for her. "It will be. You had to rush on the one that was sent to the Grafton Gallery and we got it done. Now don't be anxious."

"You are so wise, my friend."

"I try."

"And talented and I don't know what I would do without you."

"Nor I you."

And they settled down to work in companionable, creative silence.

CHRISTMAS WAS COMING and chatter sprang up throughout the day about plans for the holidays. Wish lists for presents, and suggestions for gifts for others.

Everyone entered into the spirit of things, even those who knew their Christmas would be meager. Emilie knew that at least two of the girls were the sole support of their families; others contributed to a family much larger than they could support.

A few would visit relatives in the suburbs or country for the holiday. Dora had been invited to visit her aunt and uncle in New Jersey. Grace, Emilie knew, had been invited home to Connecticut but had begged off, saying she was too tired to travel.

And Emilie believed her. Well, they would have a quiet holiday at Mrs. B's. Lotte and Maggie, having no relatives, would be there along with Miss Vanderheusen and Miss Burns. Pine boughs and red ribbons had already appeared on the mantel and above the archway to the foyer.

Emilie hadn't celebrated a family Christmas in many years, but she remembered her mother, dressed in a festive gown, sitting with her in front of the fire, or in better years, in the drawing rooms of rich patrons, their Christmas trees reaching to the ceiling, filled with shining ornaments and candles.

She looked forward to the two days off. But she didn't know how to feel about Christmas. Would they give each other presents? Little tidbits of their affection? Maybe the Tiffany girls could pool their pennies and buy something nice for Mrs. B. But what about Mrs. Driscoll? The expenses began to add up and the list seemed to grow and grow.

Maybe she would just forget about Christmas. Let others celebrate.

"But you can't forget about Christmas," Dora said one day as she placed a *W* at the bottom of the "Winter" easel. "We'll have a gay time Christmas Eve, with crackers and presents and carols. And we'll decorate the tree. It's great fun." Her brow clouded. "Though it would be more fun if there were men, or a fiancé or something." She sighed. "Maybe Grace's—I mean, Miss Griffith's—Charlie will be invited."

"He's not my Charlie," Grace called back. "And I'll thank you not to start any gossip."

Dora rolled her eyes and added the *I* of winter. "What's Paris like at Christmas, Emilie? It must be so beautiful."

It should have been. For most people Christmas consisted of dinners and parties that lasted until dawn. At which point men and women went home in time to meet their groggy-eyed children excited to see what Père Noël had left for them.

After Emilie's mother died, all semblance of celebration was snuffed out of Emilie's life. Her father would stay out late and when he did come home, he fell into bed and stayed there for most of the day, sometimes into the next. Sometimes he'd remembered to get her a present and she opened it alone over coffee she had made for herself. When she got older, she went out to meet friends, friends who lived on the edge of society, artistic friends, uninhibited friends, and Emilie tried to enjoy their company.

She never did and would soon find her way to the Pont des Arts and, shivering in the damp cold air, she would spend the day with her mother. Or at least the last memory of her mother.

"You're absolutely right," Emilie said. "We'll have a wonderful Christmas at Mrs. B's."

THE FIRST WEEK of December sped by. Mr. Tiffany was in and out at all hours, but he rarely stayed. Just walked from project to project nodding or shaking his head, sharing a quick word with Mrs. Driscoll, who seemed to catch his restless energy, which would throw them all into a case of nerves until he left and the rhythm of the studio took over once again.

One day he stood before the "Winter" easel so long without

speaking that Emilie had to force herself not to turn around and just ask him outright what the problem was.

"The cycle of life, Miss Pascal. Of all the seasons, winter is the key, both the beginning and the end. From the death of one is born the new. People must have nature to thrive, Miss Pascal, and when they can't go to it, they have Louis Tiffany. This . . ." He picked up a piece glass from the waiting stack. "See how the blue flows through it? Like an underground stream, unseen but creating life wherever it flows.

"Wherever it goes . . ." He returned the glass to the worktable, ran one finger along the vein of cobalt. "I trust you to find the nature in this glass, Miss Pascal."

Emilie pulled her eyes from his finger as it caressed the glass and looked directly at him.

Did he want her to reply? He seemed so deeply involved in his own thoughts that she was afraid to interrupt.

Fortunately, Mrs. Driscoll arrived to tell him that Mr. Belknap wished to speak to him in the business office, and he strode away, swinging his cane between taps as if brushing imaginary enemies from his path.

"Is he displeased?" Emilie ventured when Mrs. Driscoll continued to look at the easel.

"No, Miss Pascal. Quite the contrary. He's just vexed by the constant interruptions. Between the regular business and the Paris Expo he has to oversee his daughter's wedding, and the Christmas ball for which he's the guest of honor. He wants to create art, but life calls him away. It makes him . . . restive."

His daughter? No one ever talked about his family and Emilie hadn't thought to ask. Mr. Tiffany was always wrapped up with business concerns, attending gallery openings, accepting awards, attending society and art functions of all kinds.

To her, Mr. Tiffany was a being unto himself. And she just as soon he stayed that way. Sometimes a pedestal, even a lonely one, was better than being merely a man with family annoyances.

Mrs. Driscoll turned back to peruse the "Winter" panel, dismissing further conversation on the wedding. "Clever how it manages to bring a little winter inside," she said, "but without the discomfort." And she moved on to study the border panels.

More than clever, Emilie thought. It was inspired. This morning she had finished a section near the top. A branch of pine needles against a winter sky. Mr. Tiffany had chosen a type of glass called twig glass. The technique of spreading slivers of a dark glass over molten blue and green created an effect that looked just like pine needles.

No, Emilie thought. It didn't "look like"; it "became" pine needles. Probably unnoticed by the untrained eye unless they looked very closely. But she doubted many people took the time to study the details that made the whole. Critics maybe, but they rarely appreciated art in the visceral way that "Winter" elicited. It couldn't be explained. It was something that disappeared the moment you tried to define it and returned as soon as you stopped.

She reached for a sheet striated with orange and red and white. It reminded her of Amon Bronsky bent over the furnace, shaping the molten glass with deft hands. She ran her finger along the place where orange melted into red and felt a connection so powerful that she yanked her finger away.

Art could be dangerous, but it also could bring peace. Emilie longed for peace. She reached for the opalescent white streaked with cobalt. Snow. Cool. Peace.

One afternoon, the snow came for real, drifting lightly down behind the "Winter" and "Magnolia" easels as if they had created their own backdrops.

"It's so beautiful," Dora drawled, her southern accent drawn out in appreciation.

Lotte just sighed.

Grace barely looked up, her brow furrowed, her body tense; either she was having a hard time getting a cut right or she had something on her mind.

Emilie just smiled inside. Another season between herself and her old life. Sometimes, like now, watching the snow through the wide window, she could believe that she had always been here, and that other Emilie, the frightened heartsick Emilie, had never existed at all.

"Chestnuts," said someone from across the room. "I love hot chestnuts in the snow."

"Hot cocoa," said another of the girls, looking up over the edge of her decorative clock.

"Maple syrup frozen in the snow," said Miss Johnson, who had only arrived in the city two months before from Maine.

"Christmas," piped up Maggie, hugging her broom.

"Christmas," they all agreed.

And as everyone's thoughts turned to Christmas, Mrs. Driscoll appeared in the doorway and asked to see Grace and Emilie in her office.

Her timing was unfortunate, and the girls all looked from their inward imaginings to the two objects of Mrs. Driscoll's summons.

Emilie and Grace barely looked at each other before putting down their tools and walking shoulder to shoulder down the aisle between the worktables toward Mrs. Driscoll's office. Emilie could feel everyone's eyes upon them. Could they possibly be in trouble?

"What do you think she wants?" Emilie ventured as they got nearer.

Grace just shook her head. "You didn't tell her anything, did you?"

"No, did you?"

"I said I wouldn't."

"So did I," Emilie reminded her.

Grace knocked on the door. "Maybe she wants to give us a raise."

That made them both smile.

"Well," said Mrs. Driscoll when they stepped into the little office. A piece of linen had been thrown over an object that sat on her desk. It was just the shape and size her dragonfly lamp would be. Was she going to show them her latest creation?

"I have the delightful task of informing you that you have been chosen to attend the Arts Society Christmas Ball next week as one of the representatives of Tiffany Glass and Decorating Company. It's a yearly affair, and this year Mr. Tiffany is the guest of honor.

"They always invite several of the Tiffany artisans to attend. This year in addition to myself, Miss Gouvy, Miss Northrop, the two Palmié sisters, and the two of you have been invited to join us. You are both well-spoken and well-mannered and I'm certain will be shining examples of the Tiffany company."

They had both stood stock-still for this pronouncement that Mrs. Driscoll delivered in a rather wooden, memorized way. Now she let out a sigh. "I'm thrilled that Mr. Tiffany chose you to attend. You'll do us proud. Now, first order of business . . . Do you have ball gowns?"

Emilie felt Grace slump with relief. The two of them exchanged looks.

"I have last year's gown," Grace said. "I haven't bothered to have another made."

"Perhaps someone can spruce it up a bit. No one expects you, or any of us, to be at the height of fashion, just simple and tasteful will do."

"I can manage that," Grace said, and they both looked at Emilie.

Emilie just nodded.

"If it's difficult . . ."

"I will— Yes, I have something to wear."

"Good, good." Mrs. Driscoll gave them the date and the time. "You will come straight to me when you arrive. You'll be expected to stay close by at the beginning of the evening, and answer any questions the other guests may have, but then you may enjoy the rest of the ball as you would any ball. Just not too much enjoyment, if you understand what I mean."

They both nodded.

Mrs. Driscoll handed them each an invitation, scrolled in a fancy copperplate, and dismissed them back to work.

"Just like Cinderella," Grace quipped on their way back to their respective easels. "*Do* you have a gown?"

"Yes," said Emilie.

Grace sighed. "Mine's at least two years out of fashion and nothing to compare with the fashion that will be there that night. I don't even know why I've kept it. We may look like the poor country church mice."

"Ah, the folktale, yes."

"Unless you have something extravagantly Parisian in that trunk of yours . . ."

"Actually, I do."

Chapter 18

Word spread quickly that Grace and Emilie had been chosen to represent the women's division at the Arts Society Christmas Ball.

"I don't know why they never choose me to go to those special functions," Dora griped as they tramped home from work. "And the Christmas ball of all of them. Emilie's only been here for a few months."

"You're welcome to go in my place," Grace said, pulling her scarf close against the biting cold.

"Like that will ever happen," Dora said and stomped off ahead of the others.

"I want to go, too," Maggie added and stomped off after her.

"I hope this isn't going to cause strife at the boardinghouse," Emilie said.

"Just ignore them. It's a duty. Trying to drink punch with one hand while holding a plate of sandwiches with the other and carrying on ladylike conversation without spilling anything on your white gloves." Grace shivered. "Spare me."

"How is your dancing?" Emilie asked.

"Passable, but we won't be expected to dance, just stand by the artwork, looking artistic but demure, and accepting compliments for Mr. Tiffany so he doesn't have to stand there."

"Oh," said Emilie, and she was surprised at her disappointment. She was fond of dancing.

That night after dinner the two of them went upstairs and while Grace pulled a case out from under her bed, Emilie opened her trunk once again.

Her ball gown lay on the very bottom wrapped in several layers of tissue. She hadn't intended to take it out ever. She didn't know why she had decided to bring it. Perhaps as a memory of better times? A time when the Pascals were accepted, even courted, by society and she was tolerated at the Académie.

Oh, how quickly one can fall from the heights.

She glanced over at her roommate, who had retrieved an off-white taffeta gown and was clutching it tightly to her chest.

"Hold it up."

Grace frowned, but stretched the gown across her shoulders.

There was a knock at the door, followed by the entrance of Dora, Lotte, and Maggie.

"They wanted to see," Lotte explained.

"Good, maybe you have some ideas." Emilie pointed to Grace's gown.

"Oh dear," said Dora, looking disheartened.

Grace tossed the dress on her bed. "That's it. I'll just tell Mrs. Driscoll I can't attend and to invite someone else."

"You can't do that," Dora exclaimed. "She'd probably ask that horrid Miss Kruger. What have you got, Emilie?"

Emilie glanced at her trunk.

"Oh, let's see." Dora didn't wait but stepped over to the trunk and lifted out the gown, letting the tissue fall away.

There was a gasp from the others.

It was a shock even for Emilie; she had forgotten what a rich color of burgundy it was. A fine silk that had been expensive even in a time when they were flush. Her father liked her to dress well. It spoke to his success.

"Oh my lord, it really is a Paris ball gown." Dora held it up and twirled around. The burnished gold of the trim flashed in the lamplight. "It's exquisite—"

"But too splendid for a Tiffany girl," Lotte pointed out.

"True," Dora said.

"So neither of us will go," Emilie said. The last thing she wanted was to call attention to herself.

"You both have to go," Dora said. Lotte and Maggie nodded vigorously behind her.

"Maybe Miss Vanderheusen and Miss Burns would be willing to help make both of them more suitable," Lotte suggested.

"The middle-aged ladies?" Dora asked.

"Yes, they're both professional seamstresses. I'm sure they will be glad to help."

THE SEAMSTRESSES WERE more than happy to oblige and on Saturday afternoon, they all retired to the parlor where Emilie and Grace were prodded and poked and draped and tucked as the old dresses were transformed into new.

"They're going to be wonderful," Dora assured them, as she helped Grace out of her gown. "But, Grace, you still don't even have any proper dancing shoes."

"Maybe no one will notice my feet," Grace said hopefully. "Besides, I don't intend to dance."

"We'll think of something."

"Well, it will have to be later," Grace said. "Right now, I have to meet Charlie downtown."

"What is it this time?" asked Emilie as they made their way back upstairs.

"Jacob Riis is speaking before the Housing Commission on the conditions in tenements. Gotta run."

By the time Grace reached the municipal building, she was quite late, and she had to push her way through a line of policemen and the small group of protesters milling around the patch of grass outside.

She didn't see Charlie anywhere. The two of them had taken to meeting and coordinating their coverage of events. It had been at the suggestion of Charlie's editor, who called his writing and her illustrations a one-two punch to the other dailies.

He must have already gone inside.

Grace slung the strap of her sketch bag over her shoulder and held it close as she pushed through the crowd.

Inside the air was close, the number of bodies and the heat turning the air ripe and fetid.

A speaker, tall, thin, and dressed in a severe black suit, droned from the stage; his voice rose and fell with each sentence, eliciting a few cheers and shouts of derision. And demands that he sit down.

The man sat as Grace reached the other side and took a moment to catch her breath and at last caught sight of Charlie's copper hair up ahead.

He motioned to her and she pushed her way the last few feet and gratefully slid into the chair beside him.

"Where have you been?"

"Sorry," she said, unbuttoning her coat and pushing it off her shoulders. "I was busy deciding on frills and furbelows."

"What?" His blank look was comical.

It made her smile. "I'll tell you later."

"Well, shake a leg. Riis is up next. Word on the street is there's going to be a march afterward."

"Riis is leading it?"

"No. Hotheads. We'll get some initial impressions and then get the hell out before they start busting heads."

"I can always trust you to have a plan."

"I value my head more than you seem to value yours."

Grace rolled her eyes. "Will you stop bringing that up? I was a novice when I went to the sweatshop strike. I can take care of myself now."

"Yeah, you and your frills and furbelows." His eyes slid over her day dress. He raised one eyebrow and turned back to the next speaker.

Grace looked down at her dress. It was perfectly nice, wool tweed in heather colors, with an inset of simple white pleats accented by a cameo pin at the neck and corded in brown at the waist, collar, and cuffs.

And for the first time ever, she wondered what Charlie thought of the way she dressed. Or the way she looked. Did he—

She shoved that speculation aside, as Jacob Riis got up to speak. She quickly got out her notebook and pencil and focused her attention on the reason she was there.

Riis wasn't a dynamic-looking man. Wire-rimmed spectacles and a mustache that drooped to each side of his mouth gave him the look of being perpetually sad.

Considering what he had seen of how the other half of New Yorkers lived, it wasn't surprising.

His talk was accompanied by photographs projected on a screen. And what a talk; his voice never rose above normal, he didn't pound his fist or admonish the crowd. Just described the horrors of life in the tenements while photographs of starving children, and men sleeping huddled on the floor of a squalid building, appeared and disappeared in a changing slide show. "For five cents, a man may sleep on the floor. The men on the shelf above them, they pay seven cents. There is no true rest confined as they are.

"But you ask, 'What does that have to do with us?'

"And I answer." He paused. "Everything."

Grace drew quickly, he was an easy subject. She scanned the room in search of reactions, but she found mainly complacence.

Charlie seemed to have had enough, too. He nodded toward the exit door, then eased out of his seat. Grace was all too ready to follow him. Maybe there was a good restaurant nearby. She had missed lunch and now was missing dinner.

"Heard it before," Charlie said. "Worth a couple of columns. And a good illustration. You get something?"

Grace nodded. What she wanted was to see the tenements. That was where her real subject lay. Along with those wretched men huddled like so many rags on the floor.

"What do you say we finish up over some chow? There's a place right up the block, makes a decent borscht and latkes."

"Sounds delicious," Grace said, though she was only vaguely knowledgeable about what latkes were—or borscht for that matter.

They stopped a half block away, and Charlie guided her down three steps to a darkened doorway.

Grace glanced up at him.

He opened the door and light spilled out. It was quiet inside, small with only four tables, scrubbed cleaned. And only one of the tables was occupied, by two old men.

"Marta!" one of them called out and followed it with a string of words Grace thought might be Polish or German. Then he nodded to Charlie, frowned at Grace, and went back to eating with his silent companion.

Charlie seated Grace at a table away from the men, then sat across from her.

A short woman bustled in from the back, pushing a strand of gray hair from her forehead. "Ah, Charlie Murray. Haven't seen you lately."

She cut a look toward Grace, then back to Charlie.

"A colleague," Charlie said.

"Sure, sure," the woman who must be Marta said. "You hungry?"

"Starving," Charlie said.

Grace nodded her agreement.

And Marta turned around and left.

"How does she know what we want?" Grace whispered across the table.

"We want whatever she's cooking." His brow furrowed. "Is that okay with you?"

"Sure. I could eat a horse."

"I don't recommend it. They're very tough."

Grace laughed. She chose to assume it was a joke. With Charlie she didn't always know.

While they waited, Charlie worked over his notes and Grace came up with a depiction of Jacob Riis at the podium. It wasn't a very exciting depiction. She didn't even have a clear idea of what a tenement looked like really. Not from the inside anyway. If she did, she could have shown Riis driving the greedy landlords away. Like Jesus and the Pharisees. *Too many church windows*, she thought.

"I know," said Charlie, sighing and stretching back in his chair. "Not an exciting news night."

"But important," Grace said.

"Jake says there's going to be a big raid soon. He'll give me a heads-up as soon as they tell him."

"And you'll tell me."

He dipped his chin and considered Grace. He'd begun to grow on her. She'd actually grown fond of that bump in his nose. She waited for him to say okay, but when Charlie spoke, it was not at all what she expected.

"It might be dangerous. Actually there's no 'might' about it. It will be dangerous. People are desperate for decent places to live."

Marta came back carrying a heavy pot with two tin bowls balanced on the lid. She put it down on the table between them. "Don't touch. It's hot. I'll serve it."

Her accent was thick, but the affection came through.

"Plus this big galumph might spill it on your pretty dress." She lifted off the top and steam rose in a delicious curl that made Grace's mouth water.

Marta filled the bowls, then bustled away only to return with a loaf of heavy rye bread, before winking at Charlie and hurrying off again.

Across the room the two men continued to eat silently and slowly.

Grace took a sip. "It's delicious. What is it?"

"Bigos." Charlie said. "Don't ask for a further description. It has meat, vegetables. It tastes good. Everything Marta cooks tastes good."

The two old men grunted in tandem.

"See? Everyone agrees," Charlie said and took a bite.

Grace was stuffed when they left Marta's. She had handed over her drawing to Charlie to make the deadline and they caught the trolley uptown. Grace insisted that she didn't need an escort, but Charlie insisted on seeing her all the way home, even though they passed by the *Sun* on their way.

He walked her all the way to Mrs. B's door, where Grace

stopped him. "Charlie, I appreciate you seeing me home. And taking me to dinner. But remember, we're colleagues. You said so yourself. Equals . . . well, almost. And will be one day.

"I want to be where the action is. That's where I find dynamic subjects, not just people giving speeches. Some of my best work came from that night at the sweatshop strike, even if it didn't get used. I say the more of those, the better. Besides, it isn't your job to take care of me."

"I know," Charlie said, not sounding convinced. "That's what worries me."

"I don't understand."

"I know I don't need to take care of you, but more and more I find myself wanting to. Good night."

And before Grace could react, he turned and strode off down the dark street.

Chapter 19

The week flew by in a whirlwind of glass cutting, dress fittings, and searching for Maggie, who had taken to disappearing during work hours. Each time they found her wandering along one of the long hallways that connected the three buildings and the other workshops.

"I'm worried that her mind is failing," Lotte confided to Emilie and Grace. "What if . . ." She shook her head.

Emilie squeezed her arm. There wasn't much she could say. If Maggie got to where she couldn't function at work, Lotte would have to find someone or somewhere that could care for Maggie. But on Lotte's salary the possibilities were bleak.

By the evening of the ball, everyone was in a frenzy of excitement. Dora insisted on helping Emilie and Grace with their hair, and though Grace complained and made her go easy on the curls, even she looked pleased with the final outcome.

Grace squeezed her feet into a pair of Dora's evening shoes at the last minute. They were a size too small, and Grace insisted that she would ruin them by wearing them even for a minute. But Dora insisted.

Maggie pressed her favorite "ruby," one of the pieces of glass she collected, into Emilie's hand. "That way I'll be at the ball, too, like Dora's shoes. And Lotte must send something, too." She turned to her sister. "What will you send, Lotte?"

Lotte shrugged. "I don't . . . wait a minute." She hurried out the door and Dora returned to fussing with the gowns until Miss Burns shooed her away.

Lotte returned a few minutes later. "Here, Emilie, please take it." She stretched out her hand to reveal a thin lace-trimmed handkerchief. "My mother gave this to me."

Emilie's throat constricted. "Lotte, I couldn't. It's too precious."

"Please. She never went to a real ball. Maybe you'd take her with you tonight."

Grace shot Emilie a look that said, *Damned if you do, damned if you don't.*

"She'll keep it safe in her reticule," Mrs. B interjected. "It will be an honor, won't it, Emilie?"

"A very dear one," Emilie said. "Thank you, Lotte." She gave Lotte a quick hug then took the handkerchief and carefully folded it into her reticule, which she would now never put down even to eat.

Nessa announced the carriage a few minutes later and everyone accompanied the two girls downstairs, Grace already limping slightly from her shoes. Two dark capes appeared from the closet, certainly conjured by the three older ladies.

Just as they climbed into the carriage, a siren wailed in the distance. Grace stopped with her foot on the carriage step, her attention alert.

"Get in," Emilie said. "No news for you this evening, unless you find it on the dance floor."

The carriage took them north on Fourth Avenue, the same route they traversed on foot twice a day, but they drove straight past the Tiffany building without slowing down. It didn't stop until they reached Thirty-Fifth Street and pulled in front of the entrance of an Italian Renaissance edifice that rose five stories above the ground.

"My," Emilie said as the coachman helped her to the sidewalk. "It looks like Venice without the canals."

"It's someone's house," Grace said and jumped to the pavement, flinching a bit as her shoes hit the stone.

"It certainly appears to be. Is this the Arts Society building?"

"I have no idea. As long as it has lots of rooms and places to be a wallflower in solitude, I'll be content."

"I think five floors of rooms should be enough. But no wallflowers tonight. We have a function. To be knowledgeable artists."

"I know, but—" The rest of Grace's sentence was drowned out in the blare of several sirens all moving south. "Sounds like a big one," Grace said.

"You can read about it in the *Sun* tomorrow. You can't always be changing the world. Tonight your only responsibility is to represent Mr. Tiffany and to try to have a good time. Come on." Emilie nudged Grace into the pillared portico and up a set of stone steps.

The door was opened immediately by a liveried footman with a sprig of holly in his jacket pocket.

"Festive," said Grace as they stepped inside and let the maid take their cloaks.

It was a lovely wide foyer, wainscoted in dark wood with a wide stairway festooned with pine boughs and red roses. They were shown into a reception hall filled mainly with men in evening dress and a few women listening intently to the various conversations.

Emilie heard Grace sigh. "And no political comments."

Mr. Tiffany stood by the fireplace talking with several distinguished-looking men. Mrs. Driscoll, dressed in black taffeta, and Miss Northrop, in deep green velvet with a black-and-green-embroidered corset, stood to his left.

Grace and Emilie hesitated.

"They all look very formal," Grace said. "Should we say 'reporting for duty' and salute?"

"You do, and we'll fall out," Emilie said.

Grace frowned at Emilie. "You're enjoying this, aren't you?"

"I'm hoping to. Though maybe I shouldn't." In fact, what was she thinking? There would be art patrons here. People who were familiar with Paris. . . . With her father? Her foot stuttered and for a moment she thought about turning and leaving before even saying hello.

"Too late for second thoughts now," Grace said and nudged her through the archway.

CLARA SAW EMILIE and Grace enter the foyer, excused herself, and hurried toward them.

"Good evening, ladies," she said. "How lovely you look." And they did. Grace was tastefully dressed in ecru and blue, but Emilie quite took Clara's breath away. Her gown was cut in the French style in a deep wine-colored silk that might be considered too strong a color for a young woman. But worn by Emilie, it seemed the perfect choice, bringing out the delicacy of her features and the lushness of her hair.

The men parted as Clara steered the two young women toward them. Mr. Tiffany and Leland Bishop turned as one to watch them approach.

Mr. Tiffany broke into a large smile. Bishop stood stock-still like a storybook prince suddenly cast into an enchanted spell. He certainly looked the part, but it didn't prevent Clara from wanting to roll her eyes. Leland Bishop was much too sophisticated and worldly to be smitten by two pretty girls from a glass-cutting workshop.

Though at second glance, it wasn't both girls but Emilie Pascal who held the man enthralled.

But oh to be young and . . . Clara pulled herself together. When she'd been young, she'd lived in a midsize Ohio town, lucky enough to be raised by women who made it possible for her to aspire beyond her small prospects.

Now she was a successful artist, supporting herself by her work. And though she didn't arrest attention in the way Emilie Pascal did, she'd had a good life. An artistic life. A mostly happy, though short-lived, marriage. And there was the rub. Why couldn't she have all those things? Why must she, like so many people, be satisfied with one? And if one, which one? What would make her satisfied above all things? Fame? Artistic freedom? Love?

"Welcome, welcome," Mr. Tiffany said, breaking Clara's own spell. He took first Miss Griffith's hand, then Miss Pascal's.

Then turned to Bishop.

"This is Miss, um . . ."

"Griffith," Clara supplied. "One of our best copyists."

Leland nodded and briefly took Grace's hand. "A pleasure to meet you."

Grace smiled, then greeted Mr. Tiffany.

"And Miss Pascal," Mr. Tiffany said.

"But of course," Bishop said. "I believe we were almost introduced at the Tiffany building elevator not long ago." He arched his eyebrows, waiting patiently to take her hand in welcome, which she belatedly held out to him.

"Miss Pascal has recently joined us from Paris," Mr. Tiffany continued, beaming at the two girls.

The men were both like eager puppies, thought Clara, caught between amusement and perplexity. Not something one saw often in an evening party of art patrons. Every time Mr. Tiffany visited the studio he always stopped by Miss Pascal's station, but more times than not, they ended up "discussing vehemently" the choice of glass and the number of platings to be used. And as for Leland Bishop, she didn't begrudge him an evening of flirtation as long as it didn't go beyond the line.

Still, a sense of discomfort skittered through her. Really, she was becoming as bad as Alice, seeing ulterior motives in every gesture and mood.

And where *was* Alice? Clara glanced quickly around for her missing colleague. She would have liked Alice's opinion of the exchange, especially when she realized that Mr. Bishop was still holding Miss Pascal's hand. But Alice had managed to disappear into the crowd at the first opportunity.

"I believe Alice and the other girls are in the next room," Clara said. "I'm certain they would like to say hello."

Miss Pascal managed to slip her hand from Bishop's and made a hasty nod before both girls moved away.

"Beautiful." Mr. Tiffany practically sighed the word, watching as both girls seemed to glide across the carpet. Beside him Leland Bishop was silent but his eyes hadn't left Emilie Pascal since he'd let go of her hand.

"They are both lovely young women," Clara said. "And very talented and hardworking."

"You say she's from Paris? I don't doubt it, her gown definitely is. Pascal. I know a few Pascals. Who are her parents?"

Mr. Tiffany looked at Clara.

"I have no idea. She arrived one day in July with a portfolio and a carpetbag."

"She has an eye," Mr. Tiffany said.

"Dark as onyx fire," Leland agreed.

Mr. Tiffany burst into a loud guffaw. "Thank heavens you went into the gallery business, Lee. You'd never have made it as a poet."

"I don't think I've ever seen anyone so . . . Words escape me."

"Which is a good thing, no doubt. But I agree with the sentiment. She said my vases were like air creating color."

"Did she indeed?" Bishop said distractedly.

"She did. But that color she's wearing. I'll have to ask Nash if he can reproduce it in a drapery glass."

Clara, who had begun to worry about his possible infatuation, smothered a laugh.

Bishop didn't bother. "Leave it to you to see her in terms of glass and color and form." He sighed, quite a schoolboy's reaction, and it almost made Clara more sympathetic. But he was a grown man and she wasn't surprised when Mr. Tiffany said, "And you will leave her to me and my studio."

Bishop laughed then. "You sound like an overprotective papa. I have no intentions toward the girl . . . or the secrets to your glass," he added jocularly.

"Just so we understand each other."

Clara took the opportunity to slip away. She'd been rather amused watching the older man and younger man assert themselves over an even younger woman. She didn't believe either gentleman had any serious intentions toward the girl. But the glass was a different story altogether. There was extreme competition over access to the glass, and she doubted if Mr. Bishop was any different from the others. She just hoped that Emilie Pascal wouldn't somehow get caught in the middle.

EMILIE AND GRACE readily joined Miss Gouvy and the others by the punch bowl in the larger reception room. They were in what must normally be a large parlor, cleared for the additional guests with several settees and a few occasional chairs.

Beyond them the ballroom was already filled with people. Waiters passed across the opening carrying trays of champagne glasses just like the images in a flicker show.

"I always enjoy Christmas. It's one of my favorite holidays," Miss Gouvy said. "Though there is nothing quite like Christmas back home."

Emilie listened politely to the others discuss their plans for the holidays while she took in her surroundings. The walls were covered with paintings, and statuary stood in discreet niches around the room. One of Mr. Tiffany's or possibly Mrs. Driscoll's dandelion lamps sat on a round walnut table. Several favrile glass vases were safely exhibited in a tall curio case, lit from the inside. And out of harm's way, Emilie was glad to see.

And then her eyes came to rest on a long rectangular window, framed and spotlighted. It had to be one of Mr. Tiffany's but in a style she'd never seen in Paris or in the New York studio.

Emilie excused herself and walked over to take a closer look. From a distance it had seemed uniquely out of place. A simple, almost monochromatic palette of amber and gold scroll designs of blossoms and leaves twining and interlacing from a central pear-shaped orb . . . a vase or seedpod, perhaps.

It was hard to describe, for in the moments she'd been studying it, it had changed, become vibrant with movement.

"Remarkable, isn't it?"

She started. She hadn't heard Mr. Bishop come up behind her.

"I had the same reaction the first time I saw this, myself. The sense that it was a living organism."

Emilie looked at him in surprise.

He tilted his head toward the window. "It's an early work and I had a time convincing him to sell it to me. Can you imagine, he had it stored away in one of the dark corridors of the workshops. Almost as if he had forgotten it.

"But I snatched it from obscurity." He laughed. "He was not pleased. I don't know why. I bought it for a fantastic price."

In the ballroom, the orchestra began to play.

"Ah, a waltz. Will you do me the honor?"

Emilie took a startled step back.

"Please don't be alarmed. I know all the steps and am considered not too clumsy." His eyes twinkled and she had to tighten her lips not to laugh. "You do waltz?"

"Yes, but I—"

"I thought you might." He held out his hand.

"Mr. Bishop, I don't believe I was invited in order to dance."

"I asked Louis to invite you because I wanted to see you again." He presented his elbow. "Shall we?"

Emilie stood indecisive, longing to dance but not sure of her standing. But she couldn't refuse his arm, it would be impolite, and besides, the orchestra was playing a glorious waltz. She could only hope that the dance finished before Mrs. Driscoll or Mr. Tiffany saw her.

She knew what they would think. She was no naïf in society circles. A man who requested the presence of a working girl at his ball could not have honorable intentions. A young woman who acquiesced would cause herself instant ruin. Emilie had no intention of going down that road with Leland Bishop or anyone else.

Emilie nodded politely and took his arm. Before she could even lift up her train, he had taken her in his arms and they were swirling toward certain doom.

He was an excellent dancer, a natural facility she was sure. He tried none of those little squeezes or meaningful looks that indicated he was after anything more than a few minutes of waltzing.

She swallowed hard, pushing the thought away. Surely it was merely her past reacting. He was a perfectly well-mannered, handsome young man, not to mention exceedingly rich. And she refused to let her fear destroy her enjoyment.

Emilie gave in to the music and in to her partner's dexterity, and halfway round the room she forgot to distrust him.

They talked about art and music and the state of the weather. The music enveloped them; the other dancers became bits of rotating color. Then the song ended, and they were on the far side of the ballroom, both slightly out of breath and suddenly at a loss for words.

She spent the rest of the evening alternating between dancing and talking with the other guests, though dancing seemed to demand most of her time. She whirled around, blocking out the rest of the world, allowing herself to indulge in the enjoyment if just for an evening. Free to be who she was, unfettered from her past. It wasn't until halfway through the evening that she became aware that she was being watched. She could feel the intensity of his gaze.

And irrational fear flooded back into her being.

Then she would convince herself that she'd imagined it, that it was her own fear of discovery that conjured him out of nothing.

More than once during the evening, she did catch Leland Bishop watching her as she danced with others. But Leland's expression was perfectly charming, his gaze was steady, admiring, but not aggressive. That other look, the one that had followed her . . . She shivered to think who might have such intense feelings toward her. And if he was friend or foe.

And then another gentleman would ask her to dance and she forgot about those dark moments when she was afraid she'd escaped nothing after all.

MRS. DRISCOLL COLLECTED them all a little after eleven. They gathered their cloaks and went to the curb to take the carriages home and met Mr. Nash and several of the Corona men as they were leaving.

"Mr. Nash. I didn't see you all evening. This is my friend and fellow artisan Grace Griffith."

"A pleasure, and you ladies were having such a good time, I didn't want to interrupt you." He smiled happily. "Though I did try to convince this fellow to ask you."

Emilie smiled, then recognized the man standing next to him: Amon Bronsky, looking awkward in formal black. Awkward, but powerful. And when their eyes met and held, the blood rushed in her veins.

Their carriage arrived and the spell was broken. With adieus, they climbed in. Emilie just caught sight of Amon's dark eyes before the carriage door closed after them. And in a jolt of primal recognition, she knew those eyes in the ballroom had been his.

Chapter 20

It was a short ride back to the boardinghouse. Mrs. B had promised to keep the door unlocked for them, and Grace had a feeling everyone would be awake and waiting up to hear about the ball.

So at first she wasn't surprised when Mrs. B met them at the door.

"Grace, come with me." Mrs. B relieved Grace of her cloak and handed it to Emilie. "You go on upstairs. Everyone is waiting to hear about the ball."

"What is it? Has something happened?" Grace asked as she was trundled down the hall and into the warm kitchen.

Charlie was sitting at the table. He lurched to his feet and stopped to stare at Grace.

Grace stared back; his clothes and person were black with something. Soot? His face was almost black except where a blister was covered by a greasy salve.

For an eternity they stared at each other.

"What happened to you?" Grace demanded. And then it hit her. While she'd been dancing and drinking punch, Charlie had been covering the fire whose fire engines they had heard on the drive to the ball. "Charlie."

She took a step toward him, but he stepped back. "Don't come closer. You'll ruin your dress."

"To heck—"

"Listen to the man," Mrs. B said. "And you, Charlie Murray, sit down and finish your tea."

A plate of barely touched sandwiches and a heavy earthenware mug sat next to one of Mrs. B's drying cloths, hardly recognizable for the dirt and . . . was that blood?

"What happened? I should have been there."

"Nothing you could have done in that chaos. It was bad." He sank into the chair.

"I could have captured it on the page."

"That's why I came. It needs an illustration. Can you do it if I describe it to you?"

"I'll try. I'll go get my sketchbook." Grace didn't wait for an answer but grabbed her skirts in both hands and ran full tilt out of the kitchen and up to her room. She grabbed her notebook and pencil, heedless of the faces that were clustered together along Emilie's bed. She was gone again before they could ask any questions.

When Grace returned to the kitchen, Mrs. B was hovering over Charlie cajoling him to eat and dabbing at his forehead. But she moved away when Grace sat down at the table across from him.

Mrs. B looked toward heaven, wiped her hands on her apron, and left them to it.

And Charlie began his story. "A six-story tenement. The fire started somewhere in the middle and spread quickly, devouring the building, trapping most of the inhabitants inside. It jumped to two other buildings before the fire engines arrived and was lapping at half the block before it was brought under control.

"You could hear people screaming, people who had no chance of escape. Others streamed out the doors, jumped out windows, women, carrying a child on each hip, while others clung to their mothers' skirts.

"But the fire was moving faster than they could get away." Charlie's voice broke. "That's when the reporters dropped their notebooks and cameras and tried to help. We just started pulling people out of first-floor windows. Climbing up the fire escapes to reach who we could until the walls collapsed.

"There was an old man . . ."

Grace's pencil flew over the paper as Charlie brought the scene to life, his account so vivid she could almost smell the acrid smoke, hear the cries in her head. And after half an hour she had several sketches blocked out, and the tears were running down her cheeks.

Several times Mrs. B came into the room to refill their cups. They hardly noticed her, so intent were they to get the story right.

Finally Charlie stood. Swayed slightly. But when Grace would have gone to help him, he stopped her.

"Don't come near. Grace . . ." He just looked at her with sad, tired eyes. "You're so . . . that dress . . ."

"Hang the dress." Grace handed him her sketches. "You'll miss your deadline. There's a taxi stand at Fourth and Twenty-Second. Do you need the fare?"

"No."

"I'll come with you."

"No. Stay home. I came here to get you, but you'd gone to a ball. A ball. But now I'm glad. You should have nice things. You didn't need to be there tonight. I realize that now."

"What are you saying?"

"You don't have to put your life at risk. I can tell you about it and you can draw it."

"You don't want me to be on the scene?"

"Maybe you should stick to glass cutting."

"Maybe you should go soak your head." Then she took his full meaning. They often sparred. But this was different, and Grace's stomach dropped to her feet. "No. I belong there as much as you or anyone else."

"But . . ."

"Don't say another word." Because she would burst into tears if he did. She should have been at the fire, not frittering her time away at a society ball. But then she might never have realized how he really felt. He didn't understand that it was different seeing it firsthand. No. Of course he did. He just didn't think it was a place for women.

"You'll be late." She headed toward the door not waiting to see if he followed.

"Grace, don't be mad."

"Why not? You just said I wasn't needed."

"That's not what I—"

"Just go."

"You're being stubborn."

"I have to be to survive." She held open the door, but hesitated on the threshold. "Can you make it okay?"

He nodded. "Grace. You're . . . I like your dress." And he turned and strode down the street to the corner.

Grace didn't watch but went back inside and slammed the door.

Mrs. B was waiting for her. "Ach, Grace. What happened?"

"There was a fire."

"I'm not talking about the fire. What is the matter?"

Grace bit her lip. She was trying hard not to burst into tears.

"He's so annoying. At first he was just annoying. I was okay with that. But now he's annoying and . . . and . . . protective."

That startled a laugh out of Mrs. B. "Oh lord, Grace, ninety-nine girls out of a hundred would kill for someone who cares for them the way Charlie does for you."

"Well, they can have him." And a tear trickled down her cheek no matter how hard she told herself not to succumb.

Mrs. B shook her head, sighed, and held out her arms.

Grace couldn't withstand her invitation; she fell into them and for a few moments she let Mrs. B keep her safe.

"Grace, Grace, what am I going to do with you?"

"You could start by telling Charlie not to fuss," Grace mumbled from the folds of Mrs. B's nightdress.

"That would be like telling the Hudson not to flow to the sea."

Grace lifted her face to frown at her. "What do you mean?"

"Haven't you guessed by now?"

"Guessed what?"

"The reason he wants to protect you, goose."

"Charlie? Because he's an officious, bullying— He doesn't think I'm capable of doing the job, but I am—"

Mrs. B took both Grace's shoulders and held her at arm's length. "No, Grace. It's because he loves you."

It took Grace several breaths—once she got her breath back—before she could even answer. "Charlie? He doesn't love me. We're colleagues."

Mrs. B threw up her hands. "How the two of you found each other out of all the people in the world is beyond me. He does love you. But he would never admit it; he's as bullheaded as you, maybe more."

Grace sank into the nearest chair. She'd been so close to success.

Had thought her partnership with Charlie would help her get a permanent position on the paper. Not that she'd been using him, but they were good together . . . as colleagues. But maybe he didn't want her as a colleague after all. "How do you know?"

"Oh, my dear. You only have to look at him when he looks at you. He would not be my first choice. He's older than you, and though he does have a job, it is not a comfortable one. He sees unpleasant things, places himself in danger, will never be home for dinner."

"I'm hardly ever home for dinner."

"But," Mrs. B continued, ignoring Grace's objection, "I can tell beneath the reporter's swagger, he is a kind man. And he *is* tall. A girl could do worse."

Grace pushed to her feet. "No, Mrs. B. Marriage isn't for me. I'm going to become a political cartoonist or die trying."

"No one in this world has said you can't do both."

"Charlie would."

"So far I've only ever heard him suggest that you tell the editors who you are."

"I won't. That will get me fired for certain."

"Perhaps, but I thought you were all for women receiving their due. How long will the world have to wait to know that G. L. Griffith is a woman?"

Emilie finally managed to get the others to leave her room. She'd given every detail but she wasn't really paying attention. She couldn't imagine why Mrs. B had called Grace into the kitchen. And why she still hadn't come upstairs.

Was Grace in some kind of trouble? They were up-to-date on their rent. They hadn't committed any infractions that Emilie was aware of. A death in Grace's family? Would she have to return home to Connecticut?

Then what would happen to the "Magnolia" window? To Grace's journalistic aspirations? To Emilie?

And why come get her sketchbook?

Emilie spent another few minutes after the others left pacing the small uncluttered area between their beds trying to figure out what was happening. She should have had someone undo her buttons before they left so she could get ready for bed, but what if Grace needed her?

Emilie leaned on the sill and peered out the window. The street was quiet. For a moment she could almost hear the strains of a waltz in her head. Leland Bishop had been a delightful partner, entertaining without being frivolous, elegant without being stiff, refined without being affected.

She liked him. And there would be the end of it. He was much above her in station even in America. And if he knew her past . . .

The door opened and Emilie yelped in alarm. She saw immediately Grace had been crying. "What's the matter? I was worried about you."

"You don't have to be."

"I know, you're perfectly able to take care of yourself, but still I was worried."

"Everybody should leave me alone. You should all just mind your own business." Grace threw herself on her bed.

"Very well," Emilie said. "We'll each mind our own business . . . just as soon as we help each other get out of these ball gowns."

Slowly, Grace looked up, frowning dangerously, her face twitching and grimacing. She wrestled with herself for a long moment then burst into a laugh. "I'm sorry. It's just . . ."

Charlie, Emilie thought. *This is about Charlie.*

"Charlie," Grace said.

"Tell me everything."

So Grace did as they unbuttoned each other's ball gowns, hung them in the wardrobe, and changed into their nightdresses.

Emilie just let Grace talk. Didn't ask any questions or give any advice. Not that she had any to give. Men were enticing and infuriating and always creating havoc and making everyone miserable. Yet Emilie knew—at least hoped—some men might be different, and she'd thought Charlie Murray, for all his coarse ways and ill-fitting suits, might be one of them.

But she'd been wrong before. Many times.

When Grace was wrung out with anger, disappointment, and a final question of how she could have gotten herself into such a fix, Emilie gave the only kind of advice she knew how to give.

"You're not responsible for how Charlie feels; you just keep doing what you're doing, and you'll get there."

"It seems so impossible now."

"Because one man turned out to be less than you thought he was?"

"He's *not* less. He's bright, and hardworking, and he has a way with words that really is moving."

"But you just don't love him, I understand," Emilie commiserated.

"I don't want to love him. I want to be a political cartoonist," Grace said. "Let's go to bed. We have an early day tomorrow."

They didn't speak again, but Emilie could hear Grace turning over and over and she knew she wasn't sleeping. And Emilie understood Grace's dilemma. Just a dance at a ball or the fire in a man's eyes had tempted Emilie beyond reason. And it made her sad for both of them. For if Grace had determined not to marry in pursuit of her future, Emilie was prevented the same by her past.

"THERE WILL BE snow before the day is out," Lotte pronounced the next morning as they made their dreary way to work beneath an overcast and threatening sky. The excitement of the evening had worn off during sleep and Emilie felt bone-tired. She knew that Grace felt the same. She hadn't said a word at breakfast.

But they set aside their feelings and memories along with their winter coats and went straightway to their worktables. There were now three girls assigned to the "Winter" panel and Emilie had to fight her impulse to try to control the sections and the cuts. Miss Zevesky might consult her on a particularly difficult piece but the other three, who had worked there much longer than Emilie, went about their work as undaunted as if the panel had been a parlor jigsaw puzzle.

Sometimes, Emilie had to literally bite her tongue to keep from suggesting a particular cut or to stop a mistake altogether.

It was maddening. She reminded herself a thousand times a day that this was the way Michelangelo had worked. And he created masterpieces. And so did Mr. Tiffany, and she had to be content with that.

Mrs. Driscoll made her usual rounds at the beginning of the workday each morning, then after lunch and again after tea break. She spent the rest of her time either in her office or answering summonses from the other parts of the building.

Mr. Tiffany made only one trip to the studio. And stayed only long enough to nod and tap his way from piece to piece.

Overnight the studio sprouted holly leaves and bits of pine tied with bows of brightly colored ribbons. Everyone began to talk of their holiday and waited in anticipation to learn if they, like the men, would have a whole week off.

Emilie didn't see how any of them could possibly take that much time off. The Paris Exposition opening was only three and a half months away and still there was so much to do.

Grace and the two girls working on the "Magnolia" window were making great progress. But Emilie's team still had yet to start the "Spring" panel. And then it would all have to be assembled. Not to mention all the other pieces that were in various states of completion throughout the workshop. The men at Corona must be just as busy.

AT THE BOARDINGHOUSE, talk turned to Christmas dinner. Twice Charlie Murray came around, but Grace refused to see him.

She wouldn't say why. Mrs. B just clicked her tongue and kept mum.

Dora was invited to spend Christmas with her aunt and uncle in New Jersey.

"Though really, I almost wish I weren't going," Dora said one night as they sat around the fire in the parlor, making paper chains to adorn the banister. "I'll miss you all."

"It's only for a day or two," Lotte said. "It will be nice to be with your family."

"We don't have a family," Maggie said. "I wish I had an aunt and uncle."

"Well, you don't," Lotte said, snatching a paper strip from the table and adding it to her chain.

It seemed to Emilie that Lotte had become much more sharp-tempered with her sister, though who could blame her? She never got to relax or do something for herself. So it was no wonder that when on Saturday half day, Mrs. B told her that Nessa and Jane had invited Maggie to go with them to the park, Lotte acquiesced with hardly an argument.

Lotte gave Maggie a nickel and as soon as she went with the servant girls, Lotte took herself shopping.

"Good for her," Emilie said.

"She's probably just buying Maggie a Christmas present," Grace said.

"Really," Dora said. "Sometimes you can't help but think what would happen if—"

"Don't say it," Grace warned her. "Just count your blessings."

"I know. I think I'll go shopping, too," Dora said. "Maybe I can catch up to Lotte."

As soon as she was gonc, Emilie and Grace settled into the parlor before the fire.

"Will you be going home for Christmas, too, Grace?"

Grace looked up from the magazine she'd just picked up. "No," she said a little wistfully. "My parents are wonderful people, but very conservative in their views about women's place in life. Well, my father is a Methodist minister so . . . they don't really approve of my coming to New York to work for Mr. Tiffany, and if they knew about the other . . ." Grace lifted her eyes to where Emilie thought Methodist heaven might be. "It's just best that I let them celebrate without me. My sisters and brothers and their families all live nearby. They'll make up for me not being there."

Grace also had things she had to hide in order to follow her dream.

"I'm happy we are friends," Emilie said.

"Me too."

The doorbell rang.

Grace jumped up. "If that's Charlie Murray, tell him I'm not here." And she ran out of the room and up the stairs.

Emilie heard Mrs. B answer the door. Turn whoever it was away. Then the door shut.

Emilie got up and went into the hall.

"Those two," Mrs. B said. "She hasn't gone out on a story since she missed that fire to go to the ball. And it isn't Charlie's fault."

She went back to the kitchen and Emilie went upstairs to talk to Grace.

When she got to their room, Grace was stuffing her sketchbook and pencils into her bag.

"You're going to have to face him sooner or later," Emilie told her, though who was she to extoll facing your devils, when she had merely put an ocean between herself and hers.

Grace didn't answer, just added two more pencils to her bag.

"You're a good team. He came to you, no one else, the night of the fire because he knew that you could imagine just what he was feeling. And the illustrations were amazing. There were even letters to the editor saying how moving they were."

"He was using me."

"What? I've never heard of anything more ridiculous. You're a team, and quite frankly, he's been at it much longer than you have."

Grace slung her bag's strap over her shoulder. "That's what Charlie says. To give it time. But now he's changed. I have half a mind to go down to the *Sun* office and tell them exactly who G. L. Griffith is."

"Well, bully for you. And what do you think will happen then?"

"I'll probably lose any chance of them ever buying another cartoon." Grace headed toward the door.

"Then where are you going?"

"Wherever Charlie Murray isn't."

"How do you know where he won't be?"

"I don't know, but he can't be everywhere."

"Grace, why don't you just talk to him? Explain to him why you're upset. At least tell him to his face you don't want to work with him anymore."

"But I do want to work with him."

"Then—" Emilie never finished what she was going to say. Grace strode out the door, shutting it behind her. Emilie heard her run down the stairs.

Emilie wandered over to the window in time to see Grace come out onto the street. And Charlie Murray step off the opposite curb and follow her toward the corner.

With a sigh of resignation, Emilie turned from the window. Maybe she'd do some sketching herself.

She'd barely gotten her pastels set up when there was a knock at the door and Mrs. B burst in.

"Lord, Emilie, there is a gentleman come to call."

"Charlie's back? I wonder what happened."

"Not Charlie. A gentleman. He's come to call on you."

Emilie's stomach dropped and she had to grab the brass bed frame to keep from swaying. They had come after her. They were going to arrest her after all. She glanced at the window. It had worked in Paris, but it was a sheer drop to the street here. She wouldn't escape this time.

"Lord, girl, fix your hair. And where is your good visiting dress?"

"But Mrs. B, did he say who he was?"

"He did indeed. He gave me his card." She turned and pulled the wardrobe open, rummaged through. "This will be just fine." She pulled Emilie's best visiting dress out and thrust it toward her. "Now get a move on. He'll grow old waiting for you."

"What did the card say? Who is he?"

"Mr. Bishop, and he's come to take you to tea."

Chapter 21

I don't know what you're so sore about," Charlie groused as he ran to catch up with Grace. "You've been avoiding me. I thought we had a partnership."

"Evidently not," Grace huffed out, not slowing down or looking at him.

"The editors want to know why your cartoons aren't coming in as fast as they used to. What am I supposed to say? That you're pouting because I was concerned for your safety?"

That stopped her, in the middle of the sidewalk, causing several men to jump sideways into the street to keep from walking into her. "I'm not pouting. I'm . . . I'm . . . What did you tell them?"

"That I hadn't seen you, which is the truth. What the hell— I mean the . . . oh hell . . . What the hell are you up to? Do you want this job or not?"

"Of course I want this job, but I want it on my own merit, not because you're coddling me along because I'm useful to your articles."

"What? Of all the stupid, wrongheaded, arrogant—"

"Arrogant?" Grace spat back. "You have the gall to call me arrogant? You practically said that you didn't need me on the scene because I was incapable of taking care of myself. 'Stay home and I'll tell you what to draw,'" she added in a deep, gruff voice.

Charlie snatched off his hat, scratched his head, and shoved it back on again.

"I never said any such thing and you know it. Check your source. That would be me." He jabbed his thumb into his chest so hard Grace was surprised it didn't leave an impression on his overcoat.

"You said it was dangerous."

"Well, it is."

"Well, I can handle it."

"Fine. What do you want me to tell the editors? That we're no longer working together? That you'd prefer another reporter to collaborate with?"

Grace swallowed, commanding herself not to burst into angry tears. "Is that what you want?"

He gave her a quizzical look. "I guess it doesn't matter what I want."

It might if she knew what that was. But after her talk with Mrs. B the other night, she was afraid to find out.

Charlie had hesitated, waiting, but now he shrugged. "See ya around, I guess." He turned to walk away, turned back. "But one day they're going to find out who you are. They won't be happy to know they were bamboozled by a woman. It pays to have friends to take your side."

"Are you blackmailing me?"

He snatched his hat off again. But just held it. The fire had gone out of his eyes. The brilliant blue looked almost gray. Then he shook his head and walked away.

Grace opened her mouth to call him back. Tell him she did

need him. She wanted to work with him. And she wanted a friend. But something held her back. Sheer cowardice, she suspected, so she let him go and thought that she'd never spent a more miserable Christmas season in her life.

Emilie let Mrs. B fuss over her long enough to button her dress then shooed her away. What on earth was she doing acting as nervous as a debutante, though she'd never been in company with a debutante in her life. Why had he come? What could he possibly want?

One thing came to mind. Well, he would get a surprise. She was not a gullible, innocent miss. On the other hand, she hadn't fallen entirely from good sense, either.

She swept up her hair, pulled a few tendrils out, and, deciding she looked presentable, she went downstairs.

Leland Bishop popped up from his seat in the wing chair like someone had goosed him.

Emilie found it mildly endearing.

Some men were made more beautiful by the candlelight of the ballroom and slid back into their pedestrian selves by day. But here in Mrs. B's parlor, dressed in a sack suit of fine wool, Bishop was even more striking than in his evening wear.

He recovered himself immediately, and it was a suave Leland Bishop who said, "Miss Pascal, I hope I'm not intruding. I was wondering if you would join me for tea."

Emilie looked reflexively toward the kitchen where no doubt Mrs. B was rummaging the cupboards for something up to the standards of this obviously rich, cultured, and good-looking man.

"I thought you might like the Plaza. It's quite beautifully decorated for the season."

"Mr. Bishop—"

"Leland, please." He managed to say it in an offhanded way that was no doubt meant to put her at ease.

It didn't. She shook her head. "I'm afraid . . ."

His expression changed to one of alarm. "Don't be. I'm not dangerous, though perhaps you think me ridiculous?"

Emilie was completely disarmed. And a traitorous smile played at her lips. "Just a bit. Why on earth did you come here?"

"I want to take you to tea."

She stood silent, though her knees were a bit weak. Would he proposition her right here in Mrs. B's parlor?

A flash of understanding in his eyes. "Tea. At the Plaza. That is all." He sat down suddenly, uninvited, leaving her standing before him. "God, is that what you think of me?"

"I haven't thought about you at all."

"Touché. Please sit down before your landlady comes back and thinks me an uncultured oaf."

"I doubt if she would mistake you for that," Emilie said, but she sat down across from him.

"I think you'll find that I do not have that kind of reputation. Nor is there any reason for there to be."

"You were a lot more amiable when we were dancing," said Emilie. "Are you always this stilted in the daylight?"

"Not until today. It's ridiculous. We're two people who enjoy each other's company. Or at least I had that impression. Was I wrong?"

Emilie shook her head.

"Then take tea with me at the Plaza. We'll invite Mrs. Bertolucci to chaperone."

"Oh, don't be absurd," Emilie said, giving a little. "But I'm not really dressed for the Plaza. And frankly I don't even have a dress suitable for the Plaza. I am, if you've forgotten, Mr. Bishop, a working girl."

"And so am I, not a working girl, but . . ."

"But I know what you mean. You're a gallery owner and the maker and breaker of artistic careers."

"And who are you, Emilie Pascal?"

A rush of cold fear held her breathless for a moment. "As I said. A glass cutter at Tiffany's glass studio."

"Then let us go to tea. The working girl and the shop owner." His eyes were twinkling with mischief and she was succumbing to his charm.

"What if we see someone you know?"

"Then I will gloat at their envy."

"What if I slurp my tea?"

"Then I will, too."

"You absurd man."

"Your opinion totally concurs with that of my family. Go tell Mrs. Bertolucci I will take very good care of you and have you back before dinner."

Emilie left him to consult with Mrs. B, who already had Emilie's coat in her hands. "If he tries to take liberties, get in a taxi and come straight home. There's a stand at the Plaza. I will pay the cabbie."

Emilie nodded. She didn't think Leland Bishop was going to take advantage of her person; what he could do was much, much worse.

The Plaza Hotel was situated at the south end of Central Park, at Fifth Avenue, eight stories of pure luxury, it was said. Emilie had only seen it at a distance on her trip to the Metropolitan Museum farther up Fifth Avenue. As soon as their carriage pulled to a stop, the door opened and a valet let down the steps. Leland jumped out to hand her down, and a very stately doorman bowed them inside.

It was indeed elegant, Emilie thought, as Leland escorted her down the marbled hallway to the tearoom, whose white and gold decor served as a perfect canvas for the gilt baskets of poinsettias and pink roses placed throughout the room.

Emilie soon forgot her wariness and began to enjoy herself. This was where she belonged, in cultivated society, having tea with a cultured man, who, once they left the boardinghouse and he was ensconced in his usual setting, became thoroughly charming and entertaining—and showed a surprisingly democratic view of art, including the expressionists.

When they left the hotel, Emilie was easily talked into a walk in the park, though it was already growing late. Leland took her arm and drew it through his, keeping hold of her gloved hand as it rested in the crook of his elbow. It seemed natural, and she welcomed his warmth against the deepening cold.

All too soon they were getting back into his carriage and making their way down Fifth Avenue and Emilie bit back the disappointment that her visit to fantasyland was coming to an end.

Leland saw her to the door, both of them suddenly quiet after an afternoon of conversation and laughter. Mrs. B opened it almost as soon as his hand left the bell.

He said good night under the watchful eyes of her landlady and Emilie went inside where she was barraged by questions from the others, who had evidently convened in the parlor to witness her return.

All except Grace, who didn't return until after dinner, when she went straight upstairs and pretended to be asleep until finally Emilie gave up any attempt at conversation and went to sleep with visions of the Plaza's tearoom dancing in her head.

On the Friday evening before Christmas, Dora was sent off with enthusiastic fanfare to board the ferry to New Jersey.

The others drew names for presents at breakfast Saturday morning and retired immediately upstairs for a secret meeting to discuss what to give Mrs. B and a tip for Nessa and Jane.

"Well, that cleans me out," Grace said. "But three whole days off in a row. What will we do with ourselves?"

She still hadn't said much about the misunderstanding with Charlie or what they had talked about. But Emilie guessed they weren't collaborating. Grace had sent out a couple of cartoons, but her heart just didn't seem to be in it.

Still, she packed up her sketchbook and pencils and with a "See ya later," she left the boardinghouse.

Emilie went downstairs to look for a newspaper and was on her way back upstairs again when the doorbell rang. She opened the door to find a small uniformed boy carrying a long, large box. Flowers for someone.

She took the box and glanced at the name. Miss Emilie Pascal.

She gave the boy a penny and shut the door before she snatched the card from the box. They were from Leland Bishop, saying he was spending Christmas at his parents' Long Island residence and that he hoped to see her again when he returned.

She took the box to the kitchen without opening it.

"What's this?" Mrs. B asked.

"Mr. Bishop," Emilie answered, not looking at her landlady.

"Well, open it."

Reluctantly, Emilie opened the box to reveal an overflowing bouquet of colorful blossoms.

"They're beautiful," Mrs. B said. "But be careful, my dear. Men like Mr. Bishop—"

"Thank you, but you don't have to warn me about men like Mr. Bishop. They are not for the likes of me."

"That isn't exactly what I meant."

"I know, and you don't have to say that, either. Perhaps you could just break up the bouquet and make some sprays for the house."

Mrs. B smiled, kindly, Emilie thought. "They will look lovely and will be our secret, but first . . ." Mrs. B pulled out a pale lavender freesia and handed it to Emilie. "Something to press into your keepsake book."

Emilie took the flower; she didn't have the heart to tell Mrs. B she didn't have a keepsake book. She didn't have too many things she wanted to remember. As soon as she was upstairs she dropped the freesia into the wastebasket and reluctantly pushed all thought of Leland Bishop from her mind. Allowing him to take her to the Plaza had been reckless and brought her a step closer to being recognized by someone from his world, a world that used to be hers. She would just have to be firm if she saw him again.

On Christmas Eve they all gathered in Mrs. B's parlor to decorate the tree that Jane and Nessa had put on the circular table earlier that evening.

They all sang carols and Emilie sang along in French since she didn't have time to translate the words into English and keep up with the melody.

The only one who didn't seem to have the holiday spirit was Grace. Emilie knew she was still chafing from what she felt was Charlie's defection. As for Charlie, he hadn't made an appearance and Grace hadn't mentioned him once.

Everyone at Mrs. Bertolucci's agreed that the Christmas day feast was unsurpassed by any they had ever had.

Dora arrived late that night to announce that she had been invited to return to her aunt and uncle's for the spring season. "I'm sure I'll be engaged by the summer, then no more glass cutting ever." Then she looked contrite. "Though I'll miss all my friends."

It was with filled hearts and stomachs that they all went up to bed that night.

THE DAY AFTER Christmas turned suddenly colder, and the girls hurried from the warmth of the boardinghouse to the warmth of the Tiffany glassworks studio with hardly a word passing between them.

Though twice Grace had to go back and help Lotte urge Maggie along. Recently Maggie had become less pliable, more truculent, and more ready to burst into tears.

"She's mad because she wants to stay with Nessa and Jane in the kitchen where it's warm," Lotte confided as they walked along. "How can I work and take care of her at the same time?"

Grace didn't know. "Don't you have any relatives who would take you in?"

Lotte shook her head. "I'll just have to make it work."

A sudden gust of icy wind whipped around the corner. Grace took Lotte's arm in hers, and they bent their heads into the cold as they trudged forward together, Grace's mind already turning to the plight of poor working girls and an idea that she had for a quarter-page spread.

As soon as they exchanged their winter coats for work aprons, they took their places alongside the other women in the studio and after a few minutes of talk of presents, food, and family, everyone settled into the quiet of everyday work.

The work on the "Magnolia" window was almost finished and Mr. Tiffany came down twice during the week to view the finishing touches. Miss Northrop said that she was pleased with the outcome, more than pleased. She was radiant.

"WINTER" WAS DEVELOPING beyond Emilie's hopes. The opalescent snow looked so heavy that at any moment it might drop to the ground, freeing the bare branches and leaving deep impressions in the snow below before it spilled out of the frame and covered the floor at the viewer's feet.

In the "Winter" panel, Mr. Tiffany had used the glass as if he were painting with light and shadow the way no brushstroke ever could. It was moments like this that Emilie forgave him all the annoyances, the way he stood behind her while she waited for him to pass judgment, the way he gave no thought to bringing the wrath of his cane down on glass choices he didn't like. His stubbornness, his ego, his petulance, and his complete belief that he was always right.

She forgave them all and hoped he forgave hers. He had a vision; so did she. Their visions sometimes clashed. So far they had managed always to find that special meeting place in the glass. And Emilie knew that whatever happened in the future, there would always be that place that was theirs alone. And where she felt true.

Two days after they returned to work, Mrs. Driscoll finished her new dragonfly lamp.

Mr. Tiffany invited everyone to celebrate its unveiling. They all took the elevator down to ground level to the showroom where Emilie had mistakenly entered on her first day off the ship. Mrs. Driscoll looked proud and not at all nervous as they stood before what was obviously a lamp though covered by a white linen shroud.

Then Mrs. Driscoll carefully lifted the cloth to exclamations of awe. Applause broke out. It was wonderful. They gathered closer. Someone exclaimed on the mosaic tesserae of the base, another applauded the purple variegated wings of the dragonflies spread in flight. They all agreed the filigree was exquisite. Mr. Belknap exclaimed it an ingenious idea.

Even Mr. Pringle Mitchell had not a bad word to say.

Their enthusiasm attracted several customers, and one lady went so far as to offer to buy it right out of the showroom.

Mr. Tiffany smiled graciously. "Ah, Mrs. Lilburn. We most certainly can order one especially for you, but I'm afraid this particular lamp is headed for the Paris Exposition."

Mrs. Driscoll smiled her pleasure; Emilie felt like yelling, *Brava!*

They returned to the workshop still giddy with the excitement but were soon settled back to work. There was still a lot to do.

That night Grace began work on a new political cartoon. Emilie had seen her working on several different sketches, but Grace had refused to show them to her.

"Not until I've finished" was the only thing she would say.

On New Year's Eve while the upper classes were drinking champagne in restaurants all over town, the residents at Mrs. B's drank a round of hot rum punch and went onto the street to listen to the church bells ring at midnight.

And suddenly it was a new year.

Chapter 22

Nothing had changed from one year to the next as far as Emilie could tell except that she felt even farther from Paris and her father than she'd felt the day before.

Her "Winter" panel was near completion. Even though she knew it wasn't hers, she couldn't help but feel possessive.

It's about the art, she would remind herself. Not about the artist. And for now she was content to be one of many. But she began to think about her own art, her painting, and would feel a jab of longing and curiosity to see how it would look now. Could she translate her painting into glass, or vice versa?

Then she'd chastise herself for her naïveté for believing that she might one day be a respected artist without the stigma of her forger father to mar her brilliance. And then she'd bemoan her arrogance for thinking she would ever be good enough.

Leland Bishop returned the first week of the month, but Emilie hadn't seen him. He'd invited her to the opera, which she had to decline. To tea, which she also declined. She liked Leland Bishop, enjoyed his company. But she also knew that she would only cause resentment and suspicion among the other Tiffany girls if she was found to be keeping company with a rich gallery owner.

The thought of her being gossiped about made her blood run

cold. She couldn't take the chance, not when a future was finally looking possible.

January grew colder and though they said the days were growing longer, you couldn't tell it from the fifth floor of the Tiffany studios. Eyes strained against the darkness as each workday ground to an end. More and more, the girls were having to take breaks to relieve their tired eyes.

With Christmas orders out of the way and the dragonfly lamp approved, Mrs. Driscoll oversaw the workroom with renewed vigor, driving them hard to finish all the pieces destined for the world's fair in Paris.

They were asked to come in an hour earlier to finish the day's work. Mrs. B's girls barely saw one another except as they trudged to work and home again. Even then, they hardly spoke. Snow or sun, icy rain or biting wind, the weather hardly inspired conversation, and being bundled up against the cold and concentrating on keeping their footing on the icy pavement made it nigh impossible.

Each night they ate and fell into bed. Even Grace went out less and less. She hadn't mentioned the *Sun* or Charlie since the night of the ball and Emilie didn't pry.

One morning Maggie didn't come down to breakfast.

"She's not feeling well," Lotte said tightly. "She says she needs to stay in bed today." Lotte sighed, clearly on the verge of tears. "What am I supposed to do?"

"Leave her here," Mrs. B said. "I'll give her some soup for lunch and Nessa and Jane will keep her company."

"Are you sure?" Lotte asked, her voice tremulous.

"*Absolutamente.* I only have to do the marketing this afternoon and Nessa and Jane will be here if she needs anything."

"Thank you." Lotte turned away and busied herself with putting on her mittens.

It was obvious things were getting more difficult between the two sisters. Emilie didn't think Lotte could carry on for much longer. Already she was pale with dark half-moons under her eyes. And if she couldn't keep up or got sick, what would they do? Mrs. B would have to turn them out. She couldn't afford to keep them both no matter how much she might want to help.

The thought seared into Emilie's heart. She understood what it meant to lose everything. But she'd had only herself to take care of. Lotte was not yet twenty and already she was old.

They set off for work with little flurries of snow swirling about their heads. By the time they finished for the day and started for home, several inches had fallen.

They were barely out the front door of the Tiffany building when Dora exclaimed, "Isn't that Mr. Dreamy?"

They all looked to where Leland Bishop stood at the corner, his felt hat and astrakhan overcoat dotted with snowflakes as if he'd been there for a while.

After a dart of pleasure, followed by one of panic, Emilie, pretending not to see him, turned south toward home. The others followed, but they'd barely gone five feet before Emilie felt someone fall in step beside her.

"Miss Pascal," Leland said, which had the effect of turning all heads toward him.

Emilie tried to keep walking but her foot slipped on the icy sidewalk, and he grabbed her elbow to prevent her from falling.

"What a pleasure to see you," he said as if he hadn't been waiting outside the door for that very purpose.

"Are you on your way to see Mr. Tiffany?" she asked politely, even though it was obvious from the twinkle in his eyes whom he had come to see. And her nerves raced even as she ordered them to ignore him.

"I thought perhaps you would let me take you for a hot chocolate and walk you home."

Emilie was dimly aware of Grace shuttling the others down the sidewalk, Dora's frown of curiosity as she was dragged away. And Emilie knew she would have to answer a million questions before she was allowed to sleep that night.

"What are you doing here?" Emilie asked as soon as the others were gone.

"I came to see you, since it seems like the only place I might have a chance to talk to you."

"Mr. Bishop, I have my position to think of."

"Emilie. You can't fool me."

Emilie stiffened, and she felt his fingers tighten where he still held her arm. "What I meant is I see no reason why seeing me should be an impediment to your work. I come from a good family. So I've been told."

The laughter in his eyes made it almost impossible to hold out against him.

"You know that's not what I meant, you ridiculous man. It's *my* situation that you should be concerned with. I'm a working girl."

"So you've said. More than once, if I recall correctly. But since you didn't slurp your tea at the Plaza, I thought I'd risk you with a cup of chocolate."

The laughter fled from his eyes. "You are as well-bred as any of the women who haunt the Plaza, the Tiffany showroom, or my parents' ballroom, for that matter. Certainly rungs above the ones who haunt mine."

Emilie took an involuntary step backward. "I'm not."

"Emilie, I know you."

"No, you don't."

"You're smart and brave and talented—"

"No, please don't, please . . ." She didn't know what she wanted to say. *Don't have expectations I can't fulfill—don't make me the object of gossip or jealousy—don't make me have to lie to keep from telling you the truth about me.*

But from the depths of those pleas, a little voice whispered, *Please . . . take me to the opera and to dinner and all the lovely places I long to go. Give me a safe haven and treat me with kindness.*

"Do you not like me, even a little bit?" he continued earnestly. "Is that it? Just tell me you can't abide my presence and I'll leave you in peace." His voice was slow, and questioning, and she was almost persuaded to lie and tell him just that. But before she could answer, his eyes began to twinkle again. "But wait until after hot chocolate. You wouldn't deprive me of hot chocolate on a day like this. That would be too cruel." And he smiled and she relented.

Leland Bishop could do that, change from seriousness to lightheartedness in a blink of his long lashes. Could brush away her fear with a smile.

"I wouldn't be so heartless," Emilie said and let him escort her down the street, both their reputations be damned.

When Emilie returned home feeling toasty from Leland's carriage blankets and foot warmers, she found the others having their own tea in the parlor.

At first Emilie was afraid they were waiting for her, but that was quickly dispelled when Grace jumped up and ran to meet her in the foyer.

"We can't find Maggie."

"What?" Emilie asked, unbuttoning her coat. "She's not in her room?"

"No. We've searched all the other rooms thinking she might

have fallen asleep somewhere or was playing a prank on us, hiding just to get attention, but I'm beginning to worry."

"I'll help look." Emilie was shrugging out of her coat when they heard a shriek from overhead.

Mrs. B hurried from the parlor followed by the others, who crowded into the archway. "That's Lotte. Maybe she found her."

"I hope she gives Maggie what for, for worrying us like this," Dora said.

"She has every right to be angry," Mrs. B said. "After all she does for the girl. It's enough to try anyone's patience."

But Lotte came down the steps alone, cradling an empty mason jar in both hands.

"Any sign of her?" Mrs. B asked.

"She's gone. She's taken all our money and gone." Lotte held up the empty jar. "Everything I've saved. Gone. All gone." She collapsed suddenly, sitting down hard on the stairs.

"Maybe she just got confused about Christmas and presents and took the money to buy you a surprise."

"More like she run off with her fella," said Nessa, coming from the kitchen with a hot kettle.

"What fella?" Dora demanded. "Maggie doesn't have a fella."

Nessa shrugged, glanced back at Jane, who scooted past her with a tray of milk and sugar.

Lotte buried her face in her hands. "My god. What have I done?"

Grace sank onto the step next to her and put her arm around her shoulders. "You've done nothing wrong, Lotte. You've always taken great care of Maggie. She's probably just playing a trick on you."

Grace glanced up and caught Mrs. B's eye, then Emilie's.

Something was terribly amiss. Even if Maggie had gone out by herself expecting to return after her little joke, it was late, cold, and dark, and a girl like Maggie could get easily confused—and lost.

"Maybe we should go out and look," Miss Vanderheusen said, pushing past Dora. "She may be lost."

"I'll just get my coat," said Miss Burns.

"Wait," Emilie said. "How long has she been gone? Do you know?"

Mrs. B motioned Nessa and Jane over.

"We think it was while Mrs. B was out at the grocer's. We just went down to the cellar for a second to get the potatoes and onions for tonight's stew. It's the only time when no one was in the kitchen. The front door's always locked when we're here alone. We would have heard if she tried to get out."

"So when were you in the cellar?"

Nessa and Jane looked at each other and both shrugged.

"Somewhere between two and three," said Mrs. B. "I was only gone for an hour and I checked in on her before I left. I should have checked on her when I came back."

"It's not your fault, Mrs. B. How were you to know?" Grace assured her. "Nessa, Jane. What about this fella? What do you know?"

The two girls stood shoulder to shoulder, heads lowered.

"Nothin' much, miss. She talks about him a lot. We didn't pay her no mind. 'Cause you know, she's simple."

"Have you ever seen him? Did she meet him when she went out with you?"

"No, miss. Just talked about how they were going to get married."

"And did she say who this fella was?"

"No, miss," Nessa said. "Just that his name was Jack and he

was her fiancé. She don't have a fiancé. Who would marry her? She can't cook or clean or do nothin'. Can't even sweep worth beans."

"Jack," Dora said, thoughtfully. "His name was Jack?"

Nessa and Jane nodded vigorously.

Dora's eyes narrowed. "Did she say he worked at Tiffany's?"

"Dunno," Nessa said. "She did say she met him when you were at the beach."

"Oh my god," exclaimed Dora. "Jack Ratner. He was flirting with her at the beach that day. I thought he was just being nice, on account of her being, you know . . . That louse!" Her hand flew to her cheek. "Oh my god, they've eloped. That's why she took the money."

"Where are your wits?" Grace asked, exasperated. "Jack Ratner may be a cocksure arrogant jerk, but he's not totally without brains."

Dora's eyebrows dipped. "I don't—"

"He refused to marry her."

All heads snapped toward Lotte's hunched figure on the stairs.

"Lotte, what are you saying?" asked Grace.

"I went to him. Told him . . ." Lotte choked over the words and Emilie understood with blinding clarity what had happened. She'd seen it often enough in Paris, trusting girls ruined by undisciplined men.

She looked at Mrs. B and Grace and knew they understood, too.

"You asked him to marry Maggie?" Dora asked incredulously. "He would nev— Oh no, you mean— Lotte, you don't mean . . ."

Lotte broke down completely and could only nod from behind her hands.

Dora sat down on the nearest step.

Mrs. B and Grace helped Lotte up from the stairs and practically carried her into the parlor where they settled her into the big wing chair.

The others moved to the far side of the room to discuss what they could do to find the wayward Maggie.

They decided that they would search the immediate neighborhood to make certain she hadn't lost her way and was trying to find her way home.

But an hour's search gained them nothing but odd looks and chilblained fingers.

Exhausted, they ate a dinner they hardly tasted and made plans for what to do in the morning. No one pointed out that if Maggie was alone and not with Jack, tomorrow might be too late.

"As soon as we get to work tomorrow," Grace said, "we'll go ask in the pottery department if anyone knows where they might be. If they don't know, we'll go straight to Mr. Tiffany and have him call the police. He will have more clout than we will."

"He can't know!" cried Lotte. "She'll be ruined. Mr. Tiffany will turn her out, and then how will I manage three of us?"

"*Non preoccuarti*," Mrs. B said. "I will not turn you out. It will all be fine." But she sighed. She didn't think it would be fine any more than Emilie did.

"Don't worry, Lotte," said Dora. "Mr. Tiffany will find her."

But none of them had much hope. And no one asked Lotte what she meant by "three of us."

THEY ALL WENT to bed after that. Dora, in a rare display of charity, took Lotte to sleep in her room so she wouldn't be alone.

Grace stared out the bedroom window watching the wind blow a crumpled newspaper down the street. There was hardly anyone out. No one in their right mind would venture out at all. As much as Grace felt like slugging Jack Ratner, she also just hoped he had Maggie somewhere safe.

How could Maggie put this extra burden on her sister, who was trying to be mother, father, and sister all on her own? Had it been Jack's idea to take Lotte's savings?

Grace was angry—at Jack for encouraging a helpless girl. Lord help her, she was even angry at Maggie for not being able to take care of herself. But mostly she was angry at the world for allowing such things to happen.

"Come away from the window," Emilie said. "You can't conjure her appearance even if you try."

"I keep thinking we should have seen this coming," Grace snapped back. "All those times when Maggie disappeared from the lunchroom or was found wandering the halls by herself, she wasn't getting more confused and helpless, she'd known exactly what she was doing."

"Meeting Jack," Emilie said.

"I wish I knew that he was keeping her safe."

"Me too." Emilie didn't say more, but Grace knew she must be thinking the same thing. If Maggie was alone out in the cold, she wouldn't survive the night.

"Where could she be?"

"I don't know. Hopefully with Jack. Now we'd better try to sleep. We've done all we can do tonight."

"You're right." Though Grace didn't know how any of them would sleep, not with the possibility of Maggie roaming the streets. She lay down, pulled up the covers, and after an hour of listening to Emilie tossing in her bed, she finally got up to look out the window.

She didn't know how long she sat on the sill. At first she thought she must be dreaming when she saw a huddled figure limp up the steps and scratch at the door.

"It's Maggie!" Grace grabbed her robe and ran for the door, Emilie right behind her. "It's Maggie!" she called as she flew down the stairs and heard doors open down the hall behind her.

She fumbled with the locks and yanked the door open to a blast of cold air and Maggie falling into her arms.

"It's all right, Mags. You're okay now. You're home."

Maggie's skin was cold to the touch and she was dead weight in Grace's arms.

"Emilie, get Mrs. B."

But Mrs. B was already hurrying toward them, tying up her heavy robe, her hair in a long braid over her shoulder. "Nessa, Jane, *sbrigati*! Boil water for tea. Fill the hot water bottles."

"We'll take her to the back bedroom and get her undressed and into bed."

Grace and Emilie somehow managed to drag the unresponsive Maggie down the hall and divest her of her coat. But when they sat her on the bed, she began to clutch her stomach, whimpering, "Lotte? Lotte? It hurts."

Grace and Emilie worked in tandem, without a word, untying Maggie's shoes, stripping off her bodice, and unbuttoning her skirt. Grace held the girl upright while Emilie pulled back the covers. They laid her down and Emilie then pulled her skirt off.

And froze. "*Cher dieu céleste.*"

"What?" Grace looked at the front of Maggie's petticoat and choked back bile. "Oh no, oh no."

Mrs. B pushed past them and leaned over the girl. Grace and Emilie stepped back and clung together, somehow keeping their feet.

"Cover her with blankets and keep her warm."

"But . . ." Grace began.

"Do it. I'll get Nessa to fetch the doctor." She ran out of the room, past Lotte and Dora, who were just coming in.

"Maggie," Lotte cried and rushed in, followed by Dora. Emilie grabbed at Lotte as she rushed toward her sister, but she broke away. Then she saw the blood and screamed. Dora rushed to hold her back long enough for Grace and Emilie to cover Maggie with the blankets. Blankets that would never be usable again.

As soon as they were done, they stepped to the side and Lotte fell on her knees by the bed, taking her sister's hand. "Maggie, Maggie. What have you done?"

Mrs. B came back in the room carrying a bundle of clean linen. Jane followed with a bowl of steaming water, which she placed on the bedside table.

Mrs. B took Lotte by the shoulders and tried to move her away. "I need to clean her up for the doctor."

"I'll do it."

"No, Lotte." Mrs. B cut a look to Grace.

When Grace tried to lead her from the bed, Lotte refused to budge.

"Then move out of the way," Mrs. B ordered.

They were the harshest words Grace had ever heard from her landlady and she understood. She wasn't sure if Lotte did.

Lotte moved closer to Maggie's head, brushed her hair from her eyes.

"Who did this?"

"A lady," Maggie moaned. "Jack said she would help us. But she hurt me."

She let out a wail and fought to pull her petticoats down when Mrs. B pulled them up to try to stanch the bleeding.

"Hold her," Mrs. B ordered. Grace moved Lotte out of the way and grabbed both Maggie's hands and pressed them to her chest. Emilie sat at the end of the bed keeping her legs from thrashing.

Lotte turned on Jane, who was standing at the ready with the stack of rags. "Did you and Nessa help them? Did you know what they were planning?" The tears were coursing down Lotte's face, her skin as colorless as the linen Jane held in her arms.

Jane stumbled back. "It weren't us." She turned to Mrs. B. "We didn't know anything about it, I swear it."

"Jack said it was a secret," Maggie cried. "Jack took me there. He said he would wait for me outside, but he didn't. He didn't wait for me and I was all alone and I couldn't find my way—" Her last word was cut off in a groan, and she thrashed against Mrs. B's ministrations.

Grace wanted to cover her ears, but she knew it wouldn't cut out any of what was happening.

"I'm sorry, Lotte. I'm sorry."

"It's okay. It's not your fault. It's mine. I should have taken better care of you. But I'll make it right. I'll take such good care of you. You'll see."

"Don't cry, Lotte. I don't like Jack anymore. Can I still work for Mr. Tiffany like I always have?"

"Sure you can. Everything will be fine."

Grace caught Emilie's eye. And saw the same understanding in her eyes that Grace knew was in her own.

There was a commotion on the stairs and Nessa burst into the room. "Doctor's coming." She stopped short and stared at the bed. Behind her a small, bent man with a long black overcoat and carrying a black bag huffed into the room.

Mrs. B immediately ceded her place to him, managing to pull Lotte with her.

"*Mille grazie*, Jacob," she said as he took her place. And she herded the others out of the room. "Lotte, you too. You're just in the way. Let the doctor see to her."

They took Lotte down to the parlor, settled her in a chair, and stationed themselves around her, trying to give comfort, but not holding out much hope.

It was clear to Grace that Emilie didn't. Emilie had seen more of the world than probably any of them; she looked shocked, angry, but resigned.

Well, Grace was angry, but she was not resigned. And she wanted to howl at the injustice of it all. How a man could use an unsuspecting woman in this way, one who had less than common judgment, take advantage of her, then make sure he didn't have to pay for his transgressions.

It was a crime to seek an abortion. To aid someone in seeking an abortion. But men never paid, not the ultimate price. It was the poor unsuspecting woman who was sent to jail or, escaping prison, lived a mangled, unfruitful life, if she managed to survive at all.

Grace felt a hand touch hers. She looked up to see Emilie, understanding passing between them, and also pity, anger, and acceptance of what was to come.

It seemed like hours went by. Nessa brought coffee and sandwiches and poured cup after cup, but no one wanted anything to eat.

Dora had slid into the same chair as Lotte and held her close while she sobbed quietly into Dora's shoulder. It surprised Grace that Dora, who was so concerned with her own future, her own happy ever after, was so compassionate. Maybe she had underestimated their southern belle.

The doctor stayed so long in the room with Maggie that for a moment Grace began to hope her fears had been ungrounded.

But when he finally came into the parlor, Mrs. B by his side,

Grace knew from their expressions there would be no happy ending for Maggie Wilson.

"I'm sorry," the doctor said in a heavily accented voice. "She has lost too much blood."

"The hospital?" Lotte said.

"If we take her, they will arrest her, and it won't save her. I am sorry."

"No!" Lotte let out an ungodly cry and Dora burst into sobs of her own. Even Miss Vanderheusen, who had been the rock of efficiency all night, sucked in her breath as her face contorted in suppressed emotion.

"I am so very sorry, but she will probably not last the night. I've given her something to make her comfortable. You may go to her now, if you wish." He nodded formally and left.

Lotte nearly stumbled from her chair and Dora helped her out of the room.

Grace followed them and found the doctor and Mrs. B standing at the door, their heads lowered in urgent conversation.

"Will you have to report this?" Mrs. B asked. "The poor girl is simple. She didn't understand what she was doing. Any of it."

"They can't arrest the dead . . ."

Mrs. B crossed herself. "But her sister shouldn't have to live with the stigma."

"No. This needn't have happened. There are people who can perform these things in relative safety. This butcher should be punished."

And she would be, Grace decided. Somehow they would get Jack to confess her name. Then Grace would tell the world the whole hideous story whether they wanted to hear it or not.

Chapter 23

Maggie died during the night. Mrs. Bertolucci wrote Mrs. Driscoll, informing her the Wilson sisters were ill and were being seen to at home.

Grace, Emilie, and Dora, eyes red rimmed and hearts aching, made the lonely cold walk to work in silence. None of them, not even Dora who planned to leave in the spring, felt they could take a day off. It was vital that the news of what really happened didn't leak out.

Emilie stopped them on the corner outside the studio. "Remember, not a word. Just a stomach ailment."

Grace gritted her teeth but agreed. It would be more than a scandal if it was thought that any of them, especially Lotte, knew what Maggie had planned. Knowledge even in the aftermath could have them arrested. Anthony Comstock and his Society for the Suppression of Vice had done their work too well. Had infiltrated Tammany Hall with lists of things he deemed immoral, which basically had anything to do with women being human. He was an evil, vicious man, and Grace hated him with all her heart, especially today.

It was as if Comstock himself had murdered poor Maggie. And Grace decided right there at the Tiffany building entrance that she would be one of the ones who would fight to bring him down.

If the newsboys were under the feet of the newspaper magnates Pulitzer and Hearst, all women were under the fat, smug body of Anthony Comstock.

And Grace began to sketch him in her head. A monster—a dissolute, repressed monster.

"Grace, are you coming?"

"What?" Grace realized Emilie and Dora were staring at her. "Yes. But first I'm going to the fourth floor and confront Jack Ratner."

Emilie grabbed her elbow. "Grace, think. If you accuse him, it will be all over the company before lunch."

Grace shook her elbow free. "We can't just let him get away with it."

"We won't," Emilie said. "But we have to be smart."

"You be smart; I want to grab him where it will hurt the most and make him pay."

"As do we all, but you know this isn't the way. Think." Emilie glanced at Dora, who was waiting by the door. "If we attack straight on, Lotte will never be able to show her face in here again. She might even be imprisoned."

"So we do nothing?"

"We wait for a day or two. Then Maggie will die of the influenza. Then we tell Mr. Tiffany the truth."

"And he'll fire Lotte on the spot. No one will hire her after that. Unless you think he will listen to you."

"Not me. But he will listen to Mrs. Driscoll."

"What makes you think she'll be sympathetic to Maggie's death?"

"Because she's a woman, because she cares about us, and she cares about justice. She wouldn't want her girls to be subjected to predators like Jack Ratner. And I'm sure Mr. Tiffany wouldn't either."

Grace thought about it. Emilie was probably right, and she did have more experience navigating the cutthroat world of gossip and innuendo, and—unless Grace missed her mark—scandal and the law.

"Tomorrow or the next day," Emilie said. "That should be long enough."

Grace huffed out a sigh, trying to dispel the need to exact her revenge on Jack Ratner, and nodded. Then they took the elevator upstairs to the fifth floor to give Mrs. Driscoll their landlady's note.

Mrs. Driscoll read the note, frowned with an expression rife with so many emotions—annoyance, worry, sympathy among them—that Grace was tempted just to tell her right out that Maggie was dead. But she caught Emilie's look of warning and bit back her words, clenching her fists until her fingernails dug into her palms. Emilie might be younger but she was certainly more worldly than any of them. Grace knew Emilie was angry, too, but she'd learned to hide it all too well.

"Oh, dear," exclaimed Mrs. Driscoll. "And the rest of you are feeling well?"

They all nodded.

Mrs. Driscoll shook her head, obviously torn between sympathy and worry about the loss of an efficient worker. Even for a day.

Mr. Mitchell took that moment to step into the workshop. He threw a cursory look at Grace and Emilie, lingering on Emilie, then found Mrs. Driscoll and informed her that Mr. Tiffany wanted to see her in his office. "Immediately."

Mrs. Driscoll followed him out.

"What do you think that was all about?" Grace asked, exchanging looks with Emilie.

"Nothing to do with us," Emilie said, but she didn't sound that certain to Grace.

CLARA DIDN'T EVEN have time to tidy her hair before Pringle Mitchell knocked on Mr. Tiffany's office door then opened it without waiting for an answer.

She pursed her lips in distaste. She hated the way "the powers" with their hold on the finances acted, not only toward her and the other Tiffany girls but toward Mr. Tiffany. She often found herself wanting to kick Mr. Mitchell in the shin and tell him to mind his manners and show some respect.

But she knew the futility of direct conflict.

She followed him in, wondering what in the world could have put him in such a snit.

Mr. Tiffany was sitting at his desk. "Thank you, Pringle, that will be all."

Mr. Mitchell stood for a long second as if he hadn't heard correctly.

"I won't be needing you, thank you." Mr. Tiffany smiled politely, but Clara knew that smile. Her boss and mentor was feeling pugilistic today.

Mr. Mitchell finally yielded and took himself off, shutting the door after him with a finality that put Clara's teeth on edge.

Clara waited. Then finally Mr. Tiffany pulled his stare from the door and toward her, the smile melting into a scowl that was downright foreboding.

She clasped her hands behind her back so he wouldn't see her fingers fidget.

"I've had some disturbing news," he said without preamble, then stood and walked to the window.

Oh, dear, Clara thought, her mind swinging from a new factory strike in the men's division to a fatal illness striking his wife, Louise. Mr. Tiffany had already lost one wife. A man shouldn't have to endure the death of a second.

He turned suddenly. "Infamy. Betrayal!"

Only one man could evoke such a reaction from Mr. Tiffany. "Mr. La Farge?" she asked quietly.

"La Farge? What the blazes does he have to do with it?"

"I don't as yet know what *it* is," Clara reminded him.

"I ran into Leland Bishop last night at the opera. He had the temerity to tell me he's seeing one of my girls."

Clara thought rapidly. His eldest daughter, May, had just married. That would leave . . . "You don't think his intentions are honorable toward your daughter?"

"Daughter? What daughter?"

Clara knit her brows, her head immediately started to throb. "You mean one of the Tiffany girls?"

"Exactly!" He strode back to face her, practically nose to nose. Clara tried to make herself smaller. No reason to confront him when he was in, as Alice said, "one of his restive moods."

"I must say, it seems unlikely. May I ask which one?"

"Emilie Pascal."

He hadn't finished saying the name before Clara had come to the same conclusion. Of course. Bishop had pursued Miss Pascal the night of the ball. She had acted with perfect decorum, and so had he. But she was young and not practiced in the etiquette of the ballroom. Had she accepted too much attention?

Clara didn't think Leland Bishop would have put Emilie in that position, though now she looked back on it, there had been real interest in his eyes. Still . . .

"Well, aren't you going to say something?"

"I really don't think—"

"You will, of course, put an end to it immediately."

"Me?" The question came out automatically. She wasn't the girl's mother. And besides . . . "It was only the one night."

"Au contraire. He's seen her since. Several times."

"Wherever did you come up with that notion?"

"He told me so himself. He's courting that young woman."

"Well, I still have a hard time believing it, though she is quite beautiful, and refined, and passionate about her work."

"It's the passion that I'm worried about."

"I've never heard anything to his discredit."

"He's poaching."

"What on earth are you talking about?" Surely he couldn't be interested in the girl himself? No, that wasn't possible. Not Louis C. Tiffany. Clara wouldn't believe it. "Did you accuse him of that?"

"I told him that she was mine and not to continue to bother her. But I think you should have a talk with her."

And tell her what? Clara wanted to ask. Leland Bishop was, in a word, a catch. And she'd never heard anything to his discredit. Miss Pascal may not even care for him or realize the significance of his actions. "Do you think he's serious in his intentions?"

"I don't care. I want her mind on her work. Not on some upstart gallery owner or anyone else for that matter."

Clara thought he might be whistling in the wind. Emilie Pascal had a mind and—Clara imagined—a heart of her own.

"Bishop is a good man but men are . . . well, they are men, Mrs. Driscoll . . . even the best of them. And they have no business distracting the women in my workshop."

He looked at her expectantly; Clara resisted the urge to rub her pounding head. She didn't relish the idea of meddling in other people's lives. Not even those of her girls. "I'm sure Miss Pascal is capable of taking care of her own affairs. If I notice any signs that's she's distracted, I'll have a word."

For now, her only thought was to keep Miss Pascal working until the "Four Seasons" window was completed.

THE DAY DRAGGED on and by the time they hung up their aprons again, Grace was wrung out with containing her emotions. She knew Emilie and Dora must be, too. But when a couple of the girls had laughed about Maggie, saying she could afford to lose a little weight, and another quipped at least there would be no broken glass that day, Grace saw red. She marched straight for them, ready to bring her maulstick down on their heads.

Fortunately Mrs. Driscoll arrived to put an end to their conversation, and Grace slipped back to her post.

That evening, as soon as they reached the boardinghouse they all went straight to the back bedroom. The bed had been made. Maggie had already been taken away.

Lotte was sitting in an armchair as still as death herself. She saw them and succumbed to new tears.

"Thank you, thank you for being so kind to Maggie."

"Don't be silly," Dora said and came to give her a quick hug. "We loved Maggie."

"And you," Emilie added.

As for Grace, she could only nod her agreement, afraid that the waves of anger might spill out with her words.

MAGGIE WAS BURIED the next day, with only Lotte and Mrs. B in attendance.

"It is better this way," Mrs. B told them. "The authorities, egged on by that terrible Comstock man, will make us all miscreants if they can. The less you are involved, the better."

After Maggie's interment, Lotte retired to her own room, only coming down to meals and hardly speaking to any of them. The rest of them tiptoed around her, occasionally going up to check on her, but she was disconsolate and finally they just left her alone.

Lotte showed no interest in going back to work. And the three Tiffany girls felt more and more the pressure of living a lie. "But what will she do?" Dora asked. "If she can't work, where will she live? Who will take care of her?"

"Grief cannot be hurried," Mrs. B said. "I won't turn her out."

But they all knew that Mrs. B, for all her generosity, couldn't afford to keep anyone who couldn't pay.

AND YET ANOTHER day, Clara thought as she watched the three girls from Mrs. Bertolucci's enter the studio and take their places. It had been several days since the Wilson sisters had fallen ill. Every day she asked about them. Were they feeling better? Getting proper medical treatment? And every day, Emilie, Grace, and Dora nodded and looked solemn.

Clara dreaded every morning, expecting another one to be struck down with the disease. But so far they were all still arriving at work and leaving as always. Except Clara sensed something was wrong. And she wondered if the situation was dire.

If it was, she needed to know. Each day without Lotte meant they slipped a little further behind. And Clara felt added pressure to get the work done with a diminished staff.

Mr. Tiffany had been in a particularly ominous mood lately, curt with all the girls, including Clara and Agnes, but mainly with Emilie Pascal.

Their arguments over glass, art, and the amount of sunlight coming through the window were well known, and Clara usually looked on them with a kind of indulgence, amusement even. Emilie had seemed to relish their back-and-forths until the past few days. Now it seemed almost as if she didn't care. And Mr. Tiffany chafed under her lack of passion as much as he enjoyed decrying it.

After his usual Monday morning visit to the studio and not being able to get a rise out of his protégée, he accompanied Clara back to her office and barely had shut the door when he exploded.

"What's wrong with that girl? She's going through the motions of the 'Winter' panel like it was a circus advertisement. I told her to add another plate to the flame and she agreed without an argument. That piece didn't need another layer and she knows it. And the glass she chose as a background is an abomination."

Clara didn't bother to remind him that he and Agnes had been the ones to select that particular color in the first place. Mr. Tiffany's mood was no more about glass than the price of milk in Ohio. He was worried about the lack of spirit in one of his most promising artisans.

Could this really stem from the attentions Leland Bishop was entertaining toward the girl? Or was it Mr. Tiffany's paranoia? And if Leland Bishop was interested, was it more than just a passing fancy? Oh good lord, just when she was getting the staff back up to full capacity.

"Well?"

"Her friends are ill. I think it's making everyone, including Miss Pascal, a little melancholy."

"Balderdash. It's that damn Bishop. If this is his doing, I'll—"

"Do not upset yourself. I'll put a word in her ear."

"Humph. See that you do." He nodded abruptly and strode out

of the room, tapping his cane so loudly that everyone stopped to watch, and one of the girls covered her ears as he passed.

Except for Emilie Pascal. She just kept working as if he didn't exist. Clara couldn't put it off any longer.

"Miss Pascal."

Now the girl turned. Clara gestured for her to come to her office. Miss Pascal cast a glance at Miss Griffith before she followed Clara inside.

"Have a seat, Miss Pascal."

The girl looked speculatively at Clara and slowly sat down. Clara sat in her desk chair.

"Don't be alarmed. I don't know quite how to put this, but Mr. Tiffany evidently is concerned that you are seeing Mr. Leland Bishop . . . socially."

Miss Pascal's breath whooshed out. "Oh that," she said. "He invited me to tea, and again for hot chocolate. He is just amusing himself. I know better than to take him seriously."

"As long as he's not putting you in an uncomfortable situation."

"*Non, jamais.* I would never be so stupid. Surely Mr. Tiffany understands that." She lifted her chin in that stubborn way Clara had come to recognize. "Or is it the fact that I have seen Mr. Bishop at all?"

"A little of both, I suspect."

"Bah, a tempest in a teapot . . . literally."

Clara had a hard time not smiling. She suspected Miss Pascal could take care of herself. But that didn't mean she should have to. "I'm glad to hear it, but I do feel a responsibility to my girls."

"You do?"

"Why . . . yes, of course I do. That's why I feel it's incumbent on me to remind you that men don't always think rationally when it comes to women."

"Perhaps, but it is hard to believe a man so eloquent in glass and color as Mr. Tiffany could be so graceless in expressing his concerns. He should have asked me directly."

Clara was not about to open that can of worms. "Well, do not worry about it overmuch. I think if he'd allowed his daughters to be artists, I'm sure he would have wanted them to be as efficient and talented and as strong-willed as you. You must forgive him, my dear."

Miss Pascal nodded. "I know. I always do."

A knock interrupted them, the door opened, and Miss Griffith burst into the room.

"I couldn't let you face this alone."

"What on earth?" Clara exclaimed, standing automatically.

"It's nothing, Grace," Miss Pascal said urgently. "Just a misunderstanding. It's all straightened out now."

Miss Griffith shook her head. "It isn't fair. None of it is fair." Her voice broke.

And Clara got a flash of insight that something was seriously wrong in her fifth-floor domain.

This wasn't just about Leland Bishop. Which could only leave one thing. "Is this about Lotte and Maggie Wilson? Lotte has sent no word, and the two of you and Miss Hodgins have been as tight as clams about their situation. I need them back at work as soon as possible. I would like some straight answers, please."

The two girls exchanged looks.

"What is it?" Clara asked. "What are you not telling me? Are they seriously ill? Are they not planning to come back? There are over thirty other women out there who need to know they can depend on them. Mr. Tiffany needs to know.

"And I need to know. I can do without Maggie if I must, but I need Lotte here. If she's not really sick, but staying home to take care of her sister, she must make arrangements." Clara was exasperated beyond what was tenable; she closed her eyes against her sudden nausea and rubbed her temples.

"Maggie isn't coming back." Miss Griffith's voice was so strident that Clara opened her eyes and huffed out a sigh.

"Why didn't the girl just say so? I could have replaced her easily."

"Maggie isn't coming back because she's dead."

A dart of pain pierced Clara's temple. She groped for her chair and sank into it. "Oh my god. I'm so sorry. Why didn't you tell me? Mr. Tiffany would have wanted to send flowers. We all would have sent our condolences.

"But surely Lotte is strong; she won't succumb to the influenza."

"Maggie didn't die of influenza," Miss Griffith said.

"What? I thought you said—"

"We made it up. They didn't have the influenza."

"I don't understand."

Miss Pascal went to stand next to her friend and grasped her hand.

"Maggie was taken advantage of," Miss Pascal continued, more calmly. "He said he wanted to marry her. She didn't understand what he really wanted. I doubt if she understood what he did to her. And when . . ." She shuddered visibly. "When the worst happened, he took her to a place, to a woman who he said would help her. Then he left her there. Alone."

A ragged cry broke from Miss Griffith. "She bled to death trying to find her way home."

Clara was having a hard time taking this in. "But a doctor, surely." Though she had no illusions about the chances of a full recovery.

Again that exchange of looks.

"It was too late," Miss Pascal said.

"The poor child. The poor, poor child."

"Do you want to know who the man was?" Miss Griffith asked, though her words were more of a demand.

Clara's heart stopped for a second. "Someone we know?"

Miss Griffith leaned forward so suddenly that Clara nearly jumped in her seat. "Jack Ratner from the pottery department upstairs."

"No. Oh god have mercy."

"That devil will get no mercy from me," Miss Griffith spat. "Or the other girls. Somehow we'll make him pay."

Clara had no doubt that these two young women were more than capable of doing just that, but she shuddered to think what that payment might be.

"Let me handle it," Clara said. "Mr. Tiffany will want to know about this."

"No!" both girls cried. "You know it's illegal what she did. Maggie's dead, but Lotte shouldn't have to live with the shame or the fear of being arrested. No one, no one but Jack Ratner should be made to pay."

"Oh, have no doubt he will," Clara said. "The law may not pursue him, but I'm certain Mr. Tiffany will give him his marching orders. Don't be fooled by Mr. Tiffany's bouts of artistic temperament. He has the highest respect for women and their rights. Trust me, he will do something about this. And without involving the Wilson sisters or any of you. Mr. Ratner might not go to jail, but he'll get no references but bad ones from the Tiffany glass company."

"It isn't enough," said Miss Griffith.

"But it's something," Clara said. "And the other men will be put on notice. Things will change. It will take time, but they will change. I promise you that."

THAT NIGHT GRACE set to work on a new cartoon, not one of her usual political cartoons, but the continuation of the series she'd begun a few weeks before, and until now hadn't finished. But now she had an ending. A story in pictures. An all-too-common story, never told except in order to denigrate, shame, and punish the victims.

This story would be different. Would place the blame where blame was due. On the perpetrator and the society that allowed this to happen. Mrs. Driscoll had promised that Jack would be exposed and dismissed, but that wasn't enough for Grace. Her pen had driven a point home before.

It would do so again.

She drew with a vengeance. Each night after dinner she would sit at her desk, the anger and the hurt pouring onto the page.

The morning after she completed the final scene, she rolled it up and, leaving a message for Mrs. Driscoll with Emilie, she took her artwork down to the *Sun* office.

They wanted to know who G. L. Griffith was? Today they would find out.

As luck, or perhaps bad luck, would have it, the first person Grace ran into was Charlie Murray. He was standing in the hallway with several other reporters who looked like they had been out all night.

She considered ducking into one of the doors along her way, but before she could make a move, Charlie saw her. And Grace's treacherous heart did a little skip at the sight of the unshaven, rumpled, tired-looking man whom she had to admit, she'd missed sorely.

He headed toward her and she steeled her nerves. If he thought he could dissuade her, he was mistaken.

"Grace," he said, rather superfluously. "What are you doing here? I mean, I'm glad to see you but . . . Did you come to see me?"

She tried to ignore that twinkle in his eye. She could never tell if it was humor, or deviousness, or just the ordinary appearance of those particular organs. But it was always enticing.

"I actually have something for the paper. Not a cartoon exactly."

"Let me see."

Grace pulled the roll closer.

"Grace?"

She didn't answer immediately. Now that she was here and standing before Charlie, she was unsure of the step she had decided to take. Maybe it would behoove her to get a second opinion.

"You could buy me a cup of coffee if you're not busy."

"Just finished. And I know just the place."

He always did.

The café was right around the corner from the *Sun*. Once they had steaming mugs of dark coffee in front of them, Grace untied her bundle of illustrations.

"Something happened. Something I can't tell you about because . . . well, I just can't. But I have a story to tell."

"I'm intrigued," he said, pushing his mug out of the way.

She handed the sketches over and watched Charlie's face as he perused each section, two young girls left in front of an orphanage, sleeping with rows of other girls and finally being sent back to earn their way in the world. His expression grew more intense with each section, until he reached the end, Maggie dying in the street, Lotte holding her in her arms as the snow fell around them. A dramatic liberty that Grace felt no compunction using.

After a minute, Charlie carefully rolled them up and handed them back to her.

"Well?"

"They're very powerful."

"But you don't like them."

"No decent person could."

"That's not what I meant."

"Then I tell you outright. Neither the *Sun* nor any major paper would print these. And G. L. Griffith certainly wouldn't have drawn them."

"Then I'll sell them as Grace Griffith."

Charlie sighed deeply, his tired face showing more lines than someone his age should have. Grace was afraid she'd just added to them. She understood but she was immensely disappointed.

"I expected better from you, Charlie Murray." Grace started to get up.

Charlie reached across the table and pulled her back down. "I know you're angry, and you should be, all of us should be, but you won't succeed with this maudlin portrayal."

Grace raised her fist.

Charlie grabbed it and held it.

"You're just like all the others." *Please don't let me cry in front of him.* It was just that she was tired and disappointed and . . .

"Think, Grace. It's a man's world. I know you don't like to hear it. But it's a fact. If you want to change things, you have to survive in that world long enough to make it happen."

Somehow his grabbing her wrist had turned into holding it on the table, more of a caress than a defense.

"Why was your newsboys cartoon so popular? It was widely seen, talked about. It influenced people. Why?"

"Because it was about injustice."

"Of course, but think, it was satire. You didn't bang us over the head moralizing. People hate to be moralized at. Makes them do and think just the opposite. Injustice is like a rock that has to be chipped away at, bit by bit. One big whack gets attention and is soon forgotten. But it will probably be the end of G. L. Griffith. All the railing about the injustices of the world doesn't change opinion. You have to slip into people's minds by appearing clever, not aggressive."

Like Charlie did. Why hadn't she seen it before? His articles were wildly popular, not so much for their razor-sharp reporting but for making that news relatable. All his verbatim dialogue and descriptions of people made them real.

She glanced at her scroll of paper. But this was so important.

He squeezed her arm. "Grace, I want you to succeed. I agree with you. But butting your head against a brick wall will only give you a headache. Trust me, I've learned that the hard way.

"You can pillory Comstock and the law and anything you believe in, but draw your cartoons with satire and as G. L. Griffith. You've been working for the *Sun* less than a year. In another year you will have such a following, you'll be able to call your own shots. Under any name you want. One day the world will be Grace Griffith's. They can't keep you down, but you have to be smart.

"If you want to sell this for one of the political magazines, do it anonymously. Maybe you'll light a fire somewhere. But let them take it from there.

"You've got a golden opportunity at the *Sun* to change things as you see them. I understand your impatience. I really do. You've got a foot in the door, don't yank it back because you're mad and impatient."

"I used to have a colleague at the paper," she said.

He smiled, a mere shadow of his usual cocky self.

"You still do."

"And if I continue to be G. L. Griffith, you won't stand in my way of reporting the news at the scene as it happens?"

He didn't answer at first. Somehow her hand had slipped into his. She extricated it and stood up.

"Let me know when you decide." She headed to the exit door.

He caught up to her on the street.

She didn't slow down until he grabbed her by the shoulders and turned her around.

"Okay. I may not have another night's untroubled sleep. I've realized lately that I have to be part of your reckless ambition or watch from the sidelines. I don't much relish either, but yeah, okay."

The swagger was back and Grace felt an indescribable lift to her feelings. "Then we're a team?"

"As far as I'm concerned we're even more." He pulled her closer, and kissed her, full on the lips, holding her in place until she forgot they were standing on a street corner in the light of day and kissed him back.

It all made sense. She knew which direction her career would take. She would have patience. She would succeed. And suddenly everything in the world made sense, if only for the length of that kiss.

MRS. DRISCOLL MADE a condolence call a few days later. She sat with Lotte for a few minutes, then she and Mrs. B retired to her private parlor for a few minutes more. No one knew what passed between them, but Lotte, pale and thin as a wraith, returned to work the next day. The weather grew colder and the atmosphere inside the workshop more intense. The "Winter" panel was finished and sent downstairs; the "Spring" cartoon was put in its place. The glass was brought up from the basement and the panel that would complete the circle of life was begun in earnest.

Then in mid-February the snow came down so fast and furious that several of the girls were not able to make it into the studio. Those who were caught in the storm were taken in by anyone with a spare bed, and two girls came to stay at the boardinghouse. Those who managed to make it home the first day of the storm had no recourse but to stay home until it passed.

Mrs. B's girls trudged through the knee-deep drifts, stamped the snow from their boots in the lobby downstairs, and shivered their way up to the fifth floor.

Mr. Tiffany was there in the morning when they arrived and was there when they left. It seemed impossible that his carriage could make it through the downfall, but even more impossible that he should walk from his home on Seventy-Second Street. Often he would just come to stand behind Emilie as she worked on the "Spring" panel, its oranges and purples and greens cut and foiled and put precisely into place.

It snowed for a week.

And while the weather raged outside, the "Spring" panel blossomed into hope.

Chapter 24

Two weeks later, the last piece was added to the "Spring" panel. All the Tiffany girls came to see. It felt like a closing of the circle. Life renewed. The red, yellow, and orange tulips swayed in the breeze; white clouds, not snow, floated above them in a light blue sky. And even though they might never see the whole panel assembled, they knew they had been part of something special.

The next day, the men came to take the panel away, and Mr. Tiffany made an unscheduled visit. Unlike his usual visits, he walked straight back to Mrs. Driscoll's office, leaving a silent and staring staff in his wake.

Even Emilie turned and watched when he passed her and the memorial window she'd been given to draft onto the glass easel.

The office door opened and closed. A few minutes later it opened again. Mr. Tiffany emerged and retraced his steps, not lingering but heading straight for the exit door.

An uneasy murmur rippled through the room. Was he displeased with Mrs. Driscoll or with all of them? It wasn't like Mr. Tiffany to come and go without at least leaving them with a tidbit of philosophy about art.

A few minutes later, Mrs. Driscoll called Emilie and Grace to her office.

Emilie was suddenly filled with dread. Would their disclosing Maggie's fate lead to their dismissal?

Emilie entered the office with quaking knees and a sour stomach. Grace's face was ashen. What had they done? Was it because they had accused Jack Ratner of molesting Maggie? Or was it something even worse? Something that he'd learned about them. One of them? They both had something to hide and much to lose.

"Sit down, please."

They sat across from her at her desk. And waited.

"I have two pieces of news," Mrs. Driscoll said. "One you will be glad to hear. Mr. Tiffany has fired Jack Ratner without a reference and has sent a written notice to all the men's divisions stating that anyone showing unfavorable or unwanted attentions to any of his female employees will be terminated summarily."

Emilie nodded. She knew Grace wouldn't think it was enough. But right now she was worried about what the second thing was.

"And the other piece of news is that the two of you as well as Miss Northrop, Miss Gouvy, myself, and several artisans from the men's glass department will be accompanying Mr. Tiffany to Paris for the purpose of installing and making any necessary repairs to the exhibition pieces."

Emilie heard the words, even started at the word *Paris*, but it took several seconds for the meaning of the statement to sink in.

Beside her Grace hadn't made a sound.

"I was as surprised as you are. There are craftsmen there who are more than capable of dealing with these problems, but as I'm sure you are both aware, this is to be Mr. Tiffany's triumphant moment. He doesn't intend to let anything stand in the way of success. Not even a chipped piece of glass."

Emilie began to shake. She couldn't go back to Paris. Not this soon. She clasped her hands in her lap and dug her fingernails into her palms to stay calm. She couldn't go back there. And yet she dared not say no to Mr. Tiffany.

Mrs. Driscoll stood. "We'll be leaving in ten days, so we will be prepared for the April opening of the Expo. You will be there mainly to work, so pack accordingly. Though of course there will be time to visit your family." Then she smiled. "And I'm certain there will be ample time to sightsee. They say the Expo itself will be a marvel to behold.

"But until then, there's work to be done here."

They were dismissed. It took Emilie a second to react and by the time she stood, Grace was already heading to the door.

They didn't say a word to anyone, but by the end of day, the news had somehow spread through the workroom. And garnered all sorts of looks, from envious, to surprise, to anger. And Emilie knew it must be aimed at her. She was one of the newest hires and yet she had received, in the others' eyes, the highest honor.

And she dreaded it. She would gladly give the opportunity to anyone in the studio if she could. She couldn't go back. Nothing but humiliation and danger awaited her there. She'd have to find a way not to go.

Though she had to admit that she longed to see the "Four Seasons" windows assembled all in one piece. She knew in her heart and soul that it would be astounding, but to see it whole for herself . . . That would be something else.

Lotte congratulated Grace and Emilie as soon as they left the building that afternoon. She was merely being polite; Emilie knew that she just didn't care. Even after they told her the fate of Jack Ratner, she'd barely seemed to take it in. Lotte had been completely despondent since Maggie's death. Emilie thought she would feel unburdened, free from being responsible for her dependent sister's future. But now, she only seemed to feel that loss.

Dora, on the other hand, pouted all the way home, until they reminded her that work was work whether it was in Paris or New York, and that they would be working the entire time, so no balls, no fashion, no celebrations were in store for them. And that she would be leaving her job at Tiffany's to spend the season with her aunt and uncle where she was bound to find a handsome and rich husband.

She became so enthralled with that possibility that she finally joined in the excitement and even vowed to help them pack.

The only ones who weren't excited about their trip were Emilie and Grace.

"I can't be away for weeks. You have to be out there every second in the newspaper business or other reporters will get your story." Grace sat down heavily on her bed. "But I can't leave Tiffany's outright. I don't have an aunt and uncle who can support me while I chip away at the establishment to be an accepted political cartoonist. Well, actually I do, but they don't approve of female journalists, like the rest of my family."

"Well," Emilie said, "if I were an editor at the *Sun*, I would want illustrations to accompany firsthand reportage from the exhibits. Are they sending a reporter?"

Grace frowned. "I don't know. But you're right. Even if they don't, they might at least want some firsthand illustrations. I could send them back each day. Presented so the readers feel like they are there, too." She frowned even more. "I wonder . . ."

"And you can make sure Tiffany glass is a highlight of those illustrations."

"Ooh, you're devious," said Grace, brightening.

"I don't want to be," Emilie answered, crashing back from their flight of fancy.

"I didn't mean it like that." Grace moved over to where Emilie sat on her bed. "I've been so busy thinking about myself . . . Are you afraid to go back?"

Of course she was afraid. She was terrified. She'd come to feel so much a part of the Tiffany company and Mrs. B's boardinghouse that somewhere over the months Emilie had ceased to worry about her father, or Paris, or her reputation there. She'd even ceased to think about Jean and Marie, her dearest friends. And to her discredit, she was actually dreading having to face them. That's how much of a coward she was. Yes, she was afraid. Terribly afraid. "Not really," she said.

"Good," Grace said. "There will be so many people there from all over the world, what are the chances of running into someone you know?"

"Not much," Emilie admitted, though somehow that didn't make her feel better.

So as Grace's optimism grew, Emilie sank into a dark study.

As it turned out, the *Sun* was not sending a journalist to the Exposition, so they welcomed the chance to print any illustrations that G. L. Griffith might send back from Paris. "Charlie says they think G. L. Griffith is an eccentric nob whose family disapproves of journalism, hence his working on the sly. That's probably Charlie's doing."

"So you and Charlie are partners again?"

Grace, who had been pacing with excitement, grew quiet. "Yes, I think we are."

THEY LEFT TEN days later; everyone came out from Mrs. B's to see them off.

"Have a wonderful time," Mrs. B called as they climbed into the carriage Tiffany's had sent to take them to the dock. "Bon voyage," called Miss Vanderheusen and Miss Burns. The carriage jolted ahead. The last sight Emilie saw was Dora tearfully waving her handkerchief at them as the carriage drove away.

Emilie stood on the deck of the *La Bretagne* thinking about how strange a turn her life had taken. She and Grace had been given a first-class cabin, not deluxe but definitely several steps above the cramped second-class cabin where Emilie had spent her last voyage while teaching herself the craft of stained glass. The first night they dined with Mr. Tiffany and the others at a prominently placed table in the first-class dining hall. Emilie was surprised and delighted to see Mr. Nash, followed by a jolt of electricity to see Amon Bronsky standing beside him.

He bowed seriously and helped her with her seat. Emilie shivered, inordinately aware of his presence. She could feel the heat of him as if he were still standing half naked at the furnaces. She wanted to withdraw from him, keep a safe distance between them, but like a moth to the flame . . . She sat down, straightened her spine, and forced her attention to Mr. Tiffany, who was sitting across from her.

Dinner conversation was carried by the more senior Tiffany staff while the others responded as asked and tried to look pleasant, even Amon, who answered when spoken to in a deep voice that sent chills through Emilie though she tried hard to ignore them.

She was relieved when dinner ended and she and Grace were free to walk the deck without the supervision of Mrs. Driscoll. They'd barely escaped into the sea air when Emilie felt Amon come up beside them. Mr. Nash had asked him to accompany them to see to their safety. And Emilie wondered why oh why wasn't he in second class with the other men from the foundry?

After that he joined them each night after dinner. On the

fourth night when he appeared, Grace made an excuse to slip away.

Emilie cast a frantic look toward her, but Grace just winked and hurried away. Emilie cut the walk short that evening and returned early to the cabin she shared with Grace.

"Grace, you mustn't leave me with him."

Grace looked up from her sketching and frowned. "Why not? I thought you liked him."

"I don't . . . I do, but . . ."

"Oh, for heaven's sake, it's obvious the two of you are fine without me. I have to admit he's very intense and slightly mysterious. Though I think that might be his dark, brooding manner," Grace said.

"I'm not affected by that manner," Emilie said. What she felt was much more intense, something between desire and revulsion. It was no place Emilie could afford to go.

"Liar," Grace said with a knowing smile. "Just don't get carried away."

"I have no intention of being carried away . . . by anyone."

"What about Mr. Bishop? He's *très chic*." Grace waggled her eyebrows in a gesture straight from the music hall.

"Your accent is terrible." Emilie laughed, but she felt far from laughing; she was suddenly remembering Jean, whom she'd left less than a year ago. How uncomplicated that love had been and how quickly she had let it go.

As one day rolled into the next and they sailed closer to France, Emilie's anxiety increased, at odds with her growing desire to see her home again. On the last night before they docked in Le Havre, Emilie stood at the rail, a sliver of moon reflecting off the water, dipping and rising with the swells of the waves and with the swells of her heart.

Amon came to stand beside her. She didn't have to look to feel his presence. There was a fire between them that she could no longer deny. The air around them sparked with a force so great that Emilie automatically turned toward him.

Without a word, Amon drew her closer, his powerful arms entrapping her physically as well as embracing her whole being.

Oh, Maman, what is this feeling? Shall I yield or run away?

Run! She knew she must run and yet she opened her lips to his. She went willingly. Relishing the strength of him, the heat of him, and for an infinite moment she gave in to the promise of his passion.

Run, ma petite!

Emilie drew away. It took all her strength, left her breathless, and alone. More alone it seemed than ever, now that she had tasted what she had only dreamed about before. She was tempted. But she knew the things she loved most about him could destroy her.

"I'm sorry," he said, his voice husky, his large hands cradling her face. "I let myself get carried away. Forgive me."

She shook her head, pressed her fingers against his lips. "I can't." The words were wrenched from her. "I can't," she said, resigned.

"Don't say that. Forgive me and let us start again."

"You don't understand. I can't. Any of it."

And when he reached for her hands, she turned and ran. Down the deck into the dark. *Run, ma petite. Run.*

She didn't stop until she was in her cabin and a startled Grace had jumped from her berth in surprise.

"What happened? I swear if Amon Bronsky took advantage—"

"No, he didn't. He kissed me. I let him, willingly. But . . ."

"But what? You didn't like it?"

"Just the opposite."

Grace sank back on her bed. "Mr. Tiffany will have a fit."

"He will never know. It is over."

"Why? Was he too uncouth?"

"No, not at all. He's . . . overpowering. But, Grace, I've seen firsthand what passionate men are capable of—great works of art and horrible acts of destruction."

"Not all of them," Grace said, thoughtfully.

"But you can never know until it is too late."

They arrived in Le Havre the next day and stood on the train platform while the Tiffany exhibit pieces were loaded onto the train. Crate after crate, large and small, heavy and light, blown glass, lamps, windows, and decorative items of all kinds. Plus crates of replacement glass, repair equipment, cutters, solders, and all manner of things. Mr. Tiffany planned to be prepared for anything that might happen.

Mrs. Driscoll and Miss Northrop watched each movement with held breath, but Emilie wasn't worried. Mr. Tiffany had hired skilled movers to do the job and he and Mr. Nash were overseeing their every move.

At last they all boarded the train and Emilie braced herself for Paris.

It was dark when the train pulled into the Gare Saint-Lazare, and while the others gazed in amazement at their surroundings, Emilie stared at the ground and steeled her nerves.

It wasn't easy facing your past, especially when it was not so long ago. Thousands of questions, possibilities, disasters flew across her brain. Had her father really left France? Had he been arrested in Italy or Spain? Was he languishing in prison? That was fine with her as long as she never saw him again. Every sound, every person brushing past her, made her quail with the sense that he would intrude upon her life again. Would someone recognize her, point her out? Would someone shout, "*J'accuse!*" Her freedom was so new, so vulnerable, and could be so easily lost.

"Emilie, hurry up," Grace said and nudged her toward the cab where already Miss Northrop, Miss Gouvy, and Mrs. Driscoll were waiting inside. Grace practically pushed Emilie into the opposite seat.

"Are you happy to be home again?" Mrs. Driscoll asked.

Emilie forced a smile. "It is nice, but New York is my home now."

Mrs. Driscoll smiled back and that was the end of the conversation.

The cab let them off in the Place des Pyramides near the Tuileries Gardens.

"The Hotel Regina was built just in time for the Exposition," Miss Northrop informed them. "We'll be the first guests."

"It's lovely," Mrs. Driscoll said. "And how appropriate. A grand art nouveau style to usher in the new art exhibits. What is that statue?"

"Jeanne d'Arc," Emilie answered automatically, hardly glancing at the square and the figure of the saint astride a massive horse.

"She doesn't look very comfortable," Grace noted.

"Alas, no. The statue has never been considered a great work of art, but the people love it. Love her."

"Well, I rather like it," Mrs. Driscoll said. "And consider it a good omen for the women of the Tiffany Glass and Decorating Company."

"You would, Clara," Miss Gouvy said. And laughing, the two women led the way into the hotel.

It *was* a spectacular hotel, Emilie thought as the concierge welcomed their group. They were surrounded by rich, decorative paneling. Crystal chandeliers sparkled above their heads, and mosaic tiles covered the floor.

"I feel like we're walking on one of our mosaic panels," Grace whispered as they made their way to the elevator and up to their room.

The room was large, with carved moldings and two high beds covered in sateen duvets. Heavy draperies were pulled back from a French window where from a tiny Juliet balcony, they could see La Tour Eiffel beyond the *jardins*.

"Amazing," exclaimed Grace. "That's really the Eiffel Tower? Is it made of real gold?" She was already reaching for her sketchbook.

"They must have painted it for the Exposition," Emilie said, peering out the window in a different direction. "They're always painting it for one celebration or another."

"You don't seem excited. You probably stayed in places like this when you lived here." Grace fell backward on the silky coverlets and sighed. "This is the life."

Oh, yes, "the life." Emilie had stayed in luxurious places many times, though many more times in squalor, in Montmartre and most recently the Sorbonne. She could see the lights of it from where she stood. One of them might even be the apartments on the rue Suger.

Were Jean and Marie still living there? Emilie pulled her gaze away. She wouldn't look for the Pont des Arts. She wouldn't be able to see it past the trees. She would visit there, but not tonight. Tonight she must prepare for tomorrow. She must be strong—and careful. She shut the drapes and turned away. She wasn't ready.

Grace sat up. "Don't worry, Emilie. You'll be fine. You have friends. You're a Tiffany girl. No one can hurt you when you're with us."

They spent the rest of the evening luxuriating in hot baths and washing their hair. The beds were comfortable and Emilie wished she had one of her fine lawn nightgowns befitting such elegance, rather than the muslin one she'd brought to New York that was showing signs of wear.

It didn't matter in the least. She slept the sleep of the carefree, and for the first time in months she dreamed in French.

Clara barely slept; she was excited, but even more, she worried that something had broken in transit or was lost completely. Or there might be a change in the Tiffany Pavilion space and her dragonflies would be left out of the Exhibition. She was anxious about how the Tiffany works would be received, then she felt like a traitor even thinking it. Mr. Tiffany was a genius whose time had come. But she also knew the foibles of the art world, the jealousies, and the preconceived notions of people, their tastes and closed-mindedness.

"I give up," Alice said as soon as light broke through their windows.

Clara turned over to see her friend sitting bolt upright in bed, her white cambric nightgown looking like it had just come from the ironing press. Clara was sure her own looked like she'd tossed and turned all night, which she had.

"Everything will be fine," Alice continued. "Let us have some breakfast and go see for ourselves."

Clara smiled sheepishly. "What would I do without your good sense?"

"Depend on your own, which you usually do. For myself, I'm

not up to worrying about anything until I indulge in a real French *petit dejeuner*, and some very strong café au lait."

They breakfasted downstairs and were just leaving the hotel when Miss Griffith and Miss Pascal stepped out of the elevator.

"Have you breakfasted?" Clara asked.

"Yes," Miss Griffith said. "We were just leaving for the pavilion."

"Then do share a taxi with us. It's a lovely day, but I confess I'm a bit anxious to get to the exhibition rooms. The men left early to begin the setup. Miss Northrop is joining us there later. She is meeting with several gallery owners this morning."

"Thank you," Miss Pascal said. And the four of them went outside.

They took a taxi to Les Invalides where the Tiffany Pavilion was being housed.

The four of them swiveled from one side to the other as they drove along the Tuileries Gardens.

"It's lovely," Alice exclaimed. "Spring in Paris, the buds just tipping the trees with that perfect shade of light green. I must try to paint it before the leaves mature."

Spring, thought Clara and wondered if the men had successfully finished unpacking the "Four Seasons" window.

The taxi came to a stop at the curb.

"*Le pont. Ce necessaire* . . ." The driver rattled off a string of words that Clara barely understood.

"Pardon?"

He scowled at her and scissored his fingers. "*C'est nouveau. Pour les pieton.*"

"It's only used by pedestrians," Miss Pascal translated.

"Of course." Emilie had become so much a part of the Tiffany family that Clara almost forgot she was French.

“Ah, merci,” said Clara. She paid the fare and they all climbed out to the street. And stopped, even Miss Pascal who seemed taken aback by the sight before them. The new bridge, the Pont Alexandre III, spanned the Seine to the Esplanade des Invalides. It was a masterpiece of art nouveau, with an extravagant use of pilasters and statues, flanked by rows of voluptuous lamps and anchored by four huge pillars at each corner.

“It was still under construction when I left.” Miss Pascal suddenly covered her mouth with her hand, perhaps because she had started the explanation in French before she caught herself and switched to English.

“It must feel good to be home,” Alice said.

Miss Pascal smiled, but said, “Tiffany’s is my home now.”

They gazed at the bridge for a few moments longer.

“I don’t believe I’ve ever seen so many angels even in church,” said Alice. “And gold to boot. They have certainly gone all out.”

“May they watch over us,” said Clara and set a brisk pace across the bridge; she couldn’t help herself. Alice fell in step and even Miss Pascal took Miss Griffith’s arm to hurry her along.

Clara knew Alice and Miss Griffith, who hadn’t been abroad before, must be wanting to stop and stare at everything they passed, but they would have plenty of time to sightsee later. Right now, they needed to get the exhibition in tip-top shape.

But even Clara stopped when they reached the opposite shore.

“*Qu’ont-ils fait?*” gasped Miss Pascal.

Where once the grass had lined the Esplanade all the way to the Invalides hospital, two rows of buildings of the most fantastical decorations and façades had appeared. Clara could barely make out the dome of the Invalides hospital in the distance; the rest of the building had been completely hidden with this fanciful city.

"It's all a bit much," Clara said.

"Certainly extravagant," Alice agreed.

Miss Griffith was the only one who didn't comment, just looked around as if she was memorizing every minaret, turret, pagoda, and cupola.

"Mr. Nash said our pavilion would be in the buildings on the west side of the Esplanade. It must be this way." Clara started toward the nearest entrance. She was barely aware of the others hurrying to keep up.

When they encountered the doorman, Clara stepped back to let Miss Pascal ask for directions. Clara wished she had more fastidiously kept up her French. She knew enough of the language to get by, but she thought it would boost Miss Pascal's morale to be needed. Clara hadn't failed to notice that the girl had been decidedly more quiet and a little pale on the voyage over.

She'd put it down to the sea. Well, she was home now. Clara just fervently hoped that being with family and friends again wouldn't tempt her to stay instead of returning to New York when the trip was over.

"We are to follow the aisle between the displays to the far end of the hall," Miss Pascal said. "Les Etats Unis is between Angleterre and Allemagne."

They passed several exhibits that Clara would revisit if time allowed. It concerned her that they were placed so far down the hall. The Esplanade wasn't even in the main part of the fair. And there was so much to see. She just hoped people would be able to find them.

And suddenly they were standing beneath a square lintel and overhead sign that read TIFFANY FAVRILE GLASS NEW YORK. Clara took a deep breath, and passing the gold punch bowl commissioned by the Havemeyer family and the lotus motif torchière that flanked the entrance, she parted the heavy drapes and they all slipped inside.

The first thing Clara noticed was the lack of lighting. The whole space was in shadow. Not one of the heavy wall pieces had been hung; not one glass viewing case set up. It didn't look like they had even begun work.

A shard of anxiety shot through her.

Nash appeared out of the shadows and hurried toward them.

"What's happened?" Clara demanded. "Why is it so dark?"

She peered into the shadows. "Where are all the pieces? Where are the windows? The vases? Why has nothing been installed?"

Nr. Nash held up both hands and sighed heavily. "It seems we've had a bit of a setback."

Chapter 25

For a moment there was total empty silence. Their months of hard work, their long voyage . . . Mr. Tiffany's triumph seemed to have been snatched from their fingers.

Mr. Nash cleared his throat. It sounded like a freight train in a tunnel. "As you can see, the lighting is nowhere near sufficient, so . . ."

"What will we do?" Emilie blurted out. "You can't see the work in the dark."

"Mr. Tiffany has already gone to the Westinghouse Pavilion to see about installing more lighting. It will at the least take the remainder of the day." But his expression said, *If they can do it at all.*

At that moment Mr. Tiffany strode into the pavilion, followed by two men in coveralls.

They turned as one to face him.

"Ah, I see you've discovered our predicament. Well, it will soon be remedied. Our friends from the Westinghouse exhibit have offered to take a look and rectify the situation."

"He seems awfully jolly for a man whose life's work is in danger of being undermined," Grace whispered to Emilie.

Emilie shook her head. She'd recognized that glint of fury that belied Mr. Tiffany's enthusiasm. She'd been the object of it more than once. *Please let these men be able to fix things in time.*

"This way, gentlemen." Mr. Tiffany strode through the exhibition room as assured and supple as a cat in the dark. The Westinghouse men and Mr. Nash accompanied him to the back where presumably the source of the electricity could be found.

Emilie and the others followed the men and crowded into another smaller room, which was filled with unpacked crates, empty cabinets, and construction tools.

While the Westinghouse men looked over the situation, Mr. Nash ushered the rest of them back into the exhibition space, which also seemed awfully small to Emilie. Surely Mr. Tiffany, the undisputed—to her at least—master of glass, deserved better positioning.

After several minutes Mr. Tiffany returned. "It seems we are in luck. Westinghouse has agreed to relight the space today. So you may have the rest of the day to enjoy yourselves. But don't tire yourselves out. Once the lighting is in place we will have to work indefatigably to get the exhibit ready. Unfortunately, the Corona men have already left so I can't provide you an escort, but perhaps . . ." He stalled at that and Mrs. Driscoll stepped in.

"Miss Pascal, if you would like to visit friends or family, today would be the day to do it. We will be busy after that."

"Thank you," Emilie began. *But you are my family and friends now.*

"Miss Griffith, if you would like to wait, Miss Gouvy and I should be free soon and we plan to take in some of the other exhibitions, check out the competition, so to speak."

Grace widened her eyes at Emilie.

"I thought Miss Griffith might go with me," said Emilie, picking up Grace's cue.

"Excellent," said Mr. Tiffany. "A nice relaxing day; you certainly deserve it, both of you."

"But isn't there something we can do to help?" Emilie asked.

"Not at all. And don't worry. Several exhibits are running late. A good many of the exhibitors haven't even arrived. And we heard the Palace of Electricity was completely without electricity just yesterday. Can you imagine? What a good laugh that would be. But fortunately it is now fully lit. If they can do it, so can we." He nodded as if putting a period to failure. "Now get on with you."

Emilie and Grace went back outside.

"Whew," said Grace. "I was afraid they were going to insist on chaperoning me and I'd never get any work done. Thanks for bailing me out."

"*Ce n'est rien*," Emilie said, suddenly at a loss of purpose and fighting the desire to run back into the hall and sit in the dark until it was time to work again.

"But don't worry about me. Go and see your friends, I can take care of myself."

Emilie shook her head.

"Really, I go everywhere alone in New York all the time. The world's fair can't be any more daunting than the Lower East Side. And I promise not to get lost."

"I'm not going to see my friends. Not yet." Emilie bit her lip. "I know I should but I just— I feel bad about not staying in touch, but now that I'm here . . . I just need more time."

Grace linked her arm in Emilie's. "Then why don't we explore the fair together?"

"I don't know. What if someone recognizes me?"

"There are thousands of people here from all over the world. What are the chances of someone from your past recognizing you, wearing a work skirt and shirtwaist and your hair coiled like a matron?"

Emilie sighed. "When you put it that way . . . I guess it will be fine."

ONCE THEY WERE back at the Seine, Grace stopped to get out a small sketch pad and pencil. She smiled at Emilie, trying to reassure her, but she was wound tight as a coil.

"What if I drew a mustache on your upper lip?" Grace waggled her pencil in Emilie's face.

And finally Emilie laughed. "You're right. I'm being silly. *On y va.*"

Walking toward the main thoroughfare was like taking a tour of the world. Glass pavilions, Japanese pagodas, Arabian palaces, Swiss chalets, each with properly costumed barkers urging them inside. Grace didn't know what to draw first, but every time she stopped to capture something on paper, Emilie pulled her along.

"We'll never even reach the fair if you stop to draw everything you see."

Grace couldn't help it. There was so much material everywhere she looked.

Scotsmen in kilts stood before stone houses with peat roofs; next to them geishas in elaborate kimonos welcomed visitors through torii gates. And in the distance above it all the Grande Roue de Paris, the giant Ferris wheel of Paris, circled in the background.

"I have a great idea," Emilie announced.

"I'm listening," Grace said, trying to finish up a sketch of a red-sashed Cossack who invited them to glimpse a bit of Russia.

"It's just what we need. You can draw and walk at the same time."

"Perfect. How?"

They stopped at a ticket kiosk where Emilie procured two tickets. "Voilà! *Le trottoir roulant.* The moving sidewalk." She gave Grace a little push. "*Tous à bord.*"

Grace stepped onto the sidewalk but it wasn't moving. However, next to it a moving wooden platform advanced slowly forward, and next to it, a third platform moved twice as fast.

They started their journey on the middle slow-moving sidewalk. Grace braced her feet to keep her balance as the boards vibrated beneath their feet, and her pencil bounced across the page.

All the walks were crowded, and more than one young man attempted feats of daring by jumping back and forth from one to the other and surprising unsuspecting pedestrians along the way.

Grace sketched fast, catching the fearful expressions of the ladies and the contortions of the gentlemen trying to impress them. Even when one such gentleman made a miscalculation that sent his feet flying in one direction and his hat flying in the other, hitting the ground where it rolled and bounced and finally came to rest in the trees.

It was all recorded beneath Grace's pencil. At this rate she could fill an entire book as well as weeks' worth of newspaper articles. They jumped off the walk as they passed the main entrance of the Exposition. For a few seconds, bodies still vibrating from the ride, they watched the sidewalk continue on its elliptical way around the fair.

Ahead of them rose the entrance archway looking more like the giant headdress of an Indian dancer. Near the ticket booths, maps depicted the locations of the myriad of exhibits.

"It's huge," exclaimed Grace. "It would probably take weeks to see it all."

"And this is just one side of the river. The Grand Concourse and the palaces are on the other side of the river."

They entered below the giant base of the Eiffel Tower where

tourists stood gawking, their heads falling back to peer at the iron grid that pierced the sky.

"You can ride a huge elevator to the top or at least near the top," Emilie informed her.

"Have you been up?" Grace asked as she watched the giant rectangle carry rows of tourists up the side of the tower.

"Only to the second level."

"I think I'll keep my feet firmly on the ground," Grace said.

They walked on. Emilie slowed down just past a building called La Palais de la Femme. She turned to Grace. "I don't suppose G. L. Griffith would be interested in women's work? Mr. Tiffany is on the board to present an exhibit of women's artwork at the fair."

"Let's see it anyway. There's still plenty of time for G. L."

They visited exhibit after exhibit, ate *saucisson* with sweet mustard on crusty baguettes, washed down by *citron pressés.*

They followed a crowd into La Galerie des Machines Electrique where they were immediately surrounded by giant engines, casings, trestles and girders, and huge metal wheels, all of them loud. Emilie stood with her fingers in her ears, while Grace sketched, and businessmen with an eye to the future yelled to one another to be heard over the din.

Their ears were still ringing when they finally stepped out into the brisk spring day.

After another hour of exhibits, Emilie and Grace staggered out arm in arm, overcome by fatigue and laughter, and headed for the nearest sorbet vendor.

It was when they turned from the cart, cups of raspberry ices in hand, that Grace saw Emilie's expression change. The fear invading her eyes.

She turned her face away just as several men in black top hats and morning coats passed by going in the opposite direction. One of the men was looking in Grace and Emilie's direction, a frown on his face.

Grace turned to Emilie, but Emilie was gone.

Grace turned in all directions, forgetting her sorbet, her sketches, everything but her friend, and the expression on her face. When she was sure the men were well away, she scanned the crowd for Emilie, walked up and down the path trying to catch a glimpse of her. Even stood on a bench to look over the heads of the passersby.

EMILIE SLIPPED INTO a crowd of pedestrians moving away from the Académie men. Why had she come? Why had she let down her guard? Why had she dared to spend a carefree day with a friend?

She'd lost her sorbet somewhere in her retreat. And that was the thought that brought her utterly to defeat. All those delicious raspberries. And she gulped back a sob. She'd been a fool to think she could escape her past. Now if she could only disappear.

She left the crowd and skulked along the edge of the buildings wondering if she could find Grace in the sea of people, find her without being found by anyone she knew. And then she saw Grace's head above everyone else. She must be standing on something, looking for her.

And Emilie could have wept for joy. But did she dare to come out from the shadows? She must. She might be a coward, she might not deserve her friends, but she would not make them accomplices to her cowardice. She would make it up to Grace somehow, and she would visit Marie and Jean tonight.

And the next time Grace passed by, Emilie tucked her head and went out to join her.

"Sorry, I thought I saw someone I knew," she said as they walked along.

"I saw," Grace said, linking her arm in Emilie's. "He was frowning, but I don't think he recognized you. I don't think he was even looking at you. And even if he was, how many times in a crowd have you seen someone you thought you knew, and it turned out to be a stranger? It happens all the time. He's probably forgotten all about it." Grace gave Emilie a little shake. "Okay?"

Emilie nodded. "I lost my sorbet."

"So did I. Let's get another, this time, my treat."

THEY RETURNED TO the hotel much later. Emilie had every intention of begging off from dinner with the others, but they had run into Miss Gouvy in the lobby when they returned. Fortunately Mr. Tiffany and Miss Northrop were dining out and Mr. Nash and the men had gone out in search of an English pub. Over three courses, Miss Gouvy politely asked about their day, and Grace and Emilie replied the best they could. Mrs. Driscoll informed them of the workmen's progress. But they all seemed preoccupied and readily agreed to retire for the evening directly after coffee.

When they reached their room, Grace immediately pulled out paper and pen to work on the cartoons she wanted to send back to New York the next morning.

While she was absorbed in her work, Emilie grabbed her cloak and beret and slipped off to visit those she'd left behind.

Outside the hotel, the lights of the rue Rivoli lent a festive air to the night.

Emilie wrapped her cloak more closely about her. It was always cold and damp by the river, but tonight it affected her more than usual.

She walked across the Place du Carrousel where the round orbs of the lampposts perched like fireflies above her head. The Louvre rose to her left, the Tuileries stretched out to her right. And in the distance the lights of the Exposition Universelle shone like a colorful dome to a magic city.

People filled the sidewalks in part because of the Exposition. They were in a gay mood, couples strolling in the gardens, the restaurants overflowing to the sidewalk tables. Laughter and song filled the air, and for a moment Emilie remembered the good times when she had been one of these happy people. She was happy now, even after the near miss this afternoon, but not in the same way. And then she reached the river.

She made her way down the Quai. She could see the Pont des Arts clearly in the street light. But she didn't see the little flower seller.

At first Emilie refused to believe she wasn't there. She was something—someone—Emilie had come to depend on, if only her presence. As steady as the massive building behind them. And more welcomed. Had she sought a corner away from the brisk night air? Was she just resting her weary feet somewhere? But would she give up her lucrative spot even for a moment just when the Exposition was starting? That didn't make sense. Was she ill? Suddenly it was very important to know where the little flower seller was.

The tobacconist across the street was open so Emilie crossed and went inside.

"*Excusez.*"

The little man behind the counter looked up, his shiny pate catching the lamplight before his face came into focus. He had pinched features and thin lips as if constantly glaring against cigar and pipe smoke.

"Can you tell me where the flower seller is?"

"*Quoi?*"

"The little flower seller at the base of the bridge. Can you tell me where she is?"

"Haven't seen her."

Emilie waited.

"Not for months now. . . . Two . . . maybe three."

"Oh, well, thank you." Emilie turned to go but stopped with her hand on the knob. "*Dites-moi, s'il vous plaît.* Do you know her name?"

His expression became even more squinted. "*Moi?* I am a tobacconist. Why should I know the name of a flower seller?"

She lowered her head and left him to his indignation.

The night seemed even colder now.

Emilie took a breath and started across the bridge. When she was halfway, she stopped, leaned over the rail, and looked into the murky darkness. Why was it that the streetlights never seemed to penetrate the river?

She swallowed. "Hello, Maman. I'm back in Paris, but only for a short time. I like it in New York, Maman. I work for a glass artist, Mr. Tiffany. Do you know him? He's quite famous now, but perhaps not so much from when you were . . . when you were . . . that you would recognize his name.

"He's very demanding, but he has a vision. Oh, Maman, the colors in his glass are magic. Always changing with the light. I wish painting could be like that. There must be a way. Perhaps I will find it one day.

"Mostly I cut the glass pieces that go into the windows. But it's important to choose just the right section to match the picture, the folds of a gown, the hair of a cherub. I wish you could see. I worked on one that is showing at the Exposition here. It's like the new art nouveau movement. Oh, Maman, you wouldn't recognize the new art. It's brash and bold and I'm sure it keeps the Académie members up at night plotting its demise.

"But they can't stop progress, no more in art than in life. There are automobiles on the streets now. They run on electricity and some kind of fuel and go very fast . . . without horses. And people from all over the world are here.

"I don't know why Mr. Tiffany brought me here with the others. But I'm glad I get to be with you again. I won't be able to visit much while I'm here. I'll be busy. I don't even know how long that will be, but then I will return to New York. That is my home now. With Mr. Tiffany's girls. But I'll come again before I go."

Emilie closed her eyes. There was one more thing she wanted to ask. "Maman, there is a man. He's young and strong and talented. He makes beautiful glass vases. Favrile glass, they call it.

"I feel very drawn to him. My whole body is alert when he's near. He desires me, but does he really love me, Maman? A man who loves with passion can also hate with equal passion, can't he?

"I'm afraid to love, Maman. Is that the way it must be?"

She held quite still. Sometimes when she did, she could feel the warmth of her mother's hugs, but not tonight. She felt her presence and she thought she understood what her silence meant. *Do not love. It will destroy you like it destroyed me.*

Emilie turned away at last, not toward the hotel, but to the rue Suger, torn between anxiety and a need to make things right. But when she reached the building where she had lived, where Marie and Jean still lived, she couldn't go inside. She was too tired to do what she must.

She turned away and hurried back to the hotel, her mother's words echoing in her ear. *Do not love. It will destroy you.*

GRACE LEANED BACK in the dainty escritoire chair and stretched her back muscles. Between the walking, sketching while walking, and spending the evening at this small desk, she hurt in all manner of places. But she wanted to finish her sketches and take the packet down to the concierge to be sent in the next transcontinental post.

She was rather pleased with her first day's work for the *Sun*. The hardest part was deciding which cartoons to send.

Finally she chose one of the moving sidewalk, and the flying gentleman, legs splayed in his checkered trousers. Hat sailing through the air, while ladies shrank back in horror, and the man's expression broadcast his surprise and chagrin. The caption beneath it: "This is a moving sidewalk, sir. Not a flying machine!"

And another one of those massive deafening dynamos, two businessmen who stood nose to nose in their midst, their mouths open as they shouted to be heard over the roar. *Industry* and *Commerce in conversation.* While a third man, *Redundancy*, leads away a weary horse. She'd actually taken three real men as her models; the horse was a product of her own imagination. But what a perfect symbol for the past. Soon they would be replaced by more automobiles and dynamos and, who knew, maybe even machines for plowing the fields.

Grace drew a larger panorama of the fair with all the costumed figures they'd seen that day, with the Eiffel Tower soaring upward in the center.

When she was satisfied with her copies, she slipped them in between two pieces of cardboard and put it all into a large envelope and took it downstairs. She reached the lobby just as two men from the foundry, Oskar and Clint, came through the entrance, weaving slightly. Amon wasn't with them. And Emilie was still out.

They tipped their hats and grinned at Grace as they reached her.

"What did you do with Mr. Nash and Amon?" she asked lightly.

"Mr. Nash went to bed a good hour ago. Don't know what happened to Amon, he was with us a minute ago. Maybe he wandered off and got lost. Should we go look for him?"

"No!" Grace blurted. She took a quick breath. "I'm sure he's fine."

"What are you doing up so late?" Clint asked, eyeing her packet. "Writing love letters?"

"Not to you," Grace quipped, and she tapped her foot until they took the hint and staggered off to their beds.

Grace handed her packet to the concierge with instructions about the post, but she hesitated before returning upstairs. Should she go looking for Emilie? Just because Amon and Emilie were both out didn't mean they were together. Emilie may have decided to visit her friends. She'd been used to staying out late and enjoying the company of friends when she'd lived here. She might have decided to visit Jean and Marie.

She might have even gone to visit the Pont des Arts. Grace knew the bridge was nearby but not exactly where. Paris seemed to have a plethora of bridges and she didn't relish the idea of wandering around the streets of Paris in the dark.

Which was not a sign of cowardice, she told herself. She'd done just that in Manhattan many times getting a story. But she didn't know Paris and would easily be lost, and since her French barely passed the schoolroom, she knew better than to rely on language to get her by.

Besides, she would have noticed if Emilie and Amon were getting chummier, and she hadn't. In fact, if anything, Emilie had kept her distance. And Amon? Grace had been too busy with her sketching to notice.

And if they were together, she was certain any interference by her wouldn't be appreciated. She reluctantly turned toward the elevators.

Please God she was doing the right thing. And that Emilie was, too.

EMILIE TOOK HER time going back to the hotel, and she was about to cross the street when she saw the Tiffany crew returning from their night at the pub. She stepped back, waiting for them to go inside and upstairs, before she returned to the hotel. She didn't want to see Amon; she was too tired to resist his power over her.

She slipped back into the garden and without thinking, found herself on a quiet path, a path she had often strolled with her friends. She vaguely remembered, when she was a young child, sitting with her maman beneath the trees, drawing the people who passed, while her mother read, sometimes silently and sometimes out loud to Emilie.

There were other times when they had fled here to escape the wrath of her father. Those times they would sit holding each other, trembling, pretending that everything was fine and hoping they wouldn't be found. But Dominique Pascal never went looking for his small family. Just waited until they returned. It seemed his anger had no time limits on it.

Emilie shuddered in the night air. But she wouldn't remember those times, only the good ones . . . only the good ones.

She'd turned back toward the hotel when she saw him coming toward her, so soon after the image of her father that she let out a cry and stepped back. Then she recognized Amon.

"I'm sorry. I didn't mean to frighten you," he said. "But when I saw you walking alone I was concerned."

"You saw me?"

"Yes. When we were returning to the hotel. You were across the street." He stepped closer. "I would know you anywhere, even in the dark."

Emilie smiled, she couldn't help it. "Paris is the City of Light. We're surrounded by lights. Look at the sky."

But his eyes didn't leave hers; she could feel his heat and she wanted to wrap herself in it. "I'd better get back. Grace will be wondering where I am."

"Where were you? You shouldn't be out by yourself."

"I was walking. I'm from here, remember? I feel as comfortable here as I do in New York."

"And with me?"

"Amon, I told you I can't."

They started moving toward the trees. The trees that held so many memories. Did she and Amon belong beneath those trees? Was there a place for him in her life? Would their memories be good or bad? How she wanted him. But her mother's words still echoed in her bones.

They stepped into the shadows of overhanging branches.

"You're driving me crazy," he said, turning toward her. "Just being close to you is like a torture. A sublime torture. Tell me you aren't drawn to me as I am to you."

She couldn't.

He was impatient and before she could think, he had pulled her against the tree, pressed her back against the bark, and smothered her body with his. His lips covered hers and she gave in to him.

And then his hand moved to her breast and he ground into her and she wanted him, but not here. Not here. Not her safe place, her last living memory of her mother.

"Amon, I can't. I won't. My art comes first. It must come first."

"But I love you."

"You don't know me."

"I know all I need to know. Marry me. You can pursue your art. I earn enough to support us both. It would be a simpler life than the one you knew. We can rent a cottage in Corona. We could . . ."

Marry him. Marry him. An artist who worked all day and came home expecting his dinner. She wouldn't have time for art; she would take care of his home, and his children. Any woman would be happy married to Amon, a hardworking, passionate man.

Other women, but not her.

"No, Amon. I'm sorry, but no."

He held her tighter. "Why? You need someone to take care of you. And I love you. I know you must love me a little. I can tell when we're together."

"Men can love and work, but you know I can't have both, no woman can. It's just the way life is. I have to choose. And I choose art." She pulled away with the last vestige of her willpower, and if he had pulled her back, she might have yielded right there beneath the trees. But he didn't. Just called after her as she ran down the path.

"I won't wait forever!"

And suddenly she knew how her mother felt to love a man who loved too fiercely.

She didn't look back and didn't stop running until she was in the hotel lobby. Then out of breath, and probably looking wild, she said good evening to the concierge and stepped into the elevator.

Chapter 26

It took another whole day for the lighting to be finished and to move the equipment in to install the windows. Emilie and Grace were turned back at first by a rope across the opening of the Tiffany Pavilion and then by Mrs. Driscoll, who was leaving the pavilion because she, too, had been banished from the operation. Emilie argued that they needed someone to protect the artwork during the electrical installation.

"They survived the voyage over. I think they will survive a few electricians," Mrs. Driscoll said, not sounding very convinced herself. Then Mr. Nash appeared in the doorway. "Mr. Tiffany has everything under control. Go have fun; tomorrow there will be plenty for you to do."

"If you're interested," Mrs. Driscoll said, "Miss Northrop and I are off to check out the other decorative arts exhibits."

Grace politely declined. She already had her sketchbook in hand and reminded Emilie of a racehorse at the gate, eager to subject inventions and visitors alike to her prolific pen.

Emilie accepted the invitation. She would like to see what others had brought as their best work. So Emilie and her two superiors strolled down the Esplanade, viewing first the "Foreign" side, then moving to the "French side" where it turned out that Mr. Bing had set up a separate pavilion under the French aegis.

"We thought we'd wait for a few days," Miss Northrop said, when Emilie would have gone inside. "We don't want to appear too eager to see what he's offering. He used to be Mr. Tiffany's sole exhibiter, but he's only displaying a few of the older Tiffany works."

"He's gone total art nouveau," Mrs. Driscoll added, as they passed.

Emilie glanced inside and caught glimpses of a stunning array of art. Something she would return to experience when she was quite alone. Just as she had the day she'd entered his gallery and found Mr. Tiffany.

They moved from one pavilion to the other, where Mrs. Driscoll seemed particularly interested in decorative items. Several times her eyebrows rose in astonishment. Other times she made tsking noises.

Throughout, Emilie spotted pieces that were created by the Tiffany studios. They always added a special something to each display, especially when used alongside interior decor. They "finished" the room.

Once when she saw a transom window of stained glass, Emilie asked, "Does Mr. La Farge have a pavilion here?"

Mrs. Driscoll shook her head. "Couldn't afford it. Which is just as well. To think of him and Mr. Tiffany in competition again—" She shuddered. "Such antagonism between those two."

"La Farge doesn't hold a candle to Mr. Tiffany," Miss Northrop said. "Mr. Tiffany will take all the awards whether La Farge is here or not."

"He should," Mrs. Driscoll said cautiously. "But let's not count our chickens before they hatch. Still, poor Mr. La Farge."

"Oh, Clara, only you would be so compassionate," Miss Northrop said. "The man doesn't deserve pity. I grant you he's a good designer, but he's entirely unreliable, and claiming that Mr. Tiffany stole the idea of favrile glass from him—ridiculous. Whatever has happened to John La Farge, or in his case, didn't happen, is his own fault."

"On that we can both agree." Mrs. Driscoll turned to Emilie, whose mind had stopped on the "stole."

"Don't look shocked, Miss Pascal," Mrs. Driscoll said. "You can have all the talent in the world, but if you can't produce on time and catch the public's imagination, then you're not using the gifts God gave you. And that is to be pitied."

And that was something Emilie took to heart.

FINALLY ON THEIR third day in Paris, they were let back into the pavilion. The boys came in early to open crates and help hang the heavy stained-glass pieces and had already left by the time Emilie and Grace arrived.

The two torchières at the entrance were dark. The heavy drapes were still closed and the rope still barred the entrance. A rush of panic seized Emilie. Had something else gone wrong?

Grace merely hoisted her skirts and climbed over the rope to peek through the drapes. "Mr. Nash? Are you here?"

The drapes were suddenly pulled aside, and Mr. Nash appeared in his shirtsleeves. "Good morning, good morning." He moved the rope long enough for Emilie to enter, then ushered them inside.

Emilie stopped, awestruck. She'd expected a bright light everywhere to show off the detailed work. But not Mr. Tiffany. He used light just like he used glass, to shape and focus, to draw attention then inspire. In the workshop they depended on an even wash of light to create the finished work, but here, the finished works were presented to be savored. To be discovered as if by magic. Never totally dark but with streaks of lights playing against shadow, making the vases and bowls seem to materialize out of air.

"Oh," Emilie managed, as she remembered the first time she'd seen Mr. Tiffany's work in the Bing gallery on the rue de Provence.

"The Westinghouse men did a good job, didn't they?" Mr. Nash said. "Thank god they were willing to work through the night."

"Thanks to Mr. Tiffany's reputation," Emilie said.

"And his money," Grace added to Emilie under her breath. "But look how they've lit the 'Magnolia' window." She moved to the first exhibit where the spill of lights and flowers created petals so soft and natural looking that Grace was sure she could smell the delicate scent. The leaves were rich and waxy like real leaves, the whole a nuance of subtle shading and deep shadows.

"I hope Miss Northrop is pleased."

"She's very pleased," Mr. Nash told her as he proudly surveyed the room.

"And, look," Grace exclaimed. "They've written her name as designer next to it."

"How did they manage that?" Emilie asked.

"It's the rules," Mr. Nash explained. "The Exposition makes all presenters list the individual designer."

"Excellent," Grace said.

"Will you get recognized, Mr. Nash?" Emilie asked. "All this glass is because of you."

"I think Tiffany Glass and Decorating Company furnaces will get their due. Excuse me for a moment; one of the workmen is trying to get my attention." He hurried off.

"And I'm going to find Miss Northrop," Grace added and followed after him.

Left alone, Emilie walked over to a case displaying three vases in different shapes and colors, each with its own spot of light.

One was baluster shaped in an iridescent gold with a lily pad motif that Mr. Tiffany had designed himself. Emilie thought it was the most sublime vessel she had ever seen, simple and perfect. Another was made of red favrile and etched in a leaf pattern. The third was also opalescent with flecks of white and elegant filigree but in a patently modern design that made it particularly distinctive. She leaned closer to read the designer's name. Not Louis Comfort Tiffany, but Amon Bronsky.

And Emilie felt a pang of pride and honor for the man she had come to know and, despite herself, love, and for a moment, she felt a tug of disappointment for what could never be.

She could have looked at those vases for much longer, but there was so much to see and work to be done. She moved to the next piece of art. A window she hadn't seen before called "Pumpkins and Beets," continuing Mr. Tiffany's love of nature.

This also had Mr. Tiffany's name on it and a shiver ran through Emilie as she felt the essence of the man and wondered if someday her own work would have such depth.

She moved to the next display case just as Mr. Nash returned. The case held two lamps designed by Mrs. Driscoll, one with a dandelion motif and a copper base with repoussé leaves and flowers and puffballs and a white favrile globe perched on top like it might float away on the breeze.

And next to it was the dragonfly lamp they had all watched from birth to fruition. Dragonflies and dandelions. Nature captured and reimagined to adorn the homes of those who would bring the outdoors inside.

"It's spectacular," Emilie managed.

"And bound to be very popular. They're already planning how

to produce copies quickly without losing the uniqueness of the design. If you ask me, there will be dragonfly clocks, music boxes, paperweights, candy dishes. You name it."

"That will be something," Emilie said. "But, Mr. Nash, where is the 'Four Seasons'?"

"I thought you might be anxious to see that one." Mr. Nash winked at her. "This way." He took her over to a wide archway. "He has given it a special place, but first close your eyes."

Emilie put her hands over her eyes and felt his fingers enclose her arm as he guided her through the archway. Then he stopped her, adjusted her direction, and said, "Behold."

Heart beating fast, Emilie moved her hands, slowly opened her eyes.

For a moment she could only stand and stare.

"Well?" Mr. Nash asked quietly.

"It's magnificent." More magnificent than she'd ever imagined.

It was lit from behind just enough to mimic the daylight with shafts of light beaming upon it from the front. Her four panels were contained by six-inch gold-decorated borders. At the bottom, vines sprang and curled from a row of urns; above it all were the spreading wings of an eagle.

And there in the center arranged clockwise from "Spring" to "Summer," "Fall," and "Winter," the circle of life from birth to death and into birth again, connected, world without end.

And on the wall beside it, a bronze plaque, "Designed by Louis Comfort Tiffany."

Emilie's mouth twisted, and she started to cry.

"Oh my dear," said Mr. Nash, alarmed. "What is it? Is something wrong?"

"It is so beautiful, I think I might die."

He patted her shoulder. "He has surpassed himself in this," Mr. Nash agreed. "And we were all part of it."

After that they stood, unspeaking, until someone said in her ear: "Not bad, if I do say so."

"Mr. Tiffany," Emilie exclaimed at the new voice beside her. "Not bad, indeed," she agreed.

And the three of them, designer, glass cutter, and chemist, stood gazing at their work, satisfied and a little in awe at what they had done.

Emilie and Grace spent the rest of the morning on ladders, checking their respective windows for any cracks, chips, or loose solder. Then cleaned them with chamois cloths until the glass shone even brighter.

It was several hours before Emilie at last stopped to stand back and admire her window. "Her" window. Well, it was, partially. She knew every piece of glass, who had cut it and where it was placed. But it was the culmination of its parts that really made her appreciate the minutest details. Places to discover, to excite the eye or rest the soul. The inclusion of these things uplifted the whole. A testament to Mr. Tiffany's brilliance.

Knowing that she'd participated in its construction was liberating. She would never look back now. Everything was before her. And when they returned to New York she would start painting again in earnest. Because she knew there must be a way to bring light to oils in a way that would change the very essence of painting.

She would work for Mr. Tiffany. Continue to learn. Maybe one day even "collaborate" as Miss Northrop and Mrs. Driscoll did.

Emilie would continue to work in glass, at least until she found her new path.

Her shoulders and back were aching by the time Mrs. Driscoll called a lunch break. Emilie and Grace climbed carefully down from their ladders.

The other two women had also been busy; the cabinets were gleaming with polish and the vases, lamps, and boxes were shining in the light.

Mr. Tiffany stood near the drapes that covered the entrance, Mr. Nash by his side. Emilie could hear voices outside.

Emilie's first response was to rush to her window to make certain no one got too close or, heaven forbid, tried to touch it.

But she realized before she had gone two steps that a team of uniformed security people had drawn a velvet rope between brass stanchions to cordon off the windows from the visitors. The guards then positioned themselves strategically around the small gallery as a second barrier. Emilie had no warning of their presence, no idea where they'd come from, but she was extremely relieved that they were there.

Suddenly Mrs. Driscoll gathered Emilie and Grace up and herded them and their cleaning supplies to the back storeroom, where Agnes Northrop stood amid the packing crates and tools, wringing her hands.

Mrs. Driscoll closed the door and put her finger to her lips. "The Exposition judges are here," she whispered.

Emilie watched Grace's eyes grow wider and was sure hers were doing the same. She barely breathed. She wasn't sure she could breathe if she tried.

Mrs. Driscoll tiptoed back to the door, then looking quickly over her shoulder at the others, she carefully opened it a tiny crack and peered out.

The other three moved forward. Emilie, kneeling right below Grace's crouched figure, could just catch a glimpse of bearded men in dark suits and tall black hats, looking severe. And she scrambled back on hands and knees as the memory of the stern, unyielding men of the Académie des Beaux Arts flooded back.

She knew Mr. Tiffany was better than all the other exhibitors; one only had to look around to know it. But these men. They reeked of establishment. They were the kind of men who believed the stained glass of the Middle Ages was the only true glass. Oh, she knew men like them. These purveyors of taste in art. How they passed their judgment on others' talent, their art and their futures. They thought nothing of ridiculing those who dreamed of a different kind of art, of the avant-garde, of anything that didn't follow the formula. How dare they pass judgment on Mr. Tiffany's work.

"Who are those men?" Emilie whispered.

"The official judges for the decorative arts," Miss Northrop whispered back. "They are one of many panels of judges that are assigned to various areas of expertise."

"They look like undertakers," Grace whispered, not moving from her place at the door.

Mrs. Driscoll expelled a long breath. "I confess I'm almost afraid to look." But she didn't move from her place at the door.

Emilie wasn't sure how long they stayed huddled together like opera dancers looking over the audience for a rich patron, but they didn't move, and her feet were asleep when they heard the footsteps recede and the drapes being drawn out again.

Mrs. Driscoll straightened slowly and rubbed her temples.

"Do you think they liked it?" Grace ventured.

"Most certainly they did," Mrs. Driscoll said, brooking no arguments. "Perhaps we will find out more after Mr. Tiffany returns from the opening dinner this evening. I suppose it might take a few days for them to decide, though I wish they would hurry; the public will be admitted tomorrow and it would be lovely to show what awards we may win. If we win. How could we not? I don't think anyone else could possibly show such brilliance."

She finally stopped long enough to draw breath and looked at the others. "Don't you think?"

Chapter 27

Emilie woke with a feeling of anticipation the next morning. The sun was shining and she only wished she could see her "Four Seasons" window through the filter of natural light. But she didn't feel too badly about the electric light that the Westinghouse people, obviously closely overseen by Mr. Tiffany, had installed.

She missed his presence. On the voyage over, she had gotten used to seeing him every day and at almost every meal except when he was invited to the captain's table or dined with other dignitaries sailing to France. Now even though he was staying in the hotel, he was always out meeting with other artists, officials, and friends.

Emilie missed the nearness of that mind, his passion for art.

Grace was already sitting at the escritoire drawing away. Emilie had no idea how long she'd been awake. She yawned and got out of bed.

Grace glanced over her shoulder. "'Morning."

Emilie padded over to where several sheets were spread out before her. "Please don't tell me you've been up all night completing these, which by the way are really accurate." One titled *Mediaeval Paris* showed seventeenth-century peasants being ogled by twentieth-century tourists; it also showed the contents of chamber pots being tossed out the windows, and a group of tourists below, jumping aside in feigned—or real—horror. No doubt a well-rehearsed activity planned to miss the paying public. Another showed several young men and women entering the panorama "Tour around the World" and exiting as doddering old people.

Emilie chuckled. "What an idea of Paris you'll give to the *Sun*'s readers."

"Oh, I have several straight illustrations, but I couldn't resist. I had coffee sent up an hour ago. It's probably cold by now. Get dressed and let's breakfast downstairs like the ladies of leisure we are not."

Emilie dressed in her new workday shirtwaist and skirt, purchased before the trip and laundered by the hotel's excellent laundry staff. It was almost like being a real guest.

After breakfasting in the hotel's café with the other early-rising guests, Emilie and Grace were soon making their way to the Tiffany Pavilion on the Esplanade.

"Do you think there's any chance of the winner being announced as early as this morning?"

Emilie shrugged in the chilly morning air. "If it follows the usual French custom . . . no. But considering how many things they still have to judge, it's a possibility."

"Ugh," said Grace, hurrying ahead. "You're no help."

"Why are you so impatient to find out?" Emilie asked, hurrying to catch up.

"So I can write Charlie and tell him."

"Oh?" she said archly, inviting more.

"His name appeared in a list of 'reporters to watch' right before we left. If Miss Northrop or any of the Tiffany pieces get a medal, I'll be able to crow."

Emilie slipped her arm in Grace's. "You like him, don't you?"

Grace gave her a look. "He's my partner, my conduit to the editors. Liking has nothing to do with it."

"Uh-huh. I can tell."

"Well, it doesn't."

Crowds of people were already strolling in the gardens and they all seemed to be headed to the Expo.

"Looks like it will be a busy day," Emilie said. "We haven't really been given duties except to ready the exhibit in the morning and put it to bed at night."

"Yes," Grace said. "I wonder if they'll send us home soon."

Home. "I hope so," Emilie said. She would be glad to be back in the narrow bed at Mrs. B's and see the other Tiffany girls again. She wondered how Lotte was feeling and if Dora had moved out to her aunt and uncle's in preparation for the season.

Though Emilie had to admit she would miss Paris, this new Paris with sunlight and gardens and thousands of strangers. The vibrancy here would always speak to her, but there was a future in New York. And she wondered briefly if there was a place on earth where she could have both.

A cluster of people was already waiting to get into the Tiffany Pavilion when they reached the entrance, and they had to thread their way through with many apologies to the front where a security guard waved them through.

The room was crowded with people, mainly men and a few women, among them Mr. Tiffany and the senior members of the Tiffany staff.

"What's going on?" Grace asked, slipping between the viewers to Mr. Nash.

"See for yourself, Miss Griffith. Part of it belongs to you."

They were standing before the "Magnolia" window. Miss

Northrop was standing beside it. Holding . . . a medal. *They'd won a medal.*

"That's wonderful," Emilie said, slipping in beside her.

"It is indeed. Let's see what else we got."

Emilie and Grace eased out of the crowd, which seemed to consist largely of dignitaries and newsmen, and moved to the next display case. More medals. A gold for Mr. Tiffany's vase and one for Amon's. Emilie quickly looked around but neither man was in sight.

Another crowd was gathered around Mrs. Driscoll's lamps. When they finally managed to squeeze through to the front, they found a beaming Mrs. Driscoll explaining how nature influenced her designs. Several journalists were taking notes.

She flashed them a quick smile, and Emilie felt a swell of pride and happiness for her. *Her* vase. *Her* design. *Her* name. "Mrs. Clara Wolcott Driscoll" on the plaque beside it.

Emilie backed out of the group. Surely the "Four Seasons" window warranted a *gold* medal, too. But the curtain across the arch to the window was closed. Another uniformed sentinel stood in front of it.

She lifted her chin and stepped up to him. "What's going on?"

"No one is allowed in, mademoiselle."

"Why? What has happened?"

"Nothing. Mr. Tiffany is in there by himself."

"Why?"

"I don't know, miss. He just told me to guard the door."

"He won't know I'm there," she said and slipped through the opening before he could stop her or she could think better of what she was doing. What if they hadn't won? What if he was going to take his cane to it and destroy what they'd worked so hard for? She didn't care if he was Mr. Tiffany. She wouldn't let him destroy it. It was a masterwork. It was what stained glass should be. Would become the paradigm by which all stained glass would be judged.

He was just standing there looking up at his masterpiece and for a long moment she could only do the same. It was magnificent. He must know that.

His cane was in his hand, but the tip was still on the floor. She tried to see if there was a medal displayed by the window, but he blocked her view.

She eased to the side, not wanting to call attention to herself. It would anger him for certain that she had disobeyed. But she didn't care. Not now. Because it was there, on a pedestal beneath a glass dome. Larger than the others. It was tilted so the visitor could see it. *Le Grand Prix.* The highest award granted to the exhibits. They'd won.

She must have made a sound, because he turned around. His expression brooding.

Emilie braced for his reprimand. She even braced for his stick, though he had never raised it against any person that she had ever seen.

Now he lifted the tip of his cane and motioned her forward.

She came to stand beside him. He slowly pointed the cane toward "Spring." Emilie stiffened. Ready to grab the cane if she must. But his words stopped her.

"I told you that green was the right one for the new growth of spring."

The breath whooshed out of her, leaving her dizzy. "And you were right."

"What? No argument?"

"No argument." He truly was the King of Glass.

"Then I suppose we should let the others in."

She nodded, too full of emotion to speak.

He tapped his cane on the floor. The curtains parted and the crowd poured in.

Mr. Tiffany was immediately swept up with well-wishers and congratulations. And Emilie stepped out of the way and went to find Grace.

After about twenty minutes the group of dignitaries, friends, and journalists were shown out and a few others took their place.

Mr. Nash rounded up the boys and took them to the storage rooms to prepare the empty crates and packing material to be carted to a storage bin awaiting the return of the artwork at the end of November.

. . . If Mr. Tiffany didn't sell it all first. There had already been a rumor that a representative of a Russian museum was interested in Miss Northrop's "Magnolia" window.

Mrs. Driscoll, Miss Gouvy, and Miss Northrop were in consultation most of the morning. Probably working on the schedule for the studio's spring work. Just because Mrs. Driscoll was in Paris didn't mean that all work stopped in New York. When the crates were at last removed, they began reorganizing the back storage area to serve as a workshop for repair and maintenance of the exhibit.

The stream of visitors was steady throughout the morning. Mr. Tiffany was there to meet those whom he knew or wanted to know. It was midmorning when another surge of visitors entered, and a voice rose above the appreciative murmurs of the others. Emilie recognized it right away. Leland Bishop.

Bishop spotted Mr. Tiffany and made a beeline toward him.

"Hello, Louis. I heard you had arrived all right and tight, had the place rewired, and hung everything in time to sweep the gold medals in the decorative arts division."

They shook hands heartily. "Hello, Lee. I thought you planned to stay in London until next month."

"I did, but my curiosity got the better of me. And, besides, I didn't want to miss any latent talent that might be wandering around.

"I heard last night you had swept the field, so I dropped everything to come right over to see the exhibit, and congratulate you on your awards.

"And I must say, the display is a marvel. The lighting . . ." He kissed his fingers to his lips.

Mr. Tiffany broke out laughing. "Lee, Lee, you're spending too much time in Paris, my friend."

"Not at all," he said, glancing around. "Actually I also came to ask if I might take the Misses Pascal and Griffith to see the latest in paintings at the Grand Palais. I'm sure you haven't given them a moment off since you arrived, and I want to make sure they stay up-to-date on the current trends."

"Do you?" Mr. Tiffany said drily.

"You should, also. An educated artisan is a cut above."

Emilie knew he knew that she had heard every word. The man was incorrigible. It was hard not to laugh at his insouciance. And his subterfuge. He wanted someone to play with.

Mr. Tiffany beetled his thick eyebrows. "You young people. Always looking for entertainment."

"You being such a middle-aged old geezer?" Bishop asked innocently, setting off another laugh from Mr. Tiffany.

"You know, your father was just like you in his younger years."

"Well, there you have it. I feel honor bound to keep up the side. What do you say? May I have them?"

"I suppose. But you'll have to ask Mrs. Driscoll if she can spare them. You're coming to the Train Bleu dinner tonight, of course."

"I wouldn't be anywhere else. Until tonight." Bishop clapped his friend's arm, winked over his head at Emilie, and went off in search of Mrs. Driscoll.

A few minutes later Emilie and Grace had permission to accompany Leland Bishop to the art exhibits. Emilie had had just enough time to grab her hat and smooth her work skirt while Grace slung her drawing bag over her shoulder.

"You seem to have a plethora of men gadding about you," Grace said.

Emilie frowned at her. "What do you mean? I'm not sure what plethora is."

"A whole lot of."

"Oh, *pléthore*. I don't."

Grace raised one eyebrow.

"He's merely being polite, and I am looking forward to seeing the artwork at the Grand Palais. I just wish I didn't look like a . . . a . . ."

"Poor working girl?" Grace steered her out the door.

Leland Bishop was talking with two men when they entered the showroom.

"Ah, *mes belles dames*," he said, smiling at the two young women.

"*Sans merci*," Grace said under her breath.

Emilie cut her a look, then smiled pleasantly at the three men.

"*Excusez*." Bishop turned from the men, offered an elbow to each girl, and escorted them out the door.

They made small talk in English and French until they reached the Pont Alexandre. Then Grace released his arm. "If you don't mind terribly, I'll leave you here. There's another exhibit I'd like to see."

Leland blinked. "Shall we all see it? I don't think Mrs. Driscoll would be happy with me if anything happened to you."

"Well, we just won't tell her." Then she relented. "Please? Emilie wants to see the latest art and I really don't think you'd like where I'm going."

"That is alarming."

"Let me guess," Emilie said. "The mine tour."

Grace gave her a hopeful look. "Please, Mama."

Emilie winced. "Go ahead and have a good time. I'll see you back at the pavilion."

Grace hurried off without a backward look.

"She wants to go on a tour of mines?"

"She's studying light and dark and—" Emilie stopped, appalled that she'd been about to lie. It had come so easily. But no more lies, even a harmless one. "She has many interests."

His look said that he suspected there was more than she was telling, but he let it pass. "Shall we do the Grand Palais? There is only history at Le Petit."

"Therefore, nothing that would be a good addition to your galleries?"

"Exactly. But we shall go where you prefer. Either one gives me a good excuse to spend time with you."

Usually she enjoyed his banter, but having just shunned Amon, Emilie didn't want to appear a flirt. Not that anyone had seen. And she wasn't a flirt. But she had to admit, Leland Bishop was relaxing to be around, always amusing, sometimes funny—and very astute.

"What are you thinking, Miss Pascal?"

"About what to call you, Mr. Bishop."

"Leland would work unless we're around Louis. He is convinced I'm trying to lure you away for some nefarious purpose that he can't seem to name. It's not like I'm a competing artist. Not my forte, I'm afraid."

They fell silent as they walked across the Pont Alexandre.

"Have you been able to stop by the Bing gallery?" he asked.

"Not yet."

"Interesting. I did manage to stop in yesterday, but don't tell Louis."

"I never *tell* him anything. He is my employer and . . ." She hesitated.

"And?"

"At least I try not to. I've learned so much from him."

He laughed. "I can imagine. Actually so have I," he continued, more seriously. "He's the perfect combination of artist, entrepreneur, and sleight-of-hand man."

"Like a magician?"

"Well, yes. That, too. Do you not agree?"

"Yes, he does create magic. Better than anyone I've ever known."

"A lot of people would agree with you."

"Not you?"

"Of course I do, but part of his success is because he is smart enough to have a highly functioning atelier and knows how to select the best artists to work for him."

"And with all these gold medals," Emilie added enthusiastically, "he will be the undisputed . . . king . . . of stained glass."

Leland laughed out loud. "You French and your kings. So many of them met an ignominious end."

She was a little shocked at his reaction. "Not Mr. Tiffany." And she would bask in the brightness of his glory . . . until one day she would have the vision to create on her own. She sighed; it still seemed like a dream. A dream she'd never thought possible just a few months ago.

They stopped on the sidewalk at the entrance of the Grand Palais.

"Majestic Beaux-Arts façade," Leland said, as if quoting a guidebook. "Three different architects, the building cut up like a side of beef at the market. Details, details, details. Everywhere you look, more details."

"They say the devil is in the detail," Emilie said, laughing.

"Devil take the detail then and give me a unified whole."

"You're a classicist then."

"Me? Not at all. One day you'll have to visit my galleries and see for yourself."

"The one in Paris, London, or New York?" Emilie said, her practiced demeanor slipping for a second.

"All of them, of course," he retorted smoothly. "Shall we go inside?"

"By all means," she said primly, and avoiding his eyes, she gracefully lifted the hem of her work skirt and started up the steps.

They entered the building at the center hall, full of light that streamed in the steel-and-glass-domed ceiling. The hall was crowded with statuary. A stairway of elegant iron scrollwork led to a second level.

They both stood for so long that several people had to pardon themselves to be able to brush past.

"Do you want to see the statues?" Leland asked.

Emilie looked across the large space filled with statuary. "I wouldn't know where to begin," she answered.

"True. It's a little like a department store before Christmas. This way."

She was still recovering from his *petite blague*, when he took her elbow.

"Now we must choose. In the right wing is the best of the last decade of French art. But there is an international wing that's bound to be hit-and-miss. I recommend that, thinking you might have had enough of Beaux-Arts to last a lifetime."

Emilie started. "What on earth do you mean?" she asked in alarm. He couldn't know about her ousting from the Académie. She'd told no one, not even Grace.

"I mean nothing. Just that having lived in Paris you might want to see what the rest of the world has been doing during the last decade. L'Art de La Belle Epoque . . . *et les belles femmes*," he added quietly.

She darted a quick look at him, but he merely took her arm. "I believe it's this way."

They strolled from one country's exhibits to the next, lingering over one painting, hurrying past another, commenting and critiquing enthusiastically. Every now and then, he would stop, study a painting, seeming to forget he wasn't alone, then he'd turn back to her and take her arm.

"Occupational habit, I'm afraid. Heaven forbid I let some up-and-coming young artist manage to slip through my fingers."

Emilie looked curiously at him. He talked so carefree. But he was in a rarefied and serious business. Gallery owners could dash the hopes of an artist in the blink of an eye. Or make someone's career. Leland often made her forget that he was an internationally respected dealer. Most of the time he acted like one of the students at *université*. As if life were a delightful party.

She said so.

He raised both eyebrows at her. "Oh, don't be fooled by my youthful folly. I can be as ruthless as the next man, if need be."

"I don't believe you."

He broke into a grin. "Good. Shall we see what the Spaniards are up to?"

They were admiring a painting by Joaquin Sorolla y Bastida, discussing his technique of creating light and arguing about whether a sense of light could actually be attained without a medium like glass to enhance it, when Emilie became aware of a young man standing almost motionless beside them. He was staring at the painting next to the Sorolla.

She followed his gaze to a dark, moody depiction of a dying woman, a priest at her deathbed, and . . . a skeletal form leaning over to deliver the kiss of death.

The painting was called *Last Moments.*

Emilie shivered.

The young man glanced at her. Dark hair framed his narrow face; an intense energy glimmered in the even darker eyes and radiated down his long nose to his pointed chin.

"Hmm," Leland said from her other side.

The young man leaned past Emilie to address Leland. "Just what do you mean by 'Hmm'?"

"No more, no less," Leland answered. "Can I presume that you are the artist of this work?"

Emilie stared at Leland with surprise. His demeanor had changed so rapidly that she could almost believe he was a different person altogether.

"I am."

Leland stuck out his hand. "Leland Bishop."

The man looked at his hand, then slowly took it. "Ruiz Pablo Picasso."

"Well, Señor Picasso," Leland said, dropping into Spanish. "Do you have others?"

"Yes, but not on display at the Exposition. I'm here covering the fair for a Spanish newspaper."

Leland slipped his hand into his pocket and produced a business card. "When you have something more to show, look me up."

The young man looked at the card, then took it and shoved it into his vest pocket. Then he bowed and hurried away.

"How did you know he was the artist?" Emilie asked, still in awe of the sudden change in Leland's demeanor.

"That crazy look in his eyes when I said 'Hmm.'"

"You really want him to look you up?"

"I do."

"Just by one painting?"

"You can usually tell. Some of them never follow up with anything more, but the ones who do . . . *très interessant*."

They left the Palais a few minutes later, both sated with international art and comfortable conversation.

Once outside, Leland turned toward her. "Well, this was quite an afternoon. Shall we have an early dinner at the Bosnia Herzegovinian Pavilion under the watchful eyes of Alphonse Mucha? They make an excellent *cevapi*."

"Don't you have an official dinner this evening?"

He frowned at her.

"Le Train Bleu?"

"I completely forgot." He consulted his pocket watch. "Egads. I'll have to hurry."

"Go ahead. I've had a delightful time, but I can walk to the pavilion by myself, I am from Paris, after all."

"I wouldn't think of it. If Louis didn't have my head for escorting you to the exhibit this afternoon, Mrs. Driscoll would certainly have it if I didn't see you home again."

He smiled suddenly. "Unless you'd rather be my dinner companion?"

"Don't be ridiculous. Now hurry up if you plan on getting there before dessert."

They arrived back at the pavilion just as Mr. Nash and the boys were closing up for the day. Mrs. Driscoll, Miss Gouvy, and Miss Northrop were already dressed for the walk to the hotel.

"Ah, I'll leave you with Mrs. Driscoll."

"So you won't be grilled by Mr. Tiffany?" Emilie quipped.

"*Exactement.* Good evening. And thank you for a delightful afternoon." He tipped his head toward Mrs. Driscoll, then to Mr. Nash and strode out the door.

"We lost Grace to the panoramas," Emilie explained to Mrs. Driscoll.

"I'm not at all surprised. Will you walk to the hotel with us?"

"Yes, thank you."

Emilie turned to call good evening to Mr. Nash and just managed to catch Amon's eye before he turned on his heel and strode back into the storeroom.

Chapter 28

One day flowed into the next, Emilie and Grace dusting the display cases and the windows in the mornings and spending their lunchtime and early afternoons visiting different aspects of the fair. They saw moving pictures, rode the Ferris wheel, and made a tour of the Seine on a *bateau mouche*. They had lunch at the Herzegovinian Pavilion, complete with menus designed by Alphonse Mucha, the current darling of the art deco world, and even dodged the chamber pots of Mediaeval Paris to much laughter.

And amid the carefree fun, Mrs. Driscoll began to talk of returning to New York. After two weeks she was anxious to get back to the studio. Miss Northrop was perfectly ready to go back; she had several works in progress that she was missing.

As soon as Emilie and Grace realized their trip might be coming to an end, Grace grabbed her sketchbook and documented the events even more furiously than she had done before.

Grace had sent off packets every two or three days. She'd drawn enough to illustrate an entire magazine. Not all were cartoons but also accurate illustrations of the fair: depictions of buildings and contraptions and Expo landscapes with the occasional tourist viewing the sights. But they all had a distinct look that told you they were G. L. Griffiths.

"Have you heard from Charlie?" Emilie asked one afternoon as they strolled with the boys along the Colonial exhibits near the Champs de Mars.

"Once. To say that my first batch of cartoons arrived and everyone was very pleased."

"And that he misses you?"

"No. Why should he?"

"Don't be dense," Emilie said. "It's as plain as day that he's crazy about you. Don't you miss him a little?"

Grace sighed, scowled, lifted her eyes to the sky. "Yes. I haven't had a good argument since we set sail."

Emilie laughed. "You are incorrigible."

"I don't *want* to miss him. But I am ready to go home."

"Me too," Emilie admitted. "Mr. Tiffany doesn't really need us. We hardly ever see him and there are plenty of glass craftsmen to make repairs if something untoward occurs. I'm kind of anxious to get back to work myself."

"So no thought about staying here when it's over?"

Emilie stared at her friend. "Heavens, no. Why would you even think that?"

"I don't really. It's just it is quite wonderful here."

"Well, not for me." Emilie had had a good time, and she had managed the whole trip without being recognized. There actually had been long stretches of time when she didn't think about her father and his reputation at all. She'd stayed away from all the exhibits where her associates from the Académie might be seen. Avoided her old friends.

But it was best not to push her luck. She would be glad to return to her normal life in New York.

Each afternoon when the group returned from their excursions to prepare to close for the evening, Emilie would stop before the "Four Seasons" window. She could never pass it without lingering to bask in its color. It didn't matter that her name would never be associated with it, she was an inseparable part of it. The very essence of her was in the glass. She would miss it when they returned home.

The last visitors of the day hurried in. Emilie started back to the storage room, when someone called her name.

"Emilie! Emilie Pascal?"

Even as she turned to see who it was, she knew. Jean. Jean, who had once been the be-all of her life. Her solace and strength.

She had a wild moment of denying that it could be so, but he called again. "Emilie!" Could she pretend she hadn't heard and slip back into the storeroom before they reached her?

But it was too late. They were rushing toward her. *They. Jean and Marie.*

And Emilie stood, unable to flee.

Jean and Marie. Marie, petite and full fleshed, though instead of her usual aesthetic flowing gowns and shawls, she was wearing a rose-striped day dress and her coarse hair was pulled up in a pompadour beneath a stylish hat. The only nod to her usual bohemian air was a paisley shawl draped at her elbows.

Emilie might not have recognized Jean on the street. He was excessively thin, as if he'd been ill. His hair was long, almost to his shoulders, and he sported a Vandyke beard. As a bohemian artist, he looked the part. She wondered if he had developed any of the other habits of the bohemians. And whether his art suffered in the same way his physical appearance had.

Then she kicked herself for her ingratitude. She forced a smile that she should really have felt but didn't. All she felt was apprehension. It wasn't their fault. They only meant her good. They'd helped her start on her new life. At the end, they had been her only friends.

Still, just seeing them was like an electric jolt that left her sick and reeling.

Marie rushed ahead of Jean, holding out both hands. Emilie quickly dropped her cleaning supplies and took them.

"*C'est incroyable.* I can't believe it's really you," Marie said. "We knew Tiffany had a pavilion and decided to come and see if you might have something represented in the exhibit. We never dreamed you would be here *en personne.*"

Her eyebrows quirked in an expression Emilie well remembered. "How long have you been here? Why didn't you let us know you were here?"

It wasn't an accusation. Just enthusiasm.

But Emilie stood justly accused. Because she hadn't wanted to see them. Hadn't wanted to be reminded of her former life, even the good. Because she was afraid that any touch would taint her future.

Jean hadn't said a word, just stood studying her face. Looking for answers? Waiting for her to come to him?

"*Comme c'est bon de te voir,*" Emilie said. "I've meant to visit, but I haven't had a moment to spare. When we arrived there was improper electricity and it had to be completely rewired, which has put us behind; then there was the installations, and the cleaning, and I—" She was talking too much, making excuses. Lying again. She'd been right to stay away. With this one reunion, she had become a liar, just like before. "I haven't had a moment to spare. But now you are here. *Quelle fortuit.*"

Finally Jean stepped forward. Looked into her eyes. Looking for the truth, she knew.

"Is it safe for you to return here?"

His words drove a chill up her spine.

"Why? What news is there?"

"None at all." He paused to look around the room and moved closer. "He was seen in Italy a couple of months back, but not since." His voice was raspy, his breath smelled like old wine.

"So not in jail," she said, trying to move away.

"Not yet. Does anyone with you know?"

Emilie shook her head. "Only one. My friend. I room with her at the boardinghouse."

"You shouldn't have told . . . anyone."

"Why? Is my reputation still so bad?"

"You are not spoken of."

"You mean I'm forgotten?" Which normally would be the kiss of death for an artist, but for Emilie, it would give her the freedom to have a future.

"I have not forgotten you." He took her hand and brought it to his lips, not in a conventional kiss but in a possessive, encompassing way that might as well have been a public embrace.

"Jean," Marie said gently. And looked past him to catch Emilie's eye.

"Why did you not let us know you were here?" he asked.

Where Marie's questions had just exuded excitement, Jean's was accusatory. His feelings were hurt. "Why? Why did you not tell me?"

He deserved more from her. They both did.

She looked quickly around as if she thought someone might be watching. "Look, I can't talk now. I have duties and Mr. Tiffany won't be happy to see me shirking them." Another lie.

Jean frowned, but Marie jumped in. "A taskmaster, is he? I would expect so. We won't bother you now. But meet us later. After you've finished. Are you free tonight?"

Emilie hesitated. "Yes. I think I can get away. Your flat?"

"Excellent," Marie began.

"No," said Jean. "We'll meet at Le Couchon Jaune. Like the old days."

"We'll order champagne," said Marie. "And celebrate your success."

Emilie swallowed the lump of fear rising in her throat. Marie's gaiety seemed forced; Jean didn't even attempt to hide his bitterness. He looked tired and gaunt. Had she made him thus? She'd never meant to hurt him. "I'll meet you there."

She could feel Jean's gaze upon her, but if he was going to speak, he didn't have the chance.

Marie grabbed his arm. "Come, brother, there are other things I want to see before tonight. And you don't want to get Emilie in trouble, do you?"

A last quick look at Emilie, before Marie pulled Jean away.

Emilie waited until they were gone before she even tried to move. Then she ran to the storeroom, where she sat down on one of the remaining crates and covered her face with her hands.

Maybe she should have just visited them when she first arrived. Gone to their flat and not taken a chance of seeing anyone else. But then she would have felt compelled to visit them again . . . and again. They would expect it. They would deserve it. But Emilie had moved on. Which was a terrible thing. Friends should be for life.

"What are you doing?"

Emilie looked up quickly to see Grace, a smudge of pencil lead across her cheek. "Jean and Marie." It was as much as she could manage.

"Your friends?"

Emilie nodded. "They came to see the exhibit."

"Oh dear." Grace sank down on the crate beside her. "*Quelle* surprise."

Emilie blew out a long breath. "I'm a terrible person."

"No, you aren't. Life goes on. Sometimes you have to leave the old behind."

"Even good friends?"

Grace nodded.

"How did you get so wise?"

"I'm nineteen, almost twenty."

Emilie almost smiled.

"Are you going to see them again?"

"Tonight. At a café we used to go to. Would you like to go with me?"

Grace shook her head. "But I'll be there in spirit. Just do what you have to do." She gave Emilie a hard look. "Whatever that is."

It was a few minutes after eight when Emilie turned the corner of rue Christine. The street was busy as people made their way to one bistro or restaurant or another. Some had gotten an early start and were making boisterous noises as they wove down the sidewalk.

The bistro was halfway down the block and she walked toward it, head down. She could hear the laughter and conversation before she reached the double doors, closed tonight, though in summer they would be open so the tables and patrons could spill onto the sidewalk.

Emilie walked resolutely ahead. She should have insisted on meeting somewhere else, even their apartment, regardless of the loathing she felt for the very building from which she'd made her escape less than a year ago. It seemed like a lifetime. Until this morning it seemed like someone else's life altogether.

She stepped into the recess and the door set back from the sidewalk. Put her hand on the latch. But when it came to opening it, she froze. Then the door was opened, pushing her back on the walk, and two staggering couples practically fell onto the street.

She went inside.

It was crowded, as it always was. It was where artists went to drink their success or their lack of it. To argue ideas. To gossip, to eat their fill on the cheap food and wine. To forget the world waiting outside.

Emilie stood just inside, looking for her two friends, and was surprised not to see them. She'd made sure not to arrive before them.

Then a group standing just ahead of her found a table and rushed over to claim it, leaving her view to the back of the room clear for just an instant. And she saw Jean, sitting at the very back, his head lowered over a glass and an almost empty carafe of wine. He must have been here for a while. But where was Marie?

Had he sat in the very back for privacy or to punish her? Emilie stepped forward, easing past garrulous conversations and morose solo drinkers. The barman looked up just as she passed and his eyes widened as he recognized her.

She gave him a half smile, not stopping to say hello, but she saw him lean toward two of the patrons standing at the bar. She felt their eyes following her even after she was swallowed up by the crowd.

When she reached him, Jean didn't stand, just gestured for her to sit in the chair next to him. In a seat where half the bar could see her face. And a cold chill fell over her.

Jean filled a glass from the carafe. There was one empty glass left, so he was expecting Marie. Emilie wished she would hurry. It would be easier with the three of them together again.

He pushed the glass across the table toward her.

"Why didn't you write? Why didn't you let me know you were here?"

She looked across at her once best friend in the world. And she felt . . . pity. Even in the murky light of the bistro, his eyes were sunken. He was already slurring his words. What had happened to that bright young boy she'd left? Had she done this to him?

"I've been so busy. It's been hard."

"It didn't have to be."

"You know why I had to leave."

"I would have come with you. Taken care of you."

Sacrebleu, why did men always want to take care of her? She didn't want to be taken care of. She wanted to create, and to do that, she would have to take care of herself.

"Jean, be reasonable. Your life is here. You've made connections here. How is your work coming?" she asked, hoping to change the turn of conversation.

"My work." He practically spit the words at her. "I have no inspiration. No muse. And the Académie has turned their backs on the friends of Dominique Pascal and his daughter."

Emilie's hand came to her mouth. "*Non*, they would not punish you."

"No. Merely ignore."

"I'm sorry."

"Then come back to me."

"What? How will that help you?"

"You belong to me."

"Jean. You are my friend. And I care for you . . . and Marie. But I told you when I left that you must forget me. You must forget me now. I am no longer the girl I was."

A strangled cry escaped his lips and he knocked down the rest of the wine in his glass and raised his hand to order more.

"Jean, don't." She tried to take his hand, but he pulled it away.

"I knew it would be like this. Marie said no, but I could see it in your eyes this afternoon."

What could she say to that? He was right, even though she had tried not to show her feelings. She hadn't even known them herself, until she saw him. She was grateful to him, would always cherish the special bond their younger selves had shared. But she didn't love him. Not in the way she had, in the way he still wanted her to.

"Where is Marie?" she asked in a lighter tone. "Is she coming?"

He didn't seem to hear her. "Emilie, why? I never thought to see you again. And then today, there you were, *une ange* right out of one of the pre-Raphaelite paintings, staring up at that window . . . I thought— I thought you had come back to me."

"Jean, *mon chére*, you know I can't. I can't have a life or a career in Paris. I've made a place for myself in New York. You wouldn't have me give that up, would you?"

"Yes, I would." He looked at her with pleading, blurry eyes. What had happened to him? While she'd been finding her way, he had been losing his. Was that her fault, too?

"It is not to be."

He laughed, a bitter, acrid sound that she would never have thought to hear from him.

He reached across the table, knocking over her glass, and gripped her wrist so hard she winced. "You don't want me. Have you found a new lover in New York? Will he protect you when they find out who you are?"

She wrenched her arm away. “I am Emilie Pascal, glass cutter and window maker.”

“Ha! When they know what you really are, no one will have you. Here they all think you helped your father with the forgeries.”

“You know I didn’t, Jean.”

But he was past listening to reason.

“What will your new friends think when they, too, know your history? Eh? They will think the same thing people in Paris thought. What will the judges think when they know Tiffany has hired an art forger?”

“I’m not. And you know that. Would you spread lies about me? You who was once my friend.”

“I would destroy you as you have destroyed me.”

Emilie could only stare. Her dear sweet friend had turned into something she didn’t recognize. And yet, she did; the stench of failure radiated from him. The walls of the bar began to close in on her. She was a young girl crouching beneath the table to avoid the groping hands of her father’s drunk friends. Jean had become one of them. It was as if she’d only dreamed of her life in New York, her friends, her work, Mr. Tiffany.

“You’ll be sorry. Your father may have escaped but you never will. You are no better than he!” His voice broke. He pushed to his feet and swayed. Lifting his empty glass to the room, he cried out, “See her, Emilie Pascal, the forger’s daughter.”

His words were slurred, but everyone understood. Slowly the conversation died, people began to turn toward his voice as she stared back at them in horror and disbelief. She couldn’t breathe. It was happening all over again. She jumped up; her chair fell against the wall and she ran, pushing startled patrons out of the way.

She pushed the door open right into Marie.

Marie grabbed for her, "Emilie, wait! What did he do? He hasn't been well."

"I'm sorry," Emilie cried and ran out into the night.

"It isn't your fault" were the last words she heard. But it was. Her fault. She never should have come back. She didn't stop until she was standing outside the Hotel Regina.

Then she collected herself and walked inside.

Chapter 29

Emilie barely managed to hold herself together until she reached her room, where the dam of emotion broke and she threw herself on the bed and sobbed. She didn't even feel the hand that touched her shoulder until Grace's voice said softly, "I guess the meeting didn't go so well."

"I'm ruined. I should never have come back." Emilie buried her face in her pillow to muffle her despair.

"Come on, Emilie. It can't be so bad. Was he very upset? What happened?"

Emilie forced herself to sit up. Grace handed her a handkerchief.

It was the one Lotte had given her for the Christmas ball and had sent with her to Paris. Instead of wiping her tears away, Emilie brought it to her breast and held it tightly against her racing heart.

"He was drunk. I don't know what has happened to him. He's become like one those hopeless failed artists, the passion, the fury, the drink, maybe even drugs. He had the eyes of an opium eater. And he's not yet twenty.

"He was never like that. Not until I . . . until I— Did I do that to him? Is it my fault? Did my leaving destroy his life?"

"Good god, no. You're not responsible for another's choices. What did his sister say?"

"She wasn't there. He was sitting at a back table as if he wanted to make me walk through the regulars, people I probably knew. As if he wanted them to recognize me. I was afraid to look at any of them. The barman recognized me. Not that it matters now. Everyone knows. Jean made certain of that."

"Maybe it isn't as bad as you think."

"It is. He was crazed with drink and he hates me. And I looked at him and saw my father." Her voice cracked on another sob.

Her father. The same degenerate bitterness. The anger at the world, the threatening air. "I had to get away. I tried to leave, but he grabbed me and begged me to come back to him. When I said I couldn't, that I didn't love him in that way, he stood up and announced to the room that I was the forger's daughter."

"Oh. Oh. Then what happened?"

"I ran. Marie was just coming in, but I couldn't face her. I just ran back here. What am I going to do? What will Mr. Tiffany say?"

Grace frowned, bit her lip. "I doubt if he'll ever hear about what happened at a local bar. He was at dinner with a bunch of important art dealers this evening. Your father will be the last thing on his mind, if it's on his mind at all. So stop worrying."

"Jean threatened to tell the judges. Though maybe he won't remember when he is sober. But what if they do find out? It will spread all over town, it may reach their ears, that the forger's daughter is working for Tiffany.

"I wish we could just go home."

Grace smiled.

"What?"

"You called New York 'home.' Now get some sleep."

"How can I sleep after what's happened? I can't lose this. It's my whole life. Even if it means I'll always be alone, like Miss Northrop and Mrs. Driscoll. If one must choose, I choose art. *Mon dieu, mon dieu.* I should never have come back."

"Too late for second thoughts," Grace said sympathetically. "Though I do think that perhaps this is the time to tell Mrs. Driscoll about your past."

Emilie shook her head. "She would fire me and then I would be stranded in Paris. I'd rather die than have to stay here."

"Don't be so melodramatic. I know it was very unnerving, but now that the first meeting is over, it will pass. Maybe he took the hint and will leave you alone." She gave Emilie a sympathetic shake. "So see? You don't have to die, and you won't have to stay. Mrs. Driscoll will understand."

BUT MRS. DRISCOLL wasn't even at the pavilion when they arrived the next morning. And Emilie felt weak with the temporary reprieve. In the morning light, she thought maybe she *had* overreacted since the atmosphere in the bistro had been so charged to begin with. Everyone had probably forgotten all about Jean's outburst with the rising sun, when they were probably just staggering home—if they remembered it at all.

"Mrs. Driscoll and Miss Northrop have taken the morning off," Mr. Nash said. "They're visiting the American building, then dropping by to say hello to Siegfried Bing, where others of our decorative pieces are also being displayed."

But halfway through the morning, when Emilie and Grace were having a cup of tea, Mr. Nash came into the storeroom, followed by Amon.

"Miss Pascal, a word if you please."

Emilie stood, mentally going over her morning inspection to see if she could have possibly overlooked something. "Yes, Mr. Nash."

"Perhaps if you could step outside for a moment."

Emilie's blood stopped in her veins.

"Of course." She started toward the door, but Amon stood in her way.

"Is it true?"

She just stared at him.

"Amon," Mr. Nash snapped. "This is not your concern."

"If she's a forger, it is all of our concern," Amon answered back. His eyes, which flashed with that dark fire she'd found so enticing, now brought on the cold shame and fear of discovery.

Emilie sucked in her breath as the world went out of focus.

Nothing from Grace.

Emilie pulled her gaze from Amon and turned to Mr. Nash.

"My dear," Mr. Nash said. "Amon tells me the men heard a most disturbing rumor at the pub last night. And this morning a man came to the pavilion to ask if it was true that Mr. Tiffany had knowingly hired the daughter of Dominique Pascal, the notorious art forger."

Emilie slowly rose to her feet. *So Jean had made true his threat.* "It is true."

A low growl erupted from deep in Amon's chest.

"I am his daughter, but I am not a forger."

"But surely you must see how it puts the company in an awkward position," Mr. Nash said.

Emilie didn't know how to answer.

Grace did. "I hardly think she should be punished for the sins of her father."

"Nor do I, Miss Griffith. But you see how it could be misconstrued."

"No, frankly, Mr. Nash, I don't. What does someone's father copying paintings of the old masters in France have to do with Emilie cutting glass in America?"

Emilie cast Grace a thankful smile, but it was no use.

"Well, hopefully this will go no further and we can all count our blessings. But you must inform Mrs. Driscoll at once. She will decide what, if any, future you will have at Tiffany Glass. Now I suggest we all get back to work."

"But if she's a cheat," said Amon, "that will make us all cheats."

"No," Emilie cried, but the word came out in a whisper.

"Speak for yourself," Grace piped in. "No one is guilty here."

"Maybe not," said Mr. Nash. "But the perception may be that we are not what we profess to be. It's important in business to have an impeccable reputation."

"They'll say we hire forgers," Amon said, his voice rising in pitch and loudness. "That we steal ideas even, that La Farge was right all along, that Mr. Tiffany is a cheat and stole his ideas.

"The other men are already angry. They say we'll be stripped of our medals! Our entries will be disqualified, and we'll be disgraced in front of the world."

"Keep your voice down, Amon," Mr. Nash demanded. "There is no reason for this hysteria. All may turn out fine. Now no more chatter. Come, let us get back to work. I will go with you and speak with the others. We must all stay mum and hopefully this will pass without doing too much damage."

Emilie stood watching the door long after they'd gone.

"Buck up, Emilie. It will all be cleared up and life will get back to normal. You'll see."

"I hope so. For Mr. Tiffany and all of you. But it is too late for me."

"Never mind," Grace said. "They're men; they react first and reason later—the few who do get to the second stage. You should hear some of the things that Charlie says before I remind him that reason carries the day."

Emilie hoped Grace was right. But in her lifetime she had hardly ever seen reason win out over emotion.

And she lost even that hope when Mrs. Driscoll and Miss Northrop returned midafternoon.

"We were just at the Bing Pavilion," Mrs. Driscoll said. "Evidently there is a nasty rumor going around that . . . I can hardly believe it but . . . Miss Pascal, Emilie, is it true? Are you the daughter of this art forger everyone is talking about?"

Emilie nodded. There was no reason to deny it. She was Dominique Pascal's daughter and she was going to carry his sin for the rest of her life.

"She's done nothing wrong," Grace insisted.

"I know, my dear. And this could have all been avoided if I had vetted Emilie more carefully and learned the truth at the beginning. I blame myself."

Emilie shook her head. She wanted to tell her it wasn't her fault. That it was Emilie's alone. And that she had cherished every minute working under her aegis. But the words wouldn't come. It was over. Maybe the police had been looking for her all this time and she'd been foolish to think she could have a normal life. Maybe she would be arrested after all. And if she didn't have Tiffany, she wouldn't really care.

"I would have said that you should tell Mr. Tiffany everything and then we'd get on with it, but Mr. Tiffany has been called to the board of commissioners. Everyone at the Bing Pavilion thinks it's because of you."

There was a universal gasp among the group.

"But why?" cried Emilie. "I will go and explain to the board that he knew nothing."

"Best you just stay out of it," Miss Northrop said in her calm way.

But it didn't calm Emilie. The men had already found her guilty. And perhaps with good reason. They'd given her a chance for a new life—offered her hope—and she had betrayed them by her silence.

Because in her heart, Emilie knew that what they believed about her must be true. She'd been a fool to think she could escape her fate. She was accursed. Had always been accursed. For she had betrayed every person who cared for her. Betraying her father had been a moral necessity. But never would she intentionally hurt Grace or Mrs. Driscoll or any of the other Tiffany girls, whom she had grown to love.

And above all she would never hurt Mr. Tiffany.

Emilie wanted to explain this to them, but how could they ever understand? She should have risked telling the truth long before it came to this, but she'd been afraid to lose what she cherished most in the world. For the first time in her life she had almost been free.

"All is not lost," Mrs. Driscoll said. "But perhaps you should go back to the hotel and give everyone time to calm down. Hopefully this was all a false alarm and tomorrow we can go about mending our reputational fences, so to speak."

Emilie groped for her bag, lowered her head, slipped through the storeroom door, and walked right into Amon, who was waiting outside. He reached for her. But she ducked away, not able to look him in the eye. And for the first time ever, she left the building without even looking at her "Four Seasons."

GRACE GRABBED HER art bag and started after Emilie.

"You can fire me, but you can't stop me. She's only done her best by the Tiffany company. And this is what she gets? Everyone automatically assumes the worst?" She only made it as far as the door and ran into Mr. Nash and Amon on their way back inside.

"Move out of my way. How dare either of you accuse her of these things. She would never cheat Mr. Tiffany. What do you suspect her of doing? Did she ever try to finagle formulas out of you, Mr. Nash?"

Mr. Nash's mouth twitched. "Never. She was interested, yes, but with an artist's interest. I would swear that was all it was."

Grace whirled around. "Or you, Mrs. Driscoll? Did she steal your dragonfly design?"

"Of course not. She made some rather good suggestions."

"She would not cheat us, any of us," Amon said in a way that made Grace look sharply at him.

"Then you shouldn't have accused her. Any of you. She is an artist. She is devoted to Mr. Tiffany. She wouldn't do any of the things you say she might have done. Might? What does that even mean? She didn't and that's what is important. The truth is what matters."

"Then why didn't she tell us?" Amon asked.

Grace turned on Mrs. Driscoll. "Would you have hired her if you knew her past?"

Mrs. Driscoll looked chagrined. "I should have vetted her more carefully, but, yes, I would have hired her anyway. Just kept a better eye on her."

"Well, you didn't need to. She is completely honest. She was running away from her father. Risked everything to come to New York to work in the studio. Would give her life for any of us. Quite frankly, if Mr. Tiffany's reputation is so fragile that one destitute French girl could destroy it because of who she's related to, maybe it isn't so great as we think."

"Miss Griffith!" Mrs. Driscoll exclaimed. "Let us keep cool heads until we know exactly what this outcome will be."

"I'll go to the committee and explain," Grace said. "I am her friend, we room together. I'd know if she had done anything—any little thing—that was suspect. I promise you."

"I am quite certain you would. It's the perception of the thing. The rumors that are flying."

"All because of an unhappy man who she knew before in Paris, who wanted vengeance and set the lie about. Men!" Grace spat out. "So eager to blame someone else."

"Really, Miss Griffith," Mr. Nash said. "That's hardly fair."

"Isn't it? Not one of you asked her for her side of the story. So busy worrying about *your* medals, and *your* reputations, and *your* careers. I think I hate you all." And to Grace's utter humiliation she burst into angry tears.

"Now, now," Mr. Nash said helplessly. "Maybe it isn't so bad."

Amon didn't say anything.

"Well, Amon," Grace said.

"I didn't want to believe it. I never thought she was guilty of anything but blindly worshipping his majesty."

"Amon Bronsky!" Mrs. Driscoll exclaimed.

"Well, it's true. She will not have one bad word said against Mr. Tiffany. Everyone should have such a loyal friend."

And Grace thought he looked a little sad.

"Then let me tell her she's not blamed," Grace said.

"Not quite yet," Mrs. Driscoll said. "Let us ascertain how bad the situation is before you give her any false hopes. Maybe all is not lost."

EMILIE STUMBLED ALONG the street, not caring what people thought of her, drunk or demented or a criminal fleeing the police. Let them think what they wanted. They couldn't think worse of her than her friends did. Or she herself did.

She had risked everything to go to Mr. Tiffany. Now it was all unraveling. Her friends thought she had betrayed them. She had deceived them, but only to survive. She'd done nothing else to warrant their disgust. Except not to love.

Her father's deceptions were unforgivable, and yet hers had been far worse. She had ruined her new friends. And she had ruined Mr. Tiffany, a true genius, though she had never told him so.

It was too much to bear. She would have to flee once again, but this time there was nowhere else she could go.

She didn't slow down in the foyer of the hotel. Once in her room, she stood for a moment. She would disappear once again but not before trying to explain to the one who mattered most to her.

She went to the escritoire, moved Grace's sketches aside, and took out a sheet of the hotel's stationery. Made use of one of Grace's pens. This was to be her final letter, and this time it would all be true.

Dear Mr. Tiffany. I hope you will forgive me. I never meant to hurt you. Tell them you knew nothing of me. Tell them I lied.

That I tricked you. But I didn't. I only wanted to learn. I see now that my desire has led you to ruin. And now I must leave you. I am so very sorry. To me you will always be the king of stained glass. Emilie Pascal

She folded the letter, scratched a quick note of farewell to Grace. Then she tossed her cloak around her shoulders. She'd worn it to New York and she would wear it again tonight, ending her journey. And with a final look back at her room and the life that had briefly been hers, she went downstairs to leave her letter with the concierge.

When Mr. Tiffany didn't return to the pavilion, Mr. Nash suggested that they return to the hotel and wait for him there. So they locked up and left whatever maintenance that was needed to be done for the morrow.

They all waited in the hotel foyer while Mr. Nash went to ask the concierge if there had been word from Mr. Tiffany. There hadn't been, and since none of them were hungry, they decided to order a bottle of wine and wait for him at one of the tables in the loggia where they would have a view of the entrance.

Fortunately they didn't have long to wait. They were silently sipping their wine when Mr. Tiffany strode through the door.

Grace could barely keep herself from running to him and demanding he tell them immediately what had happened. Though part of her didn't want to know.

But as he passed the desk, the concierge called him over.

"*Bon soir,* Monsieur Laurence. *Quelle journée.*"

"*Oui,* Monsieur. This was left for you to be read immediately." He handed a letter to Mr. Tiffany. "And your staff is waiting for you just there."

He motioned down the long corridor to where tables were set up for the guests' relaxation. Though none of his staff were the least bit relaxed.

"*Merci.*" Mr. Tiffany strode toward them, opening the letter and moving with such a bounce in his step that Grace couldn't imagine that he'd been recently disgraced. Perhaps there was hope yet.

"I didn't expect such a welcoming committee. You want to hear the news, I expect," he said cheerfully.

"Yes, please," said Mrs. Driscoll, nervously.

"Mm-hmm, just a minute," he said as he read his letter. He frowned, looked at them. "Odd."

"Mr. Tiffany," Mr. Nash prodded.

Tiffany looked up and shook the stationery at them. "What is this nonsense?"

"What nonsense?" Miss Northrop asked and stood.

"A letter from Miss Pascal. Saying she didn't mean to harm me. Thanking me and saying she's going away. I swear if Leland has eloped with her, I'll have his head."

"No," Mrs. Driscoll said, coming to stand beside Miss Northrop. "There were rumors. And you were called before the Expo commission, and we just assumed . . . Have they not stripped us of our medals?"

Mr. Tiffany blinked. "What? I never heard of anything so absurd. They called me to the commission to praise our work and present me with—"

"So they hadn't heard the rumors?" Grace blurted out.

"What rumors?"

"Mr. Tiffany," Mrs. Driscoll said, giving Grace a look to be quiet. "Someone started a rumor that Miss Pascal was the daughter of the infamous art forger Dominique Pascal."

"It's perfectly true," Mr. Tiffany said.

"You knew?"

"Yes. Lee Bishop told me at the Christmas Ball. It's probably why she is so good with color. Learned it at the knee of her father while he copied the old masters."

"You're not outraged?"

"Well, Leland assured me that she wasn't part of any defrauding."

"How did he know?" Grace demanded.

Mr. Tiffany shrugged. "He's an art dealer. He has a gallery here in Paris. He's very sociable. He recognized her almost immediately. The art community here is quite small."

Mrs. Driscoll sat down quickly as if her knees had given out. Grace knew her own were none too steady with the rush of relief she felt.

"You're not going to fire her?"

"Why on earth would I do that? She has an eye. She's stubborn. And she's good. I would be a fool to let her go."

"May I go tell her?" Grace asked Mrs. Driscoll.

"Yes, of course. Go right ahead. I'm so relieved."

But Emilie wasn't in their room. She'd left Grace a note. *I'm sorry. You were the best friend I ever had. Emilie.*

Grace clutched the note and ran back to the elevator. As soon as the doors opened on the lobby floor, she burst out, nearly bumping into a couple on their way upstairs.

"She's gone!" Grace cried before she even reached the group, who had ordered another bottle in her absence.

"Gone?" asked Mr. Tiffany. "Out to dinner already?"

"No. Not to dinner."

"Then where? She shouldn't be traipsing around the streets of Paris at night without being accompanied, no matter how well she knows the area." He lifted his glass. "She should be here and not missing the hotel's excellent claret."

Grace shook her head. She didn't like the idea that was forming in her mind. But she couldn't ignore it. "I don't think she's coming back."

"Don't be ridiculous. She hasn't run off with Bishop, has she? I'll have his head. I swear I don't know why girls will get married."

"She has friends here," Mrs. Driscoll assured him.

"Not married," said Grace. "Not to friends. Oh god. I think I know where she's gone. I have to go."

"Where?"

Grace could hardly form the words. "To the river."

"Why on earth—" Mr. Tiffany didn't get to finish the question.

"To the Pont des Arts. We must hurry."

Chapter 30

Emilie stood at the top of the bridge looking down at the dark waters where so many unhappy souls had ended their lives. She carried no rose tonight. The little flower seller had still not returned, but she didn't think her mother would mind. Soon she would have Emilie instead.

In the distance a dome of colored light hovered over the Exposition, rising from the darkness like one of Mrs. Driscoll's lamps. All around her, the lights of Paris that had once cocooned her in a warmth of living, breathing colors were cold and accusing.

Emilie sighed and leaned on the iron parapet.

"Maman, Maman. I never understood how you could leave me. But I do now, Maman. There was no place left to go, was there? Nowhere that you could breathe free, without fear, without despair.

"And now I have nowhere to go but to you."

Emilie looked down into the river and felt . . . nothing.

"Are you there, Maman? You won't turn against me like the others, will you?"

There was a commotion at the end of the bridge. Revelers. She had come too early to be alone. But she would wait. She knew patience.

She straightened a little so no one would stop to ask if she was okay. She wasn't okay. How could she be? She had destroyed everything that mattered in her life. But soon it wouldn't matter.

Footsteps. She braced herself, stared ahead until they stopped beside her.

It was Grace.

Emilie shook her head, grabbed the rail with both hands.

"Emilie, wait!"

She couldn't wait. Even now she felt her mother slipping away. She couldn't wait. It must be now.

"Please. Everything is fine. Mr. Tiffany knows. He already knew."

Maman, wait. Don't leave me. Slipping away. Slipping away into the dark waters, away from Emilie. How would she ever find her if she didn't follow now?

"Emilie, no! Don't do this terrible thing. Listen to me. They were mistaken. All is set right."

Emilie gripped the rail. *Maman, wait!* She was crying. She could taste her tears. *But her inner voice is weak, and she's afraid that her plea has fallen on emptiness.*

"I have nothing left." *Even Maman is gone.*

Now there are more footsteps, coming closer.

And Mr. Tiffany's voice, calling her. "Emilie Pascal, you silly girl. Get away from the parapet. Do you want to catch your death?"

Yes. Yes, I do, thought Emilie, but her hands seemed frozen to the iron handrail.

Mr. Tiffany skidded to a stop beside her. She recoiled and stumbled back until her back was pressed into the opposite railing.

"Stop this instant. Get away from that rail; you're like to fall in if you aren't more careful."

"I didn't betray you. You must believe me." *She says the words but they don't come out of her mouth. They are stuck inside this awful emptiness.*

He scowled at her; even in the dark she could see his heavy brows glowering over those lively eyes. "Of course you didn't. What absurdity is this?"

"I ruined you."

"Ruined me? How could you possibly ruin me, you silly girl?"

"The committee. They called you before them."

"Merely to declare me Le Chevalier de la Legion d'Honneur. It's the grandest honor of all. We should be celebrating, not standing on a dark bridge over this miasma of bad smells."

"But everyone thinks—"

"What do you care what everyone thinks? *You* certainly don't care what I think."

"I do."

"In that case, come here at once."

But she could only stare at him standing on the bridge with the night sky and the lights of Paris behind him.

"All is well, we are the pinnacle of art tonight."

Still, Emilie said nothing. It was most amazing.

"Do you hear me? Come away from there. You are exonerated of whatever you were supposed to have done."

Exonerated. I am exonerated. She wasn't ruined, and she hadn't ruined Mr. Tiffany. She is exonerated.

Mr. Tiffany frowned. "What are you looking at?"

"The light," she said finally. "The way it shines through the grillwork of the bridge behind you. You look like a Roman soldier on the parapet."

"Indeed? Ha! I like it. Caesar, perhaps. Emperor of Rome . . . You will design it for me."

He held out his hand and when she moved toward him, he took her arm in his.

"Of course, I must wear a gold chest plate. I know just the glass for it."

"And a plumed headdress. *I* know just the glass for *it*."

"With a spear."

"In a soldier's kilt."

"I'm not sure about the kilt."

"It must be. I will make sure your knees aren't knobbly."

"I'll have you know, I don't have knobbly knees."

"And leather sandals . . ."

Clara shook her head in bemused affection as she watched them, master and apprentice, as they walked back toward the hotel, forgetting the others and the reason they were here, already arguing about how best to portray the King of Stained Glass.

Epilogue

January 1933
Green-Wood Cemetery
Brooklyn, NY

It is a frigid day and Emilie stands at a distance, away from the others, a single red rose in her hand.

They are all there: Grace, a paid political cartoonist now, with her Charlie by her side; Clara and her husband, Edward. Agnes, still unmarried but standing with Arthur Nash and others she doesn't recognize. She does recognize Amon. Older, a little thicker, his hair streaked with silver. He's standing at the end of the group with a plump woman who must be his wife.

A quick, bittersweet moment fills her before it is gone.

It is over. A biting wind sweeps across the grass and everyone begins to drift away.

Only Emilie stays. Then she walks toward the open grave. He was gone the first time she came to New York, and now he is gone once again.

Much time has passed; tastes in art and decoration have changed. His brilliant light has faded, but . . .

You are still my dear Mr. Tiffany, the undisputed King of Stained Glass. She drops the rose into the deep swell of memories. *I won't forget you.*

Someone comes to stand beside her. Emilie looks up and smiles. She takes his arm. "Come, Leland, let us join the others."

Author's Note

Where to start? Perhaps with family. There are all kinds—biological, adopted, work, spiritual.

A novelist's job is to climb into whatever family she's chosen to write about, imagining what happens as that family's past and present form them, how they argue, love, and sacrifice.

The Tiffany girls must have been some kind of family, working together all day, some living together in boardinghouses. And that's where my story began.

What were the relationships between Clara, Agnes, and Alice and with the other Tiffany girls? Though the names and photographs of many of the real "girls" are available, there is little else written about their histories. I wish that I could have included them all. But with a novel already burgeoning with characters, I was forced to limit myself to a few. So I tried to put my mind and heart into that setting, that period, those girls, and think, what would I do and feel? And imagine what the girls who lived at Mrs. B's might be like.

I discovered Grace's prototype in Lou Rogers, a feminist and suffragist who worked a few years after Grace and is considered the first female cartoonist. Emilie sprang from wondering what would a woman do when her choices had run out? And why she might conclude her only option was to travel halfway across the world to Mr. Tiffany.

I tried to adhere as closely as possible to the actual history and timeline. But as a novelist, I did take a bit of artistic license for the sake of the story and the reader.

It is possible that Alice Gouvy had already moved to the Corona workshop in 1899, but I thought she deserved to be in the story, so I kept her on site.

In Clara's letters, she mentions having the idea of the dragonfly design in spring. But I moved that process to the summer, so that we could experience the excitement of that creative moment and witness how it might have developed into the iconic dragonfly lamp.

I purposely divided work on the Season windows to coincide with the seasons of the year.

The policeman's parade was actually held in June, but it was just so perfect an event for Grace and Charlie that I nudged it into July. An account of the actual parade can be found in the *New York Times* and the *Sun*.

Tiffany was known to stutter when he became excited or agitated. I chose not to portray this since I felt writing it out distracted from what he was saying and broke into the attention of the reader (me) and the rhythm of the story.

The Paris world's fair took place from April through November of 1900. More than fifty million visitors attended. Some 60 countries presented 85,000 exhibitions of the best of their art and culture, scientific innovations, and manufacturing accomplishments. There are some wonderful prime sources for experiencing the marvels of the largest fair in the world.

I never was able to find who, if any of the actual artisans, actually went to the Exposition, so I sent my protagonists with the excuse that Tiffany would need workers to oversee the installations, make minor repairs, etc.

There were many renditions of Clara's dragonfly motif, lamps with different bases, both oil and electric, as well as hosts of decorative pieces. A dragonfly lamp version with brass base showed at the Grafton Gallery in October 1899. A different version with arrowhead base was exhibited at the Paris Expo.

Agnes's Magnolia window is said to have been displayed at the Bing Pavilion across the Esplanade on the French side of the exhibition buildings. But again, for purposes of the dramatic line of the story, I gave it a place in the Tiffany Pavilion.

The "Fours Seasons" window (currently housed at the Morse Museum and depicted in this novel) debuted at the Paris Expo. There was an earlier Four Seasons window (now at the Metropolitan Museum of Art in New York City) that Agnes Northrop also collaborated on and was shown at the Chicago Columbia Exhibition in 1892. The two are sometimes confused.

The scene of Mr. Tiffany hiring Westinghouse to light his exhibit is based on a true event. Many exhibits were not ready on opening day. Some presenters had not yet arrived. The Palais d'Electrique, which boasted 5,000 incandescent lightbulbs for the outside decoration alone, was dark for the grand opening.

The Petit and Grande Palaises didn't open until two weeks after the fair was officially opened.

Awards were not actually presented until August of 1900, but again for the sake of the story, I pushed them up to fit my timeline.

AND IF YOU'RE wondering what happened to the real characters?

Tiffany was an artist, a philanthropist, and supporter of arts and women's rights. But as often happens, over the years, he and his iconic works passed out of style in favor of more modern pieces. Lamps were banished to people's attics or sold at yard sales. Windows were taken down, boarded up, and stored in the basements of churches.

Tiffany, on the verge of bankruptcy, moved to his home at Laurelton where he opened a retreat for artists. He died in 1933, never knowing that he would once again rise to a respected place in the history of art.

All of the contents of the workshops, including the artwork, Tiffany's private papers, and his business accounts, were stored at Laurelton. In 1957, a fire destroyed Laurelton. The ruins lay abandoned until Hugh and Jeannette McKean salvaged whatever they could and donated the items to the museum they had founded in honor of Mrs. McKean's grandfather. Today the Charles Hosmer Morse Museum of American Art is the keeper of an extensive Tiffany collection.

In the 1950s, Tiffany artworks came back into fashion. Lamps and incidentals were retrieved from attics and once again graced living rooms. And with *Downton Abbey*, interest has soared, and so have the prices.

Alice Gouvy left Tiffany Studios in early 1907 and returned to Cleveland to work as a schoolteacher while caring for her mother.

In the fall of 1909, Clara Driscoll, after a decade of living in the same boardinghouse, married Edward A. Booth and left the Tiffany company for the last time. They divided their time between New York and a house in Point Pleasant, New Jersey, until 1930 when Edward retired and they moved to Florida. Clara tried her hand at various crafts, but never reached the achievements of her years at Tiffany's. She died in 1944, followed by Edward in 1950.

Agnes Northrop continued to work at the Tiffany Studio until it closed, then she moved to an offshoot studio to continue her designs. She did finally move from the boys' school to the Grammercy Park Hotel and remained an active designer until age 94.

Acknowledgments

You never write a book alone. You might sit at your desk initially with a blank screen before you, but it soon becomes peopled with characters who become real before you know it. And then you have the really real people who turn your idea and words into a finished book.

Thanks as always to my agent, Kevan Lyon, my editor, Tessa Woodward, my William Morrow team, and my copyeditor, Laurie McGee, who always finds my tongue-tied phrases and conflicting descriptions and makes sense of them. Also heartfelt appreciation to Gail Freeman and Lois Winston, sounding boards, cheerleaders, swift kickers, and friends. Thank you all.

The internet is always an invaluable source for connecting to historical archives, and since most of this book was written during the pandemic, much of my normally in-person research was dependent on Zoom, email, and webinars.

Special thanks to the museums and curators whose lectures made their way to the internet. Thanks to Eventbrite and NY Adventure Club for bringing the world to me when I couldn't get to it. (And sending me down innumerable rabbit holes that had nothing to do with Tiffany but may be the germ of another book someday.)

Inexpressible gratitude to Clara Driscoll for her letters to her family for her descriptions of the Tiffany girls and the everyday work at Tiffany's glassworks. Little was known of the women's lives until her letters were discovered in two caches in Queens and Ohio.

I was searching for a story for this book, about women at the turn of the century who changed things. Not famous women, not splashy headlines, just the everyday working girl; "the new woman" who because of their dedication to their work, helped break the glass ceiling and set the way for professional women to come. And I found it with the Tiffany girls.

About the Author

Shelley Noble is the *New York Times* and *USA Today* bestselling author of *Whisper Beach* and *Beach Colors*. Other titles include *Stargazey Point*, *Breakwater Bay*, and *Forever Beach*—a story of foster adoption in New Jersey—and four spin-off novellas. A former professional dancer and choreographer, she lives on the Jersey Shore and loves to discover new beaches and indulge her passion for lighthouses and vintage carousels. Shelley is a member of Sisters in Crime, Mystery Writers of America, and the Women's Fiction Writers Association.